THE STORY OF
AN AFRICAN FARM

THE STORY OF
AN AFRICAN FARM

Olive Schreiner

edited by Patricia O'Neill

broadview literary texts

National Library of Canada Cataloguing in Publication

Schreiner, Olive, 1855–1920
   The story of an African farm / Olive Schreiner; edited by Patricia O'Neill.

(Broadview literary texts)
Includes bibliographical references.
ISBN 1-55111-286-8

   I. O'Neill, Patricia, 1950– II. Title. III. Series.

PR9369.2.S37S7 2003   823'.8   C2002-905456-7

Broadview Press Ltd. is an independent, international publishing house, incorporated in 1985. Broadview believes in shared ownership, both with its employees and with the general public; since the year 2000 Broadview shares have traded publicly on the Toronto Venture Exchange under the symbol BDP.

We welcome comments and suggestions regarding any aspect of our publications – please feel free to contact us at the addresses below or at broadview@broadviewpress.com.

North America
Post Office Box 1243, Peterborough, Ontario, Canada K9J 7H5
3576 California Road, Orchard Park, NY, USA 14127
Tel: (705) 743-8990; Fax: (705) 743-8353;
e-mail: customerservice@broadviewpress.com

UK, Ireland, and continental Europe
Thomas Lyster Ltd., Units 3 & 4a, Old Boundary Way,
Burscough Rd, Ormskirk, Lancashire L39 2YW
Tel: (1695) 575112; Fax: (1695) 570120
email: books@tlyster.co.uk

Australia and New Zealand
UNIREPS, University of New South Wales
Sydney, NSW, 2052
Tel: 61 2 9664 0999; Fax: 61 2 9664 5420
email: info.press@unsw.edu.au

www.broadviewpress.com

Broadview Press Ltd. gratefully acknowledges the financial support of the Government of Canada through the Book Publishing Industry Development Program for our publishing activities.

This book is printed on acid-free paper containing 30% post-consumer fibre.

Series Editor: Professor L.W. Conolly
Advisory editor for this volume: Michel Pharand
Typesetting and assembly: True to Type Inc., Mississauga, Canada.

Certified Eco-Logo
30% Post.

PRINTED IN CANADA

Contents

Acknowledgements

In putting together this edition I am indebted to all of the scholars listed in the bibliography. Their insightful books and essays enhanced my own reading of *African Farm*. I am also grateful for the encouragement and assistance of my students, especially Kate Kuykendall, John Morrell, Cory Lown, Virginia Berg, and Liam Meyer. I am indebted to Carolyn Mascaro and Terri Viglietta at Hamilton College and Barbara Conolly and Leonard Conolly at Broadview Press for their patience and help with the editing and production of this edition. Thanks, too, to Christine Ingersoll for her rendering of the map of Southern Africa. Finally, for her invaluable comments and moral support over many years, I want to thank my colleague and friend Victoria Vernon.

Introduction

Olive Schreiner's *The Story of an African Farm* challenged many of
the social and literary conventions of Victorian writing in 1883.
The title suggested an adventure tale, but its contents were, as one
puzzled critic reported, "mystical and hyper-philosophical. We are
introduced to a world of most eccentric personalities who gravitate
between the transcendental and all that is most commonplace."[1]
Such qualities make the novel as challenging to read today as it was
over a hundred years ago. Through the popular form of a coming-
of-age story, *African Farm* engages the major ideological concerns of
the Victorian age: the struggle between scientific thought and religious belief, the "woman question," and the effects of imperialist
exploitation on the lives of colonial subjects. In addition to its soci-
ological and historical interests, *The Story of an African Farm* is also
important for the experimental aspects of its literary craft. For readers accustomed to the linear narratives of most nineteenth-century
novels, this novel anticipates some of the freedoms of form and style
that have become hallmarks of modernist fiction. Thus, Schreiner,
though writing in virtual isolation, was able to combine an exploration of the metaphysical and ethical concerns of her age with a
variety of representational modes uncommon in the fiction of her
time.

Raised within the confines of a colonial framework, Schreiner
developed her richly complex narrative style not only in response
to political and social transformations in South Africa, but also to
the anxiety and promise of a new self-consciousness emerging from
the restraints of social conventions and dogmatic religious traditions. By selecting the perspective of children to present her narrative in the first part of the novel, she questions the legitimacy of
institutions of power that oppress and exploit the less powerful. In
addition, the children's perspective is able to appeal to the reader
through a certain universality of experience. The children come to
realize as they suffer the ignorant brutality of their social conditions
that neither education, nor conventional religion, nor marriage will
relieve them of the burden of selfhood. Termed an "agnostic novel"
by one reviewer (see Appendix E), Schreiner's work provides

---

1 *"The Story of an African Farm." Saturday Review of Politics, Literature, Science
and Art* 55.1 (2 April 1883): 507-8.

consolation for the individual consciousness through an allegorical tale and through the idealized monologues of the narrator of the second part of the novel. As a consequence, Victorian readers responded enthusiastically to Schreiner's novel regardless of their identification with or distance from her characters or plot. For today's reader, *The Story of an African Farm* opens up the nineteenth-century form of a coming-of-age novel to include the angst of modern life, its on-going social contradictions and metaphysical challenges.

A Brief Biography

I had grown up in a land where wars were common. From my earliest years I had heard of bloodshed and battles and hair-breadth escapes; I had heard them told of by those who had seen and taken part in them. In my native country dark men were killed and their lands taken from them by white men armed with superior weapons; even near to me such things happened....

(From Olive Schreiner, "The Dawn of Civilization," in *The Nation and Anthenaeum*, 21 March 1921.)

Although Schreiner was eventually able to break free of her family and develop a distinctive narrative voice and career as a writer, her early life provided her with many challenges and obstacles. Schreiner's father, Gottlob Schreiner, a German evangelical working for the London Missionary Society, brought Olive's mother, Rebecca Lyndall, an English minister's daughter, to South Africa in 1838.[1] By this time the British had secured the Cape from the Dutch and had ended the practice of importing slaves. Some of the native South African peoples worked for the English and Dutch immigrants, but most lived on subsistence farmlands in regions still unconquered by foreign imperialists. A large number of Dutch immigrants, known as Afrikaners or Boers, had moved north to settle in what became the Transvaal and the Orange Free State, but

---

1 Most of the biographical information in this introduction is based on the biography *Olive Schreiner* by Ruth First and Ann Scott (1980; New Brunswick, NJ: Rutgers UP, 1990).

skirmishes between the Boers and the English and between whites and native peoples continually redefined borders and territories.

Olive was the second youngest of the couple's seven surviving children and, until age 12, was educated primarily by her mother. Schreiner's biographers repeat the comments of various family members and neighbors who remarked upon Olive's intelligence and liveliness from an early age. But, given the lack of formal education or intellectual society, she was forced to develop her skills in writing on her own. In 1867, after twenty-seven years of missionary service, her father was dismissed for engaging in trade, and during the next few years, the family suffered severely. Olive went with her older sister and younger brother to live with her eldest brother Theo, who had returned from his education in England and was headmaster of a school in Cradock.

Her mother's severe religiosity and her father's kinder but incompetent management of family life left Olive with a strong need to find love and support outside her domestic circle. To some extent she found comfort in a feeling for nature and a sense of oneness with the universe at large. She began to call herself a freethinker and use her time in Cradock to pursue formal training in languages and the arts and to work on her writing. At age fifteen she was sent to her first position as a governess, but she was too young and insecure to sustain such responsibilities. Instead, she moved from one house to another until in 1870, she rejoined her brother at the New Rush diamond fields (now called Kimberley). On the face of it, the likelihood of Schreiner's success as a writer seems as remote as the wilderness of her surroundings. On the contrary, her later vivid depictions of childhood derive much of their intensity from the many trials and deprivations she herself had suffered.

At one of the homes where she visited, for example, she met an employee of the Native Affairs Department who lent her a copy of Herbert Spencer's *First Principles* (1871). This man, like the stranger who appears to Waldo in Part II of *African Farm*, was just passing through, but he had a profound effect upon Schreiner. For, Spencer's philosophy articulated and brought together many of Schreiner's own deeply felt ideas and questions about the meaning of life. His account of the "Unknowable" reconciled science and religion by seeing reason and belief as equally necessary aspects of human consciousness (see Appendix B). According to Spencer, in the material world, progress means evolution of more complex and heterogeneous types. Scientific discovery, then, would never eliminate the human need for a directive force beyond human understanding. However, Spencer also observes that the law of progress is not directed toward human happiness.

After reading Spencer, Schreiner was able to understand the role of religious belief among her family and friends and to accept her own intellectual and passionate faith in a cosmic unity underlying nature. Her interest in intellectual questions and her outspoken manner sometimes fascinated and sometimes intimidated her acquaintances. By the time she was twenty, she had read not only Spencer, but also most of the leading Victorian thinkers of the day, including Emerson, Mill, and Darwin. From such reading, she embraced several key concepts of nineteenth-century thought: first, the importance of nature as a symbol of the organic unity of life; second, the struggle for existence and an evolutionary approach to human history; and third, a strong understanding of the social forms that oppress women.

While she was developing intellectually at an extraordinary rate, emotionally she remained vulnerable and unprotected. She was sometimes able to work on her writing while she supported herself as a governess. Without family support and with the tremendous demands on her not only to educate her employers' children but also to help with any household chores deemed necessary, Schreiner could only write for a few hours in the early morning or very late at night. Her accommodations were sometimes terrible and often she complained of a chest condition that had developed during the anxious, transient years after her father's dismissal and ensuing bankruptcy. She was, nevertheless, determined to support herself and by 1880, she had a manuscript of *African Farm* ready to send to her friends in England. This was not her first novel; an earlier attempt, entitled *Undine*, would remain unpublished in her lifetime, and another, *From Man to Man,* begun in her years as a governess, was never completed. Both of these works would be published only after her death. Encouraged by the publisher's request for cuts and revisions of *African Farm*, Schreiner worked another year on the manuscript.

Her fiction writing had helped her to mature and develop as a writer, but when Schreiner prepared finally to go to England, it was with the intention of studying medicine. Exhausted but excited, Schreiner, now age 26, set sail in 1881 with her revised manuscript and her application to enter nurse's training at the Royal Infirmary in Edinburgh. Schreiner did begin nurse's training, but her weak physical condition and the gaps in her formal education prevented her from pursuing a career in health care. In the meantime, she read widely in the fields of philosophy and literature. It is interesting that she reread George Eliot's *The Mill on the Floss* at this period. Although Schreiner disliked its suffocating view of "duty," Maggie Tulliver's struggles for knowledge and love involved some of the same contradictions Schreiner's own Lyndall faces in *African Farm*. Unlike Eliot's protagonist, however, Schreiner's characters are neither hampered nor sustained by family ties. The difficulties that Lyndall and Waldo face are more directly linked to the social conditions of class and gender. After the manuscript of her work had been rejected by three other publishers, Chapman and Hall accepted Schreiner's novel on the recommendation of George Meredith.[1] Although the publishers suggested that her book would receive wider circulation from the booksellers and lending libraries if she had Lyndall marry her Stranger, Schreiner refused to make any changes and the work was published as we know it in 1883. In all, fifteen editions of *African Farm* were to appear in Schreiner's lifetime.

She was instantly treated as a celebrity and invited to join various organizations and social groups. But her family and friends in South Africa were not pleased by the unorthodox views expressed in the novel, and Schreiner's life in London was also made difficult by the lack of freedom and support for women's equality with men. Like her character Lyndall, Schreiner suffered under the gender biases of her era. Her brothers were sent to England to be educated, but she was largely self-taught. As a governess, she was subjected to the sexual advances of male employers, yet as a young Victorian woman, she was not supposed to experience sexual desire herself or express ideas outside the conventional wisdom of her community. Her reading of John Stuart Mill on the woman question had informed much of the Lyndall character's views (see Appendix C), but Schreiner's own desire for economic and moral independence was shaped by her experiences in London.

The reality of English social life for a woman and a colonial in metropolitan London was full of anxieties and conflicts. Schreiner had left home with high hopes of participating in a wider and freer

---

1   Poet and novelist, Meredith's *The Ordeal of Richard Feverel* (1859) was considered too prurient for some readers. He later attained popular success with *The Egoist* (1879). In this novel, the heroine wins respect for her intelligence and demands control of her own destiny.

world than her youth had known, but in many ways the position of women in England was no better than in South Africa. Immediately after the publication of *The Story of an African Farm*, she met Havelock Ellis, then a medical student, who may have been her lover for a brief time but certainly became a close friend. Ellis made a name for himself as a literary reviewer—he wrote one of the first important reviews of Thomas Hardy—and later became renown for his studies in sexology. Although many of Schreiner's early letters to Ellis offer interesting insights into her purposes as a writer, her relationship with him has also unduly influenced the way critics and biographers read Schreiner's life and the novel.[1] Schreiner disagreed with Ellis on several issues concerning women's sexuality and women's role in society. While both agreed that women's moral responsibility and economic independence were crucial for the progress of civilization, Ellis tended to emphasize women's moral responsibilities in terms of their role as mothers. Schreiner declared in her ground-breaking tract *Woman and Labor* (1911) that "We take all labor for our province!" (see Appendix C).

Through her acquaintance with Ellis, Schreiner met other Victorian writers and intellectuals interested in the woman question. She participated in the notorious Men and Women's Club, organized by the philosopher and mathematician Karl Pearson. There, carefully chosen men and women were supposed to talk in a disciplined and intellectual manner about woman's physical and emotional nature, including her sexuality. Unfortunately, the assumptions and conditioned responses of both the men and women in this group prevented the kind of open discussion necessary to understanding women's sexual needs, and the lack of openness proved discouraging for Schreiner. Often ill, moving constantly from one type of living quarters to another, she was very unhappy, despite the impression of energy and intelligence she gave others.

She was attracted to intelligent men, but those men did not reciprocate her feelings. When her doctor proposed marriage, she

---

1 In her edition of the Schreiner-Ellis correspondence, Yaffa Claire Draznin points out that three years after their meeting, the correspondence becomes increasingly one-sided. Most of Ellis's letters were destroyed. She also notes that Schreiner's letters to Ellis project a very different persona from her letters to other correspondents. Thus, to base our understanding of Schreiner's personality solely on her relationship with Ellis would be misleading, despite the fact that they were life-long friends.

refused. The problem for Schreiner, as for all intellectual women, was to find acceptance for her passionate feelings as well as her intellectual ambitions. Since she insisted on intellectual camaraderie, she did not permit herself sexual interest, for to admit attraction was to allow herself to be treated as a woman, someone dependent on a man. Instead, she suffered the frustration of feelings and desires that remained largely incomprehensible to her contemporaries. Some of her insights into the relations of men and women were developed in short stories published in a volume entitled *Dreams* (1890). The allegorical form of these stories allowed Schreiner to deal in symbolic terms with the ideological differences that undermined human relationships and social progress (see Appendix D).

In 1889, Schreiner returned to South Africa in part to recover from what had become chronic asthma. There she met and initially admired Cecil Rhodes, then Prime Minster of Cape Colony. Schreiner later criticized Rhodes and his imperialist policies in South Africa in her short novel *Trooper Peter Halket of Mashonaland* (1897). She hoped that her book would warn her readers about Rhodes and his plans to provoke war between Britain and South Africa. Schreiner also wrote several essays on the politics of South Africa and Boer culture. Although the original drafts were burned along with many of her possessions during the Boer War, Schreiner rewrote some of the chapters and published them as journal articles that were eventually collected as a volume in 1911 (see Appendix A).

Although Schreiner was ambivalent about the institution of marriage, she was pursued by a gentleman farmer who admired her work and claimed to be a freethinker and searcher for truth like Schreiner's characters in *African Farm*. Schreiner at first tried to test his feelings and her own by leaving for England, but she returned after a few months. Her health was not good, and Samuel Cron Cronwright's physical strength and unwavering affection won her consent. In 1894 they married and Cronwright added Schreiner's name to his own. Within a year she gave birth to a child, but it died the next morning. This was a crushing blow for both parents. In the years that followed Schreiner had several miscarriages. Her health problems meant that she could not stay on Cronwright's farm near Cradock. Reluctantly, Cronwright sold his property, and from various residences in Kimberley, Hanover, and Johannesburg, he and Schreiner participated in political debates about the constitution of the Republic of South

Africa. In 1913, she traveled alone to London where she remained during World War I as a conscientious objector. Cronwright visited her after the war, but she was in a very weakened state. In August 1920, she returned alone to South Africa, where she died four months later.

Characterization, Setting, Structure and Narrative Voice in *The Story of an African Farm*

But should one sit down to paint the scenes among which he has grown, he will find that the facts creep in upon him. Those brilliant phases and shapes which the imagination sees in far-off lands are not for him to portray. Sadly he must squeeze the color from his brush, and dip it into the gray pigments around him. He must paint what lies before him. (From Schreiner's Preface to the second edition of *African Farm*.)

Among the more fascinating aspects of the crafting of this work are its characterization, its setting, and the division of the novel into two very distinctive parts. The characterizations and setting are appropriate to Schreiner's own context and experience, but they are also deftly combined with a dualistic structure and divided narration that are experimental in form. Schreiner's focus in the novel is to show the development of the major characters in the shared isolation of their colonial setting, and she helps us visualize their struggles through their childish eyes and without the artificiality of elaborate descriptions. Her mode of narration does not allow the reader to identify with a single "heroic" figure whose narrative progress is self-serving or predictable. Instead, the landscape functions as the "title character" with its own decisive effect on the individuals caught within it. Moreover, the division of the novel into two contrasting portions permits juxtapositions of the points of view of childhood and young adulthood, and of the perspectives of the various protagonists.

A. Characterization

Knowing something of Schreiner's biography allows us to appreciate her projection of the metaphysical and social struggles that engaged her consciousness in the characterizations of Waldo and Lyndall and to see these characters, perhaps, as representative of the two sides of Schreiner's own struggle for knowledge and independence. Although all three of the children in Part I are confined to the same small farm, Em, who will inherit it, seems the most at home. In this, and in her placid nature, she seems a suitable foil to the other two characters. She does not face the same intellectual turmoil and spiritual challenges as her two companions and friends, but simply appears to accept definition from her circumstances and setting, and ultimately is in harmony with them. Schreiner's biographers and critics have been quick to equate Lyndall with her creator, largely because of her outright, and occasionally outraged, opposition to the constrains imposed on women of the Victorian era. In fact, the symmetries with Waldo may be equally instructive. Like Waldo, Schreiner was largely self-taught, and her intense idealism made her impatient with the hypocrisies of institutionalized religions. Though she was, again as Waldo, so thoroughly familiar with the Bible that it influenced the language and style of her writing, *African Farm* often alludes to the Bible as a means of expressing unconventional attitudes. From Blenkins's misuse of Biblical authority for his own gain to Waldo's naïve attempts at literal interpretations of the Old Testament, the novel undermines any orthodox approach to Christian beliefs, with the possible exception of Schreiner's sympathetic treatment of the Old German, Waldo's father.

Loneliness and the hardships of rural life encompass the children's lives; but as the narrator in "Times and Seasons" suggests in Part II, a child's sense of abandonment by cruel or hypocritical authorities is also one that we all have felt. At such times, the words of strangers and of books can be as profound as oracles. Growing up, as it is represented most particularly by Waldo, begins in "striving" and ends in "dreams." Here and in the fundamental configuration of three young children, supervised by a foolish and inadequate caretaker and isolated in an environment where their fates are obviously, but unpredictably, entwined, are the palpably mythic elements of Schreiner's narrative. The intrusion of a villainous stranger in Part I and the other, more subtle, new arrivals and departures in Part II add liveliness and suspense to the story. Much of the power of *African Farm*, however, comes from Schreiner's success in evoking the inner drama of childhood and its shaping force on each child's character.

Such a novel may seem as peculiar to today's cosmopolitan and media-driven readers as it did to some London readers in Schreiner's time. But in response to such reactions, Schreiner's preface to the second edition of the novel distinguishes her method from what she calls "the stage method" of writing or the familiar tale of adventure. The predictability of conventional narrative is foregone, according to Schreiner, for the sake of "the life we all lead." That Waldo is beaten for reading John Stuart Mill's *Political Economy*, or gratefully receives a book like Herbert Spencer's *First Principles* from an admired stranger, suggests the unusually high standards of Schreiner's intellectual life; but the importance of reading itself to any child's self-making is indisputable and suggests metatextually one of Schreiner's purposes in writing her novel. For even today, any work that soothes what Schreiner calls at the end of chapter one "the barb in the arrow of childhood's suffering" becomes a sustaining influence.

B. Setting

If in *African Farm*, books are the necessary catalyst for a child's individuality, the landscape heightens and broadens the context of his or her struggles. From the first line of the novel, Schreiner insists on the geography of her story: "The full African moon poured down its light from the blue sky into the wide, lonely plain." Though we know the earth has only one moon, Schreiner's description of the "African" moon and the landscape it illuminates situates the actions and thoughts of her characters in a world both concrete and symbolic. All of the details that describe the farm's buildings are transformed by the "peculiar brightness" of the African moon to something more beautiful than the functional reality that dominates during the day. Inside the farmhouse, the dreams of the inhabitants introduce us to their individual characters: the Boer-woman suffers from indigestion while the son of the German overseer struggles with the metaphysics of time and mortality. The opening scene thus offers a soft-focussed view of the setting and a privileged view of the inhabitants' private concerns.

By the first sentence of the second chapter, we also have a date: "At last came the year of the great drought, the year of 1862." Foregrounding a time of drought and using words such as "Karoo" and "kopje," which were introduced to English readers at this time to describe the African countryside, underscore the importance of the physical circumstances of the children. For Em, the landscape offers a perpetual present. She never leaves the social and mental confines of the farm and in the end she inherits the place and becomes iden- tified with it. Waldo is almost always seen lying on the ground, day- dreaming or imagining, his physical and social positioning suggest- ing that he is as vulnerable to exploitation and misery as the Bushmen whose paintings he discovers on the rocks. His relation to the land is nostalgic and romantic, a yearning for nature that will finally compel him to return to the farm. Only Lyndall seems to reject the gravitational force of the Karoo and desire a future some- where else instead—until we remember that her last request is to be taken away from the boarding house and toward a "blue moun- tain" which is not blue, but another "low and brown" landscape, "covered with long waving grasses and rough stones." Schreiner's spare style of writing represents both the difficult circumstances of the colonists' lives and the mysterious ways in which the landscape shapes individual consciousness.

In noting how the experiences of childhood shape the con- sciousness of the adult, Schreiner reiterates and extends the influ- ential views of the Romantics. Nature is less a consoler and moral guide in *African Farm* than a witness to the transitions in the child's understanding. If at first the wind after a thunderstorm lends sweet- ness to the "unutterable longing" of youth, or portends the forgiv- ing breath of God, experience teaches the child that nature is nei- ther a product of individual desire (a "poor, plastic thing, to be toyed with") nor the negation of desire ("a weltering chaos"). By the end of the meditative chapter "Times and Seasons," the child exchanges dreams and superstitions for knowledge: "there on the flat stone, on which we so often have sat to weep and pray, we look down and see it covered with the fossil footprints of great birds, and the beautiful skeleton of a fish." The study of nature provides the child, as it did many Victorians, with a consistency to existence, "a One." A scientific romanticism replaces the older version of roman- tic feeling. It provides an "intense satisfaction" because it offers new grounds for the child's relationship to nature and the supernatural.

C. Structure: Division and Diversification and
   the Loss of Narrative Certainty

Through its dual focus upon the external and internal landscapes of its central characters, Part I of *African Farm* establishes a compelling narrative, punctuated by events that are suitably dramatic, even ironically melodramatic, at times. Readers may feel especially drawn to Waldo's intense inner life and pity the innocence of the children amidst the fallen and materialistic adult world embodied by Tant' Sannie and Bonaparte Blenkins. Schreiner, however, takes a great risk with her novel by dividing the comparatively simple reading experience of Part I from a more challenging and varied handling of narration in Part II.

To keep the spiritual and moral as well as the historical and social consequences of her story in view, in Part II, Schreiner interrupts the narrative and the omniscient voice of the narrator. Throughout this second section, she employs a number of voices and modes of representation to convey the complexity of her critique of traditional religious and social orthodoxies. In Part I, the reader is presented with dramatic characters and events that call on our sympathy and judgement. To highlight Schreiner's focus on the self-consciousness of her characters, in Part II Waldo's, Lyndall's and Gregory's experiences are presented in retrospect or indirectly through dialogue, letters, and dreams.

The chapter entitled "Times and Seasons" is difficult to classify. Though it is introduced as an account of Waldo's spiritual development since his despair after Blenkins' mistreatment, the point of view changes from the third person to the first person and from singular to plural. Here Schreiner's reading of Spencer and Darwin inform her personal understanding of the relations of faith and knowledge. The individual's experience is presented in terms of a universal process that is shared by the author and her readers, and although the narrator seems to be addressing a specifically Christian conception of spiritual development, she substitutes nature and individual experience for traditional authority. Her language may seem unusual to contemporary readers, but her model may be found in the gospels of the New Testament. The generalized narrative of a child's faith, doubt and reconciliation with the world, a spiritual and emotional journey necessary for the attainment of self-consciousness, expresses Schreiner's conception of what nineteenth-century philosophers called "species-consciousness."

In his widely circulated work *The Essence of Christianity* (1841), Ludwig Feuerbach asserts that humanity's consciousness of a God is really self-consciousness, and what we know of God is derived from our self-knowledge.[1] Thus, for Feuerbach all religions are

---

1 Ludwig Feuerbach, *The Essence of Christianity*. Trans. George Eliot. 1854. New York: Harper and Row, 1957.

man-made; God is an ideal self-image towards which we strive. In "Times and Seasons," Schreiner writes, "Whether a man believes in a human-like God or no is a small thing. Whether he looks into the mental and physical world and sees no relation between cause and effect, no order, but a blind chance sporting, this is the mightiest fact that can be recorded in any spiritual existence. It were almost a mercy to cut his throat, if indeed he does not do it for himself." Knowledge of nature saves the soul from this tragedy by organizing experience into what Feuerbach called a "cognisance of species."

Consciousness of nature, including human nature, becomes for Feuerbach the same as consciousness of the infinite. As Schreiner concludes, "And so it comes to pass in time, that the earth ceases for us to be a weltering chaos. We walk in the great hall of life, looking up and round reverentially. Nothing is despicable—all is meaningful; nothing is small—all is part of a whole, whose beginning and end we know not. The life that throbs in us is a pulsation from it; too mighty for our comprehension, not too small." Freed from dogma, ready to explore the limits of the knowable and the unknowable, Schreiner's narrator has also led the reader to a new way of approaching the moral and social dilemmas of her characters. The seasons of the soul mark the stages of human consciousness apart from the contingencies of time and place. Moreover, by closing the gap between the narrator and the reader through the use of "we," Schreiner challenges her readers to be not only observers of the action of the text, but participants as well.

Whereas "Times and Seasons" expresses the unfolding of consciousness through the concrete details of childhood experience, the stranger's tale of the Hunter interprets Waldo's thoughts and desires for selfhood in highly symbolic terms. The formal allegory, with its personified figures, is not only about the quest for truth. It is also a self-reflective mode through which Schreiner highlights the ways in which each life represents a part of the universal life that cannot itself be represented. Thus the story is told to Waldo by a stranger who remains a shadowy and even unreliable character in the novel. He denies any special knowledge of Waldo's mind when he carved the wood's design. He says, "There is nothing so universally intelligible as truth. It has a thousand meanings and suggests a thousand more." What matters, then, is not the subject who narrates, but the object of narration. Truth, like art, will find its interpreters. But the maker of art, like the seeker of truth, must pursue a life of solitude. In reinforcing the myth of the individual artist as hero, Schreiner takes her place within a distinctly European literary tradition. The mesmerizing allegorical tale, like that of Coleridge's ancient mariner, transfixes Waldo and the reader temporarily, but there is more to Schreiner's exploration of the purposes of human life than the allegorical mode can express. Through the Hunter allegory, Schreiner presents the artist's struggle to bring truth into a world of superstitions and lies.

The stranger recommends that Waldo remain in the solitude and safety of the farm in order to protect his innocence and the purity of his conceptions, but in the end, of course, it is only the more placid Em who can tolerate such quiescence. Schreiner herself was determined to abandon the backwater of the colonial context for the cosmopolitan climate of London and managed to do so after the completion of her manuscript of *African Farm*. But it is Lyndall who best embodies this drive on Schreiner's part. Her quiet persistence in Part I of *African Farm* and her diatribes in Part II reinforce a different perspective from the other children. Lyndall's development represents Schreiner's own experience as a woman living on the margins of an empire in a time of great intellectual and social movements. The young Lyndall believes that education will bring her the knowledge and power she needs to construct her own destiny. What she learns at school is that women's education provides training only for what Schreiner described in *Woman and Labor* (1911) as "sexual parasitism," women's economic dependence on men. In allowing Lyndall to speak in her own voice and at length about the condition of women, Schreiner follows the discursive strategies of many Victorian writers who saw the novel as a means for raising social issues in a more congenial form than the essay. Moreover, by putting such controversial views in the speech of her character, Schreiner allows the reader to consider her ideas with more detachment than is possible in a chapter like "Times and Seasons." For, although Lyndall can explain the contradictions of women's social position to Waldo, she has already made a mistake that will keep her from pursuing the life of work and freedom she desires. In subsequent chapters, Lyndall's protest against social injustice becomes an internalized struggle to find "something to worship"—a phrase that suggests both the limits of Schreiner's feminism and the idealism of a woman's quest for meaningful activity.

If Lyndall is to some extent Schreiner's mouthpiece in the novel, then the desire for an ideal person or cause to give direction and meaning to life reflects the ideological limits imposed by historical circumstances on women at that time. Schreiner uses Lyndall to explore one set of contradictions that obscure and retard human consciousness. Waldo's work experiences as a wagon driver explore another. Both Lyndall's and Waldo's quests, which include the desire for something more than self-determination—"someone to belong to me" as Waldo says—represent struggles as strenuous and profound as the artist/hunter's abstract and solitary quest for truth. If gender overdetermines the form of Lyndall's quest and class overdetermines the form of Waldo's quest, Schreiner embraces both forms for herself and her readers in the novel as a whole.

The ending of the novel has sometimes perplexed readers accustomed to the strategies that give coherence and unity to most fictional works. Such readers can take comfort in the idea that Schreiner's sense of structure is based on patterns that unfold at different levels of experience rather than through a chain of cause and effect. That is why Lyndall's final look and Waldo's repose cannot be definitively interpreted. Schreiner signals her difference from conventional narratives in her preface when she notes that in her method, "when the curtain falls no one is ready." By allowing Waldo's dreams the same rhetorical power as Lyndall's discourses or Gregory's letters, Schreiner's multiple forms of narration dramatize the gaps between experience and understanding. With regard to the metaphysical issues it raises, the novel must remain open-ended. For Schreiner, the existence of God, or a "Hereafter," as well as the mysteries of sex and childbirth—"love" in its purest form—are part of the "unknowable" in Spencer's terms, that which lies beyond what human consciousness can know. For Em, Gregory, and especially Tant' Sannie, the knowable world provides answers enough and their lives, paradoxical perhaps in their juxtaposition to Lyndall's and Waldo's, allow us to see the limits of the everyday world and thus the reason or rationale for Lyndall's defiance of social norms and Waldo's refusal of any conventional consolation for her death.

The Ideological Context: Class, Race and Gender Issues in a Critical Understanding of the Novel

"It is not what is done to us, but what is made of us," she said at last, "that wrongs us. No man can be really injured but by what modifies himself. We all enter the world little plastic beings, with so much natural force, perhaps, but for the rest—blank; and the world tells us what we are to be, and shapes us by the ends it sets before us." ("Lyndall")

The Story of an African Farm may have been a watershed novel for what one Victorian critic called the "theological romance" (see Appendix D), but the racism that is taken for granted in Schreiner's work anticipates the brutal history of apartheid in South Africa. Schreiner's characterizations of the Hottentot maid and her references to "Kaffirs" rightfully make today's readers uneasy. The very word "kaffir" was insulting even in Schreiner's day, and she uses it often to refer both to the servants on the farm and to Africans in general. Moreover, the Hottentot maid is a particularly unsympathetic character. When Waldo's father and later Waldo himself are abused by Tant' Sannie and Blenkins, Schreiner describes how the maid takes delight in their suffering. When a pregnant servant is forced to leave the farm, Schreiner describes her as "sullen, ill-looking, with lips hideously protruding." Native South Africans are rarely referred to in a positive light.

Although Schreiner's work reflects the racist habits of white settler society in South Africa, her only overt reference to pseudo-scientific notions of racial types comes in a speech by Tant' Sannie, a character whose ignorance Schreiner ridicules throughout the novel. A more thoroughgoing account of her references to the indigenous peoples of Southern Africa reveals what Toni Morrison notes in white American writing as well: the dependence of white society on blacks to sustain their world and give it meaning.[1] For example, the first insights Waldo gains about art and life come from his reflections on the rock paintings of the Bushmen. Though the servant woman is described as ugly, Otto compares her plight to that of the Biblical figure Hagar, the mother of Ishmael whom God promised would father a great nation. In Part II, all of the narrator's, Waldo's, and even Lyndall's musings include references to the "kaffirs." These references often project black people as "other" to the whites. But this does not diminish their crucial significance to the characters' self-fashioning. According to Margaret Lenta, "At almost every point in the novel it is indicated that necessary physical work is being done by black people, not only on the farm but in the store where Waldo works, in the hotel where Lyndall lies sick

---

1 Toni Morrison, *Playing in the Dark: Whiteness and the Literary Imagination,* Harvard UP, 1992.

and on the transport waggons.... The dependence of whites in all areas of their lives on black labour is faithfully recorded."[1] Such recording was practically non-existent in other writings about Africa at the time. Moreover, in attempting to record "the life we all lead," as Schreiner claims in her preface, Schreiner's representation of Africans allows, perhaps, a more critical understanding of race relations than Conrad's highly symbolic depictions do in *Heart of Darkness* (1902).

After the publication of *African Farm* and her involvement in various social movements in London, Schreiner began to approach the subject of race more self-consciously. In her collected essays entitled *Thoughts on South Africa* (1923), Schreiner explains to her English readers both the problem and the promise that the multi-ethnic composition of South Africa entails for its emergence as a nation in the European mode (see Appendix A). During and after the Boer war and the consolidation of South Africa as an independent state, Schreiner opposed the white supremacists who denied blacks political rights. Critics who have analyzed Schreiner's later work, especially her essays, conclude that, although Schreiner conceived of the Boer victory over the Bushmen in evolutionary terms, she envisioned a united South African nation in which Black South Africans had the same rights as working people in Europe. According to Paula Krebs, "Schreiner's progressive political agenda meant that she could use the period's unstable definitions of race to make the Boers a race, make Africans a class, and see a future for South Africa in which a blended white people worked to replace African civilization with copies of European ones."[2]

To represent her characters and their social relations in the ethnographic terms of Victorian science, Schreiner calls our attention to the cultural identities of her characters. Tant' Sannie, the Boer-woman who is the girls' guardian, the German overseer, who is Waldo's father, and the Hottentot maid all represent for Schreiner the indigenous peoples of the region. It is significant that Em and Lyndall are of English descent and that Em's father's books are treasured by Waldo. Ignorance and superstition and the isolated nature of the place frustrate Lyndall's desire for power and Waldo's desire

---

1   Margaret Lenta, "Racism, Sexism, and Olive Schreiner's Fiction," *Theoria* 70 (1987): 25.
2   Paula Krebs, "Olive Schreiner's Racialization of South Africa," *Victorian Studies* 40 (1997): 443.

for knowledge, but while they are young, the children can imagine new possibilities for themselves. Contact with a more sophisticated culture through books or education appears a benign and necessary step toward progress.

The arrival into this world of Bonaparte Blenkins, an Irish charlatan, exposes the ignorance and cruelty of the frontier society and the hypocrisy of traditional patriarchal and religious authority. Schreiner also uses Blenkins, and later the Englishman Gregory Rose, to signify the opportunism of British policies in South Africa through their courtship and infidelities with Tant' Sannie and Em. Although Blenkins is an exaggerated figure of satire, his actions demonstrate the ways in which the structures of colonial power inhibited the minds and potential creativity of those under their rule. Blenkins' crushing of Waldo's sheep-shearing machine destroys not only Waldo's plans to better his prospects, but also the possibility of cultural progress in South Africa that such technology might have made possible.

Waldo's loss of faith and his initial turn toward technology represent the disillusionments of nineteenth-century culture. Like many of her contemporaries, Schreiner used observations of animal behavior to provide analogies to patterns in human life. After Waldo's invention has been destroyed, the narrator moves closer to the ground and in a cinematic way focuses our attention on the deadly game the dog Doss plays with an unsuspecting and hardworking black-beetle. As in the encounter between Waldo and Blenkins, there seems no justice, only "a striving and a striving and an ending in nothing." The novel as a whole, however, goes beyond both Waldo's naive idealism and his equally naïve materialism. The indifference of nature and the absence of a personal God who might intervene underscore the sufferings of individuals in the social as well as natural environment.

But if Schreiner follows Darwin in treating the struggle for existence as one of the conditions of life, her views of social evolution are more progressive than those which promoted the elimination of so-called inferior races. Schreiner echoes the views of evolutionists like Spencer who saw human history as a recapitulation of individual development. As Lyndall comments to Waldo, "sometimes what is more amusing still than tracing the likeness of man to man, is to trace the analogy there always is between the progress of one individual and a whole nation; or again, between a single nation and the entire human race." The conflicts depicted in *African Farm* reflect not only transitions occurring in South Africa from an agrarian world of traditional religious and provincial culture to the newly industrialized and freethinking attitudes of the gold and diamond mine communities; they also address the new social conditions that undermined the civilizing processes that science and empire were supposed to promote.

Part II follows the lives of four protagonists whose individual ambitions are complicated by the social conditions of class and gender. Racism and imperialism remain implicit in Schreiner's characterization of Gregory Rose's arrival to manage the farm, but he also serves, along with Lyndall, as a pragmatic correction to the tendency to generalize from the individual "man" to the "human" condition. The division of humankind into categories of men and women is examined in Schreiner's world to discriminate between matters of social convention and essential difference. Although Gregory has many thoroughly conventional opinions about men's and women's differences, he need only wear women's clothes to be allowed to act the part of Lyndall's nurse. Lyndall recognizes his true character when she tells Waldo, "there goes a true woman.... How happy he would be sewing frills into his little girls' frocks...." But her own attempts to cross gender boundaries are less successful. For some readers, Lyndall's death represents Schreiner's failure to imagine the possibility for a woman to live freely in a male-dominated society. For Victorian feminists and later for those engaged in the movement for women's suffrage, however, Lyndall's analysis of the contradictions of woman's position provided insight and encouragement for their own struggles despite her tragic end. In either case, Lyndall's autonomy remains uncompromised as long as she does not marry; her pregnancy, then, calls attention to an unresolvable difference between the experiences of men and women.

Waldo's experiences of labor raise another issue of vital interest to Victorian readers. Schreiner's interest in political economy has gone largely unnoticed by contemporary critics, but Waldo's description of the brutalizing effects of class exploitation points out another way in which *African Farm* offers a radical critique of the dominant ideology. Waldo's first job as a store clerk reveals the artificiality of distinctions between men of different races and the primacy of economics in determining social relations. Waldo's boss makes him sign an agreement to work for low wages, his co-workers are selfish and insincere, and every person he meets seems determined to lie or cheat in order to make money. In retrospect, Waldo writes, "There was one respectable thing in that store—it was the Kaffir storeman. His work was to load and unload, and he never needed to smile except when he liked, and he never told lies."

Seeking to end the degradation that wage labor engenders, Waldo becomes a transport driver in charge of carrying materials between the towns and the mining camps. Because he does not own or control the wagons, Waldo cannot protest when the master leaves him to manage the wagons by himself. Physically exhausted, his life is no better than the starved and beaten oxen that are forced to haul the heavy loads. Waldo recognizes that such work can destroy a man's soul and turn even a European man into a beast or a devil. Back in town loading and unloading wagons, Waldo has time again to read and enough energy to take a walk to the sea, but his social position as a laborer still separates him from the handsome and intelligent gentlefolk he sees in town, including the stranger whose refinement he inordinately admires. His desire for people, for Lyndall in particular, but also for the relatively communal labor of the farm, motivates Waldo to return to the homestead.

Although his account is interrupted by the news of Lyndall's death, Schreiner has clearly structured Waldo's letter to correspond to Lyndall's analysis of the miseducation and oppression of women. In both cases, the children have freed themselves from the restraints of a traditional society only to be enslaved by the cultural and economic structures of frontier capitalism. In this context, it is not so surprising that the Boer women Tant' Sannie and Em are treated with compassion and humor at the end. Their culture is narrow and antiquated, but it is finally closer to a moral order than that of Blenkins or the other strangers who pass through. The chick nestled on Waldo's arm sleeve, wiser than the good-hearted Em, is a sentimental image for Schreiner's belief that individual lives and social formations must finally be subsumed in a cosmic process that is beyond our comprehension. Her critique of social injustice remains within the frame of her agnosticism. As Waldo's final musings suggest, "Well to live long and see the new time breaking."

What are twenty-first-century readers to make of Schreiner's curiously mixed novel? If her radical critique of society has lost much of its shock value, it has not yet lost its soundness. Today's reader must consider how to locate and interpret its open racism, the vehemence of Lyndall's feminist rhetoric, and the weight of class on Waldo's expectations for the future within the novel's historical context without losing sight of the fact that none of these issues of race, class and gender has been successfully resolved in our own day. More than a century after it first appeared in print, Lyndall's statement still holds meaning for readers: "It is not what is done to us, but what is made of us that wrongs us.... The world tells what we are to be, and shapes us by the ends it sets before us." *The Story of an African Farm* may not overcome the ends that Victorian social and literary conventions set before its author, but Schreiner's consciousness of how the world shapes us still provides a telling and provocative point of view.

Olive Schreiner: A Brief Chronology

1837   Gottlob Schreiner (born 1814) marries Rebecca
        Lyndall (born 1817).
1838   Schreiners arrive at Philippolis station in the Orange
        Free State.
1855   Olive Emilie Albertina is born on March 24th. She is
        one of nine surviving children.
1842-67 Schreiners are posted to various missions. After 27
        years service Gottlob is dismissed and the family is
        dispersed. Olive is sent to Cradock to live with her
        brother Theo.
1862   Olive's sister Ellie dies at age two. Later Olive claims
        that her death made her reject organized religion and
        call herself a freethinker.
1870   Theo, Ettie and Olive's younger brother Will leave
        for the diamond fields. Olive, age 15, begins work as a
        governess.
1872-3 Olive rejoins Theo and Ettie in New Rush, later
        Kimberley, diamond fields.
1874-81 Olive works as governess on various farms. She
        begins work on three novels, *Undine*, *The Story of an
        African Farm*, and *From Man to Man*.
1880   Olive sends manuscript of *The Story of an African Farm*
        to friends in Lancashire, England.
1881-89 Olive lives in England and travels to Europe. Her
        friends include Havelock Ellis, Edward Carpenter,
        Eleanor Marx, and Karl Pearson.
1883   *The Story of an African Farm* is published by Chapman
        and Hall.
1889   Olive returns to South Africa where she meets Cecil
        Rhodes, owner of De Beers Consolidated Mines and
        later Prime Minister of Cape Colony. Olive becomes
        involved in the struggles between British and Boer
        interests in South Africa and eventually breaks with
        Rhodes' imperialist policies.
1890-2 Havelock Ellis arranges for the publication of a
        collection of Olive's allegorical tales entitled *Dreams*.
        Olive writes a series of essays and a skit on South
        African issues.

1894	Olive marries Samuel Cron Cronwright who changes his name to Cronwright-Schreiner.
1895	Olive's baby girl dies within 16 hours of birth.
1896	In the aftermath of the failure of Jameson's Raid to allow British annexation of the Transvaal, Olive and Samuel visit England to agitate for a peaceful solution to conflicts in South Africa.
1897	Olive's novel, *Trooper Peter Halket of Mashonaland*, a thinly veiled attack on Rhodes, is published in London.
1899-1902	Boer Wars. Olive lives most of the war in the village of Hanover in Cape Colony where martial law is strictly imposed. The peace settlement allows Britain to annex all of the former Dutch states of Southern Africa.
1911	Olive's life-long interests in gender and class issues involve her in debates over the new constitution of South Africa. She publishes *Woman and Labour*.
1913-20	Olive lives alone in London. During the war she writes and speaks as a conscientious objector. Her favorite brother, Will, dies in 1919. Cronwright visits Olive in London for a month before she leaves for South Africa.
1920	Olive dies on 13 August at Wynberg, near Cape Town.

A Note on the Text

The glossary and text of *The Story of an African Farm* are from the first edition, published in 1883. Schreiner added a Preface and Dedication to the second edition, which are also reproduced here. Inconsistencies in punctuation and spelling in the text have been corrected.

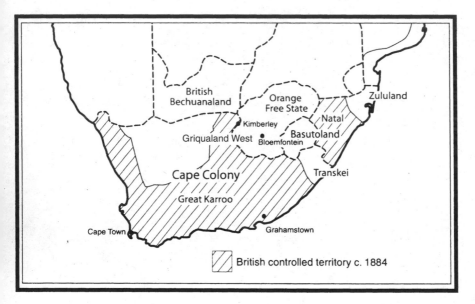

Southern Africa at the time of Schreiner's novel

THE STORY OF
AN AFRICAN FARM

To My Friend

Mrs. John Brown
Of Burnley,

This Little Firstling Of My Pen

Is Lovingly Inscribed

Ralph Iron

South Kensington, London
June, 1883

"We must see the first images which the external world casts upon the dark mirror of his mind; or must hear the first words which awaken the sleeping powers of thought, and stand by his earliest efforts, if we would understand the prejudices, the habits, and the passions that will rule his life. The entire man is, so to speak, to be found in the cradle of the child."

Alexis De Tocqueville

Preface to the Second Edition

I have to thank cordially the public and my critics for the reception they have given this little book.

Dealing with a subject that is far removed from the round of English daily life, it of necessity lacks the charm that hangs about the ideal representation of familiar things, and its reception has therefore been the more kindly.

A word of explanation is necessary. Two strangers appear on the scene, and some have fancied that in the second they have again the first, who returns in a new guise. Why this should be we cannot tell; unless there is a feeling that a man should not appear upon the scene, and then disappear, leaving behind him no more substantial trace than a mere book; that he should return later on as husband or lover to fill some more important part than that of the mere stimulator of thought.

Human life may be painted according to two methods. There is the stage method. According to that each character is duly marshalled at first, and ticketed; we know with an immutable certainty that at the right crises each one will reappear and act his part, and, when the curtain falls, all will stand before it bowing. There is a sense of satisfaction in this, and of completeness. But there is another method—the method of life we all lead. Here nothing can be prophesied. There is a strange coming and going of feet. Men appear, act and re-act upon each other, and pass away. When the crisis comes the man who would fit it does not return. When the curtain falls no one is ready. When the footlights are brightest they are blown out; and what the name of the play is no one knows. If there sits a spectator who knows, he sits so high that the players in the gaslight cannot hear his breathing. Life may be painted according to either method; but the methods are different. The canons of criticism that bear upon the one cut cruelly upon the other.

It has been suggested by a kind critic that he would better have liked the little book if it had been a history of wild adventure; of cattle driven into inaccessible 'kranzes'[1] by Bushmen; "of encounters with ravening lions, and hairbreadth escapes."[2] This could not

---

1   A wall of rocks crowning the summit of mountains in the Cape region.
2   Schreiner quotes an anonymous reviewer in the *Saturday Review* (21 April 1883). For other reviews of *African Farm*, see Appendix E.

be. Such works are best written in Piccadilly or in the Strand:[1] there the gifts of the creative imagination, untrammelled by contact with any fact, may spread their wings.

But, should one sit down to paint the scenes among which he has grown, he will find that the facts creep in upon him. Those brilliant phases and shapes which the imagination sees in far-off lands are not for him to portray. Sadly he must squeeze the colour from his brush, and dip it into the grey pigments around him. He must paint what lies before him.

R. Iron[2]

June, 1883

---

1 Fashionable and commercial areas of Central London, far from the reality of the world Schreiner describes.
2 Schreiner used the pseudonym Ralph Iron in the early editions of *The Story of an African Farm*.

Glossary[1]

Benaauwdheit	Indigestion.
Brakje	A little cur of low degree.
Bultong	Dried meat.
In-span	To harness.
Kappje	A sun-bonnet.
Karroo	The wide sandy plains in some parts of South Africa.
Karroo bushes	The bushes that take the place of grass on these plains.
Kartel	The wooden-bed fastened in an ox-waggon.
Kopje	A small hillock, or 'little head.'
Kraal	The space surrounded by a stone wall or hedged with thorn bushes, into which sheep or cattle are driven at night.
Mealies	Indian corn.
Meerkat	A small weasel-like animal.
Meiboss	Preserved and dried apricots.
Nachtmaal	The Lord's Supper.
Out-span	To unharness, or a place in the field where one unharnesses.
Predikant	Parson.
Reim	Leather rope.
Schlecht	Bad.
Sloot	A dry watercourse.
Spook	A ghost.
Stamp-block	A wooden block, hollowed out, in which mealies are placed to be pounded before being cooked.
Upsitting	In Boer courtship the man and girl are supposed to sit up together the whole night.
Velschoen	Shoes of undressed leather.

---

1   Schreiner included this glossary to help readers with words peculiar to the South African context of the novel. Her heading read, "Several Dutch and Colonial words occurring in this work, the subjoined Glossary is given, explaining the principal."

Contents.

Part I.

Chapter I.
Shadows from Child-Life.

The Watch.

The full African moon poured down its light from the blue sky into the wide, lonely plain. The dry, sandy earth, with its coating of stunted 'karroo' bushes a few inches high, the low hills that skirted the plain, the milk-bushes with their long finger-like leaves, all were touched by a weird and an almost oppressive beauty as they lay in the white light.

In one spot only was the solemn monotony of the plain broken. Near the centre a small solitary 'kopje' rose. Alone it lay there, a heap of round ironstones piled one upon another, as over some giant's grave. Here and there a few tufts of grass or small succulent plants had sprung up among its stones, and on the very summit a clump of prickly-pears lifted their thorny arms, and reflected, as from mirrors, the moon-light on their broad fleshy leaves. At the foot of the 'kopje' lay the homestead. First, the stonewalled 'sheep kraals' and Kaffir[1] huts; beyond them the dwelling-house—a square red-brick building with thatched roof. Even on its bare red walls, and the wooden ladder that led up to the loft, the moon-light cast a kind of dreamy beauty, and quite etherealised the low brick wall that ran before the house, and which enclosed a bare patch of sand and two straggling sunflowers. On the zinc roof of the great, open waggon house, on the roofs of the outbuildings that jutted from its side, the moonlight glinted with a peculiar brightness, until it seemed that every rib in the metal was of burnished silver.

Sleep ruled everywhere, and the homestead was not less quiet than the solitary plain.

In the farmhouse, on her great wooden bedstead, Tant' Sannie the Boer-woman,[2] rolled heavily in her sleep.

---

1 Dutch settlers called black Africans "Kaffirs." According to the *Dictionary of South Africa*, the word "kaffir" is "offensive in all senses and combinations." Schreiner uses it here and throughout the novel to refer to Africans of the Nguni group who lived in the eastern territories of South Africa.

2 Boer refers to rural Dutch or Afrikaans-speaking farmers in South Africa.

She had gone to bed, as she always did, in her clothes, and the night was warm and the room close, and she dreamed bad dreams. Not of the ghosts and devils that so haunted her waking thoughts; not of her second husband, the consumptive Englishman, whose grave lay away beyond the ostrich camps, nor of her first, the younger Boer; but only of the sheep's trotters she had eaten for supper that night. She dreamed that one stuck fast in her throat, and she rolled her huge form from side to side, and snorted horribly.

In the next room, where the maid had forgotten to close the shutter, the white moonlight fell in a flood, and made it light as day. There were two small beds against the wall. In one lay a yellow-haired child, with a low forehead and a face of freckles; but the loving moonlight hid defects here as elsewhere, and showed only the innocent face of a child in its first sweet sleep.

The figure in the companion bed belonged of right to the moonlight, for it was of quite elfin-like beauty. The child had dropped her cover on the floor, and the moonlight looked in at the naked little limbs. Presently she opened her eyes and looked at the moonlight that was bathing her.

"Em!" she called to the sleeper in the other bed, but received no answer. Then she drew the cover from the floor, turned her pillow, and pulling the sheet over her head, went to sleep again.

Only in one of the outbuildings that jutted from the waggon-house there was someone who was not asleep. The room was dark; door and shutter were closed; not a ray of light entered anywhere. The German overseer, to whom the room belonged, lay sleeping soundly on his bed in the corner, his great arms folded, and his bushy grey and black beard rising and falling on his breast. But one in the room was not asleep. Two large eyes looked about in the darkness, and two small hands were smoothing the patchwork quilt. The boy, who slept on a box under the window, had just awakened from his first sleep. He drew the quilt up to his chin, so that little peered above it but a great head of silky black curls and the two black eyes. He stared about it in the darkness. Nothing was visible, not even the outline of one worm-eaten rafter, nor of the deal table, on which lay the Bible from which his father had read before they went to bed. No one could tell where the toolbox was, and where the fireplace. There was something very impressive to the child in the complete darkness.

At the head of his father's bed hung a great silver hunting watch. It ticked loudly. The boy listened to it, and began mechanically to count. Tick—tick—tick—tick! One, two, three, four! He lost count presently, and only listened. Tick—tick—tick—tick!

It never waited; it went on inexorably; and every time it ticked *a man died*! He raised himself a little on his elbow and listened. He wished it would leave off.

How many times had it ticked since he came to lie down? A thousand times, a million times, perhaps.

He tried to count again, and sat up to listen better.

"Dying, dying, dying!" said the watch; "dying, dying, dying!"

He heard it distinctly. Where were they going to, all those people?

He lay down quickly, and pulled the cover up over his head; but presently the silky curls reappeared.

"Dying, dying, dying!" said the watch; "dying, dying, dying!"

He thought of the words his father had read that evening—"*For wide is the gate, and broad is the way, that leadeth to destruction, and many there be which go in thereat.*"[1]

"Many, many, many!" said the watch.

"*Because strait is the gate, and narrow is the way, that leadeth unto life, and few there be that find it.*"[2]

"Few, few, few!" said the watch.

The boy lay with his eyes wide open. He saw before him a long stream of people, a great dark multitude, that moved in one direction; then they came to the dark edge of the world, and went over. He saw them passing on before him, and there was nothing that could stop them. He thought of how that stream had rolled on through all the long ages of the past—how the old Greeks and Romans had gone over; the countless millions of China and India, they were going over now. Since he had come to bed, how many had gone!

"Stop them! stop them!" cried the child.

And all the while the watch kept ticking on; just like God's will, that never changes or alters, you may do what you please.

Great beads of perspiration stood on the boy's forehead. He climbed out of bed and lay with his face turned to the mud floor.

"Oh, God, God! save them!" he cried in agony. "Only some; only a few! Only for each moment I am praying here one!" He folded his little hands upon his head. "God! God! save them!"

---

1   Matthew 7:13.
2   Matthew 7:14.

He grovelled on the floor.

Oh, the long, long ages of the past, in which they had gone over! Oh, the long, long future, in which they would pass away! Oh, God! the long, long, long eternity, which has no end!

The child wept, and crept closer to the ground.

The Sacrifice.

The farm by daylight was not as the farm by moonlight. The plain was a weary flat of loose red sand, sparsely covered by dry karroo bushes, that cracked beneath the tread like tinder, and showed the red earth everywhere. Here and there a milk-bush lifted its pale-coloured rods, and in every direction the ants and beetles ran about in the blazing sand. The red walls of the farmhouse, the zinc roofs of the outbuildings, the stone walls of the 'kraals,' all reflected the fierce sunlight, till the eye ached and blenched. No tree or shrub was to be seen far or near. The two sunflowers that stood before the door, out-stared by the sun, drooped their brazen faces to the sand; and the little cicada-like insects cried aloud among the stones of the 'kopje.'

The Boer-woman, seen by daylight, was even less lovely than when, in bed, she rolled and dreamed. She sat on a chair in the great front room, with her feet on a wooden stove, and wiped her flat face with the corner of her apron, and drank coffee, and in Cape Dutch swore that the beloved weather was damned. Less lovely, too, by daylight was the dead Englishman's child, her little step-daughter, upon whose freckles and low, wrinkled forehead the sunlight had no mercy.

"Lyndall," the child said to her little orphan cousin, who sat with her on the floor threading beads, "how is it your beads never fall off your needle?"

"I try," said the little one gravely, moistening her tiny finger. "That is why."

The overseer, seen by daylight, was a huge German, wearing a shabby suit, and with a childish habit of rubbing his hands and nodding his head prodigiously when pleased at anything. He stood at the kraals in the blazing sun, explaining to two Kaffir boys the approaching end of the world. The boys, as they cut the cakes of dung, winked at each other, and worked as slowly as they possibly could; but the German never saw it.

Away, beyond the 'kopje,' Waldo his son herded the ewes and lambs—a small and dusty herd—powdered all over from head to foot with red sand, wearing a ragged coat and shoes of undressed leather, through whose holes the toes looked out. His hat was too large, and had sunk down to his eyes, concealing completely the silky black curls. It was a curious small figure. His flock gave him little trouble. It was too hot for them to move far; they gathered round every little milk-bush as though they hoped to find shade, and stood there motionless in clumps. He himself crept under a shelving rock that lay at the foot of the 'kopje,' stretched himself on his stomach, and waved his dilapidated little shoes in the air.

Soon, from the blue bag where he kept his dinner, he produced a fragment of slate, an arithmetic, and a pencil. Proceeding to put down a sum with solemn and earnest demeanour, he began to add it up aloud: "Six and two is eight—and four is twelve and two is fourteen—and four is eighteen." Here he paused. "And four is eighteen and four is eighteen." The last was very much drawled. Slowly the pencil slipped from his fingers, and the slate followed it into the sand. For a while he lay motionless, then began muttering to himself, folded his little arms, laid his head down upon them, and might have been asleep, but for a muttering sound that from time to time proceeded from him. A curious old ewe came to sniff at him; but it was long before he raised his head. When he did, he looked at the far-off hills with his heavy eyes.

"Ye shall receive—ye shall receive—shall, shall, shall,"[1] he muttered.

He sat up then. Slowly the dullness and heaviness melted from his face; it became radiant. Mid-day had come now, and the sun's rays were poured down vertically; the earth throbbed before the eye.

The boy stood up quickly, and cleared a small space from the bushes which covered it. Looking carefully, he found twelve small stones of somewhat the same size; kneeling down, he arranged them carefully on the cleared space in a square pile, in shape like an altar. Then he walked to the bag where his dinner was kept; in it was a mutton chop and a large slice of brown bread. The boy took them out and turned the bread over in his hand, deeply considering it. Finally he threw it away and walked to the altar with the meat, and laid it down on the stones. Close by in the red sand he knelt down. Sure, never since the beginning of the world was there so ragged and so small a priest. He took off his great hat and

---

1   Probably a reference to Mark 11:24.

placed it solemnly on the ground, then closed his eyes and folded his hands. He prayed aloud.

"Oh, God, my Father, I have made Thee a sacrifice. I have only two pence, so I cannot buy a lamb. If the lambs were mine I would give Thee one; but now I have only this meat; it is my dinner-meat. Please, my Father, send fire down from heaven to burn it. Thou hast said, Whosoever shall say unto this mountain, Be thou cast into the sea, nothing doubting, it shall be done.[1] I ask for the sake of Jesus Christ. Amen."

He knelt down with his face upon the ground, and he folded his hands upon his curls. The fierce sun poured down its heat upon his head and upon his altar. When he looked up he knew what he should see—the glory of God! For fear his very heart stood still, his breath came heavily; he was half suffocated. He dared not look up. Then at last he raised himself. Above him was the quiet blue sky, about him the red earth; there were the clumps of silent ewes and his altar—that was all.

He looked up—nothing broke the intense stillness of the blue overhead. He looked round in astonishment, then he bowed again, and this time longer than before.

When he raised himself the second time all was unaltered. Only the sun had melted the fat of the little mutton-chop, and it ran down upon the stone.

Then, the third time he bowed himself. When at last he looked up, some ants had come to the meat on the altar. He stood up and drove them away. Then he put his hat on his hot curls, and sat in the shade. He clasped his hands about his knees. He sat to watch what would come to pass. The glory of the Lord God Almighty! He knew he should see it.

"My dear God is trying me," he said; and he sat there through the fierce heat of the afternoon. Still he watched and waited when the sun began to slope; and when it neared the horizon and the sheep began to cast long shadows across the karroo, he still sat there. He hoped when the first rays touched the hills till the sun dipped behind them and was gone. Then he called his ewes together, and broke down the altar, and threw the meat far, far away into the field.

He walked home behind his flock. His heart was heavy. He reasoned so: "God cannot lie. I had faith. No fire came. I am like

---

1 Mark 11:23.

Cain—I am not His.[1] He will not hear my prayer. God hates me."

The boy's heart was heavy. When he reached the 'kraal' gate the two girls met him.

"Come," said the yellow-haired Em, "let us play 'coop.'[2] There is still time before it gets quite dark. You, Waldo, go and hide on the 'kopje'; Lyndall and I will shut eyes here, and we will not look."

The girls hid their faces in the stone wall of the sheep-kraal, and the boy clambered half way up the 'kopje.' He crouched down between two stones and gave the call. Just then the milk-herd came walking out of the cow-kraal with two pails. He was an ill-looking Kaffir.

"Ah!" thought the boy, "perhaps he will die to-night, and go to hell! I must pray for him, I must pray!"

Then he thought—"Where am *I* going to?" and he prayed desperately.

"Ah! this is not right at all," little Em said, peeping between the stones, and finding him in a very curious posture. "What *are* you doing, Waldo? It is not the play, you know. You should run out when we come to the white stone. Ah, you do not play nicely."

"I—I will play nicely now," said the boy, coming out and standing sheepishly before them; "I—I only forgot; I will play now."

"He had been to sleep," said freckled Em.

"No," said beautiful little Lyndall, looking curiously at him; "he has been crying."

She never made a mistake.

The Confession.

One night, two years after, the boy sat alone on the 'kopje.' He had crept softly from his father's room and come there. He often did, because, when he prayed or cried aloud, his father might awake and hear him; and none knew his great sorrow, and none knew his grief, but he himself, and he buried them deep in his heart.

He turned up the brim of his great hat and looked at the moon, but most at the leaves of the prickly pear that grew just

---

1   Cain was the son of Adam and Eve. In Genesis, chapter 4, Cain makes an offering of fruit while his brother Abel offers a lamb. God accepts Abel's offering. Cain is upset and kills Abel. God then banishes Cain and his offspring.

2   A game like "hide and seek". The hider calls "coop" when he/she is ready.

before him. They glinted, and glinted, and glinted, just like his own heart—cold, so hard, and very wicked. His physical heart had pain also; it seemed full of little bits of glass, that hurt. He had sat there for half an hour, and he dared not go back to the close house.

He felt horribly lonely. There was not one thing so wicked as he in all the world, and he knew it. He folded his arms and began to cry—not aloud; he sobbed without making any sound, and his tears left scorched marks where they fell. He could not pray; he had prayed night and day for so many months; and to-night he could not pray. When he left off crying, he held his aching head with his brown hands. If one might have gone up to him and touched him kindly, poor, ugly little thing! Perhaps his heart was almost broken.

With his swollen eyes he sat there on a flat stone at the very top of the 'kopje'; and the tree, with every one of its wicked leaves, blinked, and blinked, and blinked at him. Presently he began to cry again, and then stopped his crying to look at it. He was quiet for a long while, then he knelt up slowly and bent forward. There was a secret he had carried in his heart for a year. He had not dared to look at it; he had not whispered it to himself; but for a year he had carried it. "I hate God!" he said. The wind took the words and ran away them, among the stones, and through the leaves of the prickly pear. He thought it died away half down the 'kopje.' He had told it now!

"I love Jesus Christ, but I hate God."

The wind carried away that sound as it had done the first. Then he got up and buttoned his old coat around him. He knew he was certainly lost now; he did not care. If half the world were to be lost, why not he too? He would not pray for mercy any more. Better so—better to know certainly. It was ended now. Better so.

He began scrambling down the sides of the 'kopje' to go home.

Better so!—But oh, the loneliness, the agonised pain! for that night, and for nights on nights to come! The anguish that sleeps all day on the heart like a heavy worm, and wakes up at night to feed!

There are some of us who in after years say to Fate, "Now deal us your hardest blow, give us what you will; but let us never again suffer as we suffered when we were children."

The barb in the arrow of childhood's suffering is this—its intense loneliness, its intense ignorance.

Chapter II.
Plans and Bushman-Paintings.[1]

At last came the year of the great drought, the year of eighteen-sixty-two.[2] From end to end of the land the earth cried for water. Man and beast turned their eyes to the pitiless sky, that like the roof of some brazen oven arched overhead. On the farm day after day, month after month, the water in the dams fell lower and lower; the sheep died in the fields; the cattle, scarcely able to crawl, tottered as they moved from spot to spot in search of food. Week after week, month after month, the sun looked down from the cloudless sky, till the 'karroo bushes' were leafless sticks, broken into the earth, and the earth itself was naked and bare; and only the milk-bushes, like old hags, pointed their shrivelled fingers heavenwards, praying for the rain that never came.

★★★

It was on an afternoon of a long day in that thirsty summer, that on the side of the 'kopje' furthest from the homestead the two girls sat. They were somewhat grown since the days when they played hide-and-seek there, but they were mere children still.

Their dress was of dark coarse stuff; their common blue pinafores reached to their ankles, and on their feet they wore home-made 'velschoen.'

They sat under a shelving rock, on the surface of which were still visible some old Bushman-paintings, their red and black pigments having been preserved through long years from wind and rain by the overhanging ledge: grotesque oxen, elephants,

---

1   Bushman was the name given by the Dutch settlers to members of the San people, hunter-gatherers who had lived in the South and Southwest of Africa for centuries. Their stone drawings were made from natural pigments.

2   Droughts and disease were common afflictions for settlers and natives alike in the area where Schreiner grew up. Schreiner's father was moved to the eastern Cape in 1861 to run the Wesleyan training institute. In order to provide for his family and forty-four African candidates for the ministry, he engaged in trade, which was strictly forbidden by the mission. As a result, he was disgraced and eventually bankrupted. The drought that Schreiner refers to here was probably unusual only in its effects on her personal history.

rhinoceroses, and a one-horned beast, such as no man ever has seen or ever shall.

The girls sat with their backs to the paintings. In their laps were a few fern and ice-plant leaves, which by dint of much searching they had gathered under the rocks.

Em took off her big brown kappje and began vigorously to fan her red face with it; but her companion bent low over the leaves in her lap, and at last took up an ice-plant leaf and fastened it on to the front of her blue pinafore with a pin.

"Diamonds must look as these drops do," she said, carefully bending over the leaf, and crushing one crystal drop with her delicate little nail. "When I," she said, "am grown up, I shall wear real diamonds, exactly like these, in my hair."

Her companion opened her eyes and wrinkled her low forehead.

"Where will you find them, Lyndall? The stones are only crystals that we picked up yesterday. Old Otto says so."

"And you think that I am going to stay *here* always?"

The lip trembled scornfully.

"Ah, no," said her companion. " I suppose some day we shall go somewhere; but now we are only twelve, and we cannot marry till we are seventeen. Four years, five—that is a long time to wait. And we might not have diamonds if we did marry."

"And you think that I am going to stay here till then?"

"Well, where *are* you going?" asked her companion.

The girl crushed an ice-plant leaf between her fingers.

"Tant' Sannie is a miserable old woman," she said. "Your father married her when he was dying, because he thought she would take better care of the farm, and of us, than an English-woman. He said we should be taught and sent to school. Now she saves every farthing for herself, buys us not even one old book. She does not ill-use us—why? Because she is afraid of your father's ghost. Only this morning she told her Hottentot[1] that she would have beaten you for breaking the plate, but that three nights ago she heard a rustling and a grunting behind the pantry door, and knew it was your father coming to 'spook' her. She is a miserable old woman,"

---

1   Hottentot was the name given to the Khoikhoi people by early travelers and the Dutch settlers. The name refers to the linguistic clicks that are part of the Khoikhoi language.

said the girl, throwing the leaf from her; "but I intend to go to school."

"And if she won't let you?"

"I shall make her."

"How?"

The child took not the slightest notice of the last question, and folded her small arms across her knees.

"But why do you want to go, Lyndall?"

"There is nothing helps in this world," said the child slowly, "but to be very wise, and to know everything—to be clever."

"But I should not like to go to school!" persisted the small freckled face.

"And you do not need to. When you are seventeen this Boer-woman will go; you will have this farm and everything that is upon it for your own; but I," said Lyndall, "will have nothing. I must learn."

"Oh, Lyndall! *I* will give you some of my sheep," said Em, with a sudden burst of pitying generosity.

"I do not want your sheep," said the girl slowly; "I want things of my own. When I am grown up," she added, the flush on her delicate features deepening at every word, "there will be nothing that I do not know. I shall be rich, very rich; and I shall wear not only for best, but every day, a pure white silk, and little rose-buds, like the lady in Tant' Sannie's bed-room, and my petticoats will be embroidered, not only at the bottom, but all through."

The lady in Tant' Sannie's bed-room was a gorgeous creature from a fashion-sheet, which the Boer-woman, somewhere obtaining, had pasted up at the foot of her bed, to be profoundly admired by the children.

"It would be very nice," said Em; but it seemed a dream of quite too transcendent a glory ever to be realized.

At this instant there appeared at the foot of the 'kopje' two figures—the one, a dog, white and sleek, one yellow ear hanging down over his left eye; the other, his master, a lad of fourteen, and no other than the boy Waldo, grown into a heavy, slouching youth of fourteen. The dog mounted the 'kopje' quickly, his master followed slowly. He wore an aged jacket much too large for him, and rolled up at the wrists, and, as of old, a pair of dilapidated 'velschoens' and a felt hat. He stood before the two girls at last.

"What have you been doing to-day?" asked Lyndall, lifting her eyes to his face.

"Looking after ewes and lambs below the dam. Here!" he said, holding out his hand awkwardly, "I brought them for you."

There were a few green blades of tender grass.

"Where did you find them?"

"On the dam wall."

She fastened them beside the leaf on her blue pinafore.

"They look nice there," said the boy, awkwardly rubbing his great hands and watching her.

"Yes; but the pinafore spoils it all; it is not pretty."

He looked at it closely.

"Yes, the squares are ugly; but it looks nice upon you—beautiful."

He now stood silent before them, his great hands hanging loosely at either side.

"Some one has come to-day," he mumbled out suddenly, when the idea struck him.

"Who?" asked both girls.

"An Englishman on foot."

"What does he look like?" asked Em.

"I did not notice; but he has a very large nose," said the boy slowly. "He asked the way to the house."

"Didn't he tell you his name?"

"Yes—Bonaparte Blenkins."

"Bonaparte!" said Em, "why that is like the reel Hottentot Hans plays on the violin—

'Bonaparte, Bonaparte, my wife is sick;
In the middle of the week, but Sundays not,
I give her rice and beans for soup—'

It is a funny name."

"There was a living man called Bonaparte[1] once," said she of the great eyes.

---

1   Napoleon Bonaparte (1769-1821), was born in Corsica, received military
    training in France, and led important campaigns in Egypt and Italy after
    the French Revolution. His military and political skills won him appoint-
    ment as first consul of France in 1799. In 1804, he had himself crowned
    emperor. He achieved much by reforming the administrative and legal
    services of the country, but his ambitions to extend French rule through-
    out Europe brought him into conflict with England. Despite defeat and
    abdication of power in 1813, Napoleon returned from exile and ruled
    again briefly until a decisive defeat at Waterloo in 1815. He was then
    imprisoned on the island of St. Helena where he died in 1821.

"Ah yes, I know," said Em—"the poor prophet whom the lions ate. I am always so sorry for him."

Her companion cast a quiet glance upon her.

"He was the greatest man who ever lived," she said, "the man I like best."

"And what did he do?" asked Em, conscious that she had made a mistake, and that her prophet was not the man.

"He was one man, only one," said her little companion slowly, "yet all the people in the world feared him. He was not born great, he was common as we are; yet he was master of the world at last. Once he was only a little child, then he was a lieutenant, then he was a general, then he was an emperor. When he said a thing to himself he never forgot it. He waited, and waited, and waited, and it came at last."

"He must have been very happy," said Em.

"I do not know," said Lyndall; "but he had what he said he would have, and that is better than being happy. He was their master, and all the people were white with fear of him. They joined together to fight him. He was one and they were many, and they got him down at last. They were like the wild cats when their teeth are fast in a great dog, like cowardly wild cats," said the child, "they would not let him go. They were many; he was only *one*. They sent him to an island in the sea, a lonely island, and kept him there fast. He was one man, and they were many, and they were terrified at him. It was glorious!" said the child.

"And what then?" said Em.

"Then he was alone there in that island with men to watch him always," said her companion, slowly and quietly, "and in the long lonely nights he used to lie awake and think of the things he had done in the old days, and the things he would do if they let him go again. In the day when he walked near the shore it seemed to him that the sea all around him was a cold chain about his body pressing him to death.'

"And then?" said Em, much interested.

"He died there in that island; he never got away."

"It is rather a nice story," said Em; "but the end is sad."

"It is a terrible, hateful ending," said the little teller of the story, leaning forward on her folded arms; "and the worst is, it is true. I have noticed," added the child very deliberately, "that it is only the made-up stories that end nicely; the true ones all end so."

As she spoke the boy's dark, heavy eyes rested on her face.

"You have read it, have you not?"

He nodded. "Yes; but the brown history tells only what he did, not what he thought."

"It was in the brown history that I read of him," said the girl; "but I *know* what he thought. Books do not tell everything."

"No," said the boy, slowly drawing nearer to her and sitting down at her feet. "What you want to know they never tell."

Then the children fell into silence, till Doss, the dog, growing uneasy at its long continuance, sniffed at one and the other, and his master broke forth suddenly—

"If *they* could talk, if *they* could tell us now!" he said, moving his hand out over the surrounding objects—"then we would know something. This 'kopje,' if it could tell us how it came here! The 'Physical Geography' says," he went on most rapidly and confusedly, "that what are dry lands now were once lakes; and what I think is this—these low hills were once the shores of a lake; this 'kopje' is some of the stones that were at the bottom, rolled together by the water. But there is this—how did the water come to make one heap here alone, in the centre of the plain?" It was a ponderous question; no one volunteered an answer. "When I was little," said the boy, "I always looked at it and wondered, and I thought a great giant was buried under it. Now I know the water must have done it; but how? It is very wonderful. Did one little stone come first, and stopped the others as they rolled?" said the boy with earnestness, in a low voice, more as speaking to himself than to them.[1]

"Oh, Waldo, God put the little 'kopje' here," said Em with solemnity.

---

1   The first of many allusions by Waldo to the challenges that modern science posed to traditional religious belief. Nineteenth-century geologists were among the first to suggest that the earth was millions of years old and that changes had occurred through natural processes. Waldo's desire to understand how these processes worked points to a secular and evolutionary approach to nature to which Em's theistic response already appears outdated and inadequate. But Waldo's story of what the stones might say if they could speak also reflects the desires of many evolutionists to read natural history progressively, either in terms of movement toward a predetermined goal, or, as Spencer insisted, in terms of ascending levels of organization and complexity. The negative implications of the story the stones tell are apparent in Waldo's subsequent musings on the extinction not only of animals and Bushmen but also his own life and those of Em and Lyndall.

"But how did he put it here?"

"By wanting."

"But how did the wanting bring it here?"

"Because it did."

The last words were uttered with the air of one who produces a clinching argument. What effect it had on the questioner was not evident, for he made no reply, and turned away from her.

Drawing closer to Lyndall's feet, he said after a while in a low voice,

"Lyndall, has it never seemed to you that the stones *were* talking with you? Sometimes," he added in a yet lower tone, "I lie under there with my sheep, and it seems that the stones are really speaking—speaking of the old things, of the time when the strange fishes and animals lived that are turned into stone now, and the lakes were here; and then of the time when the little Bushmen lived here, so small and so ugly, and used to sleep in the wild dog holes, and in the 'sloots,' and eat snakes, and shot the bucks with their poisoned arrows. It was one of them, one of these old wild Bushmen, that painted those," said the boy, nodding towards the pictures—"one who was different from the rest. He did not know why, but he wanted to make something beautiful—he wanted to make something, so he made these. He worked hard, very hard, to find the juice to make the paint; and then he found this place where the rocks hang over and he painted them. To us they are only strange things, that make us laugh; but to him they were very beautiful."

The children had turned round and looked at the pictures.

"He used to kneel here naked, painting, painting, painting; and he wondered at the things he made himself," said the boy, rising and moving his hand in deep excitement. "Now the Boers have shot them all, so that we never see a little yellow face peeping out among the stones." He paused, a dreamy look coming over his face. "And the wild bucks have gone, and those days, and we are here. But we will be gone soon, and only the stones will lie on here, looking at everything like they look now. I know that it is I who am thinking," the fellow added slowly, "but it seems as though it were they who are talking. Has it never seemed so to you, Lyndall?"

"No, it never seems so to me," she answered.

The sun had dipped now below the hills, and the boy, suddenly remembering the ewes and lambs, started to his feet.

"Let us also go to the house and see who has come," said Em as the boy shuffled away to rejoin his flock, while Doss ran at his heels, snapping at the ends of the torn trousers as they fluttered in the wind.

Chapter III.
I Was a Stranger, and Ye Took Me In.[1]

As the two girls rounded the side of the 'kopje,' an unusual scene presented itself. A large group was gathered at the back door of the homestead.

On the door-step stood the Boer-woman, a hand on each hip, her face red and fiery, her head nodding fiercely. At her feet sat the yellow Hottentot maid, her satellite, and around stood the black Kaffir maids, with blankets twisted round their half-naked figures. Two, who stamped mealies in a wooden block, held the great stampers in their hands, and stared stupidly at the object of attraction. It certainly was not to look at the old German overseer, who stood in the centre of the group, that they had all gathered together. His salt-and-pepper suit, grizzly black beard, and grey eyes were as familiar to every one on the farm as the red gables of the homestead itself; but beside him stood the stranger, and on him all eyes were fixed. Ever and anon the new-comer cast a glance over his pendulous red nose to the spot where the Boer-woman stood, and smiled faintly.

"I'm not a child," cried the Boer-woman, in low Cape Dutch, "and I wasn't born yesterday. No, by the Lord, no! You can't take *me* in! My mother didn't wean me on Monday. One wink of my eye and I see the whole thing. I'll have no tramps sleeping on my farm," cried Tant' Sannie blowing. "No, by the Devil, no! not though he had sixty-times-six red noses."

There the German overseer mildly interposed that the man was not a tramp, but a highly respectable individual, whose horse had died by an accident three days before.

"Don't tell me," cried the Boer-woman; "the man isn't born that can take *me* in. If he'd had money, wouldn't he have bought a horse? Men who walk are thieves, liars, murderers, Rome's priests,[2] seducers! I see the Devil in his nose!"[3] cried Tant' Sannie, shaking

---

1 Matthew 25:43.
2 Roman Catholics.
3 Blenkins' red nose is a sign that he is an alcoholic.

her fist at him; "and to come walking into the house of this Boer's child, and shaking hands as though he came on horseback! Oh, no, no!"

The stranger took off his hat, a tall, battered chimney-pot, and disclosed a bald head, at the back of which was a little fringe of curled white hair; and he bowed to Tant' Sannie.

"What does she remark, my friend?" he inquired, turning his cross-wise looking eyes on the old German.

The German rubbed his old hands, and hesitated.

"Ah—well—ah—the—Dutch—you know—do not like people who walk—in this country—ah!"

"My dear friend," said the stranger, laying his hand on the German's arm, "I should have bought myself another horse, but crossing, five days ago, a full river I lost my purse—a purse with five hundred pounds in it. I spent five days on the bank of the river trying to find it—couldn't. Paid a Kaffir nine pounds to go in and look for it at the risk of his life—couldn't find it."

The German would have translated this information, but the Boer-woman gave no ear.

"No, no; he goes to-night. See how he looks at me—a poor, unprotected female! If he wrongs me, who is to do me right?" cried Tant' Sannie.

"I think," said the German in an undertone, "if you didn't look at her quite so much it might be advisable. She—ah—she—might—imagine that you liked her too well,— in fact—ah—"

"Certainly, my dear friend, certainly," said the stranger, "I shall not look at her."

Saying this, he turned his nose full upon a small Kaffir of two years old. That small naked son of Ham[1] became instantly so terrified that he fled to his mother's blanket for protection, howling horribly.

Upon this the new-comer fixed his eyes pensively on the stamp-block, folding his hands on the head of his cane. His boots were broken, but he still had the cane of a gentleman.

"You vaggabonds se Engelschman!" said Tant' Sannie, looking straight at him.

This was a near approach to plain English; but the man con-

---

1 Ham, son of Noah in the Bible, was cursed by God. Some Christians associated Ham and his descendants with black Africans; their prejudice thus assumed Biblical authority.

templated the block abstractedly, wholly unconscious that any antagonism was being displayed towards him.

"You might not be a Scotchman or anything of that kind, might you?" suggested the German. "It is the English that she hates."

"My dear friend," said the stranger, "I am Irish every inch of me—father Irish, mother Irish. I've not a drop of English blood in my veins."

"And you might not be married, might you?" persisted the German. "If you had a wife and children, now? Dutch people do not like those who are not married."

"Ah," said the stranger looking tenderly at the block, "I have a dear wife and three sweet little children—two lovely girls and a noble boy."

This information having been conveyed to the Boer-woman, she, after some further conversation, appeared slightly mollified; but remained firm to her conviction that the man's designs were evil.

"For, dear Lord!" she cried; "all Englishmen are ugly; but was there ever such a red-rag-nosed thing with broken boots and crooked eyes before? Take him to your room," she cried to the German; "but all the sin he does I lay at your door."

The German having told him how matters were arranged, the stranger made a profound bow to Tant' Sannie, and followed his host, who led the way to his own little room.

"I thought she would come to her better self soon," the German said joyously. "Tant' Sannie is not wholly bad, far from it, far." Then seeing his companion cast a furtive glance at him, which he mistook for one of surprise, he added quickly, "Ah, yes, yes; we are all a primitive people here—not very lofty. We deal not in titles. Every one is Tanta and Oom—aunt and uncle. This may be my room," he said opening the door. "It is rough, the room is rough; not a palace—not quite. But it may be better than the fields, a little better!" he said, glancing round at his companion. "Come in, come in. There is something to eat—a mouthful: not the fare of emperors or kings; but we do not starve, not yet," he said, rubbing his hands together and looking round with a pleased, half-nervous smile on his old face.

"My friend, my dear friend," said the stranger, seizing him by the hand, "may the Lord bless you, the Lord bless and reward you— the God of the fatherless and the stranger. But for you I would this night have slept in the fields, with the dews of heaven upon my head."

Late that evening Lyndall came down to the cabin with the

German's rations. Through the tiny square window the light streamed forth and without knocking she raised the latch and entered. There was a fire burning on the hearth, and it cast its ruddy glow over the little dingy room, with its worm-eaten rafters and mud floor, and broken white-washed walls. A curious little place, filled with all manner of articles. Next to the fire was a great tool-box; beyond that the little bookshelf with its well-worn books; beyond that, in the corner, a heap of filled and empty grain-bags. From the rafters hung down straps, 'reims,' old boots, bits of harness, and a string of onions. The bed was in another corner, covered by a patchwork quilt of faded red lions, and divided from the rest of the room by a blue curtain, now drawn back. On the mantelshelf was an endless assortment of little bags and stones; and on the wall hung a map of South Germany, with a red line drawn through it to show where the German had wandered. This place was the one home the girls had known for many a year. The house where Tant' Sannie lived and ruled was a place to sleep in, to eat in, not to be happy in. It was in vain she told them they were grown too old to go there; every morning and evening found them there. Were there not too many golden memories hanging about the old place for them to leave it?

Long winter nights, when they had sat round the fire and roasted potatoes, and asked riddles, and the old man had told of the little German village, where, fifty years before, a little German boy had played at snowballs, and had carried home the knitted stockings of a little girl who afterwards became Waldo's mother; did they not seem to see the German peasant girls walking about with their wooden shoes and yellow, braided hair, and the little children eating their suppers out of little wooden bowls when the good mothers called them in to have their milk and potatoes?

And were there not yet better times than these? Moonlight nights, when they romped about the door, with the old man, yet more a child than any of them, and laughed, till the old roof of the waggon-house rang?

Or, best of all, were there not warm, dark, starlight nights, when they sat together on the doorstep, holding each other's hands, singing German hymns, their voices rising clear in the still night air—till the German would draw away his hand suddenly to wipe quickly a tear the children must not see? Would they not sit looking up at the stars and talking of them—of the dear Southern Cross, red, fiery Mars, Orion, with his belt, and the Seven Mysterious Sisters—and fall to speculating over them? How old are they?

Who dwelt in them? And the old German would say that perhaps the souls we loved lived in them; *there*, in that little twinkling point was perhaps the little girl whose stockings he had carried home; and the children would look up at it lovingly, and call it "Uncle Otto's star." Then they would fall to deeper speculations—of the times and seasons wherein the heavens shall be rolled together as a scroll, and the stars shall fall as a fig-tree casteth her untimely figs, and there shall be time no longer; "when the Son of man shall come in His glory, and all His holy angels with Him."[1] In lower and lower tones they would talk, till at last they fell into whispers; then they would wish good night softly, and walk home hushed and quiet.

To-night, when Lyndall looked in, Waldo sat before the fire watching a pot which simmered there, with his slate and pencil in his hand; his father sat at the table buried in the columns of a three-weeks-old newspaper; and the stranger lay stretched on the bed in the corner, fast asleep, his mouth open, his great limbs stretched out loosely, betokening much weariness. The girl put the rations down upon the table, snuffed the candle, and stood looking at the figure on the bed.

"Uncle Otto," she said presently, laying her hand down on the newspaper, and causing the old German to look up over his glasses, "how long did that man say he had been walking?"

"Since this morning, poor fellow! A gentleman—not accustomed to walking—horse died—poor fellow!" said the German, pushing out his lip and glancing commiseratingly over his spectacles in the direction of the bed where the stranger lay, with his flabby double chin, and broken boots through which the flesh shone.

"And do you believe him, Uncle Otto?"

"Believe him? why of course I do. He himself told me the story three times *distinctly*."

"If," said the girl slowly, "he had walked for only one day his boots would not have looked so; and if——"

"*If*!" said the German, starting up in his chair, irritated that any one should doubt such irrefragable evidence—"*if*! Why, he told me *himself*! Look how he lies there," added the German pathetically, "worn out—poor fellow! We have something for him though," pointing with his forefinger over his shoulder to the saucepan that stood on the fire. "We are not cooks—not French

---

1 Matthew 25:31.

cooks, not quite; but it's drinkable, drinkable, I think; better than nothing, I think," he added, nodding his head in a jocund manner, that evinced his high estimation of the contents of the saucepan and his profound satisfaction therein. "Bish! bish! my chicken," he said, as Lyndall tapped her little foot up and down upon the floor. "Bish! bish! my chicken, you will wake him."

He moved the candle so that his own head might intervene between it and the sleeper's face; and, smoothing his newspaper, he adjusted his spectacles to read.

The child's grey-black eyes rested on the figure on the bed, then turned to the German, then rested on the figure again.

"*I* think he is a liar. Good night, Uncle Otto," she said slowly, turning to the door.

Long after she had gone the German folded his paper up methodically, and put it in his pocket.

The stranger had not awakened to partake of the soup, and his son had fallen asleep on the ground. Taking two white sheep-skins from the heap of sacks in the corner, the old man doubled them up, and lifting the boy's head gently from the slate on which it rested, placed the skins beneath it.

"Poor lambie, poor lambie!" he said, tenderly patting the great rough bear-like head; "tired, is he!"

He threw an overcoat across the boy's feet, and lifted the saucepan from the fire. There was no place where the old man could comfortably lie down himself, so he resumed his seat. Opening a much-worn Bible, he began to read, and as he read pleasant thoughts and visions thronged on him.

"I was a stranger, and ye took me in," he read.[1]

He turned again to the bed where the sleeper lay.

"I was a stranger."

Very tenderly the old man looked at him. He saw not the bloated body nor the evil face of the man; but, as it were, under deep disguise and fleshly concealment, the form that long years of dreaming had made very real to him. "Jesus, lover, and is it given to us, weak and sinful, frail and erring, to serve *Thee*, to take *Thee* in!" he said softly, as he rose from his seat. Full of joy, he began to pace the little room. Now and again as he walked he sang the lines of a German hymn, or muttered broken words of prayer. The little room was full of light. It appeared to the German that Christ was

---

1 Matthew 25:35.

very near him, and that at almost any moment the thin mist of earthly darkness that clouded his human eyes might be withdrawn, and that made manifest of which the friends at Emmaus, beholding it, said, "It is the Lord!"[1]

Again, and yet again, through the long hours of that night, as the old man walked, he looked up to the roof of his little room, with its blackened rafters, and yet saw them not. His rough bearded face was illuminated with a radiant gladness; and the night was not shorter to the dreaming sleepers than to him whose waking dreams brought heaven near.

So quickly the night fled, that he looked up with surprise when at four o'clock the first grey streaks of summer dawn showed themselves through the little window. Then the old man turned to rake together the few coals that lay under the ashes, and his son, turning on the sheep-skins, muttered sleepily to know if it were time to rise.

"Lie still, lie still! I would only make a fire," said, the old man.

"Have you been up all night?" asked the boy.

"Yes; but it has been short, very short. Sleep again, my chicken; it is yet early."

And he went out to fetch more fuel.

Chapter IV.
Blessed Is He That Believeth.[2]

Bonaparte Blenkins sat on the side of the bed. He had wonderfully revived since the day before, held his head high, talked in a full sonorous voice, and ate greedily of all the viands offered him. At his side was a basin of soup, from which he took a deep draught now and again as he watched the fingers of the German, who sat on the mud floor before him mending the bottom of a chair.

Presently he looked out, where, in the afternoon sunshine, a few half-grown ostriches might be seen wandering listlessly about, and then he looked in again at the little white-washed room, and at Lyndall, who sat in the doorway looking at a book. Then he raised

---

1 At Emmaus, Jesus met with some of his disciples who recounted to him the events of the crucifixion. Eventually, Jesus reveals himself to them as the resurrected Christ. See Luke 24:13-31.
2 See John 6:47.

his chin and tried to adjust an imaginary shirt-collar. Finding none, he smoothed the little grey fringe at the back of his head, and began—

"You are a student of history, I perceive, my friend, from the study of these volumes that lie scattered about this apartment; this fact has been made evident to me."

"Well—a little—perhaps—it may be," said the German meekly.

"Being a student of history then," said Bonaparte, raising himself loftily, "you will doubtless have heard of my great, of my celebrated kinsman, Napoleon Bonaparte?"

"Yes, yes," said the German, looking up.

"I, sir," said Bonaparte, was born at this hour, on an April afternoon, three-and-fifty years ago. The nurse, sir, she was the same who attended when the Duke of Sutherland was born,—brought me to my mother. 'There is only one name for this child,' she said: 'he has the nose of his great kinsman; and so Bonaparte Blenkins became my name—Bonaparte Blenkins. Yes, sir," said Bonaparte, "there is a stream on *my* maternal side that connects me with a stream on *his* maternal side."

The German made a sound of astonishment.

"The connection," said Bonaparte, "is one which could not be easily comprehended by one unaccustomed to the study of aristocratic pedigrees; but the connection is close."

"Is it possible!" said the German, pausing in his work with much interest and astonishment. "Napoleon an Irishman!"

"Yes," said Bonaparte, "on the mother's side, and that is how we are related. There wasn't a man to beat him," said Bonaparte, stretching himself—"not a man except the Duke of Wellington.[1] And it's a strange coincidence," added Bonaparte, bending forward, "but *he* was a connection of mine. His nephew, the Duke of Wellington's nephew, married a cousin of mine. *She* was a woman! See her at one of the court balls—amber satin—daisies in her hair. Worth going a hundred miles to look at her! Often seen her there myself, sir!"

The German moved the leather thongs in and out, and thought of the strange vicissitudes of human life, which might bring the kinsman of dukes and emperors to his humble room.

---

1 Napoleon Bonaparte was born in Corsica, became emperor of France in 1804, and was defeated at the Battle of Waterloo by the English who were led by Arthur Wellesley, Duke of Wellington.

Bonaparte appeared lost among old memories.

"Ah, that Duke of Wellington's nephew!" he broke forth suddenly; "many's the joke I've had with him. Often came to visit me at Bonaparte Hall. Grand place I had then—park, conservatory, servants. He had only one fault, that Duke of Wellington's nephew," said Bonaparte, observing that the German was deeply interested in every word: "he was a coward—what you might call a coward. You've never been in Russia, I suppose?" said Bonaparte, fixing his cross-wise looking eyes on the German's face.

"No, no," said the old man humbly. "France, England, Germany, a little in this country; it is all I have travelled."

"*I*, my friend," said Bonaparte, "have been in every country in the world, and speak every civilized language, excepting only Dutch and German. I wrote a book of my travels—noteworthy incidents. Publisher got it—cheated me out of it. Great rascals those publishers! Upon one occasion the Duke of Wellington's nephew and I were travelling in Russia. All of a sudden one of the horses dropped down dead as a door-nail. There we were—cold night—snow four feet thick—great forest—one horse not being able to move sledge—night coming on—wolves.

"'Spree!'[1] says the Duke of Wellington's nephew.

"'Spree, do you call it?' says I. 'Look out.'

"There, sticking out under a bush, was nothing less than the nose of a bear. The Duke of Wellington's nephew was up a tree like a shot; I stood quietly on the ground, as cool as I am at this moment, loaded my gun, and climbed up the tree. There was only one bough.

"'Bon,' said the Duke of Wellington's nephew, 'you'd better sit in front.'

"'All right,' said I; 'but keep your gun ready. There are more coming.' He'd got his face buried in my back.

"'How many are there?' said he.

"'Four,' said I.

"'How many are there now?' said he.

"'Eight,' said I.

"'How many are there now?' said he.

"'Ten' said I.

"'Ten! ten!' said he; and down goes his gun.

---

1 A period of time for enjoying oneself, especially by spending money or drinking (Longman's *Contemporary English*).

"'Wallie,' I said, 'what have you done? We're dead men now.'

"'Bon, my old fellow,' said he, 'I couldn't help it; my hands trembled so!'

"'Wall,' I said, turning round and seizing his hand, 'Wallie, my dear lad, good-bye. I'm not afraid to die. My legs are long—they hang down—the first bear that comes and I don't hit him, off goes my foot. When he takes it I shall give you my gun and go. You may yet be saved; but tell, oh, tell Mary Ann that I thought of her, that I prayed for her!'

"'Good-bye, old fellow!' said he.

"'God bless you!' said I.

"By this time the bears were sitting in a circle all round the tree. Yes," said Bonaparte impressively, fixing his eyes on the German, "a regular, exact circle. The marks of their tails were left in the snow, and I measured it afterwards; a drawing-master couldn't have done it better. It was that saved me. If they'd rushed on me at once, poor old Bon would never have been here to tell this story. But they came on, Sir, *systematically*, one by one. All the rest sat on their tails and waited. The first fellow came up, and I shot him; the second fellow—I shot him; the third—I shot him. At last the tenth came; he was the biggest of all—the leader, you may say.

"'Wall,' I said, 'give me your hand. My fingers are stiff with the cold; there is only one bullet left. I shall miss him. While he is eating me you get down and take your gun; and live, dear friend, live to remember the man who gave his life for you!' By that time the bear was at me. I felt his paw on my trousers.

"'Oh, Bonnie! Bonnie!' said the Duke of Wellington's nephew. But I just took my gun, and put the muzzle to the bear's ear—over he fell—dead!"

Bonaparte Blenkins waited to observe what effect his story had made. Then he took out a dirty white handkerchief, and stroked his forehead, and more especially his eyes.

"It always affects me to relate that adventure," he remarked, returning the handkerchief to his pocket. "Ingratitude—base, vile ingratitude—is recalled by it! That man, that man, who but for me would have perished in the pathless wilds of Russia, that man in the hour of my adversity forsook me." The German looked up. "Yes," said Bonaparte, "I had money, I had lands, I said to my wife, 'There is Africa, a struggling country; they want capital; they want men of talent; they want men of ability to open up that land. Let us go.'

"I bought eight thousand pounds worth of machinery—winnowing, ploughing, reaping machines; I loaded a ship with them.

Next steamer I came out—wife, children, all. Got to the Cape. Where is the ship with the things? Lost—gone to the bottom! And the box with the money? Lost—nothing saved!

"My wife wrote to the Duke of Wellington's nephew; I didn't wish her to; she did it without my knowledge.

"What did the man whose life I saved do? Did he send me thirty thousand pounds? say, 'Bonaparte, my brother, here is a crumb?' No, he sent me nothing.

"My wife, said 'Write.' I said, 'Mary Ann, NO. While these hands have power to work NO. While this frame has power to endure, NO. Never shall it be said that Bonaparte Blenkins asked of any man.'"

The man's noble independence touched the German.

"Your case is hard; yes, that *is* hard," said the German, shaking his head.

Bonaparte took another draught of the soup, leaned back against the pillows, and sighed deeply.

"I think," he said after a while, rousing himself, "I shall now wander in the benign air, and taste the gentle cool of evening. The stiffness hovers over me yet; exercise is beneficial."

So saying, he adjusted his hat carefully on the bald crown of his head, and moved to the door. After he had gone the German sighed again over his work—

"Ah, Lord! So it is! Ah!"

He thought of the ingratitude of the world.

"Uncle Otto," said the child in the doorway, "did you ever hear of ten bears sitting on their tails in a circle?"

"Well, not of ten, exactly; but bears do attack travellers every day. It is nothing unheard of," said the German. "A man of such courage too! Terrible experience that!"

"And how do we know that the story is true, Uncle Otto?"

The German's ire was roused.

"That is what I do hate!" he cried. "Know that is true! How do you know that anything is true? Because you are told so. If we begin to question everything—proof, proof, proof, what will we have to believe left? How do you know that the angel opened the prison door for Peter,[1] except that Peter said so? How do you know that God talked to Moses,[2] except that Moses wrote it? That is what I hate!"

---

1 Acts 12: 7.
2 Exodus 3.

The girl knit her brows. Perhaps her thoughts made a longer journey than the German dreamed of; for, mark you, the old dream little how their words and lives are texts and studies to the generation that shall succeed them. Not what we are taught, but what we see, makes us, and the child gathers the food on which the adult feeds to the end.

When the German looked up next there was a look of supreme satisfaction in the little mouth and the beautiful eyes.

"What dost see, chicken?" he asked.

The child said nothing, and an agonising shriek was borne on the afternoon breeze.

"Oh, God! my God! I am killed!" cried the voice of Bonaparte, as he, with wide open mouth and shaking flesh, fell into the room, followed by a half-grown ostrich, who put its head in at the door, opened its beak at him, and went away.

"Shut the door! shut the door! As you value my life, shut the door!" cried Bonaparte, sinking into a chair, his face blue and white, with a greenishness about the mouth. "Ah, my friend," he said tremulously, "eternity has looked me in the face! My life's thread hung upon a cord! The valley of the shadow of death!" said Bonaparte, seizing the German's arm.

"Dear, dear, dear!" said the German, who had closed the lower half of the door, and stood much concerned beside the stranger, "you have had a fright. I never knew so young a bird to chase before; but they will take dislikes to certain people. I sent a boy away once because a bird would chase him. Ah, dear, dear!"

"When I looked round," said Bonaparte, "the red and yawning cavity was above me, and the reprehensible paw raised to strike me. My nerves," said Bonaparte, suddenly growing faint, "always delicate—highly strung—are broken—broken! You could not give a little wine, a little brandy, my friend?"

The old German hurried away to the bookshelf, and took from behind the books a small bottle, half of whose contents he poured into a cup. Bonaparte drained it eagerly.

"How do you feel now?" asked the German, looking at him with much sympathy.

"A little, *slightly* better."

The German went out to pick up the battered chimney-pot which had fallen before the door.

"I am sorry you got the fright. The birds are bad things till you know them," he said sympathetically, as he put the hat down.

"My friend," said Bonaparte, holding out his hand, "I forgive you; do not be disturbed. Whatever the consequences, I forgive you. I know, I believe, it was with no ill-intent that you allowed me to go out. Give me your hand. I have no ill-feeling; none!"

"You are very kind," said the German, taking the extended hand, and feeling suddenly convinced that he was receiving magnanimous forgiveness for some great injury, "you are very kind."

"Don't mention it," said Bonaparte.

He knocked out the crown of his caved-in old hat, placed it on the table before him, leaned his elbows on the table and his face in his hands, and contemplated it.

"Ah, my old friend," he thus apostrophized the hat, "you have served me long, you have served me faithfully, but the last day has come. Never more shall you be borne upon the head of your master. Never more shall you protect his brow from the burning rays of summer or the cutting winds of winter. Henceforth bare-headed must your master go. Goodbye, good-bye, old hat!"

At the end of this affecting appeal the German rose. He went to the box at the foot of his bed; out of it he took a black hat, which had evidently been seldom worn and carefully preserved.

"It's not exactly what you may have been accustomed to," he said nervously, putting it down beside the battered chimney-pot, "but it might be of some use—a protection to the head you know."

"My friend," said Bonaparte, "you are not following my advice; you are allowing yourself to be reproached on my account. Do not make yourself unhappy. No; I shall go bare-headed."

"No, no, no!" cried the German energetically. "I have no use for the hat, none at all. It is shut up in the box."

"Then I will take it, my friend. It is a comfort to one's own mind when you have unintentionally injured any one to make reparation. I know the feeling. The hat may not be of that refined cut of which the old one was, but it will serve, yes, it will serve. Thank you," said Bonaparte, adjusting it on his head, and then replacing it on the table. "I shall lie down now and take a little repose," he added; "I much fear my appetite for supper will be lost."

"I hope not, I hope not," said the German, reseating himself at his work, and looking much concerned as Bonaparte stretched himself on the bed and turned the end of the patchwork quilt over his feet.

"You must not think to make your departure, not for many days," said the German presently. "Tant' Sannie gives her consent, and—"

"My friend," said Bonaparte, closing his eyes sadly, "you are kind; but were it not that to-morrow is the Sabbath, weak and trembling as I lie here, I would proceed on my way. I must seek work; idleness but for a day is painful. *Work, labour*—that is the secret of all true happiness!"

He doubled the pillow under his head, and watched how the German drew the leather thongs in and out.

After a while Lyndall silently put her book on the shelf and went home, and the German stood up and began to mix some water and meal for roaster-cakes. As he stirred them with his hands he said,—

"I make always a double supply on Saturday night; the hands are then free as the thoughts for Sunday."

"The blessed Sabbath!" said Bonaparte.

There was a pause. Bonaparte twisted his eyes without moving his head, to see if supper were already on the fire.

"You must sorely miss the administration of the Lord's word in this desolate spot," added Bonaparte. "Oh, how love I Thine house, and the place where Thine honour dwelleth!"

"Well, we do; yes," said the German; "but we do our best. We meet together, and I—well, I say a few words, and perhaps they are not wholly lost, not quite."

"Strange coincidence," said Bonaparte; "my plan always was the same. Was in the Free State[1] once—solitary farm—one neighbour. Every Sunday I called together friend and neighbour, child and servant, and said, 'Rejoice with me, that we may serve the Lord,' and then I addressed them. Ah, those were blessed times," said Bonaparte; "would they might return."

The German stirred at the cakes, and stirred, and stirred, and stirred. He could give the stranger his bed, and he could give the stranger his hat, and he could give the stranger his brandy; but his Sunday service!

After a good while he said,

"I might speak to Tant' Sannie; I might arrange; you might take the service in my place, if it—"

"My friend," said Bonaparte, "it would give me the profoundest felicity, the most unbounded satisfaction; but in these worn-out habiliments, in these deteriorated garments, it would not be possible, it would not be fitting that I should officiate in service of One,

---

1 Independent Boer Republic from 1854-1901.

whom, for respect, we shall not name. No, my friend, I will remain here; and, while you are assembling yourselves together in the presence of the Lord, I, in my solitude, will think of and pray for you. No; I will remain here!"

It was a touching picture—the solitary man there praying for them. The German cleared his hands from the meal, and went to the chest from which he had taken the black hat. After a little careful feeling about, he produced a black cloth coat, trousers, and waistcoat, which he laid on the table, smiling knowingly. They were of new shining cloth, worn twice a year, when he went to the town to 'nachtmaal.' He looked with great pride at the coat as he unfolded it and held it up.

"It's not the latest fashion, perhaps, not a West End cut,[1] not exactly; but it might do; it might serve at a push. Try it on, try it on!" he said, his old grey eyes twinkling with pride.

Bonaparte stood up and tried on the coat. It fitted admirably; the waistcoat could be made to button by ripping up the back, and the trousers were perfect; but below were the ragged boots. The German was not disconcerted. Going to the beam where a pair of top-boots hung, he took them off, dusted them carefully, and put them down before Bonaparte. The old eyes now fairly brimmed over with sparkling enjoyment.

"I have only worn them once. They might serve; they might be endured."

Bonaparte drew them on and stood upright, his head almost touching the beams. The German looked at him with profound admiration. It was wonderful what a difference feathers made in the bird.

Chapter V.
Sunday Services.

Service No. 1.

The boy Waldo kissed the pages of his book and looked up. Far over the flat lay the 'kopje,' a mere speck; the sheep wandered quietly from bush to bush; the stillness of the early Sunday rested everywhere, and the air was fresh.

---

1 Fashionable area of Central London known for its large shops, theaters and expensive hotels.

He looked down at his book. On its page a black insect crept. He lifted it off with his finger. Then he leaned on his elbow, watching its quivering antennæ and strange movements, smiling.

"Even you," he whispered, "shall not die. Even you He loves. Even you He will fold in His arms when He takes everything and makes it perfect and happy."

When the thing had gone he smoothed the leaves of his Bible somewhat caressingly. The leaves of that book had dropped blood for him once; they had taken the brightness out of his childhood; from between them had sprung the visions that had clung about him and made night horrible. Adder-like thoughts had lifted their heads, had shot out forked tongues at him, asking mockingly strange, trivial questions that he could not answer, miserable child:—

Why did the women in Mark see only one angel and the women in Luke two? Could a story be told in opposite ways and both ways be true? Could it? could it? Then again:—Is there nothing always right, and nothing always wrong? Could Jael the wife of Heber the Kenite "put her hand to the nail, and her right hand to the workman's hammer?" and could the Spirit of the Lord chant pæns over her, loud pæns, high pæns, set in the book of the Lord, and no voice cry out it was a mean and dastardly sin to lie, and kill the trusting in their sleep? Could the friend of God marry his own sister, and be beloved, and the man who does it to-day goes to hell, to hell? Was there nothing always right or always wrong?[1]

Those leaves had dropped blood for him once: they had made his heart heavy and cold; they had robbed his childhood of its gladness; now his fingers moved over them caressingly.

"My father God knows, my father knows," he said; "we cannot understand; He knows." After awhile he whispered smiling—"I heard your voice this morning when my eyes were not yet open, I felt you near me, my Father. Why do you love me so?" His face was illuminated. "In the last four months the old question has gone from me. I know you are good; I know you love everything; I

---

1 Waldo's literal reading of the Bible raised certain critical and ethical questions in his mind. If the Bible is sacred, then why do the writers disagree on details? In Judges, chapter five, Jael kills a man who seeks her tribe's protection, and in Judges, chapter 4, a man marries his own sister. Although these acts would be considered sinful in Waldo's day, they are praised as fulfilling God's will in the Old Testament. In the nineteenth century, Biblical scholars developed what was called the "Higher Criticism" to understand the intention rather than the historical or empirical veracity of the Bible.

know, I know, I know! I could not have borne it any more, not any more." He laughed softly. "And all the while I was so miserable you were looking at me and loving me, and I never knew it. But I know it now, I feel it," said the boy, and he laughed low; "I feel it!" he laughed.

After a while he began partly to sing, partly to chant the disconnected verses of hymns, those which spoke his gladness, many times over. The sheep with their senseless eyes turned to look at him as he sang.

At last he lapsed into quiet. Then as the boy lay there staring at bush and sand, he saw a vision.

He had crossed the river of Death, and walked on the other bank in the Lord's land of Beulah.[1] His feet sank into the dark grass, and he walked alone. Then, far over the fields, he saw a figure coming across the dark green grass. At first he thought it must be one of the angels; but as it came nearer he began to feel what it was. And it came closer, closer to him, and then the voice said, "Come," and he knew surely Who it was. He ran to the dear feet and touched them with his hands; yes, he held them fast! He lay down beside them. When he looked up the face was over him, and the glorious eyes were loving him; and they two were there alone together.

He laughed a deep laugh; then started up like one suddenly awakened from sleep.

"Oh, God!" he cried, "I cannot wait; I cannot wait! I want to die; I want to see Him; I want to touch Him. Let me die!" He folded his hands, trembling. "How can I wait so long—for long, long years perhaps? I want to die—to see Him. I will die any death. Oh, let me come!"

Weeping he bowed himself, and quivered from head to foot. After a long while he lifted his head.

"Yes; I will wait; I will wait. But not long; do not let it be very long, Jesus King. I want you; oh, I want you,—soon, soon!" He sat still, staring across the plain with his tearful eyes.

Service No. II.

In the front room of the farm-house sat Tant' Sannie in her elbow-chair. In her hand was her great brass-clasped hymn-book,

---

1   See Isaiah 62:4.

round her neck was a clean white handkerchief, under her feet was a wooden stove. There too sat Em and Lyndall, in clean pinafores and new shoes. There too was the spruce Hottentot in a starched white 'kappje,' and her husband on the other side of the door, with his wool oiled and very much combed out, and staring at his new leather boots. The Kaffir servants were not there, because Tant' Sannie held they were descended from apes,[1] and needed no salvation. But the rest were gathered for the Sunday service, and waited the officiator. Meanwhile Bonaparte and the German approached arm in arm—Bonaparte resplendent in the black cloth clothes, a spotless shirt, and a spotless collar; the German in the old salt-and-pepper, casting shy glances of admiration at his companion.

At the front door Bonaparte removed his hat with much dignity, raised his shirt collar, and entered. To the centre table he walked, put his hat solemnly down by the big Bible, and bowed his head over it in silent prayer.

The Boer-woman looked at the Hottentot, and the Hottentot looked at the Boer-woman.

There was one thing on earth for which Tant' Sannie had a profound reverence, which exercised a subduing influence over her, which made her for the time a better woman—that thing was new, shining black cloth. It made her think of the 'predikant'; it made her think of the elders, who sat in the top pew of the church on Sundays, with the hair so nicely oiled, so holy and respectable, with their little swallow-tailed coats; it made her think of heaven, where everything was so holy and respectable, and nobody wore tan cord, and the littlest angel had a black tail-coat. She wished she hadn't called him a thief and a Roman Catholic. She hoped the German hadn't told him. She wondered where those clothes were when he came in rags to her door. There was no doubt he was a very respectable man, a gentleman.

The German began to read a hymn. At the end of each line Bonaparte groaned, and twice at the end of every verse.

The Boer-woman had often heard of persons groaning during prayers, to add a certain poignancy and finish to them; old Jan Vanderlinde, her mother's brother, always did it after he was

---

1   According to Darwin, all human beings are descended from primates. Tant' Sannie's version of evolutionary theory makes black Africans a different species from white or other peoples.

converted; and she would have looked upon it as no especial sign of grace in any one; but to groan at hymn-time! She was startled. She wondered if he remembered that she shook her fist in his face. This was a man of God. They knelt down to pray. The Boer-woman weighed two hundred and fifty pounds, and could not kneel. She sat in her chair, and peeped between her crossed fingers at the stranger's back. She could not understand what he said; but he was in earnest. He shook the chair by the back rail till it made quite a little dust on the mud floor.

When they rose from their knees Bonaparte solemnly seated himself in the chair and opened the Bible. He blew his nose, pulled up his shirt-collar, smoothed the leaves, stroked down his capacious waistcoat, blew his nose again, looked solemnly round the room, then began,—

"All liars shall have their part in the lake which burneth with fire and brimstone, which is the second death."[1]

Having read this portion of Scripture, Bonaparte paused impressively, and looked all round the room.

"I shall not, my dear friends," he said, "long detain you. Much of our precious time has already fled blissfully from us in the voice of thanksgiving and the tongue of praise. A few, a very few words are all I shall address to you, and may they be as a rod of iron dividing the bones from the marrow, and the marrow from the bones.

"In the first place: What is a liar?"

The question was put so pointedly, and followed by a pause so profound, that even the Hottentot man left off looking at his boots and opened his eyes, though he understood not a word.

"I repeat," said Bonaparte, "what is a liar?"

The sensation was intense; the attention of the audience was riveted.

"Have you any of you ever seen a liar, my dear friends?" There was a still longer pause. "I hope not; I truly hope not. But I will tell you what a liar is. I knew a liar once—a little boy who lived in Cape Town, in Short Market Street. His mother and I sat together one day, discoursing about our souls.

"'Here, Sampson,' said his mother, 'go and buy sixpence of "meiboss" from the Malay round the corner.'

"When he came back she said, 'How much have you got?'

"'Five' he said.

---

1 Revelations 21:8.

"He was afraid if he said six and a-half she'd ask for some. And, my friends, that was a *lie*. The half of a 'meiboss' stuck in his throat, and he died, and was buried. And where did the soul of that little liar go to, my friends? It went to the lake of fire and brimstone. This brings me to the second point of my discourse.

"What is a lake of fire and brimstone? I will tell you, my friends," said Bonaparte condescendingly. "The imagination unaided cannot conceive it: but by the help of the Lord I will put it before your mind's eye.

"I was travelling in Italy once on a time; I came to a city called Rome, a vast city, and near it is a mountain which spits forth fire. Its name is Etna.[1] Now, there was a man in that city of Rome who had not the fear of God before his eyes, and he loved a woman. The woman died, and he walked up that mountain spitting fire, and when he got to the top he threw himself in at the hole that is there. The next day I went up. I was not afraid; the Lord preserves His servants. And in their hands shall they bear thee up, lest at any time thou fall into a volcano. It was dark night when I got there, but in the fear of the Lord I walked to the edge of the yawning abyss, and looked in. That sight—that sight, my friends, is impressed upon my most indelible memory. I looked down into the lurid depths upon an incandescent lake, a melted fire, a seething sea; the billows rolled from side to side, and on their fiery crests tossed the white skeleton of the suicide. The heat had burnt the flesh from off the bones; they lay as a light cork upon the melted fiery waves. One skeleton hand was raised upwards, the finger pointing to heaven; the other, with outstretched finger, pointing downwards, as though it would say, 'I go below, but you, Bonaparte, may soar above.' I gazed; I stood entranced. At that instant there was a crack in the lurid lake; it swelled, expanded, and the skeleton of the suicide disappeared, to be seen no more by mortal eye."

Here again Bonaparte rested, and then continued—

"The lake of melted stone rose in the crater, it swelled higher and higher at the side, it streamed forth at the top. I had presence of mind; near me was a rock; I stood upon it. The fiery torrent was vomited out, and streamed on either side of me. And through that long and terrible night I stood there alone upon that rock, the glowing fiery lava on every hand—a monument of the long-

---

1 Etna is a volcano located in northeast Sicily.

suffering and tender providence of the Lord, who spared me that I might this day testify in your ears of Him.

"Now, my dear friends, let us deduce the lessons that are to be learnt from this narrative.

"Firstly: let us never commit suicide. That man is a fool, my friends, that man is insane, my friends, who would leave this earth, my friends. Here are joys innumerable, such as it hath not entered into the heart of man to understand, my friends. Here are clothes my friends; here are beds, my friends; here is delicious food, my friends. Our precious bodies were given us to love, to cherish. Oh, let us do so! Oh, let us never hurt them; but care for and love them, my friends!"

Every one was impressed, and Bonaparte proceeded.

"Thirdly: let us not love too much. If that young man had not loved that young woman, he would not have jumped into Mount Etna. The good men of old never did so. Was Jeremiah ever in love, or Ezekiel, or Hosea, or even any of the minor prophets? No. Then why should we be? Thousands are rolling in that lake at this moment who would say, 'It was love that brought us here.' Oh, let us think always of our own souls first.

> "'A charge to keep I have,
> A God to glorify;
> A never-dying soul to save,
> And fit it for the sky.'[1]

"Oh, beloved friends, remember the little boy and the 'meiboss'; remember the young girl and the young man; remember the lake, the fire and the brimstone; remember the suicide's skeleton on the pitchy billows of Mount Etna; remember the voice of warning that has this day sounded in your ears; and what I say to you I say to all—watch! May the Lord add his blessing!"

Here the Bible closed with a tremendous thud. Tant' Sannie loosened the white handkerchief about her neck and wiped her eyes, and the coloured girl, seeing her do so, sniffled. They did not understand the discourse, which made it the more affecting. There hung over it that inscrutable charm which hovers for ever for the human intellect over the incomprehensible and shadowy. When the

---

1   "A Charge to Keep I Have" by Charles Wesley, from *Short Hymns on Select Passages of Holy Scripture*, 1762.

last hymn was sung the German conducted the officiator to Tant' Sannie, who graciously extended her hand, and offered coffee and a seat on the sofa. Leaving him there, the German hurried away to see how the little plum-pudding he had left at home was advancing; and Tant' Sannie remarked that it was a hot day. Bonaparte gathered her meaning as she fanned herself with the end of her apron. He bowed low in acquiescence. A long silence followed. Tant' Sannie spoke again. Bonaparte gave her no ear; his eye was fixed on a small miniature on the opposite wall, which represented Tant' Sannie as she had appeared on the day before her confirmation, fifteen years before, attired in green muslin. Suddenly he started to his feet, walked up to the picture, and took his stand before it. Long and wistfully he gazed into its features; it was easy to see that he was deeply moved. With a sudden movement, as though no longer able to restrain himself, he seized the picture, loosened it from its nail, and held it close to his eyes. At length, turning to the Boer-woman, he said, in a voice of deep emotion,—

"You will, I trust, dear madam, excuse this exhibition of my feelings; but this—this little picture recalls to me my first and best beloved, my dear departed wife, who is now a saint in heaven."

Tant' Sannie could not understand; but the Hottentot maid, who had taken her seat on the floor beside her mistress, translated the English into Dutch as far as she was able.

"Ah, my first, my beloved!" he added, looking tenderly down at the picture. "Oh, the beloved, the beautiful lineaments! My angel wife! This is surely a sister of yours, madame?" he added, fixing his eyes on Tant' Sannie.

The Dutchwoman blushed, shook her head, and pointed to herself.

Carefully, intently, Bonaparte looked from the picture in his hand to Tant' Sannie's features, and from the features back to the picture. Then slowly a light broke over his countenance; he looked up, it became a smile; he looked back at the miniature, his whole countenance was effulgent.

"Ah, yes; I see it now," he cried, turning his delighted gaze on to the Boer-woman; "eyes, mouth, nose, chin, the very expression!" he cried. "How is it possible I did not notice it before?"

"Take another cup of coffee," said Tant' Sannie. "Put some sugar in."

Bonaparte hung the picture tenderly up, and was turning to take the cup from her hand, when the German appeared, to say that the pudding was ready and the meat on the table.

"He's a God-fearing man, and one who knows how to behave himself," said the Boer-woman as he went out at the door. "If he is ugly, did not the Lord make him? And are we to laugh at the Lord's handiwork? It is better to be ugly and good than pretty and bad; though of course it's nice when one is both," said Tant' Sannie, looking complacently at the picture on the wall.

In the afternoon the German and Bonaparte sat before the door of the cabin. Both smoked in complete silence—Bonaparte with a book in his hands and his eyes half closed; the German puffing vigorously, and glancing up now and again at the serene blue sky overhead.

"Supposing—you—you, in fact, made the remark to me," burst forth the German suddenly, "that you were looking for a situation."

Bonaparte opened his mouth wide, and sent a stream of smoke through his lips.

"Now supposing," said the German—"merely supposing, of course—that some one, some one in fact, should make an offer to you, say, to become schoolmaster on their farm and teach two children, two little girls, perhaps, and would give you forty pounds a-year, would you accept it?—Just supposing, of course."

"Well, my dear friend," said Bonaparte, "that would depend on circumstances. Money is no consideration with me. For my wife I have made provision for the next year. My health is broken. Could I meet a place where a gentleman would be treated as a gentleman I would accept it, however small the remuneration. With me," said Bonaparte, "money is no consideration."

"Well," said the German, when he had taken a whiff or two more from his pipe, "I think I shall go up and see Tant' Sannie a little. I go up often on Sunday afternoon to have general conversation, to see her, you know. Nothing—nothing particular, you know."

The old man put his book into his pocket, and walked up to the farmhouse with a peculiarly knowing and delighted expression of countenance.

"He doesn't suspect what I'm going to do," soliloquised the German; "hasn't the least idea. A nice surprise for him."

The man whom he had left at his doorway winked at the retreating figure with a wink that was not to be described.

Chapter VI.
Bonaparte Blenkins Makes His Nest.

"Ah, what is the matter?" asked Waldo, stopping at the foot of the ladder with a load of skins on his back that he was carrying up to the loft. Through the open door in the gable little Em was visible, her feet dangling from the high bench on which she sat. The room, once a storeroom, had been divided by a row of 'mealie' bags into two parts, the back being Bonaparte's bedroom, the front his schoolroom.

"Lyndall made him angry," said the girl tearfully; "and he has given me the fourteenth of John to learn. He says he will teach me to behave myself, when Lyndall troubles him."

"What did she do?" asked the boy.

"You see," said Em, hopelessly turning the leaves, "whenever he talks she looks out at the door, as though she did not hear him. Today she asked him what the signs of the Zodiac were, and he said he was surprised that she should ask him; it was not a fit and proper thing for little girls to talk about. Then she asked him who Copernicus[1] was; and he said he was one of the Emperors of Rome, who burned the Christians in a golden pig, and the worms ate him up while he was still alive. I don't know why," said Em plaintively, "but she just put her books under her arm and walked out; and she will never come to his school again, she says, and she *always* does what she says. And now I must sit here every day alone," said Em, the great tears dropping softly.

"Perhaps Tant' Sannie will send him away," said the boy, in his mumbling way, trying to comfort her.

"No," said Em, shaking her head; "no. Last night when the little Hottentot maid was washing her feet, he told her he liked such feet, and that fat women were so nice to him; and she said I must always put him pure cream in his coffee now. No; he'll never go away," said Em dolorously.

The boy put down his skins and fumbled in his pocket, and produced a small piece of paper containing something. He stuck it out towards her.

"There, take it for you," he said. This was by way of comfort.

Em opened it and found a small bit of gum, a commodity prized by the children; but the great tears dropped down slowly on to it.

Waldo was distressed. He had cried so much in his morsel of life that tears in another seemed to burn him.

---

1 Nicholas Copernicus (1473-1543) was a Polish astronomer who developed the theory that the planets revolved around a motionless sun.

"If," he said, stepping in awkwardly and standing by the table, "if you will not cry I will tell you something—a secret."

"What is that?" asked Em, instantly becoming decidedly better.

"You will tell it to no human being?"

"No."

He bent nearer to her, and with deep solemnity said—

"*I have made a machine!*"

Em opened her eyes.

"Yes; a machine for shearing sheep. It is almost done," said the boy. "There is only one thing that is not right yet; but it will be soon. When you think, and think, and think, all night and day, it comes at last," he added mysteriously.

"Where is it?"

"Here! I always carry it here," said the boy, putting his hand to his breast, where a bulging-out was visible. "This is a model. When it is done they will have to make a large one."

"Show it me."

The boy shook his head.

"No, not till it is done. I cannot let any human being see it till then."

"It is a beautiful secret," said Em; and the boy shuffled out to pick up his skins.

That evening father and son sat in the cabin eating their supper. The father sighed deeply sometimes. Perhaps he thought how long a time it was since Bonaparte had visited the cabin; but his son was in that land in which sighs have no part. It is a question whether it were not better to be the shabbiest of fools, and know the way up the little stair of imagination to the land of dreams, than the wisest of men, who see nothing that the eyes do not show, and feel nothing that the hands do not touch. The boy chewed his brown bread and drank his coffee; but in truth he saw only his machine finished—that last something found out and added. He saw it as it worked with beautiful smoothness; and over and above, as he chewed his bread and drank his coffee, there was that delightful consciousness of something bending over him and loving him. It would not have been better in one of the courts of heaven, where the walls are set with rows of the King of Glory's amethysts and milk-white pearls,[1] than there, eating his supper in that little room.

---

1 In Revelations, the city of heaven is described as having twelve walls built of gems and pearls.

As they sat in silence there was a knock at the door. When it was opened the small woolly head of a little nigger showed itself. She was a messenger from Tant' Sannie: the German was wanted at once at the homestead. Putting on his hat with both hands, he hurried off. The kitchen was in darkness, but in the pantry beyond Tant' Sannie and her maids were assembled.

A Kaffir girl, who had been grinding pepper between two stones, knelt on the floor, the lean Hottentot stood with a brass candlestick in her hand, and Tant' Sannie, near the shelf, with a hand on each hip, was evidently listening intently, as were her companions.

"What may it be?" cried the old German in astonishment.

The room beyond the pantry was the store-room. Through the thin wooden partition there arose at that instant, evidently from some creature ensconced there, a prolonged and prodigious howl, followed by a succession of violent blows against the partition wall.

The German seized the churn-stick, and was about to rush round the house, when the Boer-woman impressively laid her hand upon his arm.

"That is his head," said Tant' Sannie "that is his head."

"But what might it be?" asked the German, looking from one to the other, churn-stick in hand.

A low hollow bellow prevented reply, and the voice of Bonaparte lifted itself on high.

"Mary-Ann! my angel! my wife!"

"Isn't it dreadful?" said Tant' Sannie, as the blows were repeated fiercely. "He has got a letter: his wife is dead. You must go and comfort him," said Tant' Sannie at last, "and I will go with you. It would not be the thing for me to go alone—me, who am only thirty-three, and he an unmarried man now," said Tant' Sannie, blushing and smoothing out her apron.

Upon this they all trudged round the house in company—the Hottentot maid carrying the light, Tant' Sannie and the German following, and the Kaffir girl bringing up the rear.

"Oh," said Tant' Sannie, "I see now it wasn't wickedness made him do without his wife so long—only necessity."

At the door she motioned to the German to enter, and followed him closely. On the stretcher behind the sacks Bonaparte lay on his face, his head pressed into a pillow, his legs kicking gently. The Boer-woman sat down on a box at the foot of the bed. The German stood with folded hands looking on.

"We must all die," said Tant' Sannie at last; "it is the dear Lord's will."

Hearing her voice, Bonaparte turned himself on to his back.

"It's very hard," said Tant' Sannie, "I know, for I've lost two husbands."

Bonaparte looked up into the German's face.

"Oh, what does she say? Speak to me words of comfort!"

The German repeated Tant' Sannie's remark.

"Ah, I—I also! Two dear, dear wives, whom I shall never see any more!" cried Bonaparte, flinging himself back upon the bed.

He howled, till the tarantulas, who lived between the rafters and the zinc roof, felt the unusual vibration, and looked out with their wicked bright eyes, to see what was going on.

Tant' Sannie sighed, the Hottentot maid sighed, the Kaffir girl who looked in at the door put her hand over her mouth and said "Mow—wah!"

"You must trust in the Lord," said Tant' Sannie. "He can give you more than you have lost."

"I do, I do!" he cried; "but oh, I have no wife! I have no wife!"

Tant' Sannie was much affected, and came and stood near the bed.

"Ask him if he won't have a little pap—nice, fine, flour pap. There is some boiling on the kitchen fire."

The German made the proposal, but the widower waved his hand.

"No, nothing shall pass my lips. I should be suffocated. No, no! Speak not of food to me!"

"Pap, and a little brandy in," said Tant' Sannie coaxingly.

Bonaparte caught the word.

"Perhaps, perhaps—if I struggled with myself—for the sake of my duties I might imbibe a few drops," he said, looking with quivering lip up into the German's face. "I must do my duty, must I not?"

Tant' Sannie gave the order, and the girl went for the pap.

"I know how it was when my first husband died. They could do nothing with me," the Boer-woman said, "till I had eaten a sheep's trotter, and honey, and a little roaster-cake. *I* know."

Bonaparte sat up on the bed with his legs stretched out in front of him, and a hand on each knee, blubbering softly.

"Oh, she was a woman! You are very kind to try and comfort me, but she was my wife. For a woman that is my wife I could live; for the woman that is my wife I could die! For a woman that is my wife I could—Ah! that sweet word *wife*; when will it rest upon my lips again?"

When his feelings had subsided a little he raised the corners of his turned-down mouth, and spoke to the German with flabby lips.

"Do you think she understands me? Oh, tell her every word, that she may know I thank her."

At that instant the girl reappeared with a basin of steaming gruel and a black bottle.

Tant' Sannie poured some of its contents into the basin, stirred it well, and came to the bed.

"Oh, I can't, I can't! I shall die! I shall die!" said Bonaparte, putting his hands to his side.

"Come, just a little," said Tant' Sannie coaxingly; "just a drop."

"It's too thick, it's too thick. I should choke."

Tant' Sannie added from the contents of the bottle and held out a spoonful; Bonaparte opened his mouth like a little bird waiting for a worm, and held it open, as she dipped again and again into the pap.

"Ah, this will do your heart good," said Tant' Sannie, in whose mind the relative functions of heart and stomach were exceedingly ill-defined.

When the basin was emptied the violence of his grief was much assuaged; he looked at Tant' Sannie with gentle tears.

"Tell him," said the Boer-woman, "that I hope he will sleep well, and that the Lord will comfort him, as the Lord only can."

"Bless you, dear friend, God bless you," said Bonaparte.

When the door was safely shut on the German, the Hottentot, and the Dutch-woman, he got off the bed and washed away the soap he had rubbed on his eyelids.

"Bon," he said, slapping his leg, "you're the cutest lad I ever came across. If you don't turn out the old Hymns-and-prayers, and pummel the Ragged coat, and get your arms round the fat one's waist and a wedding-ring on her finger, then you are not Bonaparte. But you *are* Bonaparte. Bon, you're a fine boy!"

Making which pleasing reflection, he pulled off his trousers and got into bed cheerfully.

Chapter VII.
He Sets His Trap.

"May I come in? I hope I do not disturb you, my dear friend," said Bonaparte, late one evening, putting his nose in at the cabin door, where the German and his son sat finishing their supper.

It was now two months since he had been installed as schoolmaster in Tant' Sannie's household, and he had grown mighty and more mighty day by day. He visited the cabin no more, sat close to Tant' Sannie drinking coffee all the evening, and walked about loftily with his hands under the coat-tails of the German's black cloth, and failed to see even a nigger who wished him a deferential good morning. It was therefore with no small surprise that the German perceived Bonaparte's red nose at his door.

"Walk in, walk in," he said joyfully. "Boy, boy, see if there is coffee left. Well, none. Make a fire. We have done supper, but—"

"My dear friend," said Bonaparte, taking off his hat, "I came not to sup, not for mere creature comforts, but for an hour of brotherly intercourse with a kindred spirit. The press of business and the weight of thought, but they alone, may sometimes prevent me from sharing the secrets of my bosom with him for whom I have so great a sympathy. You perhaps wonder when I shall return the two pounds—"

"Oh, no, no! Make a fire, make a fire, boy. We will have a pot of hot coffee presently," said the German, rubbing his hands and looking about, not knowing how best to show his pleasure at the unexpected visit.

For three weeks the German's diffident "Good evening" had met with a stately bow; the chin of Bonaparte lifting itself higher daily; and his shadow had not darkened the cabin doorway since he came to borrow the two pounds. The German walked to the head of the bed and took down a blue bag that hung there. Blue bags were a specialty of the German's. He kept above fifty stowed away in different corners of his room—some filled with curious stones, some with seeds that had been in his possession fifteen years, some with rusty nails, buckles, and bits of old harness—in all, a wonderful assortment, but highly prized.

"We have something here not so bad," said the German, smiling knowingly, as he dived his hand into the bag and took out a handful of almonds and raisins; "I buy these for my chickens. They increase in size, but they still think the old man must have something nice for them. And the old man—well, a big boy may have a sweet tooth sometimes, may he not? Ha, ha!" said the German chuckling at his own joke, as he heaped the plate with almonds. "Here is a stone—two stones to crack them—no late patent improvement—well, Adam's nut-cracker; ha, ha! But I think we shall do. We will not leave them uncracked. We will consume a few without fashionable improvements."

Here the German sat down on one side of the table, Bonaparte on the other, each one with a couple of flat stones before him, and the plate between them.

"Do not be afraid," said the German, "do not be afraid. I do not forget the boy at the fire; I crack for him. The bag is full. Why, this is strange," he said suddenly, cracking open a large nut; "three kernels! I have not observed that before. This must be retained. This is valuable." He wrapped the nut gravely in paper, and put it carefully in his waistcoat pocket. "Valuable, very valuable!" he said, shaking his head.

"Ah, my friend," said Bonaparte, "what joy it is to be once more in your society."

The German's eye glistened, and Bonaparte seized his hand and squeezed it warmly. They then proceeded to crack and eat. After a while Bonaparte said, stuffing a handful of raisins into his mouth,—

"I was so deeply grieved, my dear friend, that you and Tant' Sannie had some slight unpleasantness this evening."

"Oh, no, no," said the German; "it is all right now. A few sheep missing; but I make it good myself. I give my twelve sheep, and work in the other eight."

"It is rather hard that you should have to make good the lost sheep," said Bonaparte; "it is no fault of yours."

"Well," said the German, "this is the case. Last evening I count the sheep at the kraal—twenty are missing. I ask the herd; he tells me they are with the other flock; he tells me so *distinctly*; how can I think he lies? This afternoon I count the other flock. The sheep are not there. I come back here: the herd is gone; the sheep are gone. But I cannot—no, I will not—believe he stole them," said the German, growing suddenly excited. "Some one else, but not he. I know that boy; I knew him three years. He is a good boy. I have seen him deeply affected on account of his soul. And she would send the police after him! I say I would rather make the loss good myself. I will not have it; he has fled in fear. I know his heart. It was," said the German with a little gentle hesitation, "under my words that he first felt his need of a Saviour."

Bonaparte cracked some more almonds, then said, yawning, and more as though he asked for the sake of having something to converse about than from any interest he felt in the subject—

"And what has become of the herd's wife?"

The German was alight again in a moment.

"Yes; his wife. She has a child six days old, and Tant' Sannie would turn her out into the fields this night. That," said the German, rising, "that is what I call cruelty—diabolical cruelty. My soul abhors that deed. The man that could do such a thing I could run him through with a knife!" said the German, his grey eyes flashing, and his bushy black beard adding to the murderous fury of his aspect. Then suddenly subsiding, he said, "But all is now well; Tant' Sannie gives her word that the maid shall remain for some days. I go to Oom Muller's to-morrow to learn if the sheep may not be there. If they are not, then I return. They are gone; that is all. I make it good."

"Tant' Sannie is a singular woman," said Bonaparte, taking the tobacco bag the German passed to him.

"Singular! Yes," said the German; "but her heart is on her right side. I have lived long years with her, and I may say, I have for her an affection, which she returns. I may say," added the German with warmth, "I may say, that there is not one soul on this farm for whom I have *not* an affection."

"Ah, my friend," said Bonaparte, "when the grace of God is in our hearts, is it not so with us all? Do we not love the very worm we tread upon, and as we tread upon it? Do we know distinctions of race, or of sex, or of colour? *No!*

> 'Love so amazing, so divine,
> It fills my soul, my life, my all.'"[1]

After a time he sank into a less fervent mood, and remarked,—

"The coloured female who waits upon Tant' Sannie appears to be of a virtuous disposition, an individual who—"

"Virtuous!" said the German; "I have confidence in her. There is that in her which is pure, that which is noble. The rich and high that walk this earth with lofty eyelids might exchange with her."

The German here got up to bring a coal for Bonaparte's pipe, and they sat together talking for a while. At length Bonaparte knocked the ashes out of his pipe.

"It is time that I took my departure, dear friend," he said; "but, before I do so, shall we not close this evening of sweet communion and brotherly intercourse by a few words of prayer? Oh, how good and how pleasant a thing it is for brethren to dwell together in

---

1 From "When I Survey the Wondrous Cross," a hymn by Isaac Watts, 1707.

unity! It is like the dew upon the mountains of Hermon; for there the Lord bestowed a blessing, even life for evermore."[1]

"Stay and drink some coffee," said the German.

"No, thank you, my friend; I have business that must be done to-night," said Bonaparte. "Your dear son appears to have gone to sleep. He is going to take the waggon to the mill to-morrow! What a little *man* he is."

"A fine boy."

But though the boy nodded before the fire he was not asleep; and they all knelt down to pray.

When they rose from their knees Bonaparte extended his hand to Waldo, and patted him on the head.

"Good night, my lad," he said. "As you go to the mill to-morrow, we shall not see you for some days. Good night! Good bye! The Lord bless and guide you; and may He bring you back to us in safety to find us all *as you have left us!*" He laid some emphasis on the last words. "And you, my dear friend," he added, turning with redoubled warmth to the German, "long, long, shall I look back to this evening as a time of refreshing from the presence of the Lord, as an hour of blessed intercourse with a brother in Jesus. May such often return. The Lord bless you!" he added, with yet deeper fervour, "richly, richly."

Then he opened the door and vanished out into the darkness.

"He, he, he!" laughed Bonaparte, as he stumbled over the stones. "If there isn't the rarest lot of fools on this farm that ever God Almighty stuck legs to. He, he, he! When the worms come out then the blackbirds feed. Ha, ha, ha!" Then he drew himself up; even when alone he liked to pose with a certain dignity; it was second nature to him.

He looked in at the kitchen door. The Hottentot maid who acted as interpreter between Tant' Sannie and himself was gone, and Tant' Sannie herself was in bed.

"Never mind, Bon, my boy," he said, as he walked round to his own room, "to-morrow will do. He, he, he!"

---

1 Psalms 133:3.

Chapter VIII.
He Catches the Old Bird.

At four o'clock the next afternoon the German rode across the plain, returning from his search for the lost sheep. He rode slowly, for he had been in the saddle since sunrise and was somewhat weary, and the heat of the afternoon made his horse sleepy as it picked its way slowly along the sandy road. Every now and then a great red spider would start out of the 'karroo' on one side of the path and run across to the other, but nothing else broke the still monotony. Presently, behind one of the highest of the milk-bushes that dotted the roadside, the German caught sight of a Kaffir woman, seated there evidently for such shadow as the milk-bush might afford from the sloping rays of the sun. The German turned the horse's head out of the road. It was not his way to pass a living creature without a word of greeting. Coming nearer, he found it was no other than the wife of the absconding Kaffir herd. She had a baby tied on her back by a dirty strip of red blanket; another strip hardly larger was twisted round her waist, for the rest her black body was naked. She was a sullen, ill-looking woman, with lips hideously protruding.

The German questioned her as to how she came there. She muttered in broken Dutch that she had been turned away. Had she done evil? She shook her head sullenly. Had she had food given her? She grunted a negative, and fanned the flies from her baby. Telling the woman to remain where she was, he turned his horse's head to the road and rode off at a furious pace.

"Hard-hearted! cruel! Oh, my God! Is this the way? Is this charity?"

"Yes, yes, yes," ejaculated the old man as he rode on; but, presently, his anger began to evaporate, his horse's pace slackened, and by the time he had reached his own door he was nodding and smiling.

Dismounting quickly, he went to the great chest where his provisions were kept. Here he got out a little meal, a little 'mealies,' a few roaster-cakes. These he tied up in three blue handkerchiefs, and putting them into a sail-cloth bag, he strung them over his shoulders. Then he looked circumspectly out at the door. It was very bad to be discovered in the act of giving; it made him red up to the roots of his old grizzled hair. No one was about, however, so he rode off again. Beside the milk-bush sat the Kaffir woman still— like Hagar, he thought, thrust out by her mistress in the wilderness to die.[1] Telling her to loosen the handkerchief from her head, he poured into it the contents of his bag. The woman tied it up in sullen silence.

"You must try and get to the next farm," said the German.

The woman shook her head; she would sleep in the field.

The German reflected. Kaffir women were accustomed to sleep in the open air; but then, the child was small, and after so hot a day the night might be chilly. That she would creep back to the huts at the homestead when the darkness favoured her, the German's sagacity did not make evident to him. He took off the old brown salt-and-pepper coat, and held it out to her. The woman received it in silence, and laid it across her knee. "With that they will sleep warmly; not so bad. Ha, ha!" said the German. And he rode home, nodding his head in a manner that would have made any other man dizzy.

"I wish he would not come back to-night," said Em, her face wet with tears.

"It will be just the same if he comes back to-morrow," said Lyndall.

The two girls sat on the stop of the cabin waiting for the German's return. Lyndall shaded her eyes with her hand from the sunset light.

"There he comes," she said, "whistling 'Ach Jerusalem du schšne' so loud I can hear him here."[2]

"Perhaps he has found the sheep."

"Found them!" said Lyndall. "He would whistle just so if he knew he had to die to-night."

"You look at the sunset, eh, chickens?" the German said, as he came up at a smart canter. "Ah yes, that is beautiful!" he added, as he dismounted, pausing for a moment with his hand on the saddle to look at the evening sky, where the sun shot up long flaming

---

1 See Genesis, chapter 16. Sarah, wife of Abraham, cannot conceive so she gives her maid Hagar to Abraham. When Hagar conceives, Sarah tells Abraham that Hagar despises her. So Hagar and her child are put out. But God comforts Hagar by telling her that her child Ishmael will be the first of a great tribe.

2 This may be a line from a German hymn entitled "Alle Menschen Müssen Sterban" written by Johann G. Albinus, 1652. The hymn was translated to English ("All Men Living Are But Mortal") by Catherine Winkworth, 1863. If so, the line is "O Jerusalem how glorious/ Dost thou shine, thou city fair."

streaks, between which and the eye thin yellow clouds floated. "Ei! you weep?" said the German, as the girls ran up to him.

Before they had time to reply the voice of Tant' Sannie was heard.

"You child, of the child, of the child of a Kaffir's dog, come here!"

The German looked up. He thought the Dutch-woman, come out to cool herself in the yard, called to some misbehaving servant. The old man looked round to see who it might be.

"You old vagabond of a praying German, are you deaf?"

Tant' Sannie stood before the steps of the kitchen; upon them sat the lean Hottentot, upon the highest stood Bonaparte Blenkins, both hands folded under the tails of his coat, and his eyes fixed on the sunset sky.

The German dropped the saddle on the ground.

"Bish, bish, bish! what may *this* be?" he said, and walked toward the house. "Very strange!"

The girls followed him: Em, still weeping; Lyndall with her face rather white and her eyes wide open.

"And I have the heart of a devil did you say? You could run me through with a knife, could you?" cried the Dutch-woman. "I could not drive the Kaffir maid away because I was afraid of *you*, was I? Oh, you miserable rag! I loved you, did I? I would have liked to marry you, would I? *would* I? WOULD I?" cried the Boer-woman; "you cat's tail, you dog's paw! Be near my house to-morrow morning when the sun rises," she gasped, "my Kaffirs will drag you through the sand. They would do it gladly, any of them, for a bit of tobacco, for all your prayings with them."

"I am bewildered, I am bewildered," said the German, standing before her and raising his hand to his forehead; "I—I do not understand."

"Ask him, ask him!" cried Tant' Sannie, pointing to Bonaparte; "he knows. You thought he could not make me understand, but he did, he did, you old fool! I know enough English for that. You be here," shouted the Dutch-woman, "when the morning star rises, and I will let my Kaffirs take you out and drag you, till there is not one bone left in your old body that is not broken as fine as bobootie-meat,[1] you old beggar! All your rags are not worth that

---

1   A traditional dish (probably of Malay origin) made of lightly curried minced meat.

they should be thrown out on to the ash-heap," cried the Boer-woman, "but I will have them for my sheep. Not one rotten hoof of your old mare do you take with you; I will have her—all, all for my sheep that you have lost, you godless thing!"

The Boer-woman wiped the moisture from her mouth with the palm of her hand.

The German turned to Bonaparte, who still stood on the step absorbed in the beauty of the sunset.

"Do not address me; do not approach me, lost man," said Bonaparte, not moving his eye nor lowering his chin. "There is a crime from which all nature revolts; there is a crime whose name is loathsome to the human ear—that crime is yours; that crime is ingratitude. This woman has been your benefactress; on her farm you have lived; after her sheep you have looked; into her house you have been allowed to enter and hold Divine service—an honour of which you were never worthy; and how have you rewarded her?—Basely, basely, basely!"

"But it is all false, lies and falsehoods. I must, I will speak," said the German, suddenly looking round bewildered. "Do I dream? Are you mad? What may it be?"

"Go, dog," cried the Dutch-woman; "I would have been a rich woman this day if it had not been for your laziness. Praying with the Kaffirs behind the kraal walls. Go, you Kaffir's dog!"

"But what then is the matter? What may have happened since I left?" said the German turning to the Hottentot woman who sat upon the step.

She was his friend; she would tell him kindly the truth. The woman answered by a loud, ringing laugh.

"Give it him, old Missis! Give it him!"

It was so nice to see the white man who had been master hunted down. The coloured woman laughed, and threw a dozen mealie grains into her mouth to chew.

All anger and excitement faded from the old man's face. He turned slowly away and walked down the little path to his cabin, with his shoulders bent; it was all dark before him. He stumbled over the threshold of his own well-known door.

Em, sobbing bitterly, would have followed him; but the Boer-woman prevented her by a flood of speech which convulsed the Hottentot, so low were its images.

"Come, Em," said Lyndall, lifting her small, proud head, "let us go in. We will not stay to hear such language."

She looked into the Boer-woman's eyes. Tant' Sannie understood the meaning of the look if not the words. She waddled after them, and caught Em by the arm. She had struck Lyndall, once years before, and had never done it again, so she took Em.

"So you will defy me too, will you, you Englishman's ugliness!" she cried, as with one hand she forced the child down, and held her head tightly against her knee; with the other she beat her first upon one cheek, and then upon the other.

For one instant Lyndall looked on, then she laid her small fingers on the Boer-woman's arm. With the exertion of half its strength Tant' Sannie might have flung the girl back upon the stones. It was not the power of the slight fingers, tightly though they clenched her broad wrist—so tightly that at bedtime the marks were still there; but the Boer-woman looked into the clear eyes and at the quivering white lips, and with a half-surprised curse relaxed her hold. The girl drew Em's arm through her own.

"Move!" she said to Bonaparte, who stood in the door; and he, Bonaparte the invincible, in the hour of his triumph, moved to give her place.

The Hottentot ceased to laugh, and an uncomfortable silence fell on all the three in the doorway.

Once in their room, Em sat down on the floor and wailed bitterly. Lyndall lay on the bed with her arm drawn across her eyes, very white and still.

"Hoo, hoo!" cried Em; "and they won't let him take the grey mare; and Waldo has gone to the mill. Hoo, hoo! And perhaps they won't let us go and say good-bye to him. Hoo, hoo, hoo!"

"I wish you would be quiet," said Lyndall without moving. "Does it give you such felicity to let Bonaparte know he is hurting you? We will ask no one. It will be supper time soon. Listen,— and when you hear the chink of the knives and forks we will go out and see him."

Em suppressed her sobs and listened intently, kneeling at the door. Suddenly some one came to the window and put the shutter up.

"Who was that?" said Lyndall, starting.

"The girl, I suppose," said Em. "How early she is this evening!"

But Lyndall sprang from the bed and seized the handle of the door, shaking it fiercely. The door was locked on the outside. She ground her teeth.

"What is the matter?" asked Em.

The room was in perfect darkness now.

"Nothing," said Lyndall quietly; "only they have locked us in."

She turned, and went back to bed again. But ere long Em heard a sound of movement. Lyndall had climbed up into the window, and with her fingers felt the wood-work that surrounded the panes. Slipping down, the girl loosened the iron knob from the foot of the bedstead, and climbing up again she broke with it every pane of glass in the window, beginning at the top and ending at the bottom.

"What are you doing?" asked Em, who heard the falling fragments.

Her companion made her no reply; but leaned on every little cross-bar, which cracked and gave way beneath her. Then she pressed with all her strength against the shutter. She had thought the wooden buttons would give way, but by the clinking sound she knew that the iron bar had been put across. She was quite quiet for a time. Clambering down she took from the table a small one-bladed pen-knife, with which she began to peck at the hard wood of the shutter.

"What are you doing now?" asked Em, who had ceased crying in her wonder, and had drawn near.

"Trying to make a hole," was the short reply.

"Do you think you will be able to?"

"No; but I am trying."

In an agony of suspense Em waited. For ten minutes Lyndall pecked. The hole was three-eighths of an inch deep—then the blade sprang into ten pieces.

"What has happened now?" asked Em, blubbering afresh.

"Nothing," said Lyndall. "Bring me my night-gown, a piece of paper, and the matches."

Wondering, Em fumbled about till she found them.

"What are you going to do with them?" she whispered.

"Burn down the window."

"But won't the whole house take fire and burn down too?"

"Yes."

"But will it not be very wicked?"

"Yes, very. And I do not care."

She arranged the night-gown carefully in the corner of the window, with the chips of the frame about it. There was only one match in the box. She drew it carefully along the wall. For a moment it burnt up blue, and showed the tiny face with its glistening eyes. She held it carefully to the paper. For an instant it burnt up brightly, then flickered and went out. She blew the spark, but it died also. Then she threw the paper on to the ground, trod on it, and went to her bed, and began to undress.

Em rushed to the door, knocking against it wildly.

"Oh, Tant' Sannie! Tant' Sannie! Oh, let us out!" she cried. "Oh, Lyndall, what are we to do?"

Lyndall wiped a drop of blood off the lip she had bitten.

"I am going to sleep," she said. "If you like to sit there and howl till the morning, do. Perhaps you will find that it helps; I never heard that howling helped any one."

Long after, when Em herself had gone to bed and was almost asleep, Lyndall came and stood at her bedside.

"Here," she said, slipping a little pot of powder into her hand; "rub some on to your face. Does it not burn where she struck you?"

Then she crept back to her own bed. Long, long after, when Em was really asleep, she lay still awake, and folded her hands on her little breast, and muttered,—

"When that day comes, and I am strong, I will hate everything that has power, and help everything that is weak." And she bit her lip again.

The German looked out at the cabin door for the last time that night. Then he paced the room slowly and sighed. Then he drew out pen and paper, and sat down to write, rubbing his old grey eyes with his knuckles before he began.

"MY CHICKENS,

"You did not come to say good-bye to the old man. Might you? Ah, well, there is a land where they part no more, where saints immortal reign.

"I sit here alone, and I think of you. Will you forget the old man? When you wake to-morrow he will be far away. The old horse is lazy, but he has his stick to help him; that is three legs. He comes back one day with gold and diamonds. Will you welcome him? Well, we shall see. I go to meet Waldo. He comes back with the waggon; then he follows me. Poor boy! God knows. There is a land where all things are made right, but that land is not here.

"My little children, serve the Saviour; give your hearts to Him while you are yet young. Life is short.

"Nothing is mine, otherwise I would say, Lyndall, take my books, Em my stones. Now I say nothing. The things are mine: it is not righteous, God knows! But I am silent. Let it be. But I feel it, I must say I feel it.

"Do not cry too much for the old man. He goes out to seek his fortune, and comes back with it in a bag, it may be.

"I love my children. Do they think of me? I am Old Otto, who goes out to seek his fortune.   O. F."

Having concluded this quaint production, he put it where the children would find it the next morning, and proceeded to prepare his bundle. He never thought of entering a protest against the loss of his goods: like a child he submitted, and wept. He had been there eleven years, and it was hard to go away. He spread open on the bed a blue handkerchief, and on it put one by one the things he thought most necessary and important: a little bag of curious seeds, which he meant to plant some day, an old German hymn-book, three misshapen stones that he greatly valued, a Bible, a shirt, and two handkerchiefs; then there was room for nothing more. He tied up the bundle tightly and put it on a chair by his bed-side.

"That is not much; they cannot say I take much," he said, look-ing at it.

He put his knotted stick beside it, his blue tobacco bag and his short pipe, and then inspected his coats. He had two left—a moth-eaten overcoat and a black alpaca out at the elbows. He decided for the overcoat: it was warm certainly, but then he could carry it over his arm, and only put it on when he met someone along the road. It was more respectable than the black alpaca. He hung the great-coat over the back of the chair, and stuffed a hard bit of roaster-cake under the knot of the bundle, and then his preparations were completed. The German stood contemplating them with much satisfaction. He had almost forgotten his sorrow at leaving in plea sure at preparing. Suddenly he started; an expression of intense pain passed over his face. He drew back his left arm quickly, and then pressed his right hand upon his breast.

"Ah, the sudden pang again," he said.

His face was white, but it quickly regained its colour. Then the old man busied himself in putting everything right.

"I will leave it neat. They shall not say I did not leave it neat," he said. Even the little bags of seeds on the mantelpiece he put in rows and dusted. Then he undressed and got into bed. Under his pillow was a little story-book. He drew it forth. To the old German a story was no story. Its events were as real and as important to himself as the matters of his own life. He could not go away with-out knowing whether that wicked Earl relented, and whether the Baron married Emilina. So he adjusted his spectacles and began to read. Occasionally, as his feelings became too strongly moved, he ejaculated, "Ah, I thought so!—That was a rogue!—I saw it before!—I knew it from the beginning!" More than half an hour had passed when he looked up to the silver watch at the top of his bed.

"The march is long to-morrow; this will not do," he said, taking off his spectacles and putting them carefully into the book to mark the place. "This will be good reading as I walk along to-morrow," he added, as he stuffed the book into the pocket of the great-coat; "very good reading." He nodded his head and lay down. He thought a little of his own troubles, a good deal of the two little girls he was leaving, of the Earl, of Emilina, of the Baron; but he was soon asleep—sleeping as peacefully as a little child upon whose innocent soul sorrow and care cannot rest.

It was very quiet in the room. The coals in the fire-place threw a dull red light across the floor upon the red lions on the quilt. Eleven o'clock came, and the room was very still. One o'clock came. The glimmer had died out, though the ashes were still warm, and the room was very dark. The grey mouse, who had its hole under the tool-box, came out and sat on the sacks in the corner; then, growing bolder, the room was so dark, it climbed the chair at the bedside, nibbled at the roaster-cake, took one bite quickly at the candle, and then sat on his haunches listening. It heard the even breathing of the old man, and the steps of the hungry Kaffir dog going his last round in search of a bone or a skin that had been forgotten; and it heard the white hen call out as the wild cat ran away with one of her brood, and it heard the chicken cry. Then the grey mouse went back to its hole under the tool-box, and the room was quiet. And two o'clock came. By that time the night was grown dull and cloudy. The wild cat had gone to its home on the 'kopje;' the Kaffir dog had found a bone, and lay gnawing it.

An intense quiet reigned everywhere. Only in her room the Boer-woman tossed her great arms in her sleep; for she dreamed that a dark shadow with outstretched wings fled slowly over her house, and she moaned and shivered. And the night was very still.

But, quiet as all places were, there was a quite peculiar quiet in the German's room. Though you strained your ear most carefully you caught no sound of breathing.

He was not gone, for the old coat still hung on the chair—the coat that was to be put on when he met any one; and the bundle and stick were ready for to-morrow's long march. The old German himself lay there, his wavy black hair just touched with grey thrown back upon the pillow. The old face was lying there alone in the dark, smiling like a little child's—oh, so peacefully. There is a stranger whose coming, they say, is worse than all the ills of life, from whose presence we flee away trembling; but he comes very tenderly sometimes. And it seemed almost as though Death had known and loved the old man, so gently it touched him. And how could it deal hardly with him—the loving, simple, childlike old man?

So it smoothed out the wrinkles that were in the old-forehead, and fixed the passing smile, and sealed the eyes that they might not weep again; and then the short sleep of time was melted into the long, long sleep of eternity.

"How has he grown so young in this one night?" they said when they found him in the morning.

Yes, dear old man, to such as you time brings no age. You die with the purity and innocence of your childhood upon you, though you die in your grey hairs.

Chapter IX.
He Sees A Ghost.

Bonaparte stood on the ash-heap. He espied across the plain a moving speck, and he chucked his coat-tails up and down in expectancy of a scene.

The waggon came on slowly. Waldo laid curled among the sacks at the back of the waggon, the hand in his breast resting on the sheep-shearing machine. It was finished now. The right thought had struck him the day before as he sat, half asleep, watching the water go over the mill-wheel. He muttered to himself with half-closed eyes,–

"To-morrow smooth the cogs—tighten the screws a little— show it to them." Then after a pause—"Over the whole world— the whole world—mine, that I have made!" He pressed the little wheels and pulleys in his pocket till they cracked. Presently his muttering became louder—"And fifty pounds—a black hat for my dadda—for Lyndall a blue silk, very light; and one purple like the earth-bells, and white shoes." He muttered on—"A box full, full of books. They shall tell me all, all, all," he added, moving his fingers desiringly: "why the crystals grow in such beautiful shapes; why lightning runs to the iron; why black people are black; why the sunlight makes things warm. I shall read, read, read," he muttered slowly. Then came over him suddenly what he called "The presence of God"; a sense of a good, strong something folding him round. He smiled through his half-shut eyes. "Ah, Father, my own Father, it is so sweet to feel you, like the warm sunshine. The Bibles and books cannot tell of you and all I feel you. They are mixed with men's words; but you—"

His muttering sank into inaudible confusion, till, opening his eyes wide, it struck him that the brown plain he looked at was the old home farm. For half an hour they had been riding in it, and he had not known it. He roused the leader, who sat nodding on the front of the waggon in the early morning sunlight. They were within half a mile of the homestead. It seemed to him that he had been gone from them all a year. He fancied he could see Lyndall standing on the brick wall to watch for him, his father, passing from one house to the other, stopping to look.

He called aloud to the oxen. For each one at home he had brought something. For his father a piece of tobacco, bought at the shop by the mill; for Em a thimble; for Lyndall a beautiful flower dug out by the roots, at a place where they had 'out-spanned'; for Tant' Sannie a handkerchief. When they drew near the house he threw the whip to the Kaffir leader, and sprang from the side of the waggon to run on. Bonaparte stopped him as he ran past the ash-heap.

"Good morning, my dear boy. Where are you running to so fast with your rosy cheeks?"

The boy looked up at him, glad even to see Bonaparte.

"I am going to the cabin," he said, out of breath.

"You won't find them in just now—not your good old father," said Bonaparte.

"Where is he?" asked the lad.

"There, beyond the camps," said Bonaparte, waving his hand oratorically towards the stone-walled ostrich-camps.

"What is he doing there?" asked the boy.

Bonaparte patted him on the cheek kindly.

"We could not keep him any more, it was too hot. We've buried him, my boy," said Bonaparte, touching with his finger the boy's cheek. "We couldn't keep him any more. He, he, he!" laughed Bonaparte, as the boy fled away along the low stone wall, almost furtively, as one in fear.

At five o'clock Bonaparte knelt before a box in the German's room. He was busily unpacking it.

It had been agreed upon between Tant' Sannie and himself, that now the German was gone he, Bonaparte, was to be no longer schoolmaster, but overseer of the farm. In return for his past scholastic labours he had expressed himself willing to take possession of the dead man's goods and room. Tant' Sannie hardly liked the arrangement. She had a great deal more respect for the German dead than the German living, and would rather his goods had been allowed to descend peacefully to his son. For she was a firm believer in the chinks in the world above, where not only ears, but eyes might be applied to see how things went on in this world below. She never felt sure how far the spirit-world might overlap this world of sense, and, as a rule, prudently abstained from doing anything which might offend unseen auditors. For this reason she abstained from ill-using the dead English-man's daughter and niece, and for this reason she would rather the boy had had his father's goods. But it was hard to refuse Bonaparte anything when she and he sat so happily together in the evening drinking coffee, Bonaparte telling her in the broken Dutch he was fast learning how he adored fat women, and what a splendid farmer he was.

So at five o'clock on this afternoon Bonaparte knelt in the German's room.

"Somewhere, here it is," he said, as he packed the old clothes carefully out of the box, and, finding nothing, packed them in again. "Somewhere in this room it is; and if it's here Bonaparte finds it," he repeated. "You didn't stay here all these years without making a little pile somewhere, my lamb. You weren't such a fool as you looked. Oh, no!" said Bonaparte.

He now walked about the room, diving his fingers in every where: sticking them into the great crevices in the wall and frightening out the spiders; rapping them against the old plaster till it cracked and fell in pieces; peering up the chimney, till the soot dropped on his bald head and blackened it. He felt in little blue bags; he tried to raise the hearthstone; he shook each book, till the old leaves fell down in showers on the floor.

It was getting dark, and Bonaparte stood with his finger on his nose reflecting. Finally he walked to the door, behind which hung the trousers and waistcoat the dead man had last worn. He had felt in them, but hurriedly, just after the funeral the day before; he would examine them again. Sticking his fingers into the waistcoat pockets, he found in one corner a hole. Pressing his hand through it, between the lining and the cloth, he presently came into contact with something. Bonaparte drew it forth—a small, square parcel, sewed up in sail-cloth. He gazed at it, squeezed it; it cracked, as though full of bank notes. He put it quickly into his own waistcoat pocket, and peeped over the half-door to see if there was any one coming. There was nothing to be seen but the last rays of yellow sunset light, painting the 'karroo bushes' in the plain, and shining on the ash-heap, where the fowls were pecking. He turned and sat down on the nearest chair, and, taking out his pen-knife, ripped the parcel open. The first thing that fell was a shower of yellow faded papers. Bonaparte opened them carefully one by one, and smoothed them out on his knee. There was something very valuable to be hidden so carefully, though the German characters he could not decipher. When he came to the last one, he felt there was something hard in it.

"You've got it, Bon, my boy! you've got it!" he cried, slapping his leg hard. Edging nearer to the door, for the light was fading, he opened the paper carefully. There was nothing inside but a plain gold wedding-ring.

"Better than nothing!" said Bonaparte, trying to put it on his little finger, which, however, proved too fat.

He took it off and set it down on the table before him, and looked at it with his crosswise eyes.

"When that auspicious hour, Sannie," he said, "shall have arrived, when, panting, I shall lead thee, lighted by Hymen's torch, to the connubial altar, then upon thy fair amaranthine finger, my joyous bride, shall this ring repose.

"Thy fair body, oh, my girl,
Shall Bonaparte possess;
His fingers in thy money-bags,
He therein, too, shall mess."

Having given utterance to this flood of poesy, he sat lost in joyous reflection.

"He therein, too, *shall* mess," he repeated, meditatively.

At this instant, as Bonaparte swore, and swore truly to the end of his life, a slow and distinct rap was given on the crown of his bald head.

Bonaparte started and looked up. No 'reim,' or strap, hung down from the rafters above, and not a human creature was near the door. It was growing dark; he did not like it. He began to fold up the papers expeditiously. He stretched out his hand for the ring. The ring was gone! Gone, although no human creature had entered the room; gone, although no form had crossed the doorway. Gone!

He would not sleep there, that was certain. He stuffed the papers into his pocket. As he did so, three slow and distinct taps were given on the crown of his head. Bonaparte's jaw fell: each separate joint lost its power; he could not move; he dared not rise; his tongue lay loose in his mouth.

"Take all, take all!" he gurgled in his throat. "I—I do not want them. Take—"

Here a resolute tug at the grey curls at the back of his head caused him to leap up, yelling wildly. Was he to sit still paralysed, to be dragged away *bodily* to the devil? With terrific shrieks he fled, casting no glance behind.

When the dew was falling, and the evening was dark, a small figure moved towards the gate of the farthest ostrich-camp, driving a bird before it. When the gate was opened and the bird driven in and the gate fastened, it turned away, but then suddenly paused near the stone wall.

"Is that you, Waldo?" said Lyndall, hearing a sound.

The boy was sitting on the damp ground with his back to the wall. He gave her no answer.

"Come," she said, bending over him, "I have been looking for you all day."

He mumbled something.

"You have had nothing to eat. I have put some supper in your room. You must come home with me, Waldo."

She took his hand, and the boy rose slowly.

She made him take her arm, and twisted her small fingers among his.

"You must forget," she whispered. "Since it happened I walk, I talk, I never sit still. If we remember, we cannot bring back the dead." She knit her little fingers closer among his. "Forgetting is the best thing. He did not watch it coming," she whispered presently. "That is the dreadful thing, to *see* it coming!" She shuddered. "I want it to come so to me too. Why do you think I was driving that bird?" she added quickly. "That was Hans, the bird that hates Bonaparte. I let him out this afternoon; I thought he would chase him and perhaps kill him."

The boy showed no sign of interest.

"He did not catch him; but he put his head over the half-door of your cabin and frightened him horribly. He was there, busy stealing your things. Perhaps he will leave them alone now; but I wish the bird had trodden on him."

They said no more till they reached the door of the cabin.

"There is a candle and supper on the table. You must eat," she said authoritatively. "I cannot stay with you now, lest they find out about the bird."

He grasped her arm and brought his mouth close to her ear. "There is no God!" he almost hissed; "no God; not anywhere!" She started.

"Not anywhere!"

He ground it out between his teeth, and she felt his hot breath on her cheek.

"Waldo, you are mad," she said, drawing herself from him instinctively.

He loosened his grasp and turned away from her also.

In truth, is it not life's way? We fight our little battles alone; you yours, I mine. We must not help or find help.

When your life is most real, to me you are mad; when your agony is blackest I look at you and wonder. Friendship is good, a strong stick; but when the hour comes to lean hard, it gives.

In the day of their bitterest need all souls are alone.

Lyndall stood by him in the dark, pityingly, wonderingly. As he walked to the door she came after him.

"Eat your supper; it will do you good," she said.

She rubbed her cheek against his shoulder and then ran away.

In the front room the little woolly Kaffir girl was washing Tant' Sannie's feet in a small tub, and Bonaparte, who sat on the wooden sofa, was pulling off his shoes and stockings that his own feet might be washed also. There were three candles burning in the room, and he and Tant' Sannie sat close together, with the lean Hottentot not far off; for when ghosts are about much light is needed, there is great strength in numbers. Bonaparte had completely recovered from the effects of his fright in the afternoon, and the numerous doses of brandy that it had been necessary to administer to him to effect his restoration had put him into a singularly pleasant and amiable mood.

"That boy Waldo," said Bonaparte, rubbing his toes, "took himself off coolly this morning as soon as the waggon came, and has not done a stiver of work all day. *I'll* not have that kind of thing now I'm master of this farm."

The Hottentot maid translated.

"Ah, I expect he's sorry that his father's dead," said Tant' Sannie. "It's nature, you know. I cried the whole morning when my father died. One can always get another husband, but one can't get another father," said Tant' Sannie, casting a sidelong glance at Bonaparte.

Bonaparte expressed a wish to give Waldo his orders for the next day's work, and accordingly the little woolly-headed Kaffir was sent to call him. After a considerable time the boy appeared, and stood in the doorway.

If they had dressed him in one of the swallow-tailed coats, and oiled his hair till the drops fell from it, and it lay as smooth as an elder's on sacrament Sunday, there would still have been something unanointed in the aspect of the fellow. As it was, standing there in his strange old costume, his head presenting much the appearance of having been deeply rolled in sand, his eyelids swollen, the hair hanging over his forehead, and a dogged sullenness on his features, he presented most the appearance of an ill-conditioned young buffalo.

"Beloved Lord," cried Tant' Sannie, "how he looks! Come in, boy. Couldn't you come and say good-day to me? Don't you want some supper?"

He said he wanted nothing, and turned his heavy eyes away from her.

"There's a ghost been seen in your father's room," said Tant' Sannie. "If you're afraid you can sleep in the kitchen."

"I will sleep in our room," said the boy slowly.

"Well, you can go now," she said; "but be up early to take the sheep. The herd"

"Yes, be up early, my boy," interrupted Bonaparte, smiling. "I am to be master of this farm now; and we shall be good friends, I trust, very good friends, if you try to do your duty, my dear boy."

Waldo turned to go, and Bonaparte, looking benignly at the candle, stretched out one unstockinged foot, over which Waldo, looking at nothing in particular, fell with a heavy thud upon the floor.

"Dear me! I hope you are not hurt, my boy," said Bonaparte. "You'll have many a harder thing than that though, before you've gone through life," he added consolingly, as Waldo picked himself up.

The lean Hottentot laughed till the room rang again; and Tant' Sannie tittered till her sides ached.

When he had gone the little maid began to wash Bonaparte's feet.

"Oh, Lord, beloved Lord, how he did fall! I can't think of it," cried Tant' Sannie, and she laughed again. "I always did know he was not right; but this evening any one could see it," she added, wiping the tears of mirth from her face.

"His eyes are as wild as if the devil was in them. He never *was* like other children. The dear Lord knows, if he doesn't walk alone for hours talking to himself. If you sit in the room with him you can see his lips moving the whole time; and if you talk to him twenty times he doesn't hear you. Daft-eyes; he's as mad as mad can be."

The repetition of the word mad conveyed meaning to Bonaparte's mind. He left off paddling his toes in the water.

"Mad, mad? *I* know that kind of mad," said Bonaparte, "and I know the thing to give for it. The front end of a little horsewhip, the tip! Nice thing; takes it out," said Bonaparte.

The Hottentot laughed, and translated.

"No more walking about and talking to themselves on this farm now," said Bonaparte; "no more minding of sheep and reading of books at the same time. The point of a horsewhip is a little thing, but I think he'll have a taste of it before long." Bonaparte rubbed his hands and looked pleasantly across his nose; and then the three laughed together grimly.

And Waldo in his cabin crouched in the dark in a corner, with his knees drawn up to his chin.

Chapter X.
He Shows His Teeth.

Doss sat among the karroo bushes, one yellow ear drawn over his wicked little eye, ready to flap away any adventurous fly that might settle on his nose. Around him in the morning sunlight fed the sheep; behind him lay his master polishing his machine. He found much comfort in handling it that morning. A dozen philosophical essays, or angelically attuned songs for the consolation of the bereaved, could never have been to him what that little sheep-shearing machine was that day.

After struggling to see the unseeable, growing drunk with the endeavour to span the infinite, and writhing before the inscrutable mystery, it is a renovating relief to turn to some simple, feelable, weighable substance; to something which has a smell and a colour, which may be handled and turned over this way and that. Whether there be or be not a hereafter, whether there be any use in calling aloud to the Unseen power, whether there be an Unseen power to call to, whatever be the true nature of the *I* who call and of the objects around me, whatever be our meaning, our internal essence, our cause (and in a certain order of minds death and the agony of loss inevitably awaken the wild desire, at other times smothered, to look into these things), whatever be the nature of that which lies beyond the unbroken wall which the limits of the human intellect build up on every hand, this thing is certain—a knife will cut wood and one cogged wheel will turn another. This is sure.

Waldo found an immeasurable satisfaction in the handling of his machine; but Doss winked and blinked, and thought it all frightfully monotonous out there on the flat, and presently dropped asleep, sitting bolt upright. Suddenly his eyes opened wide; something was coming from the direction of the homestead. Winking his eyes and looking intently, he perceived it was the grey mare. Now Doss had wondered much of late what had become of her master. Seeing she carried some one on her back, he now came to his own conclusion, and began to move his tail violently up and down. Presently he pricked up one ear and let the other hang; his tail became motionless, and the expression of his mouth was one of decided disapproval bordering on scorn. He wrinkled his lips up on each side into little lines.

The sand was soft, and the grey mare came on so noiselessly that the boy heard nothing till Bonaparte dismounted. Then Doss got up and moved back a step. He did not approve of Bonaparte's appearance. His costume, in truth, was of a unique kind. It was a combination of the town and country. The tails of his black cloth coat were pinned up behind to keep them from rubbing; he had on a pair of moleskin trousers and leather gaiters, and in his hand he carried a little whip of rhinoceros hide.

Waldo started and looked up. Had there been a moment's time he would have dug a hole in the sand with his hands and buried his treasure. It was only a toy of wood, but he loved it, as one of necessity loves what has been born of him, whether of the flesh or spirit. When cold eyes have looked at it, the feathers are rubbed off our butterfly's wing forever.

"What have you here, my lad?" said Bonaparte, standing by him, and pointing, with the end of his whip to the medley of wheels and hinges.

The boy muttered something inaudible, and half-spread his hand over the thing.

"But this seems to be a very ingenious little machine," said Bonaparte, seating himself on the ant-heap, and bending down over it with deep interest. "What is it for, my lad?"

"Shearing sheep."

"It is a very nice little machine," said Bonaparte. "How does it work, now? I have never seen anything so ingenious!"

There was never a parent who heard deception in the voice that praised his child—his first-born. Here was one who liked the thing that had been created in him. He forgot everything. He showed how the shears would work with a little guidance, how the sheep would be held, and the wool fall into the trough. A flush burst over his face as he spoke.

"I tell you what, my lad," said Bonaparte emphatically, when the explanation was finished, "we must get you a patent. Your fortune is made. In three years' time there'll not be a farm in this colony where it isn't working. You're a genius, that's what *you* are!" said Bonaparte, rising.

"If it were made larger," said the boy, raising his eyes, "it would work more smoothly. Do you think there would be any one in this colony would be able to make it?"

"I'm sure they could," said Bonaparte; "and if not, why I'll do my best for you. I'll send it to England. It must be done somehow. How long have you worked at it?"

"Nine months," said the boy.

"Oh, it is such a nice little machine," said Bonaparte, "one can't help feeling an interest in it. There is only *one* little improvement, one very little improvement, I should like to make."

Bonaparte put his foot on the machine and crushed it into the sand. The boy looked up into his face.

"Looks better now," said Bonaparte, "doesn't it? If we can't have it made in England we'll send it to America. Good-bye; ta-ta," he added. "You're a great genius, a born genius, my dear boy, there's no doubt about it."

He mounted the grey mare and rode off. The dog watched his retreat with cynical satisfaction; but his master lay on the ground with his head on his arms in the sand, and the little wheels and chips of wood lay on the ground around him. The dog jumped on to his back and snapped at the black curls, till, finding that no notice was taken, he walked off to play with a black beetle. The beetle was hard at work trying to roll home a great ball of dung it had been collecting all the morning; but Doss broke the ball, and ate the beetle's hind legs, and then bit off its head. And it was all play, and no one could tell what it had lived and worked for. A striving, and a striving, and an ending in nothing.

Chapter XI.
He Snaps.

"I have found something in the loft," said Em to Waldo, who was listlessly piling cakes of fuel on the kraal wall, a week after. "It is a box of books that belonged to my father. We thought Tant' Sannie had burnt them."

The boy put down the cake he was raising and looked at her.

"I don't think they are very nice, not stories," she added, "but you can go and take any you like."

So saying, she took up the plate in which she had brought his breakfast, and walked off to the house.

After that the boy worked quickly. The pile of fuel Bonaparte had ordered him to pack was on the wall in half an hour. He then went to throw salt on the skins laid out to dry. Finding the pot empty, he went to the loft to refill it.

Bonaparte Blenkins, whose door opened at the foot of the ladder, saw the boy go up, and stood in the doorway waiting for his return. He wanted his boots blacked. Doss, finding he could not follow his master up the round bars, sat patiently at the foot of the ladder. Presently he looked up longingly, but no one appeared. Then Bonaparte looked up also, and began to call; but there was no answer. What could the boy be doing? The loft was an unknown land to Bonaparte. He had often wondered what was up there; he liked to know what was in all locked-up places and out-of-the-way corners, but he was afraid to climb the ladder. So Bonaparte looked up, and, in the name of all that was tantalizing, questioned what the boy did up there. The loft was used only as a lumber-room. What could the fellow find up there to keep him so long?

Could the Boer-woman have beheld Waldo at that instant, any lingering doubt which might have remained in her mind as to the boy's insanity would instantly have vanished. For, having filled the salt-pot, he proceeded to look for the box of books among the rubbish that filled the loft. Under a pile of sacks he found it—a rough packing-case, nailed up, but with one loose plank. He lifted that, and saw the even backs of a row of books. He knelt down before the box, and ran his hand along its rough edges, as if to assure himself of its existence. He stuck his hand in among the books, and pulled out two. He felt them, thrust his fingers in among the leaves, and crumpled them a little, as a lover feels the hair of his mistress. The fellow gloated over his treasure. He had had a dozen books in the course of his life; now here was a mine of them opened at his feet. After a while he began to read the titles, and now and again opened a book and read a sentence; but he was too excited to catch the meanings distinctly. At last he came to a dull brown volume. He read the name, opened it in the centre and where he opened began to read. 'Twas a chapter on property that he fell upon—Communism, Fourierism, St. Simonism, in a work on Political Economy.[1] He read down one page and turned over to the next; he read down that without changing his posture by an inch; he read the next, and the next, kneeling up all the while with the book in his hand, and his lips parted.

All he read he did not fully understand; the thoughts were new to him; but this was the fellow's startled joy in the book—the thoughts were his, they belonged to him. He had never thought them before, but they were his.

He laughed silently and internally, with the still intensity of triumphant joy.

So, then, all thinking creatures did not send up the one cry— "As thou, dear Lord, hast created things in the beginning, so they are now, so ought they to be, so will they be, world without end; and it doesn't concern us what they are. Amen." There were men to whom not only kopjes and stones were calling out imperative-

---

1 J.S. Mill's *Principles of Political Economy: with Some of their Applications to Social Philosophy* (1848), Book II, chapter one "Of Property," considers which of the economic systems is consistent with "the greatest amount of human liberty and spontaneity." According to Mill, "the restraints of Communism would be freedom in comparison with the present condition of the majority of the human race." Mill also examines two non-communistic forms of socialism. St. Simonism, based on ideas of French social philosopher Claude Henri de Rouvroy, comte de Saint-Simon (1760-1825), advocated a society that divided labor according to vocation or capacity and governed by a few men of genius. Fourierism, based on ideas of Charles Fourier (1772-1837), imagined communities as economic units in which both labor and capital are shared. A number of socialist movements were active in England in the nineteenth century. Although Schreiner never officially joined any socialist organization, she was an intimate friend of Eleanor Marx and was especially interested in the rights of organized labor. Waldo's joy in reading about alternative forms of social organization and ownership is that of a worker who has achieved a degree of class-consciousness, albeit in the humanist terms to which Schreiner and other Victorian disciples of Mill adhered.

ly, "What are we, and how came we here? Understand us, and know us;" but to whom even the old, old relations between man and man, and the customs of the ages called, and could not be made still and forgotten.

The boy's heavy body quivered with excitement. So he was not alone, not alone. He could not quite have told any one why he was so glad, and this warmth had come to him. His cheeks were burning. No wonder that Bonaparte called in vain, and Doss put his paws on the ladder, and whined till three-quarters of an hour had passed. At last the boy put the book in his breast and buttoned it tightly to him. He took up the salt-pot, and went to the top of the ladder. Bonaparte, with his hands folded under his coat-tails, looked up when he appeared, and accosted him.

"You've been rather a long time up there, my lad," he said, as the boy descended with a tremulous haste, most unlike his ordinary slow movements. "You didn't hear me calling, I suppose?"

Bonaparte whisked the tails of his coat up and down as he looked at him. He, Bonaparte Blenkins, had eyes which were very far-seeing. He looked at the pot. It was rather a small pot to have taken three-quarters of an hour in the filling. He looked at the face. It was flushed. And yet, Tant' Sannie kept no wine—he had not been drinking; his eyes were wide open and bright—he had not been sleeping; there was no girl up there—he had not been making love. Bonaparte looked at him sagaciously. What would account for the marvellous change in the boy coming down the ladder from the boy going up the ladder? *One* thing there was. Did not Tant' Sannie keep in the loft 'bultongs,' and nice smoked sausages? There must be something nice to *eat* up there! Aha! that was it!

Bonaparte was so interested in carrying out this chain of inductive reasoning that he quite forgot to have his boots blacked.

He watched the boy shuffle off with the salt-pot under his arm; then he stood in his doorway, and raised his eyes to the quiet blue sky, and audibly propounded this riddle to himself.

"What is the connection between the naked back of a certain boy with a greatcoat on and a salt-pot under his arm, and the tip of a horsewhip? Answer: No connection at present, but there will be soon."

Bonaparte was so pleased with this sally of his wit that he chuckled a little, and went to lie down on his bed.

There was bread-baking that afternoon, and there was a fire lighted in the brick oven behind the house, and Tant' Sannie had left the great wooden-elbowed chair in which she passed her life, and waddled out to look at it. Not far off was Waldo, who, having thrown a pail of food into the pig-sty, now leaned over the sod-wall looking at the pigs. Half of the sty was dry, but the lower half was a pool of mud, on the edge of which the mother sow lay with closed eyes, her ten little ones sucking; the father pig, knee-deep in the mud, stood running his snout into a rotten pumpkin and wriggling his curled tail.

Waldo wondered dreamily as he stared why they were pleasant to look at. Taken singly they were not beautiful; taken together they were. Was it not because there was a certain harmony about them? The old sow was suited to the little pigs, and the little pigs to their mother, the old boar to the rotten pumpkin, and all to the mud. They suggested the thought of nothing that should be added, of nothing that should be taken away. And, he wondered on vaguely, was not *that* the secret of all beauty, that you who look on——. So he stood dreaming, and leaned further and further over the sod-wall, and looked at the pigs.

All this time Bonaparte Blenkins, was sloping down from the house in an aimless sort of way; but he kept one eye fixed on the pig-sty, and each gyration brought him nearer to it. Waldo stood like a thing asleep when Bonaparte came close up to him.

In old days, when a small boy, playing in an Irish street-gutter, he, Bonaparte, had been familiarly known among his comrades under the title of Tripping Ben; this, from the rare ease and dexterity with which, by merely projecting his foot, he could precipitate any unfortunate companion on to the crown of his bead. Years had elapsed, and Tripping Ben had become Bonaparte; but the old gift was in him still. He came close to the pig-sty. All the defunct memories of his boyhood returned on him in a flood, as with an adroit movement he inserted his leg between Waldo and the wall, and sent him over into the pig-sty.

The little pigs were startled at the strange intruder, and ran behind their mother, who sniffed at him. Tant' Sannie smote her hands together and laughed; but Bonaparte was far from joining her. Lost in reverie, he gazed at the distant horizon.

The sudden reversal of head and feet had thrown out the volume that Waldo carried in his breast. Bonaparte picked it up, and began to inspect it, as the boy climbed slowly over the wall. He would have walked off sullenly, but he wanted his book, and waited till it should be given him.

"Ha!" said Bonaparte, raising his eyes from the leaves of the book which he was examining. "I hope your coat has not been injured; it is of an elegant cut. An heirloom, I presume, from your paternal grandfather? It looks nice now."

"Oh, Lord! oh, Lord!" cried Tant' Sannie, laughing and holding her sides; "how the child looks—as though he thought the mud would never wash off. Oh, Lord, I shall die! You, Bonaparte, are the funniest man I ever saw."

Bonaparte Blenkins was now carefully inspecting the volume he had picked up. Among the subjects on which the darkness of his understanding had been enlightened during his youth, Political Economy had not been one. He was not, therefore, very clear as to what the nature of the book might be; and as the name of the writer, J. S. Mill, might, for anything he knew to the contrary, have belonged to a venerable member of the British and Foreign Bible Society,[1] it by no means threw light upon the question. He was not in any way sure that Political Economy had nothing to do with the cheapest way of procuring clothing for the army and navy, which would be, certainly, both a political and economical subject.

But Bonaparte soon came to a conclusion as to the nature of the book and its contents, by the application of a simple rule now largely acted upon, but which, becoming universal, would save much thought and valuable time. It is of marvellous simplicity, of infinite utility, of universal applicability. It may easily be committed to memory, and runs thus:—

Whenever you come into contact with any book, person, or opinion of which you absolutely comprehend nothing, declare that book, person, or opinion to be immoral. Bespatter it, vituperate against it, strongly insist that any man or woman harbouring it is a fool or a knave or both. Carefully abstain from studying it. Do all that in you lies to annihilate that book, person, or opinion.

Acting on this rule, so wide in its comprehensiveness, so beautifully simple in its working, Bonaparte approached Tant' Sannie with the book in his hand. Waldo came a step nearer, eyeing it like a dog whose young has fallen into evil hands.

"This book," said Bonaparte, "is not a fit and proper study for a young and immature mind."

---

1   Many Bible Societies were established at the end of the eighteenth century to publish and distribute the Bible throughout the world. The most important was the British and Foreign Bible Society which distributed biblical texts in 700 languages.

Tant' Sannie did not understand a word and said, "What?"

"This book," said Bonaparte, bringing down his finger with energy on the cover, "this book is *sleg, sleg, Davel, Davel!*"

Tant' Sannie perceived from the gravity of his countenance that it was no laughing matter. From the words *sleg* and *Davel* she understood that the book was evil, and had some connection with the prince who pulls the wires of evil over the whole earth.

"Where did you get this book?" she asked, turning her twinkling little eyes on Waldo. "I wish that my legs may be as thin as an Englishman's if it isn't one of your father's. He had more sins than all the Kaffirs in Kaffirland, for all that he pretended to be so good all those years, and to live without a wife because he was thinking of the one that was dead! As though ten dead wives could make up for one fat one with arms and legs!" cried Tant' Sannie, snorting.

"It was not my father's book," said the boy savagely. "I got it from your loft."

"My loft! my book! How dare you?" cried Tant' Sannie.

"It was Em's father's. She gave it me," he muttered more sullenly.

"Give it here. What is the name of it? What is it about?" she asked, putting her finger upon the title.

Bonaparte understood.

"Political Economy," he said slowly.

"Dear Lord!" said Tant' Sannie, "cannot one hear from the very sound what an ungodly book it is! One can hardly say the name. Haven't we got curses enough on this farm?" cried Tant' Sannie, eloquently: "my best imported Merino ram dying of nobody knows what, and the short-horn cow casting her two calves, and the sheep eaten up with the scab and the drought? And is *this* a time to bring ungodly things about the place, to call down the vengeance of Almighty God to punish us more? Didn't the minister tell me when I was confirmed not to read any book except my Bible and hymn-book, that the Devil was in all the rest? And I never have read any other book," said Tant' Sannie with virtuous energy, "and I never will!"

Waldo saw that the fate of his book was sealed, and turned sullenly on his heel.

"So you will not stay to hear what I say!" cried Tant' Sannie. "There, take your Polity-gollity-gominy, your devil's book!" she cried, flinging the book at his head with much energy.

It merely touched his forehead on one side and fell to the ground.

"Go on," she cried; "I know you are going to talk to yourself. People who talk to themselves always talk to the Devil. Go and tell him all about it. Go, go! run!" cried Tant' Sannie.

But the boy neither quickened nor slackened his pace, and passed sullenly round the back of the waggon-house.

Books have been thrown at other heads before and since that summer afternoon, by hands more white and delicate than those of the Boer-woman; but whether the result of the process has been in any case wholly satisfactory, may be questioned. We love that with a peculiar tenderness, we treasure it with a peculiar care, it has for us quite a fictitious value, for which we have suffered. If we may not carry it anywhere else we will carry it in our hearts, and always to the end.

Bonaparte Blenkins went to pick up the volume, now loosened from its cover, while Tant' Sannie pushed the stumps of wood farther into the oven. Bonaparte came close to her, tapped the book knowingly, nodded, and looked at the fire. Tant' Sannie comprehended, and, taking the volume from his hand, threw it into the back of the oven. It lay upon the heap of coals, smoked, flared, and blazed, and the 'Political Economy' was no more—gone out of existence, like many another poor heretic of flesh and blood.[1]

Bonaparte grinned, and to watch the process brought his face so near the oven door that the white hair on his eyebrows got singed. He then inquired if there were any more in the loft.

Learning that there were, he made signs indicative of taking up armfuls and flinging them into the fire. But Tant' Sannie was dubious. The deceased Englishman had left all his personal effects specially to his child. It was all very well for Bonaparte to talk of burning the books. He had had his hair spiritually pulled, and she had no wish to repeat his experience.

She shook her head. Bonaparte was displeased. But then a happy thought occurred to him. He suggested that the key of the loft should henceforth be put into his own safe care and keeping—no one gaining possession of it without his permission. To this Tant' Sannie readily assented, and the two walked lovingly to the house to look for it.

---

1 In the middle ages, those who dissented from the accepted beliefs of the Roman Catholic church were burned at the stake. Here Waldo's book suffers a similar fate.

Chapter XII.
He Bites.

Bonaparte Blenkins was riding home on the grey mare. He had ridden out that afternoon, partly for the benefit of his health, partly to maintain his character as overseer of the farm. As he rode on slowly, he thoughtfully touched the ears of the grey mare with his whip.

"No, Bon, my boy," he addressed himself, "don't propose! You can't marry for four years, on account of the will; then why propose? Weedle her, tweedle her, teedle her, but *don't* let her make sure of you. When a woman," said Bonaparte, sagely resting his finger against the side of his nose, "when a woman is sure of you she does what she likes with you; but when she isn't, you do what you like with her. And I—" said Bonaparte.

Here he drew the horse up suddenly and looked. He was now close to the house, and leaning over the pigsty wall, in company with Em, who was showing her the pigs, was a strange female figure. It was the first visitor that had appeared on the farm since his arrival, and he looked at her with interest. She was a tall, pudgy girl of fifteen, weighing a hundred and fifty pounds, with baggy, pendulous cheeks and up-turned nose. She strikingly resembled Tant' Sannie, in form and feature, but her sleepy good eyes lacked the twinkle that dwelt in the Boer-woman's small orbs. She was attired in a bright green print, wore brass rings in her ears and glass beads round her neck, and was sucking the tip of her large finger as she looked at the pigs.

"Who is it that has come?" asked Bonaparte, when he stood drinking his coffee in the front room.

"Why, my niece, to be sure," said Tant' Sannie, the Hottentot maid translating. "She's the only daughter of my only brother Paul, and she's come to visit me. She'll be a nice mouthful to the man that can get her," added Tant' Sannie. "Her father's got two thousand pounds in the green waggon box under his bed, and a farm, and five thousand sheep, and God Almighty knows how many goats and horses. They milk ten cows in mid winter, and the young men are after her like flies about a bowl of milk. She says she means to get married in four months, but she doesn't yet know to whom. It was so with me when I was young," said Tant' Sannie: "I've sat up with the young men four and five nights a week. And they will come riding again, as soon as ever they know that the time's up that the Englishman made me agree not to marry in."

The Boer-woman smirked complacently.

"Where are you going to?" asked Tant' Sannie presently, seeing that Bonaparte rose.

"Ha! I'm just going to the kraals; I'll be in to supper," said Bonaparte.

Nevertheless, when he reached his own door he stopped and turned in there. Soon after he stood before the little glass, arrayed in his best white shirt with the little tucks, and shaving himself. He had on his very best trousers, and had heavily oiled the little fringe at the back of his head, which, however, refused to become darker. But what distressed him most was his nose—it was very red. He rubbed his finger and thumb on the wall, and put a little white-wash on it; but, finding it rather made matters worse, he rubbed it off again. Then he looked carefully into his own eyes. They certainly were a little pulled down at the outer corners, which gave them the appearance of looking crosswise; but then they were a nice blue. So he put on his best coat, took up his stick, and went out to supper, feeling on the whole well satisfied.

"Aunt," said Trana to Tant' Sannie when that night they lay together in the great wooden bed, "why does the Englishman sigh so when he looks at me?"

"Ha!" said Tant' Sannie, who was half asleep, but suddenly started, wide awake. "It's because he thinks you look like me. I tell you, Trana," said Tant' Sannie, "the man is mad with love of me. I told him the other night I couldn't marry till Em was sixteen, or I'd lose all the sheep her father left me. And he talked about Jacob working seven years and seven years again for his wife. And of course he meant me," said Tant' Sannie pompously. "But he won't get me so easily as he thinks; he'll have to ask more than once."

"Oh!" said Trana, who was a lumpish girl and not much given to talking; but presently she added, "Aunt, why does the Englishman always knock against a person when he passes them?"

"That's because you are always in the way," said Tant' Sannie.

"But, Aunt," said Trana, presently, "I think he is very ugly."

"Phugh!" said Tant' Sannie. "It's only because we're not accustomed to such noses in this country. In his country he says all the people have such noses, and the redder your nose is the higher you are. He's of the family of the Queen Victoria, you know," said Tant' Sannie, wakening up with her subject; "and he doesn't think anything of governors and Church elders, and such people; they are nothing to him. When his aunt with the dropsy dies he'll have money enough to buy all the farms in this district!"

"Oh!" said Trana. That certainly made a difference.

"Yes," said Tant' Sannie; "and he's only forty-one, though you'd take him to be sixty. And he told me last night the real reason of his baldness."

Tant' Sannie then proceeded to relate how, at eighteen years of age, Bonaparte had courted a fair young lady. How a deadly rival, jealous of his verdant locks, his golden flowing hair, had, with a damnable and insinuating deception, made him a present of a pot of pomatum. How, applying it in the evening, on rising in the morning he found his pillow strewn with the golden locks, and, looking into the glass, beheld the shining and smooth expanse which henceforth he must bear. The few remaining hairs were turned to a silvery whiteness, and the young lady married his rival.

"And," said Tant' Sannie solemnly, "if it had not been for the grace of God, and reading of the psalms, he says he would have killed himself. He says he could kill himself quite easily if he wants to marry a woman and she won't."

"A le wereld," said Trana: and then they went to sleep.

Every one was lost in sleep soon; but from the window of the cabin the light streamed forth. It came from a dung fire, over which Waldo sat brooding. Hour after hour he sat there, now and again throwing a fresh lump of fuel on to the fire, which burnt up bravely, and then sank into a great bed of red coals, which reflected themselves in the boy's eyes as he sat there brooding, brooding, brooding. At last, when the fire was blazing at its brightest, he rose suddenly and walked slowly to a beam from which an ox 'riem' hung. Loosening it, he ran a noose in one end and then doubled it round his arm.

"Mine, mine! I have a right," he muttered; and then something louder, "if I fall and am killed, so much the better!"

He opened the door and went out into the starlight.

He walked with his eyes bent upon the ground, but overhead it was one of those brilliant southern nights when every space so small that your hand might cover it shows fifty cold white points, and the Milky Way is a belt of sharp frosted silver. He passed the door where Bonaparte lay dreaming of Trana and her wealth, and he mounted the ladder steps. From those he clambered with some difficulty on to the roof of the house. It was of old rotten thatch with a ridge of white plaster, and it crumbled away under his feet at every step. He trod as heavily as he could. So much the better if he fell.

He knelt down when he got to the far gable, and began to fasten his 'riem' to the crumbling bricks. Below was the little window of the loft. With one end of the 'riem' tied round the gable, the other end round his waist, how easy to slide down to it, and to open it, through one of the broken panes, and to go in, and to fill his arms with books, and to clamber up again! They had burnt one book—he would have twenty. Every man's hand was against his[1]— his should be against every man's. No one would help him—he would help himself.

He lifted the black damp hair from his knit forehead, and looked round to cool his hot face. Then he saw what a regal night it was. He knelt silently and looked up. A thousand eyes were looking down at him, bright and so cold. There was a laughing irony in them.

"So hot, so bitter, so angry? Poor little mortal!"

He was ashamed. He folded his arms, and sat on the ridge of the roof looking up at them.

"*So* hot, *so* bitter, *so* angry?"

It was as though a cold hand had been laid upon his throbbing forehead, and slowly they began to fade and grow dim. Tant' Sannie and the burnt book, Bonaparte and the broken machine, the box in the loft, he himself sitting there—how small they all became! Even the grave over yonder. Those stars that shone on up above so quietly, they had seen a thousand such little existences, a thousand such little existences fight just so fiercely, flare up just so brightly, and go out; and they, the old, old stars, shone on for ever.

"So hot, so angry, poor little soul?" they said.

The 'riem' slipped from his fingers; he sat with his arms folded, looking up.

"We," said the stars, "have seen the earth when it was young. We have seen small things creep out upon its surface—small things that prayed and loved and cried very loudly, and then crept under it again. But we," said the stars, "are as old as the Unknown."

He leaned his chin against the palm of his hand and looked up at them. So long he sat there that bright stars set and new ones rose, and yet he sat on.

Then at last he stood up, and began to loosen the 'riem' from the gable.

What did it matter about the books? The lust and the desire for them had died out. If they pleased to keep them from him they

---

1 See Genesis 16:12. Waldo thinks of himself as one cursed like Ishmael.

might. What matter? it was a very little thing. Why hate, and struggle and fight? Let it be as it would.

He twisted the 'riem' round his arm and walked back along the ridge of the house.

By this time Bonaparte Blenkins had finished his dream of Trana, and as he turned himself round for a fresh doze he heard the steps descending the ladder. His first impulse was to draw the blanket over his head and his legs under him, and to shout; but, recollecting that the door was locked and the window carefully bolted, he allowed his head slowly to crop out among the blankets, and listened intently. Whosoever it might be, there was no danger of their getting at *him*; so he clambered out of bed, and going on tiptoe to the door, applied his eye to the keyhole. There was nothing to be seen; so walking to the window, he brought his face as close to the glass as his nose would allow. There was a figure just discernible. The lad was not trying to walk softly, and the heavy shuffling of the well-known 'velschoens' could be clearly heard through the closed window as they crossed the stones in the yard. Bonaparte listened till they had died away round the corner of the waggon-house; and, feeling that his bare legs were getting cold, he jumped back into bed again.

"What do you keep up in your loft?" inquired Bonaparte of the Boer-woman the next evening, pointing upwards and elucidating his meaning by the addition of such Dutch words as he knew, for the lean Hottentot was gone home.

"Dried skins," said the Boer-woman, "and empty bottles, and boxes, and sacks, and soap."

"You don't keep any of your provisions there—sugar, now?" said Bonaparte, pointing to the sugar-basin and then up at the loft.

Tant' Sannie shook her head.

"Only salt, and dried peaches."

"Dried peaches! Eh?" said Bonaparte. "Shut the door, my dear child, shut it tight," he called out to Em, who stood in the dining-room. Then he leaned over the elbow of the sofa and brought his face as close as possible to the Boer-woman's, and made signs of eating. Then he said something she did not comprehend; then said, "Waldo, Waldo, Waldo," pointed up to the loft, and made signs of eating again.

Now an inkling of his meaning dawned on the Boer-woman's mind. To make it clearer, he moved his legs after the manner of one going up a ladder, appeared to be opening a door, masticated vigorously, said, "Peaches, peaches, peaches," and appeared to be coming down the ladder.

It was now evident to Tant' Sannie that Waldo had been in her loft and eaten her peaches.

To exemplify his own share in the proceedings, Bonaparte lay down on the sofa, and shutting his eyes tightly, said, "Night, night, night!" Then he sat up wildly, appearing to be intently listening, mimicked with his feet the coming down a ladder, and looked at Tant' Sannie. This clearly showed how, roused in the night, he had discovered the theft.

"He must have been a great fool to eat my peaches," said Tant' Sannie. "They are full of mites as a sheep-skin, and as hard as stones."

Bonaparte, fumbling in his pocket, did not even hear her remark, and took out from his coat-tail a little horsewhip, nicely rolled up. Bonaparte winked at the little rhinoceros horsewhip, at the Boer-woman, and then at the door.

"Shall we call him—Waldo, Waldo?" he said.

Tant' Sannie nodded, and giggled. There was something so exceedingly humorous in the idea that he was going to beat the boy, though for her own part she did not see that the peaches were worth it. When the Kaffir maid came with the wash-tub she was sent to summon Waldo; and Bonaparte doubled up the little whip and put it in his pocket. Then he drew himself up, and prepared to act his important part with becoming gravity. Soon Waldo stood in the door, and took off his hat.

"Come in, come in, my lad," said Bonaparte, "and shut the door behind."

The boy came in and stood before them.

"You need not be so afraid, child," said Tant' Sannie. "I was a child myself once. It's no great harm if you have taken a few."

Bonaparte perceived that her remark was not in keeping with the nature of the proceedings, and of the little drama he intended to act. Pursing out his lips, and waving his hand, he solemnly addressed the boy.

"Waldo, it grieves me beyond expression to have to summon you for so painful a purpose; but it is at the imperative call of duty, which I dare not evade. I do not state that frank and unreserved confession will obviate the necessity of chastisement, which if requisite shall be fully administered; but the nature of that chastisement may be mitigated by free and humble confession. Waldo, answer me as you would your own father, in whose place I now stand to you: have you, or have you not, did you, or did you not, eat of the peaches in the loft?"

"Say you took them, boy, say you took them, then he won't beat you much," said the Dutch-woman good-naturedly, getting a little sorry for him.

The boy raised his eyes slowly and fixed them vacantly upon her, then suddenly his face grew dark with blood.

"*So*, you haven't got anything to say to us, my lad?" said Bonaparte, momentarily forgetting his dignity, and bending forward with a little snarl. "But what I mean is just this, my lad—when it takes a boy three-quarters of an hour to fill a salt-pot, and when at three o'clock in the morning he goes knocking about the doors of a loft, it's natural to suppose there's mischief in it. It's certain there *is* mischief in it; and where there's mischief *in* it must be taken *out*," said Bonaparte, grinning into the boy's face. Then, feeling that he had fallen from that high gravity which was as spice to the pudding, and the flavour of the whole little tragedy, he drew himself up. "Waldo," he said, "confess to me instantly, and without reserve, that you ate the peaches."

The boy's face was white now. His eyes were on the ground, his hands doggedly clasped before him.

"What, you do not intend to answer?"

The boy looked up at them once from under his bent eyebrows, and then looked down again.

"The creature looks as if all the devils in hell were in it," cried Tant' Sannie. "Say you took them, boy. Young things will be young things; I was older than you when I used to eat 'bultong' in my mother's loft, and get the little niggers whipped for it. Say you took them."

But the boy said nothing.

"I think a little solitary confinement might perhaps be beneficial," said Bonaparte. "It will enable you, Waldo, to reflect on the enormity of the sin you have committed against our Father in heaven. And you may also think of the submission you owe to those who are older and wiser than you are, and whose duty it is to check and correct you."

Saying this, Bonaparte stood up and took down the key of the fuel-house, which hung on a nail against the wall.

"Walk on, my boy," said Bonaparte, pointing to the door; and as he followed him out he drew his mouth expressively on one side, and made the lash of the little horsewhip stick out of his pocket and shake up and down.

Tant' Sannie felt half sorry for the lad; but she could not help laughing, it was always so funny when one was going to have a whipping, and it would do him good. Anyhow he would forget all about it when the places were healed. Had not she been beaten many times and been all the better for it?

Bonaparte took up a lighted candle that had been left burning on the kitchen table, and told the boy to walk before him. They went to the fuel-house. It was a little stone erection that jutted out from the side of the waggon-house. It was low, and without a window; and the dried dung was piled in one corner, and the coffee-mill stood in another, fastened on the top of a short post about three feet high. Bonaparte took the padlock off the rough door.

"Walk in my lad," he said.

Waldo obeyed sullenly; one place to him was much the same as another. He had no objection to being locked up.

Bonaparte followed him in, and closed the door carefully. He put the light down on the heap of dung in the corner, and quietly introduced his hand under his coat-tails, and drew slowly from his pocket the end of a rope, which he concealed behind him.

"I'm very sorry, exceedingly sorry, Waldo, my lad, that you should have acted in this manner. It grieves me," said Bonaparte.

He moved round towards the boy's back. He hardly liked the look in the fellow's eyes though he stood there motionless. If he should spring on him!

So he drew the rope out very carefully, and shifted round to the wooden post. There was a slip-knot in one end of the rope, and a sudden movement drew the boy's hands to his back and passed it round them. It was an instant's work to drag it twice round the wooden post: then Bonaparte was safe.

For a moment the boy struggled to free himself; then he knew that he was powerless, and stood still.

"Horses that kick must have their legs tied," said Bonaparte, as he passed the other end of the rope round the boy's knees. "And now, my dear Waldo," taking the whip out of his pocket, "I am going to beat you."

He paused for a moment. It was perfectly quiet; they could hear each other's breath.

"'Chasten thy son while there is hope,'" said Bonaparte, "'and let not thy soul spare for his crying.'[1] Those are God's words. I shall

---

1 Proverbs 19:18.

act as a father to you, Waldo. I think we had better have your naked back."

He took out his pen-knife, and slit the shirt down from the shoulder to the waist.

"Now," said Bonaparte, "I hope the Lord will bless and sanctify to you what I am going to do to you."

The first cut ran from the shoulder across the middle of the back; the second fell exactly in the same place. A shudder passed through the boy's frame.

"Nice, eh?" said Bonaparte, peeping round into his face, speaking with a lisp, as though to a very little child. "*Nith, eh?*"

But the eyes were black and lustreless, and seemed not to see him. When he had given sixteen Bonaparte paused in his work to wipe a little drop of blood from his whip.

"Cold, eh? What makes you shiver so? Perhaps you would like to pull up your shirt? But I've not quite done yet."

When he had finished he wiped the whip again, and put it back in his pocket. He cut the rope through with his pen-knife, and then took up the light.

"You don't seem to have found your tongue yet. Forgotten how to cry?" said Bonaparte, patting him on the cheek.

The boy looked up at him—not sullenly, not angrily. There was a wild, fitful terror in the eyes. Bonaparte made haste to go out and shut the door, and leave him alone in the darkness. He himself was afraid of that look.

It was almost morning. Waldo lay with his face upon the ground at the foot of the fuel-heap. There was a round hole near the top of the door, where a knot of wood had fallen out, and a stream of grey light came in through it.

Ah, it was going to end at last! Nothing lasts forever, not even the night. How was it he had never thought of that before? For in all that long dark night he had been very strong, had never been tired, never felt pain, had run on and on, up and down, up and down; he had not dared to stand still, and he had not known it would end. He had been so strong, that when he struck his head with all his force upon the stone wall it did not stun him nor pain him—only made him laugh. That was a dreadful night. When he clasped his hands frantically and prayed—"O God, my beautiful God, my sweet God, once, only once, let me feel you near me tonight!" he could not feel Him. He prayed aloud, very loud, and he got no answer; when he listened it was all quite quiet—like when the priests of Baal cried aloud to their god—

"Oh, Baal, hear us! Oh, Baal, hear us!" but Baal was gone a-hunting.[1]

That was a long wild night, and wild thoughts came and went in it; but they left their marks behind them for ever: for, as years cannot pass without leaving their traces behind them, neither can nights into which are forced the thoughts and sufferings of years. And now the dawn was coming, and at last he was very tired. He shivered, and tried to draw the shirt up over his shoulders. They were getting stiff. He had never known they were cut in the night. He looked up at the white light that came in through the hole at the top of the door and shuddered. Then he turned his face back to the ground and slept again.

Some hours later Bonaparte came towards the fuel-house with a lump of bread in his hand. He opened the door and peered in; then entered, and touched the fellow with his boot. Seeing that he breathed heavily, though he did not rouse, Bonaparte threw the bread down on the ground. He was alive, that was one thing. He bent over him, and carefully scratched open one of the cuts with the nail of his forefinger, examining with much interest his last night's work. He would have to count his sheep himself that day; the boy was literally cut up. He locked the door and went away again.

"Oh, Lyndall," said Em, entering the dining-room, and bathed in tears, that afternoon, "I have been begging Bonaparte to let him out, and he won't."

"The more you beg the more he will not," said Lyndall.

She was cutting out aprons on the table.

"Oh, but it's late, and I think they want to kill him," said Em, weeping bitterly; and finding that no more consolation was to be gained from her cousin, she went off blubbering—"I wonder you can cut out aprons when Waldo is shut up like that."

For ten minutes after she was gone Lyndall worked on quietly; then she folded up her stuff, rolled it tightly together, and stood before the closed door of the sitting-room with her hands closely clasped. A flush rose to her face: she opened the door quickly, and walked in, went to the nail on which the key of the fuel-room hung. Bonaparte and Tant' Sannie sat there and saw her.

"What do you want?" they asked together.

"This key," she said, holding it up, and looking at them.

---

1   See 1 Kings 18:26.

"Do you mean her to have it?" said Tant' Sannie in Dutch.

"Why don't you stop her?" asked Bonaparte in English.

"Why don't you take it from her?" said Tant' Sannie.

So they looked at each other, talking, while Lyndall walked to the fuel-house with the key, her underlip bitten in.

"Waldo," she said, as she helped him to stand up, and twisted his arm about her waist to support him, "we will not be children always; we shall have the power too, some day." She kissed his naked shoulder with her soft little mouth. It was all the comfort her young soul could give him.

Chapter XIII.
He Makes Love.

"Here," said Tant' Sannie to her Hottentot maid, "I have been in this house four years, and never been up in the loft. Fatter women than I go up ladders; I will go up today and see what it is like, and put it to rights up there. You bring the little ladder, and stand at the bottom."

"There's one would be sorry if you were to fall," said the Hottentot maid, leering at Bonaparte's pipe, that lay on the table.

"Hold your tongue, jade," said her mistress, trying to conceal a pleased smile, "and go and fetch the ladder."

There was a never-used trap-door at one end of the sitting-room; this the Hottentot maid pushed open, and setting the ladder against it, the Boer-woman with some danger and difficulty climbed into the loft. Then the Hottentot maid took the ladder away, as her husband was mending the waggon-house, and needed it; but the trap-door was left open.

For a little while Tant' Sannie poked about among the empty bottles and skins, and looked at the bag of peaches that Waldo was supposed to have liked so; then she sat down near the trap-door beside a barrel of salt mutton. She found that the pieces of meat were much too large, and took out her clasp-knife to divide them.

That was always the way when one left things to servants, she grumbled to herself; but when once she was married to her husband Bonaparte it would not matter whether a sheep spoiled or no—when once his rich aunt with the dropsy was dead. She smiled as she dived her hand into the pickle-water.

At that instant her niece entered the room below, closely followed by Bonaparte, with his head on one side, smiling mawkishly. Had Tant' Sannie spoken at that moment the life of Bonaparte Blenkins would have run a wholly different course; as it was, she remained silent, and neither noticed the open trap-door above their heads.

"Sit there, my love," said Bonaparte, motioning Trana into her aunt's elbow-chair, and drawing another close up in front of it, in which he seated himself. "There, put your feet upon the stove too. Your aunt has gone out somewhere. Long have I waited for this auspicious event!"

Trana, who understood not one word of English, sat down in the chair and wondered if this was one of the strange customs of other lands, that an old gentleman may bring his chair up to yours, and sit with his knees touching you. She had been five days in Bonaparte's company, and feared the old man, and disliked his nose.

"How long have I desired this moment!" said Bonaparte. "But that aged relative of thine is always casting her unhallowed shadow upon us. Look into my eyes, Trana."

Bonaparte knew that she comprehended not a syllable; but he understood that it is the eye, the tone, the action, and not at all the rational word, that touches the love-chords. He saw she changed colour.

"All night," said Bonaparte, "I lie awake; I see nought but thy angelic countenance. I open my arms to receive thee—where art thou, where? Thou art not there!" said Bonaparte, suiting the action to the words, and spreading out his arms and drawing them to his breast.

"Oh, please, I don't understand," said Trana, "I want to go away."

"Yes, yes," said Bonaparte, leaning back in his chair, to her great relief, and pressing his hands on his heart, "since first thy amethystine countenance was impressed here—what have I not suffered, what have I not felt? Oh, the pangs unspoken, burning as an ardent coal in a fiery and uncontaminated bosom!" said, Bonaparte, bending forward again.

"Dear Lord!" said Trana to herself, "how foolish I have been! The old man has a pain in his stomach, and now, as my aunt is out, he has come to me to help him."

She smiled kindly at Bonaparte, and pushing past him, went to the bed-room, quickly returning with a bottle of red drops in her hand.

"They are very good for 'benaawdheit;'[1] my mother always drinks them," she said, holding the bottle out.

---

1 A tightness of the chest or shortness of breath.

The face in the trap-door was a fiery red. Like a tiger-cat ready to spring, Tant' Sannie crouched, with the shoulder of mutton in her hand. Exactly beneath her stood Bonaparte. She rose and clasped with both arms the barrel of salt meat.

"What, rose of the desert, nightingale of the colony, that with thine amorous lay whilest the lonesome night!" cried Bonaparte, seizing the hand that held the 'vonlicsense.' "Nay, struggle not! Fly as a stricken fawn into the arms that would embrace thee, thou—"

Here a stream of cold pickle-water, heavy with ribs and shoulders, descending on his head abruptly terminated his speech. Half-blinded, Bonaparte looked up through the drops that hung from his eye-lids, and saw the red face that looked down at him. With one wild cry he fled. As he passed out at the front door a shoulder of mutton, well-directed, struck the black coat in the small of the back.

"Bring the ladder! bring the ladder! I will go after him!" cried the Boer-woman, as Bonaparte Blenkins wildly fled into the fields.

Late in the evening of the same day Waldo knelt on the floor of his cabin. He bathed the foot of his dog, which had been pierced by a thorn. The bruises on his own back had had five days to heal in, and, except a little stiffness in his movements, there was nothing remarkable about the boy.

The troubles of the young are soon over; they leave no external mark. If you wound the tree in its youth the bark will quickly cover the gash; but when the tree is very old, peeling the bark off, and looking carefully, you will see the scar there still. All that is buried is not dead.

Waldo poured the warm milk over the little swollen foot; Doss lay very quiet, with tears in his eyes. Then there was a tap at the door. In an instant Doss looked wide awake, and winked the tears out from between his little lids.

"Come in," said Waldo, intent on his work; and slowly and cautiously the door opened.

"Good evening, Waldo, my boy," said Bonaparte Blenkins in a mild voice not venturing more than his nose within the door. "How are you this evening?"

Doss growled and showed his little teeth, and tried to rise, but his paw hurt him so he whined.

"I'm very tired, Waldo, my boy," said Bonaparte, plaintively.

Doss showed his little white teeth again. His master went on with his work without looking round. There are some people at whose hands it is best not to look. At last he said,

"Come in."

Bonaparte stopped cautiously a little way into the room, and left the door open behind him. He looked at the boy's supper on the table.

"Waldo, I've had nothing to eat all day—I'm very hungry," he said.

"Eat!" said Waldo after a moment, bending lower over his dog.

"You won't go and tell her that I am here, will you, Waldo?" said Bonaparte most uneasily. "You've heard how she used me, Waldo? I've been *badly* treated; you'll know yourself what it is some day when you can't carry on a little conversation with a lady without having salt meat and pickle-water thrown at you. Waldo, look at me; do I look as a gentleman should?"

But the boy neither looked up nor answered, and Bonaparte grew more uneasy.

"You wouldn't go and tell her that I am here, would you?" said Bonaparte, whiningly. "There's no knowing what she would do to me. I've such trust in you, Waldo; I've always thought you such a promising lad, though you mayn't have known it, Waldo."

"Eat," said the boy, "I shall say nothing."

Bonaparte, who knew the truth when another spoke it, closed the door, carefully putting on the button. Then he looked to see that the curtain of the window was closely pulled down, and seated himself at the table. He was soon munching the cold meat and bread. Waldo knelt on the floor, bathing the foot with hands which the dog licked lovingly. Once only he glanced at the table, and turned away quickly.

"Ah, yes! I don't wonder that you can't look at me, Waldo," said Bonaparte: "my condition would touch any heart. You see, the water was fatty, and that has made all the sand stick to me; and my hair," said Bonaparte, tenderly touching the little fringe at the back of his head, "is all caked over like a little plank: you wouldn't think it was hair at all," said Bonaparte plaintively. "I had to creep all along the stone walls for fear she'd see me, and with nothing on my head but a red handkerchief tied under my chin, Waldo; and to hide in a 'sloot' the whole day, with not a mouthful of food, Waldo. And she gave me such a blow, just here," said Bonaparte.

He had cleared the plate of the last morsel, when Waldo rose and walked to the door.

"Oh, Waldo, my dear boy, you are not going to call her," said Bonaparte, rising anxiously.

"I am going to sleep in the waggon," said the boy, opening the door.

"Oh, we can both sleep in this bed: there's plenty of room. Do stay, my boy, please."

But Waldo stepped out.

"It was such a little whip, Waldo," said Bonaparte, following him deprecatingly. "I didn't think it would hurt you so much. It was such a *little* whip. I'm *sure* you didn't take the peaches. You aren't going to call her, Waldo, are you?"

But the boy walked off.

Bonaparte waited till his figure had passed round the front of the waggon-house, and then slipped out. He hid himself round the corner, but kept peeping out to see who was coming. He felt sure the boy was gone to call Tant' Sannie. His teeth chattered with inward cold as he looked round into the darkness and thought of the snakes that might bite him, and the dreadful things that might attack him, and the dead that might arise out of their graves if he slept out in the field all night. But more than an hour passed, and no footstep approached.

Then Bonaparte made his way back to the cabin. He buttoned the door and put the table against it, and, giving the dog a kick to silence his whining when the foot throbbed, he climbed into bed. He did not put out the light for fear of the ghost, but, worn out with the sorrows of the day, was soon asleep himself.

About four o'clock Waldo, lying between the seats of the horse-waggon, was awakened by a gentle touch on his head.

Sitting up, he espied Bonaparte looking through one of the windows with a lighted candle in his hand.

"I'm about to depart, my dear boy, before my enemies arise; and I could not leave without coming to bid you farewell," said Bonaparte.

Waldo looked at him.

"I shall always think of you with affection," said Bonaparte. "And there's that old hat of yours, if you could let me have it for a keepsake—"

"Take it," said Waldo.

"I thought you would say so, so I brought it with me," said Bonaparte, putting it on. "The Lord bless you, my dear boy. You haven't a few shillings,—just a trifle you don't need,—have you?"

"Take the two shillings that are in the broken vase."

"May the blessing of my God rest upon you, my dear child," said Bonaparte; "may He guide and bless you. Give me your hand."

Waldo folded his arms closely, and lay down.

"Farewell, adieu!" said Bonaparte. "May the blessing of my God and my father's God rest on you, now, and evermore."

With these words the head and nose withdrew themselves, and the light vanished from the window.

After a few moments the boy, lying in the waggon, heard stealthy footsteps as they passed the waggon-house and made their way down the road. He listened as they grew fainter and fainter, and at last died away altogether! And from that night the footstep of Bonaparte Blenkins was heard no more at the old farm.

End of Part I.

Part II.

"And it was all play, and no one could tell what it had lived and worked for. A striving, and a striving, and an ending in nothing."

Chapter I.
Times and Seasons.

Waldo lay on his stomach on the sand. Since he prayed and howled to his God in the fuel-house three years had passed.

They say that in the world to come time is not measured out by months and years. Neither is it here. The soul's life has seasons of its own; periods not found in any calendar, times that years and months will not scan, but which are as deftly and sharply cut off from one another as the smoothly-arranged years which the earth's motion yields us.

To stranger eyes these divisions are not evident; but each, looking back at the little track his consciousness illuminates, sees it cut into distinct portions, whose boundaries are the termination of mental states.

As man differs from man, so differ these souls' years. The most material life is not devoid of them; the story of the most spiritual is told in them. And it may chance that some, looking back, see the past cut out after this fashion:—

1.

The year of infancy, where from the shadowy background of forgetfulness start out pictures of startling clearness, disconnected, but brightly coloured, and indelibly printed in the mind. Much that follows fades, but the colours of those baby-pictures are permanent.

There rises, perhaps, a warm summer's evening; we are seated on the door-step; we have yet the taste of the bread and milk in our mouth, and the red sunset is reflected in our basin.

Then there is a dark night, where, waking with a fear that there is some great being in the room, we run from our own bed to another, creep close to some large figure, and are comforted.

Then there is remembrance of the pride when, on some one's shoulder, with our arms around their head, we ride to see the little pigs, the new little pigs with their curled tails and tiny snouts—where do they come from?

Remembrance of delight in the feel and smell of the first orange we ever see; of sorrow which makes us put up our lip, and cry hard, when one morning we run out to try and catch the dew-drops, and they melt and wet our little fingers; of almighty and despairing sorrow when we are lost behind the kraals, and cannot see the house anywhere.

And then one picture starts out more vividly than any.

There has been a thunder-storm; the ground, as far as the eye can reach, is covered with white hail; the clouds are gone, and overhead a deep blue sky is showing; far off a great rainbow rests on the white earth. We, standing in a window to look, feel the cool, unspeakably sweet wind blowing in on us, and a feeling of longing comes over us—unutterable longing, we cannot tell for what. We are so small, our head only reaches as high as the first three panes. We look at the white earth, and the rainbow, and the blue sky; and oh, we want it, we want—we do not know what. We cry as though our heart was broken. When one lifts our little body from the window we cannot tell what ails us. We run away to play.

So looks the first year.

II.

Now the pictures become continuous and connected. Material things still rule, but the spiritual and intellectual take their places.

In the dark night when we are afraid we pray and shut our eyes. We press our fingers very hard upon the lids, and see dark spots moving round and round, and we know they are heads and wings of angels sent to take care of us, seen dimly in the dark as they move round our bed. It is very consoling.

In the day we learn our letters, and are troubled because we cannot see why k-n-o-w should be know, and p-s-a-l-m psalm. They tell us it is so because it *is* so. We are not satisfied; we hate to learn; we like better to build little stone houses. We can build them as we please, and know the reason for them.

Other joys too we have incomparably greater than even the building of stone houses.

We are run through with a shudder of delight when in the red sand we come on one of those white wax flowers that lie between their two green leaves flat on the sand. We hardly dare pick them, but we feel compelled to do so; and we smell and smell till the delight becomes almost pain. Afterwards we pull the green leaves softly into pieces to see the silk threads run across.

Beyond the 'kopje' grow some pale-green, hairy-leaved bushes. We are so small, they meet over our head; and we sit among them, and kiss them, and they love us back; it seems as though they were alive.

One day we sit there and look up at the blue sky, and down at our fat little knees; and suddenly it strikes us, Who are we? This *I*, what is it? We try to look in upon ourself, and ourself beats back upon ourself. Then we get up in great fear and run home as hard as we can. We can't tell any one what frightened us. We never quite lose that feeling of self again.

III.

And then a new time rises. We are seven years old. We can read now—read the Bible. Best of all we like the story of Elijah in his cave at Horeb, and the still small voice.[1]

One day, a notable one, we read on the 'kopje,' and discover the fifth chapter of Matthew, and read it all through.[2] It is a new gold-mine. Then we tuck the Bible under our arm and rush home. They didn't know it was wicked to take your things again if some one took them, wicked to go to law, wicked to—! We are quite breathless when we get to the house; we tell them we have discovered a chapter they never heard of; we tell them what it says. The old wise people tell us they knew all about it. Our discovery is a mare's-nest to them; but to us it is very real. The ten commandments and the old "Thou shalt" we have heard about long enough, and don't care about it; but this new law sets us on fire. We will deny ourself. Our little waggon that we have made, we give to the little Kaffirs. We keep quiet when they throw sand at us (feeling, oh, so happy). We conscientiously put the cracked teacup for ourselves at breakfast, and take the burnt roaster-cake. We save our money, and buy three pence of tobacco for the Hottentot maid who calls us names. We are exotically virtuous. At night we are profoundly religious; even the ticking watch says, "Eternity, eternity! hell, hell, hell!" and the silence talks of God, and the things that shall be.

---

1 See 1 Kings, chapter 19.
2 Beginning with the Beatitudes, this chapter of the Gospels also instructs the faithful to return good for evil, revising the "eye for an eye" precepts and ten commandments of the Old Testament.

Occasionally, also, unpleasantly shrewd questions begin to be asked by some one, we know not who, who sits somewhere behind our shoulder. We get to know him better afterwards. Now we carry the questions to the grown-up people, and they give us answers. We are more or less satisfied for the time. The grown-up people are very wise, and they say it was kind of God to make hell, and very loving of Him to send men there; and besides, He couldn't help Himself; and they are very wise, we think, so we believe them—more or less.

IV.

Then a new time comes, of which the leading feature is that the shrewd questions are asked louder. We carry them to the grown-up people; they answer us, and we are not satisfied.

And now between us and the dear old world of the senses the spirit-world begins to peep in, and wholly clouds it over. What are the flowers to us? They are fuel waiting for the great burning. We look at the walls of the farm-house and the matter-of-fact sheep-kraals, with the merry sunshine playing over all; and do not see it. But we see a great white throne, and Him that sits on it. Around Him stand a great multitude that no man can number, harpers harping with their harps, a thousand times ten thousand, and thousands of thousands. How white are their robes, washed in the blood of the Lamb! And the music rises higher, and rends the vault of heaven with its unutterable sweetness. And we, as we listen, ever and anon, as it sinks on the sweetest, lowest note, hear a groan of the damned from below. We shudder in the sunlight.

"The torment," says Jeremy Taylor, whose sermons our father reads aloud in the evening, "comprises as many torments as the body of man has joints, sinews, arteries, &c., being caused by that penetrating and real fire of which this temporal fire is but a painted fire. What comparison will there be between burning for a hundred years' space and to be burning without intermission as long as God is God!"[1]

---

1 Jeremy Taylor (1613-1667) was chaplain to King Charles. Imprisoned during the Puritan revolution, he was made Bishop of two Irish counties after the Restoration. His sermons were popular and influential. John Wesley, the founder of Methodism, and his brother Charles, who wrote many of the hymns that Schreiner knew as a child, were both admirers of Taylor's works.

We remember the sermon there in the sunlight. One comes and asks why we sit there nodding so moodily. Ah, they do not see what we see.

> "A moment's time, a narrow space,
> Divides me from that heavenly place,
> Or shuts me up in hell."

So says Wesley's hymn, which we sing evening by evening. What matter sunshine and walls, men and sheep?

"The things which are seen are temporal, but the things which are not seen are eternal."[1] They are real.

The Bible we bear always in our breast; its pages are our food; we learn to repeat it; we weep much, for in sunshine and in shade, in the early morning or the late evening, in the field or in the house, the Devil walks with us. He comes to us a real person, copper-coloured face, head a little on one side, forehead knit, asking questions. Believe me, it were better to be followed by three deadly diseases than by him. He is never silenced—without mercy. Though the drops of blood stand out on your heart he will put his question. Softly he comes up (we are only a wee bit child); "Is it good of God to make hell? Was it kind of Him to let no one be forgiven unless Jesus Christ died?"

Then he goes off, and leaves us writhing. Presently he comes back.

"Do you love Him?"—waits a little. "Do you love Him? You will be lost if you don't."

We say we try to.

"But do you?" Then he goes off.

It is nothing to him if we go quite mad with fear at our own wickedness. He asks on, the questioning Devil; he cares nothing what he says. We long to tell some one, that they may share our pain. We do not yet know that the cup of affliction is made with such a narrow mouth that only one lip can drink at a time, and that each man's cup is made to match his lip.

One day we try to tell some one. Then a grave head is shaken solemnly at us. We are wicked, very wicked, they say; we ought not to have such thoughts. God is good, very good. We are wicked, very wicked. That is the comfort we get. Wicked! Oh, Lord! do we

---

1 2 Corinthians 4:18.

not know it? Is it not the sense of our own exceeding wickedness that is drying up our young, heart, filling it with sand, making all life a dust-bin for us?

Wicked? We know it! Too vile to live, too vile to die, too vile to creep over this, God's earth, and move among His believing men. Hell is the one place for him who hates his master, and there we do not want to go. This is the comfort we get from the old.

And once again we try to seek for comfort. This time great eyes look at us wondering, and lovely little lips say,—

"If it makes you so unhappy to think of these things, why do you not think of something else, and forget?"

Forget! We turn away and shrink into ourself. Forget, and think of other things! Oh, God! Do they not understand that the material world is but a film, through every pore of which God's awful spirit-world is shining through on us? We keep as far from others as we can.

One night, a rare, clear moonlight night, we kneel in the window; every one else is asleep, but we kneel reading by the moonlight. It is a chapter in the prophets, telling how the chosen people of God shall be carried on the Gentiles' shoulders.[1] Surely the Devil might leave us alone; there is not much handle for him there. But presently he comes.

"Is it right there should be a chosen people? To Him, who is father to all, should not all be dear?"

How can we answer him? We were feeling so good till he came. We put our head down on the Bible and blister it with tears. Then we fold our hands over our head and pray, till our teeth grind together. Oh, that from that spirit-world, so real and yet so silent, that surrounds us, one word would come to guide us! We are left alone with this devil; and God does not whisper to us. Suddenly we seize the Bible, turning it round and round, and say hurriedly,—

"It will be God's voice speaking to us; His voice as though we heard it."

We yearn for a token from the inexorably Silent One.

We turn the book, put our finger down on a page, and bend to read by the moonlight. It is God's answer. We tremble.

---

1 See Isaiah 49:22-26.

"Then fourteen years after I went up again to Jerusalem with Barnabas, and took Titus with me also."[1]

For an instant our imagination seizes it; we are twisting, twirling, trying to make an allegory. The fourteen years are fourteen months; we are Paul and the devil is Barnabas, Titus is—Then a sudden loathing comes to us: we are liars and hypocrites, we are trying to deceive ourselves. What is Paul to us—and Jerusalem? Who are Barnabas and Titus? We know not the men. Before we know we seize the book, swing it round our head, and fling it with all our might to the farther end of the room. We put down our head again and weep. Youth and ignorance; is there anything else that can weep so? It is as though the tears were drops of blood congealed beneath the eyelids; nothing else is like those tears. After a long time we are weak with crying, and lie silent, and by chance we knock against the wood that stops the broken pane. It falls. Upon our hot stiff face a sweet breath of wind blows. We raise our head, and with our swollen eyes look out at the beautiful still world, and the sweet night-wind blows in upon us, holy and gentle, like a loving breath from the lips of God. Over us a deep peace comes, a calm, still joy; the tears now flow readily and softly. Oh, the unutterable gladness! At last, at last we have found it! "*The peace with God.*" "*The sense of sins forgiven.*" All doubt vanished, God's voice in the soul, the Holy Spirit filling us! We feel Him! We feel Him! Oh, Jesus Christ! Through you, through you this joy! We press our hands upon our breast and look upward with adoring gladness. Soft waves of bliss break through us. "*The peace with God.*" "*The sense of sins forgiven.*" Methodists and Revivalists[2] say the words, and the mocking world shoots out its lip, and walks by smiling—"Hypocrite!"

There are more fools and fewer hypocrites than the wise world dreams of. The hypocrite is rare as icebergs in the tropics; the fool

---

1 Galatians 2:1.
2 Methodists are followers of the church founded by John Wesley in 1703 to reform the Church of England. It became a separate church in 1795 and grew rapidly in the nineteenth century. Methodists were active in the London Missionary Society, which sent Schreiner's father to South Africa. Revivalists are also associated with Protestantism and the Great Awakening of the 1720s. Reformed Dutch, Baptists, Presbyterians and Congregationalists share the Revivalist concern with the terrors of eternal damnation for non-believers. These sects were also actively engaged in missionary work in South Africa.

common as butter-cups beside a water-furrow: whether you go this way or that you tread on him; you dare not look at your own reflection in the water but you see one. There is no cant phrase, rotten with age, but it was the dress of a living body; none but at heart it signifies a real bodily or mental condition which some have passed through.

After hours and nights of frenzied fear of the supernatural desire to appease the power above, a fierce quivering excitement in every inch of nerve and blood-vessel, there comes a time when nature cannot endure longer, and the spring long bent recoils. We sink down emasculated. Up creeps the deadly delicious calm.

"I have blotted out as a cloud thy sins, and as a thick cloud thy trespasses, and will remember them no more for ever."[1] We weep with soft transporting joy.

A few experience this; many imagine they experience it; one here and there lies about it. In the main, "The peace with God; a sense of sins forgiven," stands for a certain mental and physical reaction. Its reality those know who have felt it.

And we, on that moonlight night, put down our head on the window, "Oh, God! we are happy, happy; thy child for ever. Oh, thank you, God!" and we drop asleep.

Next morning the Bible we kiss. We are God's for ever. We go out to work, and it goes happily all day, happily all night; but hardly so happily, not happily at all, the next day; and the next night the Devil asks us, "Where is your Holy Spirit?"

We cannot tell.

So month by month, summer and winter, the old life goes on— reading, praying, weeping, praying. They tell us we become utterly stupid. We know it. Even the multiplication table we learnt with so much care we forget. The physical world recedes further and further from us. Truly we love not the world, neither the things that are in it. Across the bounds of sleep our grief follows us. When we wake in the night we are sitting up in bed weeping bitterly, or find ourself outside in the moonlight, dressed, and walking up and down, and wringing our hands, and we cannot tell how we came there. So pass two years, as men reckon them.

---

1   Isaiah 44:22.

V.

Then a new time.

Before us there were three courses possible—to go mad, to die, to sleep.

We take the latter course; or nature takes it for us.

All things take rest in sleep; the beasts, birds, the very flowers close their eyes, and the streams are still in winter; all things take rest; then why not the human reason also? So the questioning Devil in us drops asleep, and in that sleep a beautiful dream rises for us. Though you hear all the dreams of men, you will hardly find a prettier one than ours. It ran so:—

In the centre of all things is a Mighty Heart, which, having begotten all things, loves them; and, having born them into life, beats with great throbs of love towards them. No death for his dear insects, no hell for His dear men, no burning up for His dear world—His own, own world that he has made. In the end all will be beautiful. Do not ask us how we make our dream tally with facts; the glory of a dream is this—that it despises facts, and makes its own. Our dream saves us from going mad; that is enough.

Its peculiar point of sweetness lay here. When the Mighty Heart's yearning of love became too great for other expression, it shaped itself into the sweet Rose of heaven, the beloved Man-god.

Jesus! you Jesus of our dream! how we loved you; no Bible tells of you as we knew you. Your sweet hands held ours fast; your sweet voice said always, "I am here, my loved one, not far off; put your arms about Me, and hold fast."

We find Him in everything in those days. When the little weary lamb we drive home drags its feet, we seize on it, and carry it with its head against our face. His little lamb! We feel we have got Him.

When the drunken Kaffir lies by the road in the sun we draw his blanket over his head, and put green branches of milk-bush on it. His Kaffir; why should the sun hurt him?

In the evening, when the clouds lift themselves like gates, and the red lights shine through them, we cry; for in such glory He will come, and the hands that ache to touch Him will hold Him, and we shall see the beautiful hair and eyes of our God. "Lift up your heads, O ye gates; and be ye lifted up, ye everlasting doors, and our King of glory shall come in!"[1]

---

1 Psalms 24:9.

The purple flowers, the little purple flowers, are His eyes, looking at us. We kiss them, and kneel alone on the flat, rejoicing over them. And the wilderness and the solitary place shall be glad for Him, and the desert shall rejoice and blossom as a rose.[1]

If ever in our tearful, joyful ecstasy the poor sleepy, half-dead Devil should raise his head, we laugh at him. It is not his hour now.

"If there should be a hell, after all!" he mutters. "If Your God should be cruel! If there should be no God! If you should find out it is all imagination! If——"

We laugh at him. When a man sits in the warm sunshine, do you ask him for proof of it? He feels—that is all. And we feel—that is all. We want no proof of our God. We feel, we feel!

We do not believe in our God because the Bible tells us of Him. We believe in the Bible because He tells us of it. We feel Him, we feel Him, we feel—that is all! And the poor half-swamped Devil mutters—

"But if the day should come when you do not feel?"

And we laugh, and cry him down.

"It will never come—never," and the poor Devil slinks to sleep again, with his tail between his legs. Fierce assertion many times repeated is hard to stand against; only time separates the truth from the lie. So we dream on.

One day we go with our father to town, to church. The townspeople rustle in their silks, and the men in their sleek cloth, and settle themselves in their pews, and the light shines in through the windows on the artificial flowers in the women's bonnets. We have the same miserable feeling that we have in a shop where all the clerks are very smart. We wish our father hadn't brought us to town, and we were out on the karroo. Then the man in the pulpit begins to preach. His text is "He that believeth not shall be damned."[2]

The day before the magistrate's clerk, who was an atheist, has died in the street struck by lightning.

The man in the pulpit mentions no name; but he talks of "The hand of God made visible among us." He tells us how, when the white stroke fell, quivering and naked, the soul fled, robbed of his earthly filament, and lay at the footstool of God; how over its head has been poured out the wrath of the Mighty One, whose exis-

---

1 Isaiah 35:1.
2 Mark 16:16.

tence it has denied; and, quivering and terrified, it has fled to the everlasting shade.

We, as we listen, half start up; every drop of blood in our body has rushed to our head. He lies! he lies! he lies! That man in the pulpit lies! Will no one stop him? Have none of them heard—do none of them know, that when the poor dark soul shut its eyes on earth it opened them in the still light of heaven? that there is no wrath where God's face is? that if one could once creep to the footstool of God, there is ever-lasting peace there? like the fresh stillness of the early morning. While the atheist lay wondering and afraid, God bent down and said, "My child, *here* I am—I, whom you have not known; I, whom you have not believed in; I am here. I sent My messenger, the white sheet lightning, to call you home. I am here."

Then the poor soul turned to the light,—its weakness and pain were gone for ever.

Have they not known, have they not heard, who it is rules?

"For a little moment have I hidden my face from thee; but with everlasting kindness will I have mercy upon thee, saith the Lord thy Redeemer."[1]

We mutter on to ourselves, till some one pulls us violently by the arm to remind us we are in church. We see nothing but our own ideas.

Presently every one turns to pray. There are six hundred souls lifting themselves to the Everlasting light.

Behind us sit two pretty ladies; one hands her scent-bottle softly to the other, and a mother pulls down her little girl's frock. One lady drops her handkerchief, a gentleman picks it up; she blushes. The women in the choir turn softly the leaves of their tune-books, to be ready when the praying is done. It is as though they thought more of the singing than the Everlasting Father. Oh, would it not be more worship of Him to sit alone in the 'karroo' and kiss one little purple flower that he had made? Is it not mockery? Then the thought comes, "*What doest thou here, Elijah?*"[2] We who judge, what are we better than they?—rather worse. Is it any excuse to say, "I am but a child and must come"? Does God allow any soul to step in between the spirit he made and himself? What do we there in that place, where all the words are lies against the All Father? Filled

---

1 Isaiah 54:8.
2 1 Kings 19:9.

with horror, we turn and flee out of the place. On the pavement we smite our foot, and swear in our child's soul never again to enter those places where men come to sing and pray. We are questioned afterwards. Why was it we went out of the church.

How can we explain?—we stand silent. Then we are pressed further, and we try to tell. Then a head is shaken solemnly at us. No one *can* think it wrong to go to the house of the Lord; it is the idle excuse of a wicked boy. When will we think seriously of our souls, and love going to church? We are wicked, very wicked. And we— we slink away and go alone to cry. Will it be always so? Whether we hate and doubt, or whether we believe and love, to our dearest, are we to seem always wicked?

We do not yet know that in the soul's search for truth the bitterness lies here, the striving cannot always hide itself among the thoughts; sooner or later it will clothe itself in outward action; then it steps in and divides among the soul and what it loves. All things on earth have their price; and for truth we pay the dearest. We barter it for love and sympathy. The road to honour is paved with thorns; but on the path to truth, at every step you set your foot down on your own heart.

VI.

Then at last a new time—the time of waking: short, sharp, and not pleasant, as wakings often are.

Sleep and dreams exist on this condition—that no one wake the dreamer.

And now life takes us up between her finger and thumb, shakes us furiously, till our poor nodding head is well-nigh rolled from our shoulders, and she sets us down a little hardly on the bare earth, bruised and sore, but preternaturally wide awake.

We have said in our days of dreaming, "Injustice and wrong are a seeming; pain is a shadow. Our God, He is real, He who made all things, and He only is Love."

Now life takes us by the neck and shows us a few other things,—new-made graves with the red sand flying about them; eyes that we love with the worms eating them; evil men walking sleek and fat, the whole terrible hurly-burly of the thing called life,—and she says, "What do you think of these?" We dare not say "Nothing." We feel them; they are very real. But we try to lay our hands about and feel that other thing we felt before. In the dark night in the fuel-room we cry to our Beautiful dream-god—"Oh, let us come near you, and lay our head against your feet. Now in our hour of need be near us." But He is not there; He is gone away. The old questioning Devil is there.

We must have been awakened sooner or later. The imagination cannot always triumph over reality, the desire over truth. We must have been awakened. If it was done a little sharply, what matter? it was done thoroughly, and it had to be done.

VII.

And a new life begins for us—a new time, a life as cold as that of a man who sits on the pinnacle of an iceberg and sees the glittering crystals all about him. The old looks indeed like a long hot delirium, peopled with phantasies. The new is cold enough.

Now we have no God. We have had two: the old God that our fathers handed down to us, that we hated, and never liked; the new one that we made for ourselves, that we loved; but now he has flitted away from us, and we see what he was made of—the shadow of our highest ideal, crowned and throned. Now we have no God.

"The fool hath said in his heart, There is no God."[1] It may be so. Most things said or written have been the work of fools.

This thing is certain—he is a fool who says, "No man hath said in his heart, There is no God."

It has been said many thousand times in hearts with profound bitterness of earnest faith.

We do not cry and weep; we sit down with cold eyes and look at the world. We are not miserable. Why should we be? We eat and drink, and sleep all night; but the dead are not colder.

And, we say it slowly, but without sighing, "Yes, we see it now: there is no God."

And, we add, growing a little colder yet, "There is no justice. The ox dies in the yoke, beneath its master's whip; it turns its anguish-filled eyes on the sunlight, but there is no sign of recompense to be made it. The black man is shot like a dog, and it goes well with the shooter. The innocent are accused, and the accuser triumphs. If you will take the trouble to scratch the surface anywhere, you will see under the skin a sentient being writhing in impotent anguish."

And, we say further, and our heart is as the heart of the dead for

---

1 Psalms 14:1; 53:1.

coldness, "There is no order: all things are driven about by a blind chance."

What a soul drinks in with its mother's milk will not leave it in a day. From our earliest hour we have been taught that the thought of the heart, the shaping of the rain-cloud, the amount of wool that grows on a sheep's back, the length of a draught, and the growing of the corn, depend on nothing that moves immutable, at the heart of all things; but on the changeable will of a changeable being, whom our prayers can alter. To us, from the beginning, nature has been but a poor plastic thing, to be toyed with this way or that, as man happens to please his deity or not; to go to church or not; to say his prayers right or not; to travel on a Sunday or not. Was it possible for us in an instant to see Nature as she is—the flowing vestment of an unchanging reality? When a soul breaks free from the arms of a superstition, bits of the claws and talons break themselves off in him. It is not the work of a day to squeeze them out.

And so, for us, the human-like driver and guide being gone, all existence, as we look out at it with our chilled, wondering eyes, is an aimless rise and swell of shifting waters. In all that weltering chaos we can see no spot so large as a man's hand on which we may plant our foot.

Whether a man believes in a human-like God or no is a small thing. Whether he looks into the mental and physical world and sees no relation between cause and effect, no order, but a blind chance sporting, this is the mightiest fact that can be recorded in any spiritual existence. It were almost a mercy to cut his throat, if indeed he does not do it for himself.

We, however, do not cut our throats. To do so would imply some desire and feeling, and we have no desire and no feeling; we are only cold. We do not wish to live, and we do not wish to die. One day a snake curls itself round the waist of a Kaffir woman. We take it in our hand, swing it round and round, and fling it on the ground—dead. Everyone looks at us with eyes of admiration. We almost laugh. Is it wonderful to risk that for which we care nothing?

In truth, nothing matters. This dirty little world full of confusion, and the blue rag, stretched overhead for a sky, is so low we could touch it with our hand.

Existence is a great pot, and the old Fate who stirs it round cares nothing what rises to the top and what goes down, and laughs when the bubbles burst. And we do not care. Let it boil about. Why should we trouble ourselves? Nevertheless the physical sensations are real. Hunger hurts, and thirst, therefore we eat and drink: inaction pains us, therefore we work like galley-slaves. No one demands it, but we set ourselves to build a great dam in red sand beyond the graves. In the grey dawn before the sheep are let out we work at it. All day, while the young ostriches we tend feed about us, we work on through the fiercest heat. The people wonder what new spirit has seized us now. They do not know we are working for life. We bear the greatest stones, and feel a satisfaction when we stagger under them, and are hurt by a pang that shoots through our chest. While we eat our dinner we carry on baskets full of earth, as though the Devil drove us. The Kaffir servants have a story that at night a witch and two white oxen come to help us. No wall, they say, could grow so quickly under one man's hands.

At night, alone in our cabin, we sit no more brooding over the fire. What should we think of now? All is emptiness. So we take the old arithmetic; and the multiplication table, which with so much pains we learnt long ago and forgot directly, we learn now in a few hours, and never forget again. We take a strange satisfaction in working arithmetical problems. We pause in our building to cover the stones with figures and calculations. We save money for a Latin Grammar and an Algebra, and carry them about in our pockets, poring over them as over our Bible of old. We have thought we were utterly stupid, incapable of remembering anything, of learning anything. Now we find that all is easy. Has a new soul crept into this old body, that even our intellectual faculties are changed? We marvel; not perceiving that what a man expends in prayer and ecstacy he cannot have over for acquiring knowledge. You never shed a tear, or create a beautiful image, or quiver with emotion, but you pay for it at the practical, calculating end of your nature. You have just so much force; when the one channel runs over the other runs dry.

And now we turn to Nature. All these years we have lived beside her, and we have never seen her; now we open our eyes and look at her.

The rocks have been to us a blur of brown; we bend over them, and the disorganised masses dissolve into a many-coloured, many-shaped, carefully-arranged form of existence. Here masses of rainbow-tinted crystals, half-fused together; there bands of smooth grey and red methodically overlying each other. This rock here is covered with a delicate silver tracery, in some mineral, resembling leaves and branches; there on the flat stone, on which we so often have sat to weep and pray, we look down, and see it covered with the fossil footprints of great birds, and the beautiful skeleton of a fish. We have often tried to picture in our mind what the fossiled remains of creatures must be like, and all the while we sat on them. We have been so blinded by thinking and feeling that we have never seen the world.

The flat plain has been to us a reach of monotonous red. We look at it, and every handful of sand starts into life. That wonderful people, the ants, we learn to know; see them make war and peace, play and work, and build their huge palaces. And that smaller people we make acquaintance with, who live in the flowers. The bitto flower has been for us a mere blur of yellow; we find its heart composed of a hundred perfect flowers, the homes of the tiny black people with red stripes, who move in and out in that little yellow city. Every bluebell has its inhabitant. Every day the karroo shows us a new wonder sleeping in its teeming bosom. On our way to work we pause and stand to see the ground-spider make its trap, bury itself in the sand, and then wait for the falling in of its enemy. Farther on walks a horned beetle, and near him starts open the door of a spider, who peeps out carefully, and quickly pulls it down again. On a karroo-bush a green fly is laying her silver eggs. We carry them home, and see the shells pierced, the spotted grub come out, turn to a green fly, and flit away. We are not satisfied with what Nature shows us, and will see something for ourselves. Under the white hen we put a dozen eggs, and break one daily, to see the white spot wax into the chicken. We are not excited or enthusiastic about it; but if a man is not to lay his throat open, he must think of something. So we plant seeds in rows on our dam-wall, and pull one up daily to see how it goes with them. Alladeen buried her wonderful stone, and a golden palace sprang up at her feet.[1] We do far more. We put a brown seed in the earth, and a living thing starts out—starts upwards—why, no more than Alladeen can we say— starts upwards, and does not desist till it is higher than our heads, sparkling with dew in the early morning, glittering with yellow blossoms, shaking brown seeds with little embryo souls on to the

---

1 Alladeen may be Schreiner's name for the wife of Aladdin. Aladdin uses the magic lantern's powers to build a palace of precious stones and thus win the hand of a Princess named Bardroulboudour. But because she does not know of the lantern's significance, she gives it away and the palace disappears. But there is no burying of a stone in this tale.

ground. We look at it solemnly, from the time it consists of two leaves peeping above the ground and a soft white root, till we have to raise our faces to look at it; but we find no reason for that upward starting.

We look into dead ducks and lambs. In the evening we carry them home, spread newspapers on the floor, and lie working with them till midnight. With a startled feeling near akin to ecstasy we open the lump of flesh called a heart, and find little doors and strings inside. We feel them, and put the heart away; but every now and then return to look, and to feel them again. Why we like them so we can hardly tell.

A gander drowns itself in our dam. We take it out, and open it on the bank, and kneel, looking at it. Above are the organs divided by delicate tissues; below are the intestines artistically curved in a spiral form, and each tier covered by a delicate network of blood-vessels standing out red against the faint blue background. Each branch of the blood-vessels is comprised of a trunk, bifurcating and rebifurcating into the most delicate, hair-like threads, symmetrically arranged. We are struck with its singular beauty. And, moreover—and here we drop from our kneeling into a sitting posture—this also we remark: of that same exact shape and outline is our thorn-tree seen against the sky in mid-winter: of that shape also is delicate metallic tracery between our rocks; in that exact path does our water flow when without a furrow we lead it from the dam; so shaped are the antlers of the horned beetle. How are these things related that such deep union should exist between them all? Is it chance? Or, are they not all the fine branches of one trunk, whose sap flows through us all? That would explain it.[1] We nod over the gander's inside.

This thing we call existence; is it not a something which has its roots far down below in the dark, and its branches stretching out into the immensity above, which we among the branches cannot see? Not a chance jumble; a living thing, a *One*. The thought gives us intense satisfaction, we cannot tell why.

We nod over the gander; then start up suddenly, look into the

---

1   The "argument from design" was popular among naturalists and theologians in the early nineteenth century. "Unaided nature never could have produced such structures; therefore, divine will had to be invoked as the only reasonable explanation of their existence" (See Peter J. Bowler, *Evolution: The History of an Idea*. University of California Press, 1989, 5).

blue sky, throw the dead gander and the refuse into the dam, and go to work again.

And so, it comes to pass in time, that the earth ceases for us to be a weltering chaos. We walk in the great hall of life, looking up and round reverentially. Nothing is despicable—all is meaning-full; nothing is small—all is part of a whole, whose beginning and end we know not. The life that throbs in us is a pulsation from it; too mighty for our comprehension, not too small.

And so, it comes to pass at last, that whereas the sky was at first a small blue rag stretched out over us, and so low that our hands might touch it, pressing down on us, it raises itself into an immeasurable blue arch over our heads, and we begin to live again.

Chapter II.
Waldo's Stranger.

Waldo lay on his stomach on the red sand. The small ostriches he herded wandered about him, pecking at the food he had cut, or at pebbles and dry sticks. On his right lay the graves; to his left the dam; in his hand was a large wooden post covered with carvings, at which he worked. Doss lay before him basking in the winter sunshine, and now and again casting an expectant glance at the corner of the nearest ostrich-camp. The scrubby thorn-trees under which they lay yielded no shade, but none was needed in that glorious June weather, when in the hottest part of the afternoon the sun was but pleasantly warm; and the boy carved on, not looking up, yet conscious of the brown serene earth about him and the intensely blue sky above.

Presently, at the corner of the camp, Em appeared, bearing a covered saucer in one hand, and in the other a jug with a cup in the top. She was grown into a premature little old woman of sixteen, ridiculously fat. The jug and saucer she put down on the ground before the dog and his master, and dropped down beside them herself, panting and out of breath. "Waldo, as I came up the camps I met some one on horseback; and I do believe it must be the new man that is coming."

The new man was an Englishman to whom the Boer-woman had hired half the farm.

"Hum!" said Waldo.

"He is quite young," said Em, holding her side, "and he has brown hair, and beard curling close to his face, and such dark blue eyes. And, Waldo, I was so ashamed! I was just looking back to see, you know, and he happened just to be looking back too, and we looked right into each other's faces; and he got red, and I got so red. I believe he is the new man."

"Yes," said Waldo.

"I must go now. Perhaps he has brought us letters from the post from Lyndall. You know she can't stay at school much longer, she must come back soon. And the new man will have to stay with us till his house is built. I must get his room ready. Good-bye!"

She tripped off again, and Waldo carved on at his post. Doss lay with his nose close to the covered saucer, and smelt that some one had made nice little fat cakes that afternoon. Both were so intent on their occupation that not till a horse's hoofs beat beside them in the sand did they look up to see a rider drawing in his steed.

He was certainly not the stranger whom Em had described. A dark, somewhat French-looking little man of eight-and-twenty, rather stout, with heavy, cloudy eyes and pointed moustaches. His horse was a fiery creature, well caparisoned; a highly-finished saddle-bag hung from the saddle; the man's hands were gloved, and he presented the appearance—an appearance rare on that farm—of a well-dressed gentleman.

In an uncommonly melodious voice he inquired whether he might be allowed to remain there for an hour. Waldo directed him to the farm-house, but the stranger declined. He would merely rest under the trees, and give his horse water. He removed the saddle, and Waldo led the animal away to the dam. When he returned, the stranger had settled himself under the trees, with his back against the saddle. The boy offered him of the cakes. He declined, but took a draught from the jug; and Waldo lay down not far off, and fell to work again. It mattered nothing if cold eyes saw it. It was not his sheep-shearing machine. With material loves, as with human, we go mad once, love out, and have done. We never get up the true enthusiasm a second time. This was but a thing he had made, laboured over, loved and liked—nothing more—not his machine.

The stranger forced himself lower down in the saddle and yawned. It was a drowsy afternoon, and he objected to travel in these out-of-the-world parts. He liked better civilised life, where at every hour of the day a man may look for his glass of wine, and his easy-chair, and paper; where at night he may lock himself into his room with his books and a bottle of brandy, and taste joys mental and physical. The world said of him—the all-knowing, omnipotent world whom no locks can bar, who has the cat-like propensity of seeing best in the dark—the world said, that better than the books he loved the brandy, and better than books or brandy that which it had been better had he loved less. But for the world he cared nothing; he smiled blandly in its teeth. All life is a dream; if wine and philosophy and women keep the dream from becoming a nightmare, so much the better. It is all they are fit for, all they can be used for. There was another side to his life and thought; but of that the world knew nothing, and said nothing, as the way of the wise world is.

The stranger looked from beneath his sleepy eyelids at the brown earth that stretched away, beautiful in spite of itself in that June sunshine; looked at the graves, the gables of the farm-house showing over the stone walls of the camps, at the clownish fellow at his feet, and yawned. But he had drunk of the hind's tea, and must say something.

"Your father's place, I presume?" he inquired sleepily.

"No; I am only a servant."

"Dutch people?"

"Yes."

"And you like the life?"

The boy hesitated.

"On days like these."

"And why on these?"

The boy waited.

"They are very beautiful."

The stranger looked at him. It seemed that as the fellow's dark eyes looked across the brown earth they kindled with an intense satisfaction; then they looked back at the carving.

What had that creature, so coarse-clad and clownish, to do with the subtle joys of the weather? Himself, white-handed and delicate, *he* might hear the music which shimmering sunshine and solitude play on the finely-strung chords of nature; but that fellow! Was not the ear in that great body too gross for such delicate mutterings?

Presently he said,

"May I see what you work at?"

The fellow handed his wooden post. It was by no means lovely. The men and birds were almost grotesque in their laboured resemblance to nature, and bore signs of patient thought. The stranger turned the thing over on his knee.

"Where did you learn this work?"

"I taught myself."

"And these zigzag lines represent——"

"A mountain."

The stranger looked.

"It has some meaning, has it not?"

The boy muttered confusedly,

"Only things."

The questioner looked down at him—the huge, unwieldy figure, in size a man's, in right of its childlike features and curling hair a child's; and it hurt him—it attracted him and it hurt him. It was something between pity and sympathy.

"How long have you worked at this?"

"Nine months."

From his pocket the stranger drew his pocket-book, and took something from it. He could fasten the post to his horse in some way, and throw it away in the sand when at a safe distance.

"Will you take this for your carving?"

The boy glanced at the five-pound note and shook his head.

"No; I cannot."

"You think it is worth more?" asked the stranger with a little sneer.

He pointed with his thumb to a grave.

"No; it is for him."

"And who is there?" asked the stranger.

"My father."

The man silently returned the note to his pocket-book, and gave the carving to the boy; and, drawing his hat over his eyes, composed himself to sleep. Not being able to do so, after a while he glanced over the fellow's shoulder to watch him work. The boy carved letters into the back.

"If," said the stranger, with his melodious voice, rich with a sweetness that never showed itself in the clouded eyes—for sweetness will linger on in the voice long after it has died out in the eyes— "if for such a purpose, why write that upon it?"

The boy glanced round at him, but made no answer. He had almost forgotten his presence.

"You surely believe," said the stranger, "that some day, sooner or later, these graves will open, and those Boer-uncles with their wives walk about here in the red sand, with the very fleshly legs with which they went to sleep? Then why say, 'He sleeps forever?' You believe he will stand up again?"

"Do you?" asked the boy, lifting for an instant his heavy eyes to the stranger's face.

Half taken aback, the stranger laughed. It was as though a curious little tadpole which he held under his glass should suddenly lift its tail and begin to question him.

"I?—no." He laughed his short thick laugh. "I am a man who believes nothing, hopes nothing, fears nothing, feels nothing. I am beyond the pale of humanity; no criterion of what you should be who live here among your ostriches and bushes."

The next moment the stranger was surprised by a sudden movement on the part of the fellow, which brought him close to the stranger's feet. Soon after, he raised his carving and laid it across the man's knee.

"Yes, I will, tell you," he muttered; "I will tell you all about it."

He put his finger on the grotesque little mannikin at the bottom (Ah! that man who believed nothing, hoped nothing, felt nothing; *how he loved him!*), and with eager finger the fellow moved upwards, explaining over fantastic figures and mountains, to the crowning bird from whose wing dropped a feather. At the end he spoke with broken breath—short words, like one who utters things of mighty import.

The stranger watched more the face than the carving; and there was now and then a show of white teeth beneath the moustaches as he listened.

"I think," he said blandly, when the boy had done, "that I partly understand you. It is something after this fashion, is it not?" (He smiled.) "In certain valleys there was a hunter." (He touched the grotesque little figure at the bottom.) "Day by day he went to hunt for wild-fowl in the woods; and it chanced that once he stood on the shores of a large lake. While he stood waiting in the rushes for the coming of the birds, a great shadow fell on him, and in the water he saw a reflection. He looked up to the sky; but the thing was gone. Then a burning desire came over him to see once again that reflection in the water, and all day he watched and waited; but night came, and it had not returned. Then he went home with his empty bag, moody and silent. His comrades came questioning about him to know the reason, but he answered them nothing; he sat alone and brooded. Then his friend came to him, and to him he spoke.

"'I have seen to-day,' he said, 'that which I never saw before—a vast white bird, with silver wings outstretched, sailing in the everlasting blue. And now it is as though a great fire burnt within my breast. It was but a sheen, a shimmer, a reflection in the water; but now I desire nothing more on earth than to hold her.'

His friend laughed.

'It was but a beam playing on the water, or the shadow of your own head. To-morrow you will forget her,' he said.

But to-morrow, and to-morrow, and to-morrow the hunter walked alone. He sought in the forest and in the woods, by the lakes and among the rushes, but he could not find her. He shot no more wild-fowl; what were they to him?

'What ails him?' said his comrades.

'He is mad,' said one.

'No; but he is worse,' said another; 'he would see that which none of us have seen, and make himself a wonder.'

'Come, let us forswear his company,' said all.

So the hunter walked alone.

One night, as he wandered in the shade, very heart-sore and weeping, an old man stood before him, grander and taller than the sons of men.

'Who are you?' asked the hunter.

'I am Wisdom,' answered the old man; 'but some men called me Knowledge. All my life I have grown in these valleys; but no man sees me till he has sorrowed much. The eyes must be washed with tears that are to behold me; and, according as a man has suffered, I speak.'

And the hunter cried—

'Oh, you who have lived here so long, tell me, what is that great wild bird I have seen sailing in the blue? They would have me believe she is a dream; the shadow of my own head.'

The old man smiled.

'Her name is Truth. He who has once seen her never rests again. Till death he desires her.'

And the hunter cried—

'Oh, tell me where I may find her.'

But the man said,

'You have not suffered enough,' and went.

Then the hunter took from his breast the shuttle of Imagination, and wound on it the thread of his Wishes; and all night he sat and wove a net.

In the morning he spread the golden net open on the ground, and into it he threw a few grains of credulity, which his father had left him, and which he kept in his breast-pocket. They were like white puff-balls, and when you trod on them a brown dust flew out. Then he sat by to see what would happen. The first that came into the net was a snow-white bird, with dove's eyes, and he sang a beautiful song—'A human-God! a human-God! a human-God!' it sang. The second that came was black and mystical, with dark, lovely eyes, that looked into the depths of your soul, and he sang only this—'Immortality!'

And the hunter took them both in his arms, for he said—

'They are surely of the beautiful family of Truth.'

Then came another, green and gold, who sang in a shrill voice, like one crying in the market-place,—'Reward after Death! Reward after Death!'

And he said—

'You are not so fair; but you are fair too,' and he took it.

And others came, brightly coloured, singing pleasant songs, till all the grains were finished. And the hunter gathered all his birds together, and built a strong iron cage called a new creed, and put all his birds in it.

Then the people came about dancing and singing.

'Oh, happy hunter!' they cried. 'Oh, wonderful man! Oh, delightful birds! Oh lovely songs!'

No one asked where the birds had come from, nor how they had been caught; but they danced and sang before them, And the hunter too was glad, for he said—

'Surely Truth is among them. In time she will moult her feathers, and I shall see her snow-white form.'

But the time passed, and the people sang and danced; but the hunter's heart grew heavy. He crept alone, as of old, to weep; the terrible desire had awakened again in his breast. One day, as he sat alone weeping, it chanced that Wisdom met him. He told the old man what he had done.

And Wisdom smiled sadly.

'Many men,' he said, 'have spread that net for Truth; but they have never found her. On the grains of credulity she will not feed; in the net of wishes her feet cannot be held; in the air of these valleys she will not breathe. The birds you have caught are of the brood of Lies. Lovely and beautiful, but still lies; Truth knows them not.'

And the hunter cried out in bitterness—

'And must I then sit still to be devoured of this great burning?'

And the old man said,

'Listen, and in that you have suffered much and wept much, I will tell you what I know. He who sets out to search for Truth must leave these valleys of superstition for ever, taking with him not one shred that has belonged to them. Alone he must wander down into the

Land of Absolute Negation and Denial; he must abide there; he must resist temptation; when the light breaks he must arise and follow it into the country of dry sunshine. The mountains of stern reality will rise before him; he must climb them; *beyond* them lies Truth.'

'And he will hold her fast! he will hold her in his hands!' the hunter cried.

Wisdom shook his head.

'He will never see her, never hold her. The time is not yet.'

'Then there is no hope?' cried the hunter.

'There is this,' said Wisdom. 'Some men have climbed on those mountains; circle above circle of bare rock they have scaled; and, wandering there, in those high regions, some have chanced to pick up on the ground, one white, silver feather dropped from the wing of Truth. And it shall come to pass,' said the old man, raising himself prophetically and pointing with his finger to the sky, 'it shall come to pass, that, when enough of those silver feathers shall have been gathered by the hands of men, and shall have been woven into a cord, and the cord into a net, that in *that* net Truth may be captured. *Nothing but Truth can hold Truth.*'

The hunter arose. 'I will go,' he said.

But Wisdom detained him.

'Mark you well—who leaves these valleys *never* returns to them. Though he should weep tears of blood seven days and nights upon the confines, he can never put his foot across them. Left—they are left for ever. Upon the road which you would travel there is no reward offered. Who goes, goes freely—for the great love that is in him. The work is his reward.'

'I go,' said the hunter, 'but upon the mountains, tell me, which path shall I take?'

'I am the child of The-Accumulated-Knowledge-of-Ages,' said the man; 'I can walk only where many men have trodden. On those mountains few feet have passed; each man strikes out a path for himself. He goes at his own peril: my voice he hears no more. I may follow after him, but I cannot go before him.'

Then Knowledge vanished.

And the hunter turned. He went to his cage, and with his hands broke down the bars, and the jagged iron tore his flesh. It is sometimes easier to build than to break.

One by one he took his plumed birds and let them fly. But, when he came to his dark-plumed bird, he held it, and looked into its beautiful eyes, and the bird uttered its low deep cry—'Immortality!'

And he said quickly, 'I cannot part with it. It is not heavy; it eats no food. I will hide it in my breast; I will take it with me.' And he buried it there, and covered it over with his cloak.

But the thing he had hidden grew heavier, heavier, heavier—till it lay on his breast like lead. He could not move with it. He could not leave those valleys with it. Then again he took it out and looked at it.

'Oh, my beautiful, my heart's own!' he cried, 'may I not keep you?'

He opened his hands sadly.

'Go,' he said. 'It may happen that in Truth's song one note is like to yours; but I shall never hear it.'

Sadly he opened his hand, and the bird flew from him for ever.

Then from the shuttle of imagination he took the thread of his wishes, and threw it on the ground; and the empty shuttle he put into his breast, for the thread was made in those valleys, but the shuttle came from an unknown country. He turned to go, but now the people came about him, howling.

'Fool, hound, demented lunatic!' they cried. 'How dared you break your cage and let the birds fly?'

The hunter spoke; but they would not hear him.

'Truth! who is she? Can you eat her? can you drink her? Who has ever seen her? Your birds were real: all could hear them sing! Oh, fool! vile reptile! atheist!' they cried, 'you pollute the air.'

'Come, let us take up stones and stone him,' cried some.

'What affair is it of ours?' said others. 'Let the idiot go,' and went away. But the rest gathered up stones and mud and threw at him. At last, when he was bruised and cut, the hunter crept away into the woods. And it was evening about him."

At every word the stranger spoke the fellow's eyes flashed back on him—yes, and yes, and yes! The stranger smiled. It was almost worth the trouble of exerting oneself, even on a lazy afternoon, to win those passionate flashes, more thirsty and desiring than the love-glances of a woman.

"He wandered on and on," said the stranger, "and the shade grew deeper. He was on the borders now of the land where it is always night. Then he stepped into it, and there was no light there. With his hands he groped; but each branch as he touched it broke off, and the earth was covered with cinders. At every step his foot sank in, and a fine cloud of impalpable ashes flew up into his face; and it was dark. So he sat down upon a stone and buried his face in his hands, to wait in that Land of Negation and Denial till the light came.

And it was night in his heart also.

Then from the marshes to his right and left cold mists arose and closed about him. A fine, imperceptible rain fell in the dark, and great drops gathered on his hair and clothes. His heart beat slowly, and a numbness crept through all his limbs. Then, looking up, two merry whisp lights came dancing. He lifted his head to look at them. Nearer, nearer they came. So warm, so bright, they danced like stars of fire. They stood before him at last. From the centre of the radiating flame in one looked out a woman's face, laughing, dimpled, with streaming yellow hair. In the centre of the other were merry laughing ripples, like the bubbles on a glass of wine. They danced before him.

'Who are you,' asked the hunter, 'who alone come to me in my solitude and darkness?'

'We are the twins Sensuality,' they cried. 'Our father's name is Human-Nature, and our mother's name is Excess. We are as old as the hills and rivers, as old as the first man; but we never die,' they laughed.

'Oh, let me wrap my arms about you!' cried the first; 'they are soft and warm. Your heart is frozen now, but I will make it beat. Oh, come to me!'

'I will pour my hot life into you,' said the second; 'your brain is numb, and your limbs are dead now; but they shall live with a fierce free life. Oh, let me pour it in!'

'Oh, follow us,' they cried, 'and live with us. Nobler hearts than yours have sat here in this darkness to wait, and they have come to us and we to them; and they have never left us, never. All else is a delusion, but *we* are real, we are real. Truth is a shadow; the valleys of superstition are a farce; the earth is of ashes, the trees all rotten; but we—feel us—we live! You cannot doubt us. Feel us, how warm we are! Oh, come to us! Come with us!'

Nearer and nearer round his head they hovered, and the cold drops melted on his forehead. The bright light shot into his eyes, dazzling him, and the frozen blood began to run. And he said—

'Yes, why should I die here in this awful darkness? They are warm, they melt my frozen blood!' and he stretched out his hands to take them.

Then in a moment there arose before him the image of the thing he had loved, and his hand dropped to his side.

'Oh, come to us!' they cried.

But he buried his face.

'You dazzle my eyes,' he cried, 'you make my heart warm; but you cannot give me what I desire. I will wait here—wait till I die. Go!'

He covered his face with his hands and would not listen; and when he looked up again they were two twinkling stars, that vanished in the distance.

And the long, long night rolled on.

All who leave the valley of superstition pass through that dark land; but some go through it in a few days, some linger there for months, some for years, and some die there."

The boy had crept closer; his hot breath almost touched the stranger's hand; a mystic wonder filled his eyes.

"At last for the hunter a faint light played along the horizon, and he rose to follow it; and he reached that light at last, and stepped into the broad sunshine. Then before him rose the almighty mountains of Dry-facts and Realities. The clear sunshine played on them, and the tops were lost in the clouds. At the foot many paths ran up. An exultant cry burst from the hunter. He chose the straightest and began to climb; and the rocks and ridges resounded with his song. They had exaggerated; after all, it was not so high, nor was the road so steep! A few days, a few weeks, a few months at most, and then the top! Not one feather only would he pick up; he would gather all that other men had found—weave the net—capture Truth— hold her fast—touch her with his hands—clasp her!

He laughed in the merry sunshine, and sang loud. Victory was very near. Nevertheless, after a while the path grew steeper. He needed all his breath for climbing, and the singing died away. On the right and left rose huge rocks, devoid of lichen or moss, and in the lava-like earth chasms yawned. Here and there he saw a sheen of white bones. Now too the path began to grow less and less marked; then it became a mere trace, with a foot-mark here and there; then it ceased altogether. He sang no more, but struck forth a path for himself, until he reached a mighty wall of rock, smooth and without break, stretching as far as the eye could see. 'I will rear a stair against it; and, once this wall climbed, I shall be almost there,' he said bravely; and worked. With his shuttle of imagination he dug out stones; but half of them would not fit, and half a month's work would roll down because those below were ill chosen. But the hunter worked on, saying always to himself, 'Once this wall climbed, I shall be almost there. This great work ended!'

At last he came out upon the top, and he looked about him. Far below rolled the white mist over the valleys of superstition, and above him towered the mountains. They had seemed low before;

they were of an immeasurable height now, from crown to foundation surrounded by walls of rock, that rose tier above tier in mighty circles. Upon them played the eternal sunshine. He uttered a wild cry. He bowed himself onto the earth, and when he rose his face was white. In absolute silence he walked on. He was very silent now. In those high regions the rarefied air is hard to breathe by those born in the valleys; every breath he drew hurt him, and the blood oozed out from the tips of his fingers. Before the next wall of rock he began to work. The height of this seemed infinite, and he said nothing. The sound of his tool rang night and day upon the iron rocks into which he cut steps. Years passed over him, yet he worked on; but the wall towered up always above him to heaven. Sometimes he prayed that a little moss or lichen might spring up on those bare walls to be a companion to him; but it never came." The stranger watched the boy's face.

"And the years rolled on: he counted them by the steps he had cut—a few for a year—only a few. He sang no more; he said no more, 'I will do this or that'—he only worked. And at night, when the twilight settled down, there looked out at him from the holes and crevices in the rocks strange wild faces.

'Stop your work, you lonely man, and speak to us,' they cried.

'My salvation is in work. If I should stop but for one moment you would creep down upon me,' he replied. And they put out their long necks further.

'Look down into the crevice at your feet,' they said. 'See what lie there—white bones! As brave and strong a man as you climbed to these rocks. And he looked up. He saw there was no use in striving; he would never hold Truth, never see her, never find her. So he lay down here, for he was very tired. He went to sleep for ever. He put himself to sleep. Sleep is very tranquil. You are not lonely when you are asleep, neither do your hands ache, nor your heart.' And the hunter laughed between his teeth.

'Have I torn from my heart all that was dearest; have I wandered alone in the land of night; have I resisted temptation; have I dwelt where the voice of my kind is never heard, and laboured alone, to lie down and be food for you, ye harpies?'

He laughed fiercely; and the Echoes of Despair slunk away, for the laugh of a brave, strong heart is as a death-blow to them.

Nevertheless they crept out again and looked at him.

'Do you know that your hair is white?' they said, 'that your hands begin to tremble like a child's? Do you see that the point of your shuttle is gone?—it is cracked already. If you should ever climb this stair,' they said, 'it will be your last. You will never climb another.'

And he answered, *'I know it!'* and worked on.

The old, thin hands cut the stones ill and jaggedly, for the fingers were stiff and bent. The beauty and the strength of the man was gone.

At last, an old, wizened, shrunken face looked out above the rocks. It saw the eternal mountains rise with walls to the white clouds; but its work was done.

The old hunter folded his tired hands and lay down by the precipice where he had worked away his life. It was the sleeping time at last. Below him over the valleys rolled the thick white mist. Once it broke; and through the gap the dying eyes looked down on the trees and fields of their childhood. From afar seemed borne to him the cry of his own wild birds, and he heard the noise of people singing as they danced. And he thought he heard among them the voices of his old comrades; and he saw far off the sunlight shine on his early home. And great tears gathered in the hunter's eyes.

'Ah! they who die there do not die alone,' he cried.

Then the mists rolled together again; and he turned his eyes away.

'I have sought,' he said, 'for long years I have laboured; but I have not found her. I have not rested, I have not repined, and I have not seen her; now my strength is gone. Where I lie down worn out other men will stand, young and fresh. By the steps that I have cut they will climb; by the stairs that I have built they will mount. They will never know the name of the man who made them. At the clumsy work they will laugh; when the stones roll they will curse me. But they will mount, and on *my* work; they will climb, and by *my* stair! They will find her, and through me! And no man liveth to himself, and no man dieth to himself.'[1]

The tears rolled from beneath the shriveled eyelids. If Truth had appeared above him in the clouds now he could not have seen her, the mist of death was in his eyes.

'My soul hears their glad step coming,' he said; 'and they shall mount! they shall mount!' He raised his shrivelled hand to his eyes.

Then slowly from the white sky above, through the still air, came something falling, falling, falling. Softly it fluttered down, and

---

1 Romans 14:7.

dropped on to the breast of the dying man. He felt it with his hands. It was a feather. He died holding it."

The boy had shaded his eyes with his hand. On the wood of the carving great drops fell. The stranger must have laughed at him, or remained silent. He did so.

"How did you know it?" the boy whispered at last. "It is not written there—not on that wood. How did you know it?"

"Certainly," said his stranger, "the whole of the story is not written here, but it is suggested. And the attribute of all true art, the highest and the lowest, is this—that it says more than it says, and takes you away from itself. It is a little door that opens into an infinite hall where you may find what you please. Men, thinking to detract, say, 'People read more in this or that work of genius than was ever written in it,' not perceiving that they pay the highest compliment. If we pick up the finger and nail of a real man, we can decipher a whole story—could almost reconstruct the creature again, from head to foot. But half the body of a Mumboo-jumbow idol leaves us utterly in the dark as to what the rest was like. We see what we see, but nothing more. There is nothing so universally intelligible as truth. It has a thousand meanings, and suggests a thousand more." He turned over the wooden thing. "Though a man should carve it into matter with the least possible manipulative skill, it will yet find interpreters. It is the soul that looks out with burning eyes through the most gross fleshly filament. Whosoever should portray truly the life and death of a little flower—its birth, sucking in of nourishment, reproduction of its kind, withering and vanishing—would have shaped a symbol of all existence. All true facts of nature or the mind are related. Your little carving represents some mental facts as they really are, therefore fifty different true stories might be read from it. What your work wants is not truth, but beauty of external form, the other half of art." He leaned almost gently towards the boy. "Skill may come in time, but you will have to work hard. The love of beauty and the desire for it must be born in a man; the skill to reproduce it he must make. He must work hard."

"All my life I have longed to see you," the boy said.

The stranger broke off the end of his cigar, and lit it. The boy lifted the heavy wood from the stranger's knee and drew yet nearer him. In the dog-like manner of his drawing near there was something superbly ridiculous, unless one chanced to view it in another light. Presently the stranger said, whiffing, "Do something for me."

The boy started up.

"No; stay where you are. I don't want you to go anywhere; I want you to talk to me. Tell me what you have been doing all your life."

The boy slunk down again. Would that the man had asked him to root up bushes with his hands for his horse to feed on; or to run to the far end of the plain for the fossils that lay there; or to gather the flowers that grew on the hills at the edge of the plain; he would have run and been back quickly—but now!

"I have never done anything," he said.

"Then tell me of that nothing. I like to know what other folks have been doing whose word I can believe. It is interesting. What was the first thing you ever wanted very much?"

The boy waited to remember, then began hesitatingly; but soon the words flowed. In the smallest past we find an inexhaustible mine when once we begin to dig at it.

A confused, disordered story—the little made large and the large small, and nothing showing its inward meaning. It is not till the past has receded many steps that before the clearest eyes it falls into co-ordinate pictures. It is not till the I we tell of has ceased to exist that it takes its place among other objective realities, and finds its true niche in the picture. The present and the near past is a confusion, whose meaning flashes on us as it slinks away into the distance.

The stranger lit one cigar from the end of another, and puffed and listened with half-closed eyes.

"I will remember more to tell you if you like," said the fellow.

He spoke with that extreme gravity common to all very young things who feel deeply. It is not till twenty that we learn to be in deadly earnest and to laugh. The stranger nodded, while the fellow sought for something more to relate. He would tell all to this man of his—all that he knew, all that he had felt, his most inmost sorest thought. Suddenly the stranger turned upon him.

"Boy," he said, "you are happy to be here."

Waldo looked at him. Was his delightful one ridiculing him? Here, with this brown earth and these low hills, while the rare wonderful world lay all beyond. Fortunate to be here!

The stranger read his glance.

"Yes," he said; "here with the 'karroo bushes' and red sand. Do you wonder what I mean? To all who have been born in the old faith there comes a time of danger, when the old slips from us, and we have not yet planted our feet on the new. We hear the voice from Sinai thundering no more, and the still small voice of reason is not yet heard. We have proved the religion our mothers fed us on to be a delusion; in our bewilderment we see no rule by which to guide our steps day by day; and yet every day we must step somewhere." The stranger leaned forward and spoke more quickly. "We have never once been taught by word or act to distinguish between religion and the moral laws on which it has artfully fastened itself, and from which it has sucked its vitality. When we have dragged down the weeds and creepers that covered the solid wall and have found them to be rotten wood, we imagine the wall itself to be rotten wood too. We find it is solid and standing only when we fall headlong against it. We have been taught that all right and wrong originate in the will of an irresponsible being. It is some time before we see how the inexorable 'Thou shalt and shalt not,' are carved into the nature of things. This is the time of danger."

His dark, misty eyes looked into the boy's.

"In the end experience will inevitably teach us that the laws for a wise and noble life have a foundation infinitely deeper than the fiat of any being, God or man, even in the groundwork of human nature. She will teach us that whoso sheddeth man's blood, though by man his blood be not shed, though no man avenge and no hell await, yet every drop shall blister on his soul and eat in the name of the dead. She will teach that whoso takes a love not lawfully his own, gathers a flower with a poison on its petals; that whoso revenges, strikes with a sword that has two edges—one for his adversary, one for himself; that who lives to himself is dead, though the ground is not yet on him; that who wrongs another clouds his sun; and that who sins in secret stands accused and condemned before the one Judge who deals eternal justice—his own all-knowing self.

"Experience *will* teach us this, and reason will show us why it *must* be so; but at first the world swings before our eyes, and no voice cries out, 'This is the way, walk ye in it!' You are happy to be here, boy! When the suspense fills you with pain you build stone walls and dig earth for relief. Others have stood where you stand today, and have felt as you feel; and another relief has been offered them, and they have taken it.

"When the day has come when they have seen the path in which they might walk, they have not the strength to follow it. Habits have fastened on them from which nothing but death can free them; which cling closer than his sacerdotal sanctimony to a priest; which feed on the intellect like a worm sapping energy, hope, creative power, all that makes a man higher than a beast— leaving only the power to yearn, to regret, and to sink lower in the abyss.

"Boy," he said, and the listener was not more unsmiling now than the speaker, "you are happy to be here! Stay where you are, If you ever pray, let it be only the one old prayer—'Lead us not into temptation.' Live on here quietly. The time may yet come when you will be that which other men have hoped to be and never will be now."

The stranger rose, shook the dust from his sleeve, and, ashamed at his own earnestness, looked across the bushes for his horse.

"We should have been on our way already," he said. "We shall have a long ride in the dark to-night."

Waldo hastened to fetch the animal; but he returned leading it slowly. The sooner it came the sooner would its rider be gone.

The stranger was opening his saddle-bag, in which were a bright French novel and an old brown volume. He took the last and held it out to the boy.

"It may be of some help to you," he said carelessly. "It was a gospel to me when I first fell on it. You must not expect too much; but it may give you a centre round which to hang your ideas, instead of letting them lie about in a confusion that makes the head ache. We of this generation are not destined to eat and be satisfied as our fathers were; we must be content to go hungry."

He smiled his automaton smile, and rebuttoned the bag. Waldo thrust the book into his breast, and while he saddled the horse the stranger made inquiries as to the nature of the road and the distance to the next farm.

When the bags were fixed Waldo took up his wooden post and began to fasten it on to the saddle, tying it with the little blue cotton handkerchief from his neck. The stranger looked on in silence. When it was done the boy held the stirrup for him to mount.

"What is your name?" he inquired, ungloving his right hand when he was in the saddle.

The boy replied.

"Well, I trust we shall meet again some day, sooner or later."

He shook hands with the ungloved hand; then drew on the glove, and touched his horse, and rode slowly away. The boy stood to watch him.

Once when the stranger had gone half across the plain he looked back.

"Poor devil," he said, smiling and stroking his moustache. Then he looked to see if the little blue handkerchief were still safely knotted. "Poor devil!"

He smiled, and then he sighed wearily, very wearily.

And Waldo waited till the moving speck had disappeared on the horizon; then he stooped and kissed passionately a hoof-mark in the sand. Then he called his young birds together, and put his book under his arm, and walked home along the stone wall. There was a rare beauty to him in the sunshine that evening.

Chapter III.
Gregory Rose Finds His Affinity.

The new man, Gregory Rose, sat at the door of his dwelling, his arms folded, his legs crossed, and a profound melancholy seeming to rest over his soul. His house was a little square daub-and-wattle building, far out in the 'karroo,' two miles from the homestead. It was covered outside with a sombre coating of brown mud, two little panes being let into the walls for windows. Behind it were the 'sheep-kraals,' and to the right a large dam, now principally containing baked mud. Far off the little 'kopje' concealed the homestead, and was not itself an object conspicuous enough to relieve the dreary monotony of the landscape.

Before the door sat Gregory Rose in his shirt-sleeves, on a camp-stool, and ever and anon he sighed deeply. There was that in his countenance for which even his depressing circumstances failed to account. Again and again he looked at the little 'kopje,' at the milk-pail at his side, and at the brown pony, who a short way off cropped the dry bushes—and sighed.

Presently he rose and went into his house. It was one tiny room, the whitewashed walls profusely covered with prints cut from the *Illustrated London News*,[1] and in which there was a noticeable preponderance of female faces and figures. A stretcher filled one end of the hut, and a rack for a gun and a little hanging looking-glass

---

1 One of the leading newspapers of the day, appreciated especially for its many finely engraved images. The fact that Gregory has covered his walls with these prints is not surprising. What is peculiar is that he has preferred images from the fashion pages rather than sports, industry or politics.

diversified the gable opposite, while in the centre stood a chair and table. All was scrupulously neat and clean, for Gregory kept a little duster folded in the corner of his table-drawer, just as he had seen his mother do, and every morning before he went out he said his prayers, and made his bed, and dusted the table and the legs of the chairs, and even the pictures on the wall and the gun-rack.

On this hot afternoon he took from beneath his pillow a watch-bag made by his sister Jemima, and took out the watch. Only half-past four! With a suppressed groan he dropped it back and sat down beside the table. Half-past four! Presently he roused himself. He would write to his sister Jemima. He always wrote to her when he was miserable. She was his safety-valve. He forgot her when he was happy; but he used her when he was wretched.

He took out ink and paper. There was a family crest and motto on the latter, for the Roses since coming to the colony had discovered that they were of distinguished lineage. Old Rose himself, an honest English farmer, knew nothing of his noble descent; but his wife and daughter knew—especially his daughter. There were Roses in England who kept a park and dated from the Conquest. So the colonial "Rose Farm" became "Rose Manor" in remembrance of the ancestral domain, and the claim of the Roses to noble blood was established—in their own minds at least.

Gregory took up one of the white, crested sheets; but on deeper reflection he determined to take a pink one, as more suitable to the state of his feelings. He began—

"Kopje Alone
"Monday Afternoon.

"MY DEAR JEMIMA,—"

Then he looked up into the little glass opposite. It was a youthful face reflected there, with curling brown beard and hair; but in the dark blue eyes there was a look of languid longing that touched him. He re-dipped his pen and wrote,—
"When I look up into the little glass that hangs opposite me, I wonder if that changed and sad face—"
Here he sat still and reflected. It sounded almost as if he might be conceited or unmanly to be looking at his own face in the glass. No, that would not do. So he looked for another pink sheet and began again.

"Kopje Alone

"Monday Afternoon.

"DEAR SISTER,

"It is hardly six months since I left you to come to this spot, yet could you now see me I know what you would say, I know what mother would say—'Can that be our Greg—that thing with the strange look in his eyes?'

"Yes, Jemima, it is your Greg, and the change has been coming over me ever since I came here; but it is greatest since yesterday. You know what sorrows I have passed through, Jemima: how unjustly I was always treated at school, the masters keeping me back and calling me a blockhead, though, as they themselves allowed, I had the best memory of any boy in the school, and could repeat whole books from beginning to end. You know how cruelly father always used me, calling me a noodle and a milksop, just because he couldn't understand my fine nature. You know how he has made a farmer of me instead of a minister, as I ought to have been; you know it all, Jemima; and how I have borne it all, not as a woman, who whines for every touch, but as a man should—in silence.

"But there are things, there is *a* thing, which the soul longs to pour forth into a kindred ear.

"Dear sister, have you ever known what it is to keep wanting and wanting and wanting to kiss some one's mouth, and you may not; to touch some one's hand, and you cannot? I am in love, Jemima.

"The old Dutch-woman from whom I hire this place has a little step-daughter, and her name begins with *E*.

"She is English. I do not know how her father came to marry a Boer-woman. It makes me feel so strange to put down that letter, that I can hardly go on writing—E. I've loved her ever since I came here. For weeks I have not been able to eat or drink; my very tobacco when I smoke has no taste; and I can remain for no more than five minutes in one place, and sometimes feel as though I were really going mad.

"Every evening I go there to fetch my milk. Yesterday she gave me some coffee. The spoon fell on the ground. She picked it up; when she gave it me her finger touched mine. Jemima, I do not know if I fancied it—I shivered hot, and she shivered too! I thought, 'It is all right; she will be mine; she loves me!' Just then, Jemima, in came a fellow, a great coarse fellow, a German—a ridiculous fellow, with curls right down to his shoulders; it makes one *sick* to look at him. He's only a servant of the Boer-woman's, and a low, vulgar, uneducated thing, that's never been to boarding-school in his life. He had been to the next farm seeking sheep. When he came in she said, 'Good evening, Waldo. Have some coffee!' *and she kissed him.*

"All last night I heard nothing else but 'Have some coffee; have some coffee.' If I went to sleep for a moment I dreamed that her finger was pressing mine; but when I woke with a start I heard her say, 'Good evening, Waldo. Have some coffee!'

"Is this madness?

"I have not eaten a mouthful to-day. This evening I go and propose to her. If she refuses me I shall go and kill myself to-morrow. There is a dam of water close by. The sheep have drunk most of it up, but there is still enough if I tie a stone to my neck.

"It is a choice between death and madness. I can endure no more. If this should be the last letter you ever get from me, think of me tenderly, and forgive me. Without her, life would be a howling wilderness, a long tribulation. She is my affinity; the one love of my life, of my youth, of my manhood; my sunshine; my God-given blossom.

"'They never loved who dreamed that they loved once,
And who saith, 'I loved once'?—

Not angels, whose deep eyes look down through realms of light:
"Your disconsolate brother, on what is, in all probability, the last and distracted night of his life,

"GREGORY NAZIANZEN ROSE.

"P.S.—Tell mother to take care of my pearl studs. I left them in the wash-hand-stand drawer. Don't let the children get hold of them.
"P.P.S.—I shall take this letter with me to the farm. If I turn down one corner you may know I have been accepted; if not, you may know it is all up with your heart-broken brother,
"G. N. R."

Gregory having finished this letter, read it over with much approval, put it in an envelope, addressed it, and sat contemplating the ink-pot, somewhat relieved in mind.

The evening turned out chilly and very windy after the day's heat. From afar off, as Gregory neared the homestead on the brown pony, he could distinguish a little figure in a little red cloak at the door of the cow 'kraal.' Em leaned over the poles that barred the gate, and watched the frothing milk run through the black fingers of the herdsman, while the unwilling cows stood with tethered heads by the milking poles. She had thrown the red cloak over her own head, and held it under her chin with a little hand, to keep from her ears the wind, that playfully shook it, and tossed the little fringe of yellow hair into her eyes.

"Is it not too cold for you to be standing here?" said Gregory, coming softly close to her.

"Oh, no; it is so nice. I always come to watch the milking. That red cow with the short horns is bringing up the calf of the white cow that died. She loves it so—just as if it were her own. It is so nice to see her lick its little ears. Just look!"

"The clouds are black. I think it is going to rain tonight," said Gregory.

"Yes," answered Em, looking up as well as she could for the little yellow fringe.

"But I'm sure you must be cold," said Gregory, and put his hand under the cloak, and found there a small fist doubled up, soft, and very warm. He held it fast in his hand.

"Oh, Em, I love you better than all the world besides! Tell me, *do* you love me a little?"

"Yes, I do." said Em, hesitating, and trying softly to free her hand.

"Better than everything; better than all the world, darling?" he asked, bending down so low that the yellow hair was blown into his eyes.

"I don't know," said Em gravely. "I do love you very much; but I love my cousin who is at school, and Waldo, very much. You see I have known them so long!"

"Oh, Em, do not talk to me so coldly," Gregory cried, seizing the little arm that rested on the gate, and pressing it till she was half afraid. The herdsman had moved away to the other end of the 'kraal' now, and the cows, busy with their calves, took no notice of the little human farce "Em, if you talk so to me I will go mad! You must love me, love me better than all! You must give yourself to me. I have loved you since that first moment when I saw you walking by the stone wall with the jug in your hands. You were made for me, created for me! I will love you till I die! Oh, Em, do not be so cold, so cruel to me!"

He held her arm so tightly that her fingers relaxed their hold, and the cloak fluttered down on to the ground, and the wind played more roughly than ever with the little yellow head.

"I do love you very much," she said; "but I do not know if I want to marry you. I love you better than Waldo, but I can't tell if I love you better than Lyndall. If you would let me wait for a week, I think perhaps I could tell you."

Gregory picked up the cloak and wrapped it round her.

"If you could but love me as I love you," he said; but no woman *can* love as a man can. I will wait till next Saturday. I will not once come near you till then. Good-bye! Oh, Em," he said, turning again, and twining his arm about her, and kissing her surprised little mouth, "if you are not my wife I cannot live. I have never loved another woman, and I never shall!—never, never!"

"You make me afraid," said Em. "Come let us go, and I will fill your pail."

"I want no milk.—Good-bye! You will not see me again till Saturday."

Late that night, when every one else had gone to bed, the yellow-haired little woman stood alone in the kitchen. She had come to fill the kettle for the next morning's coffee, and now stood before the fire. The warm reflection lit the grave old-womanish little face, that was so unusually thoughtful this evening.

"Better than all the world; better than everything; he loves me better than everything!" She said the words aloud, as if they were more easy to believe if she spoke them so. She had given out so much love in her little life, and had got none of it back with interest. Now one said, "I love you better than all the world." One loved her better than she loved him. How suddenly rich she was. She kept clasping and unclasping her hands. So a beggar feels who falls asleep on the pavement wet and hungry, and who wakes in a palace-hall with servants and lights, and a feast before him. Of course the beggar's is only a dream, and he wakes from it; and this was real.

Gregory had said to her, "I will love you as long as I live." She said the words over and over to herself like a song.

"I will send for him to-morrow, and I will tell him how I love him back," she said.

But Em needed not to send for him. Gregory discovered on reaching home that Jemima's letter was still in his pocket. And, therefore, much as he disliked the appearance of vacillation and weakness, he was obliged to be at the farmhouse before sunrise to post it.

"If I see her," Gregory said, "I shall only bow to her. She shall see that I am a man, who keeps his word."

As to Jemima's letter, he had turned down one corner of the page, and then turned it back, leaving a deep crease. That would show that he was neither accepted nor rejected, but that matters were in an intermediate condition. It was a more poetical way than putting it in plain words.

Gregory was barely in time with his letter, for Waldo was starting when he reached the homestead, and Em was on the door-step to see him off. When he had given the letter, and Waldo had gone, Gregory bowed stiffly and prepared to remount his own pony, but somewhat slowly. It was still early; none of the servants were about. Em came up close to him and put her little hand softly on his arm as he stood by his horse.

"I do love you best of all," she said. She was not frightened now, however much he kissed her. "I wish I was beautiful and nice," she added, looking up into his eyes as he held her against his breast.

"My darling, to me you are more beautiful than all the women in the world; dearer to me than everything it holds. If you were in hell I would go after you to find you there! If you were dead, though my body moved, my soul would be under the ground with you. All life as I pass it with you in my arms will be perfect to me. It will pass, pass like a ray of sunshine."

Em thought how beautiful and grand his face was as she looked into it. She raised her hand gently and put it on his forehead.

"You are so silent, so cold, my Em," he cried. "Have you nothing to say to me?"

A little shade of wonder filled her eyes.

"I will do everything you tell me," she said.

What else could she say? Her idea of love was only service.

"Then, my own precious one, promise never to kiss that fellow again. I cannot bear that you should love anyone but me. You must not! I will not have it! If every relation I had in the world were to die to-morrow, I would be quite happy if I still only had you! My darling, my love, why are you so cold? Promise me not to love him any more. If you asked *me* to do anything for *you*, I would do it, though it cost my life."

Em put her hand very gravely round his neck.

"I will never kiss him," she said, "and I will try not to love any one else. But I do not know if I will be able."

"Oh, my darling, I think of *you* all night, all day. I think of nothing else, love, nothing else," he said, folding his arms about her.

Em was a little conscience-stricken; even that morning she had found time to remember that in six months her cousin would come back from school, and she had thought to remind Waldo of the lozenges for his cough, even when she saw Gregory coming.

"I do not know how it is," she said humbly, nestling to him, "but I cannot love you so much as you love me. Perhaps it is because I am only a woman; but I *do* love you as much as I can."

Now the Kaffir maids were coming from the huts. He kissed her again, eyes and mouth and hands, and left her.

Tant' Sannie was well satisfied when told of the betrothment. She herself contemplated marriage within the year with one or other of her numerous 'vrijers,'[1] and she suggested that the weddings might take place together.

Em set to work busily to prepare her own household linen and wedding garments. Gregory was with her daily, almost hourly, and the six months which elapsed before Lyndall's return passed, as he felicitously phrased it, "like a summer night, when you are dreaming of some one you love."

Late one evening, Gregory sat by his little love, turning the handle of her machine as she drew her work through it, and they talked of the changes they would make when the Boer-woman was gone, and the farm belonged to them alone. There should be a new room here, and a kraal there. So they chatted on. Suddenly Gregory dropped the handle, and impressed a fervent kiss on the fat hand that guided the linen.

"You are so beautiful, Em," said the lover. "It comes over me in a flood suddenly, how I love you."

Em smiled.

"Tant' Sannie says when I am her age no one will look at me; and it is true. My hands are as short and broad as a duck's foot, and my forehead is so low, and I haven't any nose. I *can't* be pretty."

She laughed softly. It was so nice to think he should be so blind.

"When my cousin comes to-morrow you will see a beautiful woman, Gregory," she added presently. "She is like a little queen: her shoulders are so upright, and her head looks as though it ought to have a little crown upon it. You must come to see her to-morrow as soon as she comes. I am sure you will love her."

"Of course I shall come to see her, since she is your cousin; but do you think I could *ever* think any woman as lovely as I think you?"

---

1   Lover or sweetheart.

He fixed his seething eyes upon her.

"You could not help seeing that she is prettier," said Em, slipping her right hand into his; "but you will never be able to like any one so much as you like me."

Afterwards, when she wished her lover good night, she stood upon the doorstep to call a greeting after him; and she waited, as she always did, till the brown pony's hoofs became inaudible behind the 'kopje.'

Then she passed through the room where Tant' Sannie lay snoring, and, through the little room that was all draped in white, waiting for her cousin's return, on to her own room.

She went to the chest of drawers to put away the work she had finished, and sat down on the floor before the lowest drawer. In it were the things she was preparing for her marriage. Piles of white linen, and some aprons and quilts; and in the little box in the corner a spray of orange-blossom which she had brought from a smouse.[1] There too was a ring Gregory had given her, and a veil his sister had sent, and there was a little roll of fine embroidered work which Trana had given her. It was too fine and good even for Gregory's wife—just right for something very small and soft. She would keep it. And she touched it gently with her forefinger, smiling; and then she blushed and hid it far behind the other things. She knew so well all that was in that drawer, and yet she turned them all over as though she saw them for the first time, packed them all out, and packed them all in, without one fold or crumple; and then sat down and looked at them.

To-morrow evening when Lyndall came she would bring her here, and show it her all. Lyndall would so like to see it—the little wreath, and the ring, and the white veil! It would be so nice! Then Em fell to seeing pictures. Lyndall should live with them till she herself got married some day.

Every day when Gregory came home, tired from his work, he would look about and say, "Where is my wife? Has no one seen my wife? Wife, some coffee!" and she would give him some.

Em's little face grew very grave at last, and she knelt up and extended her hands over the drawer of linen.

"Oh, God!" she said, "I am so glad! I do not know what I have done that I should be so glad. Thank you!"

---

1 Itinerant trader.

Chapter IV.
Lyndall.

She was more like a princess, yes, far more like a princess, than the lady who still hung on the wall in Tant' Sannie's bedroom. So Em thought. She leaned back in the little armchair; she wore a grey dressing-gown, and her long hair was combed out and hung to the ground. Em, sitting before her, looked up with mingled respect and admiration.

Lyndall was tired after her long journey, and had come to her room early. Her eyes ran over the familiar objects. Strange to go away for four years, and come back, and find that the candle standing on the dressing-table still cast the shadow of an old crone's head in the corner beyond the clothes-horse. Strange that even a shadow should last longer than man! She looked about among the old familiar objects; all was there, but the old self was gone.

"What are you noticing?" asked Em.

"Nothing and everything. I thought the windows were higher. If I were you, when I get this place I should raise the walls. There is not room to breathe here; one suffocates."

"Gregory is going to make many alterations," said Em; and drawing nearer to the grey dressing-gown respectfully. "Do you like him, Lyndall? Is he not handsome?"

"He must have been a fine baby," said Lyndall, looking at the white dimity curtain that hung above the window.

Em was puzzled.

"There are some men," said Lyndall, "whom you never can believe were babies at all; and others you never see without thinking how very nice they must have looked when they wore socks and pink sashes."

Em remained silent; then she said with a little dignity, "When you know him you will love him as I do. When I compare other people with him, they seem so weak and little. Our hearts are so cold, our loves are mixed up with so many other things. But he— no one is worthy of his love. I am not. It is so great and pure."

"You need not make yourself unhappy on that point—your poor return for his love, my dear," said Lyndall. "A man's love is a fire of olive-wood. It leaps higher every moment; it roars, it blazes, it shoots out red flames; it threatens to wrap you round and devour you—you who stand by like an icicle in the glow of its fierce warmth. You are self-reproached at your own chilliness and want of reciprocity. The next day, when you go to warm your hands a little, you find a few ashes! 'Tis a long love and cool against a short love and hot—men, at all events, have nothing to complain of."

"You speak so because you do not know men," said Em, instantly assuming the dignity of superior knowledge so universally affected by affianced and married women in discussing man's nature with their uncontracted sisters.

"You will know them too some day, and then you will think differently," said Em, with the condescending magnanimity which superior knowledge can always afford to show to ignorance.

Lyndall's little lip quivered in a manner indicative of intense amusement. She twirled a massive ring upon her forefinger—a ring more suitable for the hand of a man, and noticeable in design—a diamond cross let into gold, with the initials "R.R." below it.

"Ah, Lyndall," Em cried, "perhaps you are engaged yourself—that is why you smile. Yes; I am sure you are. Look at this ring!"

Lyndall drew the hand quickly from her.

"I am not in so great a hurry to put my neck beneath any man's foot; and I do not so greatly admire the crying of babies," she said, as she closed her eyes half wearily and leaned back in the chair. "There are other women glad of such work."

Em felt rebuked and ashamed. How could she take Lyndall and show her the white linen and the wreath, and the embroidery? She was quiet for a little while, and then began to talk about Trana and the old farm-servants, till she saw her companion was weary; then she rose and left her for the night. But after Em was gone Lyndall sat on, watching the old crone's face in the corner, and with a weary look, as though the whole world's weight rested on these frail young shoulders.

The next morning, Waldo, starting off before breakfast with a bag of mealies slung over his shoulder to feed the ostriches, heard a light step behind him.

"Wait for me; I am coming with you," said Lyndall adding as she came up to him, "If I had not gone to look for you yesterday you would not have come to greet me till now. Do you not like me any longer, Waldo?"

"Yes—but—you are changed."

It was the old clumsy, hesitating mode of speech.

"You liked the pinafores better?" she said quickly. She wore a dress of a simple cotton fabric, but very fashionably made, and on her head was a broad white hat. To Waldo she seemed superbly attired. She saw it. "My dress has changed a little," she said, "and I also; but not to you. Hang the bag over your other shoulder, that I may see your face. You say so little that if one does not look at you you are an uncomprehended cipher." Waldo changed the bag, and they walked on side by side. "You have improved," she said. "Do you know that I have sometimes wished to see you while I was away; not often, but still sometimes."

They were at the gate of the first camp now. Waldo threw over a bag of mealies, and they walked on over the dewy ground.

"Have you learnt much?" he asked her simply, remembering how she had once said, "When I come back again I shall know everything that a human being can."

She laughed.

"Are you thinking of my old boast? Yes; I have learnt something, though hardly what I expected, and not *quite* so much. In the first place, I have learnt that one of my ancestors must have been a very great fool; for they say nothing comes out in a man but one of his forefathers possessed it before him. In the second place, I have discovered that of all cursed places under the sun, where the hungriest soul can hardly pick up a few grains of knowledge, a girls' boarding-school is the worst. They are called finishing schools, and the name tells accurately what they are. They finish everything but imbecility and weakness, and that they cultivate. They are nicely adapted machines for experimenting on the question, 'Into how little space a human soul can be crushed?' I have seen some souls so compressed that they would have fitted into a small thimble, and found room to move there—wide room. A woman who has been for many years at one of those places carries the mark of the beast on her till she dies, though she may expand a little afterwards, when she breathes in the free world."

"Were you miserable?" he asked, looking at her with quick anxiety.

"I?—no. I am never miserable and never happy. I wish I were. But I should have run away from the place on the fourth day, and hired myself to the first Boer-woman whose farm I came to, to make fire under her soap-pot, if I had to live as the rest of the drove did. Can you form an idea, Waldo, of what it must be to be shut up with cackling old women, who are without knowledge of life, without love of the beautiful, without strength, to have your soul cultured by them? It is suffocation only to breathe the air they breathe; but I made them give me room. I told them I should leave, and they knew I came there on my own account; so they gave me a bedroom without the companionship of one of those things that were having their brains slowly diluted and squeezed out of them.

I did not learn music, because I had no talent; and when the drove made cushions, and hideous flowers that the roses laugh at, and a footstool in six weeks that a machine would have made better in five minutes, I went to my room. With the money saved from such work I bought books and newspapers, and at night I sat up. I read, and epitomised what I read; and I found time to write some plays, and find out how hard it is to make your thoughts look anything but imbecile fools, when you paint them with ink on paper. In the holidays I learnt a great deal more. I made acquaintances, saw a few places and many people, and some different ways of living, which is more than any books can show one. On the whole, I am not dis satisfied with my four years. I have not learnt what I expected; but I have learnt something else. What have you been doing?"

"Nothing."

"That is not possible. I shall find out by-and-by."

They still stepped on side by side over the dewy bushes. Then suddenly she turned on him.

"Don't you wish you were a woman, Waldo?"

"No," he answered readily.

She laughed.

"I thought not. Even you are too worldly-wise for that. I never met a man who did. This is a pretty ring," she said, holding out her little hand, that the morning sun might make the diamonds sparkle. "Worth fifty pounds at least. I will give it to the first man who tells me he would like to be a woman. There might be one on Robbin Island[1] who would win it perhaps, but I doubt it even there. It is delightful to be a woman; but every man thanks the Lord devoutly that he isn't one."

She drew her hat to one side to keep the sun out of her eyes as she walked. Waldo looked at her so intently that he stumbled over the bushes. Yes, this was his little Lyndall who had worn the check pinafores; he saw it now, and he walked closer beside her. They reached the next camp.

"Let us wait at this camp and watch the birds," she said, as an ostrich hen came bounding towards them, with velvety wings outstretched, while far away over the bushes the head of the cock was visible as he sat brooding on the eggs.

---

1   Robbin Island in Table Bay was used as a leper-colony, an asylum, and, later, as a detention camp for political prisoners. In the first edition of *African Farm*, Schreiner footnotes it as a place for lunatics.

Lyndall folded her arms on the gate bar, and Waldo threw his empty bag on the wall and leaned beside her.

"I like these birds," she said; "they share each other's work, and are companions. Do you take an interest in the position of women, Waldo?"

"No."

"I thought not. No one does, unless they are in need of a subject upon which to show their wit. And as for you, from of old you can see nothing that is not separated from you by a few millions of miles, and strewed over with mystery. If women were the inhabitants of Jupiter, of whom you had happened to hear something, you would pore over us and our condition night and day; but because we are before your eyes you never look at us. You care nothing that *this* is ragged and ugly," she said, putting her little finger on his sleeve; "but you strive mightily to make an imaginary leaf on an old stick beautiful. I'm sorry you don't care for the position of women: I should have liked us to be friends; and it is the only thing about which I think much or feel much—if, indeed, I have any feeling about anything," she added flippantly, readjusting her dainty little arms. "When I was a baby, I fancy my parents left me out in the frost one night, and I got nipped internally—it feels so!"

"I have only a few old thoughts," he said, "and I think them over and over again; always beginning where I left off. I never get any further. I am weary of them."

"Like an old hen that sits on its eggs month after month and they never come out?" she said quickly. "I am so pressed in upon by new things that, lest they should trip one another up, I have to keep forcing them back. My head swings sometimes. But this one thought stands, never goes—if I might but be one of those born in the future, then, perhaps, to be born a woman will not be to be born branded."

Waldo looked at her. It was hard to say whether she were in earnest or mocking, "I know it is foolish. Wisdom never kicks at the iron walls it can't bring down," she said. "But we are cursed, Waldo, born cursed from the time our mothers bring us into the world till the shrouds are put on us. Do not look at me as though I were talking nonsense. Everything has two sides—the outside that is ridiculous, and the inside that is solemn."

"I am not laughing," said the boy sedately enough; "but what curses you?"

He thought she would not reply to him, she waited so long.

"It is not what is done to us, but what is made of us," she said at last, "that wrongs us. No man can be really injured but by what modifies himself. We all enter the world little plastic beings, with so much natural force, perhaps, but for the rest—blank; and the world tells us what we are to be, and shape us by the ends it sets before us. To you it says—*Work*; and to us it says—*Seem!* To you it says—As you approximate to man's highest ideal of God, as your arm is strong and your knowledge great, and the power to labour is with you, so you shall gain all that human heart desires. To us it says—Strength shall not help you, nor knowledge, nor labour. You shall gain what men gain, but by other means. And so the world makes men and women.[1]

"Look at this little chin of mine, Waldo, with the dimple in it. It is but a small part of my person; but though I had a knowledge of all things under the sun, and the wisdom to use it, and the deep loving heart of an angel, it would not stead me through life like this little chin. I can win money with it, I can win love; I can win power with it, I can win fame. What would knowledge help me? The less a woman has in her head the lighter she is for climbing. I once heard an old man say, that he never saw intellect help a woman so much as a pretty ankle; and it was the truth. They begin to shape us to our cursed end," she said, with her lips drawn in to look as though they smiled, "when we are tiny things in shoes and socks. We sit with our little feet drawn up under us in the window, and look out at the boys in their happy play. We want to go. Then a loving hand is laid on us: 'Little one, you cannot go,' they say; 'your little face will burn, and your nice white dress be spoiled! We feel it must be for our good, it is so lovingly said; but we cannot understand; and we kneel still with one little cheek wistfully pressed against the pane. Afterwards we go and thread blue beads, and make a string for our neck; and we go and stand before the glass. We see the complexion we were not to spoil, and the white frock, and we look into our own great eyes. Then the curse begins to get on us. It finishes its work when we are grown women, who no more look out wistfully at a more healthy life; we are contented. We fit our sphere as a Chinese woman's foot fits

---

1 See Appendix C for Schreiner's essay on "Woman and Labor" and Appendix D for her allegory "Three Dreams in a Desert." In both works, Schreiner criticizes social conventions that reinforce women's dependence on men.

her shoe, exactly, as though God had made both—and yet he knows nothing of either. In some of us the shaping to our end has been quite completed. The parts we are not to use have been quite atrophied, and have even dropped off; but in others, and we are not less to be pitied, they have been weakened and left. We wear the bandages, but our limbs have not grown to them; we know that we are compressed, and chafe against them.

"But what does it help? A little bitterness, a little longing when we are young, a little futile searching for work, a little passionate striving for room for the exercise of our powers,— and then we go with the drove. A woman must march with her regiment. In the end she must be trodden down or go with it; and if she is wise she goes.

"I see in your great eyes what you are thinking," she said, glancing at him; "I always know what the person I am talking to is thinking of. How is this woman who makes such a fuss worse off than I? I will show you by a very little example. We stand here at this gate this morning, both poor, both young, both friendless; there is not much to choose between us. Let us turn away just as we are, to make our way in life. This evening you will come to a farmer's house. The farmer, albeit you come alone and on foot, will give you a pipe of tobacco and a cup of coffee and a bed. If he has no dam to build and no child to teach, to-morrow you can go on your way with a friendly greeting of the hand. I, if I come to the same place to-night, will have strange questions asked me, strange glances cast on me. The Boer-wife will shake her head and give me food to eat with the Kaffirs, and a right to sleep with the dogs. That would be the first step in our progress—a very little one, but every step to the end would repeat it. We were equals once when we lay new-born babes on our nurse's knees. We will be equals again when they tie up our jaws for the last sleep."

Waldo looked in wonder at the little quivering face; it was a glimpse into a world of passion and feeling wholly new to him.

"Mark you," she said, "we have always this advantage over you— we can at any time step into ease and competence, where you must labour patiently for it. A little weeping, a little wheedling, a little self-degradation, a little careful use of our advantages, and then some man will say—'Come, be my wife!' With good looks and youth marriage is easy to attain. There are men enough; but a woman who has sold herself, even for a ring and a new name, need hold her skirt aside for no creature in the street. They both earn their bread in one way. Marriage for love is the beautifulest external symbol of the union of souls; marriage without it is the uncleanest traffic that defiles the world." She ran her little finger savagely along the topmost bar, shaking off the dozen little dew-drops that still hung there. "And they tell us we have men's chivalrous attention!" she cried. "When we ask to be doctors, lawyers, law-makers, anything but ill-paid drudges, they say,—No; but you have men's chivalrous attention; now think of that and be satisfied! What would you do without it?"

The bitter little silvery laugh, so seldom heard, rang out across the bushes. She bit her little teeth together.

"I was coming up in Cobb and Co.'s the other day. At a little wayside hotel we had to change the large coach for a small one. We were ten passengers, eight men and two women. As I sat in the house the gentlemen came and whispered to me, 'There is not room for all in the new coach, take your seat quickly.' We hurried out, and they gave us the best seat, and covered me with rugs, because it was drizzling. Then the last passenger came running up to the coach—an old woman with a wonderful bonnet, and a black shawl pinned with a yellow pin.

"'There is no room,' they said; 'you must wait till next week's coach takes you up;' but she climbed on to the step, and held on at the window with both hands.

"'My son-in-law is ill, and I must go and see him,' she said.

"'My good woman,' said one, 'I am really exceedingly sorry that your son-in-law is ill; but there is absolutely no room for you here.'

"'You had better get down,' said another, 'or the wheel will catch you.'

I got up to give her my place.

"'Oh, no, no!' they cried, 'we will not allow that.'

"'I will rather kneel,' said one, and he crouched down at my feet; so the woman came in.

"There were nine of us in that coach, and only one showed chivalrous attention—and that was a woman to a woman.

"I shall be old and ugly too one day, and I shall look for men's chivalrous help, but I shall not find it.

"The bees are very attentive to the flowers till their honey is done, and then they fly over them. I don't know if the flowers feel grateful to the bees; they are great fools if they do."

"But some women," said Waldo, speaking as though the words forced themselves from him at that moment, "some women have power."

She lifted her beautiful eyes to his face.

"Power! Did you ever hear of men being asked whether other souls should have power or not? It is born in them. You may dam up the fountain of water, and make it a stagnant marsh, or you may let it run free and do its work; but *you* cannot say whether it shall be there; *it is there*. And it will act, if not openly for good, then covertly for evil; but it will act. If Goethe had been stolen away as a child, and reared in a robber horde in the depths of a German forest, do you think the world would have had 'Faust' and 'Iphegenie'? But he would have been Goethe still—stronger, wiser than his fellows. At night, round their watch-fire, he would have chanted wild songs of rapine and murder, till the dark faces about him were moved and trembled. His songs would have echoed on from father to son, and nerved the heart and arm—for evil. Do you think if Napoleon had been born a woman that he would have been contented to give small tea-parties and talk small scandal? He would have risen; but the world would not have heard of him as it hears of him now—a man great and kingly, with all his sins; he would have left one of those names that stain the leaf of every history—the names of women, who, having power, but having denied the right to exercise it openly, rule in the dark, covertly, and by stealth, through the men whose passions they feed on and by whom they climb.

"Power!" she said suddenly, smiting her little hand upon the rail. "Yes, we have power; and since we are not to expend it in tunneling mountains, nor healing diseases, nor making laws, nor money, nor on any extraneous object, we expend it on *you*. You are our goods, our merchandise, our material for operating on; we buy you, we sell you, we make fools of you, we act the wily old Jew with you, we keep six of you crawling to our little feet, and praying only for a touch of our little hand; and they say truly, there was never an ache or pain or a broken heart but a woman was at the bottom of it. We are not to study law, nor science, nor art, so we study you. There is never a nerve or fibre in your man's nature but we know it. We keep six of you dancing in the palm of one little hand," she said, balancing her outstretched arm gracefully, as though tiny beings disported themselves in its palm. "There—we throw you away, and you sink to the Devil," she said, folding her arms composedly. "There was never a man who said one word for woman but he said two for man, and three for the whole human race."

She watched the bird pecking up the last yellow grains; but Waldo looked only at her.

When she spoke again it was very measuredly.

"They bring weighty arguments against us when we ask for the perfect freedom of women," she said; "but, when you come to the objections, they are like pumpkin devils with candles inside, hollow, and can't bite. They say that women do not wish for the sphere and freedom we ask for them, and would not use it!

"If the bird *does* like its cage, and *does* like its sugar, and will not leave it, why keep the door so very carefully shut? Why not open it, only a little? Do they know, there is many a bird will not break its wings against the bars, but would fly if the doors were open." She knit her forehead, and leaned further over the bars.

"Then they say, 'If the women have the liberty you ask for, they will be found in positions for which they are not fitted!' If two men climb one ladder, did you ever see the weakest anywhere but at the foot? The surest sign of fitness is success. The weakest never wins but where there is handicapping. Nature left to herself will as beautifully apportion a man's work to his capacities as long ages ago she graduated the colours on the bird's breast. If we are not fit you give us to no purpose the right to labour; the work will fall out of our hands into those that are wiser."

She talked more rapidly as she went on, as one talks of that over which they have brooded long, and which lies near their hearts.

Waldo watched her intently.

"They say women have one great and noble work left them, and they do it ill.—That is true; they do it execrably. It is the work that demands the broadest culture, and they have not even the narrowest. The lawyer may see no deeper than his lawbooks, and the chemist see no further than the windows of his laboratory, and they may do their work well. But the woman who does woman's work needs a many-sided, multiform culture; the heights and depths of human life must not be beyond the reach of her vision; she must have knowledge of men and things in many states, a wide catholicity of sympathy, the strength that springs from knowledge, and the magnanimity which springs from strength. *We* bear the world, and *we* make it. The souls of little children are marvellously delicate and tender things, and keep for ever the shadow that first falls on them, and that is the mother's, or at best a woman's. There was never a great man who had not a great mother—it is hardly an exaggeration. The first six years of our life make us; all that is added later is veneer; and yet some say, if a woman can cook a dinner or dress herself well she has culture enough.

"The mightiest and noblest of human work is given to us, and we do it ill. Send a navvie[1] to work into an artist's studio, and see what you will find there! And yet, thank God, we have this work," she added quickly: "it is the one window through which we see into the great world of earnest labour. The meanest girl who dances and dresses becomes something higher when her children look up into her face and ask her questions. It is the only education we have and which they cannot take from us."

She smiled slightly; "They say that we complain of woman's being compelled to look upon marriage as a profession; but that she is free to enter upon it or leave it as she pleases.

"Yes—and a cat set afloat in a pond is free to sit in the tub till it dies there, it is under no obligation to wet its feet; and a drowning man may catch at a straw or not, just as he likes—it is a glorious liberty! Let any man think for five minutes of what old maidenhood means to a woman—and then let him be silent. Is it easy to bear through life a name that in itself signifies defeat? to dwell, as nine out of ten unmarried women must, under the finger of another woman? Is it easy to look forward to an old age without honour, without the reward of useful labour, without love? I wonder how many men there are who would give up everything that is dear in life for the sake of maintaining a high ideal purity."

She laughed a little laugh that was clear without being pleasant. "And then, when they have no other argument against us, they say— 'Go on; but when you have made women what you wish, and her children inherit her culture, you will defeat yourself. Man will gradually become extinct from excess of intellect, the passions which replenish the race will die.' Fools!" she said, curling her pretty lip. "A Hottentot sits at the road-side and feeds on a rotten bone he has found there, and takes out his bottle of Cape-smoke and swills at it, and grunts with satisfaction; and the cultured child of the nineteenth century sits in his arm-chair, and sips choice wines with the lip of a connoisseur, and tastes delicate dishes with a delicate palate, and with a satisfaction of which the Hottentot knows nothing. Heavy jaw and sloping forehead—all have gone with increasing intellect; but the animal appetites are there still—refined, discriminative, but immeasurably intensified. Fools! Before men forgave or worshipped, while they still were weak on their hind legs, did they not eat and drink, and fight for wives? When all the

---

1 Variant of "navvy": a laborer in excavation or construction of earth-works.

later additions to humanity have vanished, will not the foundation on which they are built remain?"

She was silent then for a while, and said somewhat dreamily, more as though speaking to herself than to him—

"They ask, What will you gain, even if man does not become extinct?—you will have brought justice and equality on to the earth, and sent love from it. When men and women are equals they will love no more. Your highly-cultured women will not be lovable, will not love.

"Do they see nothing, understand nothing? It is Tant' Sannie who buries husbands one after another, and folds her hands resignedly,—'The Lord gave, and the Lord hath taken away, and blessed be the name of the Lord,'—and she looks for another. It is the hard-headed, deep thinker who, when the wife who has thought and worked with him goes, can find no rest, and lingers near her till he finds a sleep beside her.

"A great soul draws and is drawn with a more fierce intensity than any small one. By every inch we grow in intellectual height our love strikes down its roots deeper, and spreads out its arms wider. It is for love's sake yet more than for any other that we look for that new time." She had leaned her head against the stones, and watched with her sad, soft eyes the retreating bird. "Then when that time comes," she said lowly, "when love is no more bought or sold, when it is not a means of making bread, when each woman's life is filled with earnest, independent labour, then love will come to her, a strange sudden sweetness breaking in upon her earnest work; not sought for, but found. Then, but not now——"

Waldo waited for her to finish the sentence, but she seemed to have forgotten him.

"Lyndall," he said, putting his hand upon her—she started—"if you think that that new time will be so great, so good, you who speak so easily——"

She interrupted him.

"Speak! speak!" she said; "the difficulty is not to speak; the difficulty is to keep silence."

"But why do you not try to bring that time?" he said with pitiful simplicity. "When you speak I believe all you say; other people would listen to you also."

"I am not so sure of that," she said with a smile.

Then over the small face came the weary look it had worn last night as it watched the shadow in the corner. Ah, so weary!

"I, Waldo, I?" she said. "I will do nothing good for myself, nothing for the world, till someone wakes me. I am asleep, swathed, shut up in self; till I have been delivered I will deliver no one."

He looked at her wondering, but she was not looking at him.

"To see the good and the beautiful," she said, "and to have no strength to live it, is only to be Moses on the mountain of Nebo,[1] with the land at your feet and no power to enter. It would be better not to see it. Come," she said, looking up into his face, and seeing its uncomprehending expression, "let us go, it is getting late. Doss is anxious for his breakfast also," she added, wheeling round and calling to the dog, who was endeavouring to unearth a mole, an occupation to which he had been zealously addicted from the third month, but in which he had never on any single occasion proved successful.

Waldo shouldered his bag, and Lyndall walked on before in silence, with the dog close to her side. Perhaps she thought of the narrowness of the limits within which a human soul may speak and be understood by its nearest of mental kin, of how soon it reaches that solitary land of the individual experience, in which no fellow-footfall is ever heard. Whatever her thoughts may have been, she was soon interrupted. Waldo came close to her, and standing still, produced with awkwardness from his breast-pocket a small carved box.

"I made it for you," he said, holding it out.

"I like it," she said, examining it carefully.

The workmanship was better than that of the grave-post. The flowers that covered it were delicate, and here and there small conical protuberances were let in among them. She turned it round critically. Waldo bent over it lovingly.

"There is one strange thing about it," he said earnestly, putting a finger on one little pyramid. "I made it without these, and I felt something was wrong; I tried many changes, and at last I let these in, and then it was right. But why was it? They are not beautiful in themselves."

"They relieve the monotony of the smooth leaves, I suppose."

He shook his head as over a weighty matter.

"The sky is monotonous," he said, "when it is blue, and yet it is beautiful. I have thought of that often; but it is not monotony and it is not variety makes beauty. What is it? The sky, and your face,

---

1 Deuteronomy 34:1.

and this box—the same thing is in them all, only more in the sky and in your face. But what is it?"

She smiled.

"So you are at your old work still. Why, why, why? What is the reason? It is enough for me," she said, "if I find out what is beautiful and what is ugly, what is real and what is not. Why it is there, and over the final cause of things in general, I don't trouble myself; there must be one, but what is it to me? If I howl to all eternity I shall never get hold of it; and if I did I might be no better off. But you Germans are born with an aptitude for burrowing; you can't help yourselves.[1] You must sniff after reasons, just as that dog must after a mole. He knows perfectly well he will never catch it, but he's under the imperative necessity of digging for it."

"But he *might* find it."

"*Might!*—but he never has and never will. Life is too short to run after mights; we must have certainties."

She tucked the box under arm and was about to walk on, when Gregory Rose, with shining spurs, an ostrich feather in his hat, and a silver-headed whip, careered past. He bowed gallantly as he went by. They waited till the dust of the horse's hoofs had laid itself.

"There," said Lyndall, "goes a true woman—one born for the sphere that some women have to fill without being born for it. How happy he would be sewing frills into his little girl's frocks, and how pretty he would look sitting in a parlour, with a rough man making love to him! Don't you think so?"

"I shall not stay here when he is master," Waldo answered, not able to connect any kind of beauty with Gregory Rose.

"I should imagine not. The rule of a woman is tyranny, but the rule of a man-woman grinds fine. Where are you going?"

"Anywhere."

"What to do?"

"See—see everything."

"You will be disappointed."

"And were you?"

---

1 Lyndall links Waldo's questions to those of German idealists as opposed to her own more English and Utilitarian philosophy. In the work of German writers like F.W.J. von Schelling (1775-1854) and G.W.F. Hegel (1770-1831), individual will is the primary reality and the universal will the driving force in history. Spencer's synthetic philosophy, which Lyndall advocates, combines a progressive view of human society with the idea of biological evolution through "survival of the fittest."

"Yes; and you will be more so. I want some things that men and the world give, you do not. If you have a few yards of earth to stand on, and a bit of blue over you, and something that you cannot see to dream about, you have all that you need, all that you know how to use. But I like to see real men. Let them be as disagreeable as they please, they are more interesting to me than flowers, or trees, or stars, or any other thing under the sun. Sometimes," she added, walking on, and shaking the dust daintily from her skirts, "when I am not too busy trying to find a new way of doing my hair that will show my little neck to better advantage, or over other work of that kind, sometimes it amuses me intensely to trace out the resemblance between one man and another: to see how Tant' Sannie and I, you and Bonaparte, St. Simon on his pillar,[1] and the Emperor dining off larks' tongues, are one and the same compound, merely mixed in different proportions. What is microscopic in one is largely developed in another; what is a rudimentary in one man is an active organ in another; but all things are in all men, and one soul is the model of all. We shall find nothing new in human nature after we have once carefully dissected and analysed the one being we ever shall truly know—ourself. The Kaffir girl threw some coffee on my arm in bed this morning; I felt displeased, but said nothing. Tant' Sannie would have thrown the saucer at her and sworn for an hour; but the feeling would be the same irritated displeasure. If a huge animated stomach like Bonaparte were put under a glass by a skilful mental microscopist, even he would be found to have an embryonic doubling somewhere indicative of a heart, and rudimentary buddings that might have become conscience and sincerity.—Let me take your arm, Waldo. How full you are of mealie dust.—No, never mind. It will brush off.—And sometimes what is more amusing still than tracing the likeness between man and man, is to trace the analogy there always is between the progress and development of one individual and of a whole nation; or again, between a single nation and the entire human race. It is pleasant when it dawns on you that the one is just the other written out in large letters; and very odd to find all the little follies and virtues, and developments and retrogressions, written out in the big world's

---

1 St. Simeon the Elder of Syria (c. 390–459) was a Christian ascetic who lived on a pillar exposed to the elements. Schreiner may have read about him in Edward Gibbons's *The Decline and Fall of the Roman Empire* (1776–88).

book that you find in your little internal self.[1] It is the most amusing thing I know of; but of course, being a woman, I have not often time for such amusements. Professional duties always first, you know. It takes a great deal of time and thought always to look perfectly exquisite, even for a pretty woman. Is the old buggy still in existence, Waldo?"

"Yes; but the harness is broken."

"Well, I wish you would mend it. You must teach me to drive. I must learn something while I am here. I got the Hottentot girl to show me how to make 'sarsarties'[2] this morning; and Tant' Sannie is going to teach me to make 'kapjes.' I will come and sit with you this afternoon while you mend the harness."

"Thank you."

"No, don't thank me; I come for my own pleasure. I never find any one I can talk to. Women bore me, and men, I talk so to— 'Going to the ball this evening?—Nice little dog that of yours.— Pretty little ears.—So fond of pointer pups!'—And they think me fascinating, charming! Men are like the earth and we are the moon; we turn always one side to them, and they think there is no other, because they don't see it—but there is."

They had reached the house now.

"Tell me when you set to work," she said, and walked towards the door.

Waldo stood to look after her, and Doss stood at his side, a look of painful uncertainty depicted on his small countenance, and one little foot poised in the air. Should he stay with his master or go? He looked at the figure with the wide straw hat moving towards the house, and he looked up at his master; then he put down the little paw and went. Waldo watched them both in at the door and then walked away alone. He was satisfied that at least his dog was with her.

---

1 Lyndall's musings on the parallels between the development of individual lives, nations, and humanity in general reflect several currents of thought derived from evolutionary theory in the nineteenth century. The "recapitulation theory" saw in the growth of the human embryo a repetition of the stages of development of the species as a whole, and therefore an underlying unity in nature. Analogies between human biological development and social evolution helped lend a scientific character to nineteenth-century social thought. In addition to Spencer (see Appendix B), Schreiner read Darwin's *Variations of Plants and Animals* (1868) and Carl Vogt's *Lectures on Man* (1864).

2 Variant of sosatie: cubes of curried or spiced meat on a skewer.

Chapter V.
Tant' Sannie Holds an Upsitting,
and Gregory Writes a Letter.

It was just after sunset, and Lyndall had not yet returned from her first driving-lesson, when the lean coloured woman standing at the corner of the house to enjoy the evening breeze, saw coming along the road a strange horseman. Very narrowly she surveyed him, as slowly he approached. He was attired in the deepest mourning, the black crape round his tall hat totally concealing the black felt, and nothing but a dazzling shirt-front relieving the funereal tone of his attire. He rode much forward in his saddle, with his chin resting on the uppermost of his shirt-studs, and there was an air of meek subjection to the will of Heaven, and to what might be in store for him, that bespoke itself even in the way in which he gently urged his steed. He was evidently in no hurry to reach his destination, for the nearer he approached to it the slacker did his bridle hang. The coloured woman having duly inspected him, dashed into the dwelling.

"Here is another one," she cried— "a widower; I see it by his hat."

"Good Lord!" said Tant' Sannie; "it's the seventh I've had this month; but the men know where sheep and good looks and money in the bank are to be found," she added, winking knowingly. "How does he look?"

"Nineteen, weak eyes, white hair, little round nose," said the maid.

"Then it's he! then it's he!" said Tant' Sannie triumphantly: "Little Piet Vander Walt, whose wife died last month—two farms, twelve thousand sheep. I've not seen him, but my sister-in-law told me about him, and I dreamed about him last night."

Here Piet's black hat appeared in the doorway, and the Boer-woman drew herself up in dignified silence, extended the tips of her fingers, and motioned solemnly to a chair. The young man seated himself, sticking his feet as far under it as they would go, and said mildly—

"I am Little Piet Vander Walt, and my father is Big Piet Vander Walt."

Tant' Sannie said solemnly, "Yes."

"Aunt," said the young man, starting up spasmodically, "can I off-saddle?"

"Yes."

He seized his hat, and disappeared with a rush through the door. "I told you so! I knew it!" said Tant' Sannie. "The dear Lord doesn't send dreams for nothing. Didn't I tell you this morning that I dreamed of a great beast like a sheep, with red eyes, and I killed it? Wasn't the white wool his hair, and the red eyes his weak eyes, and my killing him meant marriage? Get supper ready quickly: the sheep's inside and roaster-cakes. We shall sit up to-night."

To young Piet Vander Walt that supper was a period of intense torture. There was something overawing in that assembly of English people, with their incomprehensible speech; and moreover, it was his first courtship: his first wife had courted him, and ten months of severe domestic rule had not raised his spirit nor courage. He ate little, and when he raised a morsel to his lips glanced guiltily round to see if he were not observed. He had put three rings on his little finger, with the intention of sticking it out stiffly when he raised a coffee-cup; now the little finger was curled miserably among its fellows. It was small relief when the meal was over, and Tant' Sannie and he repaired to the front room. Once seated there, he set his knees close together, stood his black hat upon them, and wretchedly turned the brim up and down. But supper had cheered Tant' Sannie, who found it impossible longer to maintain that decorous silence, and whose heart yearned over the youth.

"I was related to your aunt Selena who died," said Tant' Sannie. "My mother's step-brother's child was married to her father's brother's step-nephew's niece."

"Yes, aunt," said the young man, "I knew we were related."

"It was her cousin," said Tant' Sannie, now fairly on the flow, "who had the cancer cut out of her breast by the other doctor, who was not the right doctor they sent for, but who did it quite as well."

"Yes, aunt," said the young man.

"I've heard about it often," said Tant' Sannie. "And he was the son of the old doctor that they say died on Christmas day; but I don't know if that's true. People do tell such awful lies. Why should he die on Christmas day more than any other day?"

"Yes, aunt, why?" said the young man meekly.

"Did you ever have the toothache?" asked Tant' Sannie.

"No, aunt."

"Well, they say that doctor,—not the son of the old doctor that died on Christmas day, the other that didn't come when he was sent for,—he gave such good stuff for the toothache that if you opened the bottle in the room where any one was bad they got better directly. You could see it was good stuff," said Tant' Sannie. "It tasted horrid. *That* was a real doctor! He used to give a bottle so high," said the Boer-woman, raising her hand a foot from the table, "you could drink at it for a month and it wouldn't get done, and the same medicine was good for all sorts of sicknesses—croup, measles, jaundice, dropsy. *Now* you have to buy a new kind for each sickness. The doctors aren't so good as they used to be."

"No, aunt," said the young man, who was trying to gain courage to stick out his legs and clink his spurs together. He did so at last.

Tant' Sannie had noticed the spurs before; but she thought it showed a nice manly spirit, and her heart warmed yet more to the youth.

"Did you ever have convulsions when you were a baby?" asked Tant' Sannie.

"Yes," said the young man.

"Strange!" said Tant' Sannie; "I had convulsions too. Wonderful that we should be so much alike!"

"Aunt," said the young man explosively, "can we sit up to-night?"

Tant' Sannie hung her head and half closed her eyes; but finding that her little wiles were thrown away, the young man staring fixedly at his hat, she simpered "Yes," and went away to fetch candles.

In the dining-room Em worked at her machine, and Gregory sat close beside her, his great blue eyes turned to the window where Lyndall leaned out talking to Waldo.

Tant' Sannie took two candles out of the cupboard and held them up triumphantly, winking all round the room.

"He's asked for them," she said.

"Does he want them for his horse's rubbed back?" asked Gregory, new to up-country life.

"No," said Tant' Sannie indignantly; "we're going to sit-up!" and she walked off in triumph with the candles.

Nevertheless, when all the rest of the house had retired, when the long candle was lighted, when the coffee-kettle was filled, when she sat in the elbow-chair, with her lover on a chair close beside her, and when the vigil of the night was fairly begun, she began to find it wearisome. The young man looked chilly, and said nothing.

"Won't you put your feet on my stove?" said Tant' Sannie.

"No, thank you, aunt," said the young man, and both lapsed into silence.

At last Tant' Sannie, afraid of going to sleep, tapped a strong cup of coffee for herself and handed another to her lover. This visibly revived both.

"How long were you married, cousin?"

"Ten months, aunt."

"How old was your baby?"

"Three days when it died."

"It's very hard when we must give our husbands and wives to the Lord," said Tant' Sannie.

"Very," said the young man; "but it's the Lord's will."

"Yes," said Tant' Sannie, and sighed.

"She was such a good wife, aunt: I've known her break a churn-stick over a maid's head for only letting dust come on a milk-cloth."

Tant' Sannie felt a twinge of jealousy. She had never broke a churn-stick on a maid's head.

"I hope your wife made a good end," she said.

"Oh, beautiful, aunt: she said up a psalm and two hymns and a half before she died."

"Did she leave any messages?" asked Tant' Sannie.

"No," said the young man; "but the night before she died I was lying at the foot of her bed; I felt her foot kick me.

"'Piet,' she said.

"'Annie, my heart,' said I.

"'My little baby that died yesterday has been here, and it stood over the waggon-box,' she said.

"'What did it say?' I asked.

"'It said that if I died you must marry a fat woman.'

"'I will,' I said, and I went to sleep again. Presently she woke me.

"The little baby has been here again, and it says you must marry a woman over thirty, and who's had two husbands.'

"I didn't go to sleep after that for a long time, aunt; but when I did she woke me.

"'The baby has been here again,' she said, 'and it says you must-n't marry a woman with a mole.' I told her I wouldn't; and the next day she died."

"That was a vision from the Redeemer," said Tant' Sannie.

The young man nodded his head mournfully. He thought of a younger sister of his wife's who was not fat, and who *had* a mole, and of whom his wife had always been jealous, and he wished the little baby had liked better staying in heaven than coming and standing over the waggon-chest.

"I suppose that's why you came to me," said Tant' Sannie.

"Yes, aunt. And pa said I ought to get married before shearing-time. It is bad if there's no one to see after things then; and the maids waste such a lot of fat."

"When do you want to get married?"

"Next month, aunt," said the young man in a tone of hopeless resignation. "May I kiss you, aunt?"

"Fie! fie!" said Tant' Sannie, and then gave him a resounding kiss. "Come, draw your chair a little closer," she said, and, their elbows now touching, they sat on through the night.

The next morning at dawn, as Em passed through Tant' Sannie's bedroom, she found the Boer-woman pulling off her boots preparatory to climbing into bed.

"Where is Piet Vander Walt?"

"Just gone," said Tant' Sannie; "and I am going to marry him this day four weeks. I am dead sleepy," she added; "the stupid thing doesn't know how to talk love-talk at all," and she climbed into the four-poster, clothes and all, and drew the quilt up to her chin.

On the day preceding Tant' Sannie's wedding, Gregory Rose sat in the blazing sun on the stone wall behind his daub-and-wattle house. It was warm, but he was intently watching a small buggy that was being recklessly driven over the bushes in the direction of the farmhouse. Gregory never stirred till it had vanished; then, finding the stones hot, he slipped down and walked into the house. He kicked the little pail that lay in the doorway, and sent it into one corner; that did him good. Then he sat down on the box, and began cutting letters out of a piece of newspaper. Finding that the snippings littered the floor, he picked them up and began scribbling on his blotting paper. He tried the effect of different initials before the name Rose: G. Rose, E. Rose, L. Rose, L. Rose, L. L. L. L. Rose. When he had covered the sheet, he looked at it discontentedly a little while, then suddenly began to write a letter.

"Beloved Sister,

"It is a long while since I last wrote to you, but I have had no time. This is the first morning I have been at home since I don't know when. Em always expects me to go down to the farm-house in the morning; but I didn't feel as though I could stand the ride to-day.

"I have much news for you.

"Tant' Sannie, Em's Boer step-mother, is to be married to-morrow. She is gone to town today, and the wedding feast is to be at her brother's farm. Em and I are going to ride over on horseback, but her cousin is going to ride in the buggy with that German. I don't think I've written to you since she came back from school. I don't think you would like her at all, Jemima; there's something so proud about her. She thinks just because she's handsome there's nobody good enough to talk to her, and just as if there had nobody else but her been to boarding-school before.

"They are going to have a grand affair to-morrow: all the Boers about are coming, and they are going to dance all night; but I don't think I shall dance at all; for, as Em's cousin says, these Boer dances are low things. I am sure I only danced at the last to please Em. I don't know why she is fond of dancing. Em talked of our being married on the same day as Tant' Sannie; but I said it would be nicer for her if she waited till the shearing was over, and I took her down to see you. I suppose she will have to live with us (Em's cousin, I mean), as she has not anything in the world but a poor fifty pounds. I don't like her *at all*, Jemima, and I don't think you would. She's got such queer ways: she's always driving about in a gig with that low German; and I don't think it's at all the thing for a woman to be going about with a man she's not engaged to. Do you? If it was me now, of course, who am a kind of connection, it would be different. The way she treats me, considering that I am so soon to be her cousin, is not at all nice. I took down my album the other day with your likenesses in it, and I told her she could look at it, and put it down close to her; but she just said, Thank you, and never even touched it, as much as to say—What are your relations to me?

"She gets the wildest horses in that buggy, and a horrid snappish little cur belonging to the German sitting in front, and then she drives out alone. I don't think it's at all proper for a woman to drive out alone; I wouldn't allow it if she was *my* sister. The other morning, I don't know how it happened, I was going in the way from which she was coming, and that little beast—they call him Doss— began to bark when he saw me—he always does, the little wretch— and the horses began to spring, and kicked the splash-board all to pieces. It was a sight to see, Jemima! She has got the littlest hands I ever saw—I could hold them both in one of mine, and not know that I'd got anything except that they were so soft; but she held those horses in as though they were made of iron. When I wanted to help her she said, 'No, thank you; I can manage them myself. I've got a pair of bits that would break their jaws if I used them well,' and she laughed and drove away. It's so unwomanly.

"Tell father my hire of the ground will not be out for six months, and before that Em and I will be married. My pair of birds is breeding now, but I haven't been down to see them for three days. I don't seem to care about anything any more. I don't know what it is: I'm not well. If I go into town on Saturday I will let the doctor examine me; but perhaps she'll go in herself. It's a very strange thing, Jemima, but she never will send her letters to post by me. If I ask her she has none, and the very next day she goes in and posts them herself. You mustn't say anything about it, Jemima, but twice I've brought her letters from the post in a gentleman's hand, and I'm sure they were both from the same person, because I noticed every little mark, even the dotting of the *i*'s. Of course it's nothing to *me*; but for Em's sake I can't help feeling an interest in her, however much I may dislike her myself; and I hope she's up to nothing. I pity the man who marries *her*; I wouldn't be him for *anything*. If I had a wife with pride I'd make her give it up, *sharp*. I don't believe in a man who can't make a woman obey him. Now Em— I'm very fond of her, as you know—but if I tell her to put on a certain dress, that dress she puts on; and if I tell her to sit on a certain seat, on that seat she sits; and if I tell her not to speak to a certain individual, she does not speak to them. If a man lets a woman do what he doesn't like *he's a muff*.

"Give my love to mother and the children. The 'veld' here is looking pretty good, and the sheep are better since we washed them. Tell father the dip he recommended is very good.

"Em sends her love to you. She is making me some woollen shirts; but they don't fit me so nicely as those mother made me.

"Write soon to
"Your loving brother,
"Gregory.

"P.S.—She drove past just now; I was sitting on the kraal wall right before her eyes, and she never even bowed.
"G. N. R."

Chapter VI.
A Boer-Wedding.

"I didn't know before you were so fond of riding hard," said Gregory to his little betrothed.

They were cantering slowly on the road to Oom Muller's on the morning of the wedding.

"Do you call this riding hard?" asked Em in some astonishment.

"Of course I do! It's enough to break the horses' necks, and knock one up for the whole day besides," he added testily; then twisted his head to look at the buggy that came on behind. "I thought Waldo was such a mad driver; they are taking it easily enough to-day," said Gregory. "One would think the black stallions were lame."

"I suppose they want to keep out of our dust," said Em. "See, they stand still as soon as we do."

Perceiving this to be the case, Gregory rode on.

"It's all that horse of yours: she kicks up such a confounded dust, I can't stand it myself," he said.

Meanwhile the cart came on slowly enough.

"Take the reins," said Lyndall, "and make them walk. I want to rest and watch their hoofs today—not to be exhilarated; I am so tired."

She leaned back in her corner, and Waldo drove on slowly in the grey dawn light along the level road. They passed the very milk-bush behind which so many years before the old German had found the Kaffir woman. But their thoughts were not with him that morning: they were the thoughts of the young, that run out to meet the future, and labour in the present. At last he touched her arm.

"What is it?"

"I feared you had gone to sleep, and might be jolted out," he said; "you sat so quietly."

"No; do not talk to me; I am not asleep;" but after a time she said suddenly, "It must be a terrible thing to bring a human being into the world."

Waldo looked round; she sat drawn into the corner, her blue cloud wound tightly about her, and she still watched the horses' feet. Having no comment to offer on her somewhat unexpected remark, he merely touched up his horses.

"I have no conscience, none," she added; "but I would not like to bring a soul into this world. When it sinned and when it suf-fered something like a dead hand would fall on me,—'You did it, you, for your own pleasure you created this thing! See your work!' If it lived to be eighty it would always hang like a millstone round my neck, have the right to demand good from me, and curse me for its sorrow. A parent is only like to God: if his work turns out bad so much the worse for him; he *dare* not wash his hands of it. Time and years can never bring the day when you can say to your child, 'Soul, what have I to do with you?'"

Waldo said dreamily,—

"It is a marvellous thing that one soul should have power to cause another."

She heard the words as she heard the beating of the horses' hoofs; her thoughts ran on in their own line.

"They say, 'God sends the little babies.' Of all the dastardly revolting lies men tell to suit themselves, I hate that most. I suppose my father said so when he knew he was dying of consumption, and my mother when she knew she had nothing to support me on, and they created me to feed like a dog from stranger hands. Men do not say God sends the books, or the newspaper articles, or the machines they make; and then sigh, and shrug their shoulders, and say they can't help it. Why do they say so about other things? Liars! 'God sends the little babies!'" She struck her foot fretfully against the splashboard. "The small children say so earnestly. *They* touch the little stranger reverently who has just come from God's far country, and they peep about the room to see if not one white feather has dropped from the wing of the angel that brought him. On their lips the phrase means much; on all others it is a *deliberate lie*. Noticeable too," she said, dropping in an instant from the passionate into a low, mocking tone, "when people are married, though they should have sixty children, they throw the whole *onus* on God. When they are not, we hear nothing about God's having sent them. When there has been no legal contract between the parents, who sends the little children then? The Devil perhaps!" she laughed her little silvery, mocking laugh. "Odd that some men should come from hell and some from heaven, and yet all look so much alike when they get here."

Waldo wondered at her. He had not the key to her thoughts, and did not see the string on which they were strung. She drew her cloud tighter about her.

"It must be very nice to believe in the Devil," she said; "I wish I did. If it would be of any use I would pray three hours night and morning on my bare knees, 'God, let me believe in Satan.' He is so useful to those people who do. They may be as selfish and as sensual as they please, and, between God's will and the Devil's action, always have some one to throw their sin on. But we, wretched unbelievers, we bear our own burdens; we must say, 'I myself did it, I. Not God, not Satan; I myself!' That is the sting that strikes deep.

Waldo," she said gently, with a sudden and complete change of manner, "I like you so much, I love you." She rested her cheek softly against his shoulder. "When I am with you I never know that I am a woman and you are a man; I only know that we are both things that think. Other men when I am with them, whether I love them or not, they are mere bodies to me; but you are a spirit; I like you. Look," she said quickly, sinking back into her corner, "what a pretty pinkness there is on all the hilltops! The sun will rise in a moment."

Waldo lifted his eyes to look round over the circle of golden hills; and the horses, as the first sunbeams touched them, shook their heads and champed their bright bits, till the brass settings in their harness glittered again.

It was eight o'clock when they neared the farmhouse: a red-brick building, with kraals to the right and a small orchard to the left. Already there were signs of unusual life and bustle: one cart, a waggon, and a couple of saddles against the wall betokened the arrival of a few early guests, whose numbers would soon be largely increased. To a Dutch country wedding guests start up in numbers astonishing to one who has merely ridden through the plains of sparsely-inhabited 'karroo.'

As the morning advances, riders on many shades of steeds appear from all directions, and add their saddles to the long rows against the walls, shake hands, drink coffee, and stand about outside in groups to watch the arriving carts and ox-waggons, as they are unburdened of their heavy freight of massive Tantes and comely daughters, followed by swarms of children of all sizes, dressed in all manner of print and moleskin, who are taken care of by Hottentot, Kaffir, and half-caste nurses, whose many-shaded complexions, ranging from light yellow up to ebony black, add variety to the animated scene. Everywhere is excitement and bustle, which gradually increases as the time for the return of the wedding party approaches. Preparations for the feast are actively advancing in the kitchen; coffee is liberally handed round, and amid a profound sensation, and the firing of guns, the horse-waggon draws up, and the wedding party alight. Bride and bridegroom, with their attendants, march solemnly to the marriage-chamber, where bed and box are decked out in white, with ends of ribbon and artificial flowers, and where on a row of chairs the party solemnly seat themselves. After a time bridesmaid and best man rise, and conduct in with ceremony each individual guest, to wish success and to kiss bride and bridegroom. Then the feast is set on the table, and it is almost sunset before the dishes are cleared away, and the pleasure of the day begins. Everything is removed from the great front room, and the mud floor, well rubbed with bullock's blood, glistens like polished mahogany. The female portion of the assembly flock into the side-rooms to attire themselves for the evening; and re-issue clad in white muslin, and gay with bright ribbons and brass jewellery. The dancing begins as the first tallow candles are stuck up about the walls, the music coming from a couple of fiddlers in a corner of the room. Bride and bridegroom open the ball, and the floor is soon covered with whirling couples, and every one's spirits rise. The bridal pair mingle freely in the throng, and here and there a musical man sings vigorously as he drags his partner through the Blue Water or John Speriwig; boys shout and applaud, and the enjoyment and confusion are intense, till eleven o'clock comes. By this time the children who swarm in the side-rooms are not to be kept quiet longer, even by hunches of bread and cake; there is a general howl and wail, that rises yet higher than the scraping of fiddles, and mothers rush from their partners to knock small heads together, and cuff little nursemaids, and force the wailers down into unoccupied corners of beds, under tables, and behind boxes. In half-an-hour every variety of childish snore is heard on all sides, and it has become perilous to raise or set down a foot in any of the side-rooms lest a small head or hand should be crushed. Now too the busy feet have broken the solid coating of the floor, and a cloud of fine dust arises, that makes a yellow halo round the candles, and sets asthmatic people coughing, and grows denser, till to recognise any one on the opposite side of the room becomes impossible, and a partner's face is seen through a yellow mist.

At twelve o'clock the bride is led to the marriage-chamber and undressed; the lights are blown out, and the bridegroom is brought to the door by the best man, who gives him the key; then the door is shut and locked, and the revels rise higher than ever. There is no thought of sleep till morning, and no unoccupied spot where sleep may be found.

It was at this stage of the proceedings on the night of Tant' Sannie's wedding that Lyndall sat near the doorway in one of the side-rooms, to watch the dancers as they appeared and disappeared in the yellow cloud of dust. Gregory sat moodily in a corner of the large dancing-room. His little betrothed touched his arm.

"I wish you would go and ask Lyndall to dance with you," she said; "she must be so tired; she has sat still the whole evening."

"I have asked her three times," replied her lover shortly. "I'm not

going to be *her* dog, and creep to`her` feet, just to give her the pleasure of kicking me—not for you, Em, nor for anybody else."

"Oh, I didn't know you had asked her, Greg," said his little
betrothed humbly; and she went away to pour out coffee.

Nevertheless, some time after Gregory found he had shifted so
far round the room as to be close to the door where Lyndall sat.
After standing for some time he inquired whether he might not
bring her a cup of coffee. She declined: but still he stood on (why
should he not stand there as well as anywhere else?), and then he
stepped into the bedroom.

"May I not bring you a stove, Miss Lyndall, to put your feet
on?"

"Thank you."

He sought for one, and put it under her feet.

"There is a draught from that broken window; shall I stuff
something in the pane?"

"No; we want air."

Gregory looked round, but, nothing else suggesting itself, he sat
down on a box on the opposite side of the door. Lyndall sat before
him, her chin resting in her hand; her eyes, steel-grey by day but
black by night, looked through the doorway into the next room.
After a time he thought she had entirely forgotten his proximity,
and he dared to inspect the little hands and neck as he never dared
when he was in momentary dread of the eyes being turned upon
him. She was dressed in black, which seemed to take her yet further from the white-clad, gewgawed[1] women about her; and the
little hands were white, and the diamond ring glittered. Where had
she got that ring? He bent forward a little and tried to decipher the
letters, but the candle-light was too faint. When he looked up her
eyes were fixed on him. She was looking at him—not, Gregory
felt, as she had ever looked at him before; not as though he were a
stump or a stone that chance had thrown in her way. To-night,
whether it were critically, or kindly, or unkindly he could not tell,
but she looked at him, at the man, Gregory Rose, with attention.
A vague elation filled him. He clenched his fist tight to think of
some good idea he might express to her; but of all those profound
things he had pictured himself as saying to her, when he sat alone
in the daub-and-wattle house,[2] not one came. He said at last,

---

1 Gewgaw is a gaudy trifle, ornament, or bauble.
2 Cottage made from interwoven twigs plastered with clay or mud.

"These Boer dances are very low things;" and then, as soon as it had gone from him, he thought it was not a clever remark, and wished it back.

Before Lyndall replied Em looked in at the door.

"Oh, come," she said; "they are going to have the cushion-dance. I do not want to kiss any of these fellows. Take me quickly." She slipped her hand into Gregory's arm.

"It is so dusty, Em, do you care to dance any more?" he asked, without rising.

"Oh, I do not mind the dust, and the dancing rests me."

But he did not move.

"I feel tired; I do not think I shall dance again," he said.

Em withdrew her hand, and a young farmer came to the door and bore her off.

"I have often imagined," remarked Gregory—but Lyndall had risen.

"I am tired," she said. "I wonder where Waldo is; he must take me home. These people will not leave off till morning, I suppose; it is three already."

She made her way past the fiddlers, and a bench full of tired dancers, and passed out at the front door. On the 'stoep'[1] a group of men and boys were smoking, peeping in at the windows, and cracking coarse jokes. Waldo was certainly not among them, and she made her way to the carts and waggons drawn up at some distance from the homestead.

"Waldo," she said, peering into a large cart, "is that you? I am so dazed with the tallow candles, I see nothing."

He had made himself a place between the two seats. She climbed up and sat on the sloping floor in front.

"I thought I should find you here," she said, drawing her skirt up about her shoulders. "You must take me home presently, but not now."

She leaned her head on the seat near to his, and they listened in silence to the fitful twanging of the fiddles as the night-wind bore it from the farmhouse, and to the ceaseless thud of the dancers, and the peals of gross laughter. She stretched out her little hand to feel for his.

"It is so nice to lie here and hear that noise," she said. "I like to

---

1 A raised, paved platform or terrace running the whole length of the front of a house.

feel that strange life beating up against me. I like to realise forms of life utterly unlike mine." She drew a long breath. "When my own life feels small, and I am oppressed with it, I like to crush together, and see it in a picture, in an instant, a multitude of disconnected unlike phases of human life—a mediæval monk with his string of beads pacing the quiet orchard, and looking up from the grass at his feet to the heavy fruit-trees; little Malay boys playing naked on a shining sea-beach; a Hindoo philosopher alone under his banyan tree, thinking, thinking, thinking, so that in the thought of God he may lose himself; a troop of Bacchanalians[1] dressed in white, with crowns of vine-leaves, dancing along the Roman streets; a martyr on the night of his death looking through the narrow window to the sky, and feeling that already he has the wings that shall bear him up" (she moved her hand dreamily over her face); "an epicurean[2] discoursing at a Roman bath to a knot of his disciples on the nature of happiness; a Kaffir witch-doctor seeking for herbs by moonlight, while from the huts on the hill-side come the sound of dogs barking, and the voices of women and children; a mother giving bread and milk to her children in little wooden basins and singing the evening song. I like to see it all; I feel it run through me—that life belongs to me; it makes my little life larger, it breaks down the narrow walls that shut me in."

She sighed, and drew a long breath.

"Have you made any plan?" she asked him presently.

"Yes," he said, the words coming in jets, with pauses between; "I will take the grey mare,—I will travel first—I will see the world—then I will find work."

"What work?"

"I do not know."

She made a little impatient movement.

"That is no plan; travel—see the world—find work! If you go into the world aimless, without a definite object, dreaming—dreaming, you will be definitely defeated, bamboozled, knocked this way and that. In the end you will stand with your beautiful life all spent, and nothing to show. They talk of genius—it is nothing but

---

1 Bacchus was the Roman name for Dionysus, god of wine. Festivals called Bacchanalia were celebrated in Rome until 186 B.C.

2 One who follows the Greek philosophy of Epicurus. Epicurus (341-270 B.C.) believed that freedom from bodily pain, friendship, and the pleasures of intellectual life were the grounds for human happiness.

this, that a man knows what he can do best, and does it, and nothing else. Waldo," she said, knitting her little fingers closer among his, "I wish I could help you; I wish I could make you see that you must decide what you will be and do. It does not matter what you choose,—be a farmer, business-man, artist, what you will,—but know your aim, and live for that one thing. We have only one life. The secret of success is concentration; wherever there has been a great life, or a great work that has gone before. Taste everything a little, look at everything a little; but live for one thing. Anything is possible to a man who knows his end and moves straight for it, and for it alone. I will show you what I mean," she said, concisely; "words are gas till you condense them into pictures."

"Suppose a woman, young, friendless as I am, the weakest thing on God's earth. But she must make her way through life. What she would be she cannot be because she is a woman; so she looks carefully at herself and the world about her, to see where her path must be made. There is no one to help her; she must help herself. She looks. These things she has—a sweet voice, rich in subtle intonations; a fair, very fair face, with a power of concentrating in itself, and giving expression to, feelings that otherwise must have been dissipated in words; a rare power of entering into other lives unlike her own, and intuitively reading them aright. These qualities she has. How shall she use them? A poet, a writer, needs only the mental; what use has he for a beautiful body that registers clearly mental emotions? And the painter wants an eye for form and colour, and the musician an ear for time and tune, and the mere drudge has no need for mental gifts. But there is one art in which all she has would be used, for which they are all necessary—the delicate expressive body, the rich voice, the power of mental transposition. The actor, who absorbs and then reflects from himself other human lives, needs them all, but needs not much more. This is her end; but how to reach it? Before her are endless difficulties: seas must be crossed, poverty must be endured, loneliness, want. She must be content to wait long before she can even get her feet upon the path. If she has made blunders in the past, if she has weighted herself with a burden which she must bear to the end, she must but bear the burden bravely, and labour on. There is no use in wailing and repentance here: the next world is the place for that; this life is too short. By our errors we see deeper into life. They help us." She waited for a while. "If she does all this,—if she waits patiently, if she is never cast down, never despairs, never forgets her end, moves straight towards it, bending men and things most unlikely to her purpose,—she must succeed at last. Men and things are plastic; they part to the right and left when one comes among them moving in a straight line to one end. I know it by my own little experience," she said. "Long years ago I resolved to be sent to school. It seemed a thing utterly out of my power; but I waited, I watched, I collected clothes, I wrote, took my place at the school; when all was ready I bore with my full force on the Boer-woman, and she sent me at last. It was a small thing; but life is made up of small things, as a body is built up of cells. What has been done in small things can be done in large. Shall be," she said softly.

Waldo listened. To him the words were no confession, no glimpse into the strong, proud, restless heart of the woman. They were general words with a general application. He looked up into the sparkling sky with dull eyes.

"Yes," he said, "but when we lie and think, and think, we see that there is nothing worth doing. The universe is so large, and man is so small——"

She shook her head quickly.

"But we must not think so far; it is madness, it is a disease. We know that no man's work is great, and stands for ever. Moses is dead, and the prophets, and the books that our grandmothers fed on the mould is eating. Your poet and painter and actor,—before the shouts that applaud them have died their names grow strange, they are milestones that the world has passed. Men have set their mark on mankind for ever, as they thought; but time has washed it out as it has washed out mountains and continents." She raised herself on her elbow. "And what, if we *could* help mankind, and leave the traces of our work upon it to the end? Mankind is only an ephemeral blossom on the tree of time; there were others before it opened; there will be others after it has fallen. Where was man in the time of the dicynodont,[1] and when hoary monsters wallowed in the mud? Will he be found in the æons that are to come? We are sparks, we are shadows, we are pollen, which the next wind will carry away. We are dying already; it is all a dream.

"I know that thought. When the fever of living is on us, when the desire to become, to know, to do, is driving us mad, we can use it as an anodyne, to still the fever and cool our beating pulses. But it is a poison, not a food. If we live on it will turn our blood to ice; we might as well be dead. We must not, Waldo; I want your life to

---

1 A fossil reptile found only in the red sandstone of South Africa.

be beautiful, to end in something. You are nobler and stronger than I," she said; "and as much better as one of God's great angels is better than a sinning man. Your life must go for something."

"Yes, we will work," he said.

She moved closer to him and lay still, his black curls touching her smooth little head.

Doss, who had lain at his master's side, climbed over the bench, and curled himself up in her lap. She drew her skirt up over him, and the three sat motionless for a long time.

"Waldo," she said, suddenly, "they are laughing at us."

"Who?" he asked, starting up.

"They—the stars!" she said, softly. "Do you not see? there is a little, white, mocking finger pointing down at us from each one of them! We are talking of to-morrow, and to-morrow, and our hearts are so strong; we are not thinking of something that can touch us softly in the dark, and make us still for ever. They are laughing at us, Waldo."

Both sat looking upwards.

"Do you ever pray?" he asked her in a low voice.

"No."

"I never do; but I might when I look up there. I will tell you," he added, in a still lower voice, "where I could pray. If there were a wall of rock on the edge of a world, and one rock stretched out far, far into space, and I stood alone upon it, alone, with stars above me, and stars below me,—I would not say anything; but the feeling would be prayer."

There was an end to their conversation after that, and Doss fell asleep on her knee. At last the night-wind grew very chilly.

"Ah," she said, shivering, and drawing the skirt about her shoulders, "I am cold. Span-in the horses, and call me when you are ready."

She slipped down and walked towards the house, Doss stiffly following her, not pleased at being roused. At the door she met Gregory.

"I have been looking for you everywhere; may I not drive you home?" he said.

"Waldo drives me," she replied, passing on; and it appeared to Gregory that she looked at him in the old way, without seeing him. But before she had reached the door an idea had occurred to her, for she turned.

"If you wish to drive me you may."

Gregory went to look for Em, whom he found pouring out coffee in the back room. He put his hand quickly on her shoulder.

"You must ride with Waldo; I am going to drive your cousin home."

"But I can't come just now, Greg; I promised Tant' Annie Muller to look after the things while she went to rest a little."

"Well, you can come presently, can't you? I didn't say you were to come now. I'm sick of this thing," said Gregory, turning sharply on his heel. "Why must I sit up the whole night because your step-mother chooses to get married?"

"Oh, its all right, Greg, I only meant——"

But he did not hear her, and a man had come up to have his cup filled.

An hour after Waldo came in to look for her, and found her still busy at the table.

"The horses are ready," he said; "but if you would like to have one dance more I will wait."

She shook her head wearily.

"No; I am quite ready. I want to go."

And soon they were on the sandy road the buggy had travelled an hour before. Their horses, with heads close together, nodding sleepily as they walked in the starlight, you might have counted the rise and fall of their feet in the sand; and Waldo in his saddle nodded drowsily also. Only Em was awake, and watched the starlit road with wide-open eyes. At last she spoke.

"I wonder if all people feel so old, so very old, when they get to be seventeen?"

"Not older than before," said Waldo sleepily, pulling at his bridle.

Presently, she said again,

"I wish I could have been a little child always. You are good then. You are never selfish; you like every one to have everything; but when you are grown-up there are some things you like to have all to yourself, you don't like any one else to have any of them."

"Yes," said Waldo sleepily, and she did not speak again.

When they reached the farmhouse all was dark, for Lyndall had retired as soon as they got home.

Waldo lifted Em from her saddle, and for a moment she leaned her head on his shoulder and clung to him.

"You are very tired," he said, as he walked with her to the door; "let me go in and light a candle for you."

"No, thank you; it is all right," she said. "Good night, Waldo dear."

But when she went in she sat long alone in the dark.

Chapter VII.
Waldo Goes Out to Taste Life,
and Em Stays at Home and Tastes It.

At nine o'clock in the evening, packing his bundles for the next morning's start, Waldo looked up, and was surprised to see Em's yellow head peeping in at his door. It was many a month since she had been there. She said she had made him sandwiches for his journey, and she stayed a while to help him put his goods into the saddle-bags.

"You can leave the old things lying about," she said, "I will lock the room, and keep it waiting for you to come back someday."

To come back some day! Would the bird ever return to its cage? But he thanked her. When she went away he stood on the doorstep holding the candle till she had almost reached the house. But Em was that evening in no hurry to enter, and, instead of going in at the back door, walked with lagging footsteps round the low brick wall that ran before the house. Opposite the open window of the parlour she stopped. The little room, kept carefully closed in Tant' Sannie's time, was well lighted by a paraffin lamp; books and work lay strewn about it, and it wore a bright, habitable aspect. Beside the lamp at the table in the corner sat Lyndall, the open letters and papers of the day's post lying scattered before her, while she perused the columns of a newspaper. At the centre table, with his arms folded on an open paper, which there was not light enough to read, sat Gregory. He was looking at her. The light from the open window fell on Em's little face under its white 'kapje' as she looked in, but no one glanced that way.

"Go and fetch me a glass of water," Lyndall said at last.

Gregory went out to find it; when he put it down at her side she merely moved her head in recognition, and he went back to his seat and his old occupation. Then Em moved slowly away from the window, and through it came in spotted, hard-winged insects, to play round the lamp, till, one by one, they stuck to its glass, and fell to the foot dead.

Ten o'clock struck. Then Lyndall rose, gathered up her papers and letters, and wished Gregory good night. Some time after Em entered; she had been sitting all the while on the loft ladder, and had drawn her 'kapje' down very much over her face.

Gregory was piecing together the bits of an envelope when she came in.

"I thought you were never coming," he said, turning round

quickly, and throwing the fragments on to the floor. "You know I have been shearing all day, and it is ten o'clock already."

"I'm sorry. I did not think you would be going so soon," she said in a low voice.

"I can't hear what you say. What makes you mumble so? Well, good night, Em."

He stooped down hastily to kiss her.

"I want to talk to you, Gregory."

"Well, make haste," he said pettishly. "I'm awfully tired. I've been sitting here all the evening. Why couldn't you come and talk before?"

"I will not keep you long," she answered, very steadily now. "I think Gregory, it would be better if you and I were never to be married."

"Good heavens! Em, what do you mean? I thought you were so fond of me? You always *professed* to be. What on earth have you taken into your head now?"

"I think it would be better," she said, folding her hands over each other, very much as though she were praying.

"Better, Em! What do you mean? Even a woman can't take a freak all about nothing! You must have *some* reason for it, and I'm sure I've done nothing to offend you. I wrote only today to my sister to tell her to come up next month to our wedding, and I've been as affectionate and happy as possible. Come—what's the matter?"

He put his arm half round her shoulder, very loosely.

"I think it would be better," she answered slowly.

"Oh, well," he said, drawing himself up, "if you won't enter into explanations you won't; and I'm not the man to beg and pray—not to any woman, and you know that! If you don't want to marry me I can't oblige you to, of course."

She stood quite still before him.

"You women never *do* know your own minds for two days together; and of course you know the state of your own feelings best; but it's very strange. Have you really made up your mind, Em?"

"Yes."

"Well, I'm very sorry. I'm sure I've not been in anything to blame. A man can't always be billing and cooing; but, as you say, if your feeling for me has changed, it's much better you shouldn't marry me. There's nothing so foolish as to marry some one you don't love; and I only wish for your happiness, I'm sure. I daresay you'll find some one can make you much happier than *I* could; the first person we love is seldom the right one. You are very young; it's quite natural you should change."

She said nothing.

"Things often seem hard at the time, but Providence makes them turn out for the best in the end," said Gregory. "You'll let me kiss you, Em, just for old friendship's sake." He stooped down. "You must look upon me as a dear brother, as a cousin at least; as long as I am on the farm I shall always be glad to help you, Em."

Soon after the brown pony was cantering along the footpath to the daub-and-wattle house, and his master as he rode whistled John Speriwig and the Thorn Kloof Schottische.

The sun had not yet touched the outstretched arms of the prickly pear upon the 'kopje,' and the early cocks and hens still strutted about stiffly after the night's roost, when Waldo stood before the waggon-house saddling the grey mare. Every now and then he glanced up at the old familiar objects: they had a new aspect that morning. Even the cocks, seen in the light of parting, had a peculiar interest, and he listened with conscious attention while one crowed clear and loud as it stood on the pigsty wall. He wished good morning softly to the Kaffir woman who was coming up from the huts to light the fire. He was leaving them all to that old life, and from his height he looked down on them pityingly. So they would keep on crowing, and coming to light fires, when for him that old colourless existence was but a dream.

He went into the house to say good-bye to Em, and then he walked to the door of Lyndall's room to wake her; but she was up, and standing in the doorway.

"So you are ready," she said.

Waldo looked at her with sudden heaviness; the exhilaration died out of his heart. Her grey dressing-gown hung close about her, and below its edge the little bare feet were resting on the threshold.

"I wonder when we shall meet again, Waldo? What you will be, and what I?"

"Will you write to me?" he asked of her.

"Yes; and if I should not, you can still remember, wherever you are, that you are not alone."

"I have left Doss for you," he said.

"Will you not miss him?"

"No; I want you to have him. He loves you better than he loves me."

"Thank you." They stood quiet.

"Good-bye!" she said, putting her little hand in his, and he turned away; but when he reached the door she called to him: "Come back, I want to kiss you." She drew his face down to hers, and held it with both hands, and kissed it on the forehead and mouth. "Good-bye, dear!"

When he looked back the little figure with its beautiful eyes was standing in the doorway still.

Chapter VIII
The Kopje.

"Good morning!"

Em, who was in the store-room measuring the Kaffir's rations, looked up and saw her former lover standing betwixt her and the sunshine. For some days after that evening on which he had ridden home whistling he had shunned her. She might wish to enter into explanations, and he, Gregory Rose, was not the man for that kind of thing. If a woman had once thrown him overboard she must take the consequences, and stand by them. When, however, she showed no inclination to revert to the past, and shunned him more than he shunned her, Gregory softened.

"You must let me call you Em still, and be like a brother to you till I go," he said; and Em thanked him so humbly that he wished she hadn't. It wasn't so easy after that to think himself an injured man.

On that morning he stood some time in the doorway switching his whip, and moving rather restlessly from one leg to the other.

"I think I'll just take a walk up to the camps and see how your birds are getting on. Now Waldo's gone you've no one to see after things. Nice morning, isn't it?" Then he added suddenly, "I'll just go round to the house and get a drink of water first;" and somewhat awkwardly walked off. He might have found water in the kitchen, but he never glanced towards the buckets. In the front room a monkey and two tumblers stood on the centre table; but he merely looked round, peeped into the parlour, looked round again, and then walked out at the front door, and found himself again at the store-room without having satisfied his thirst. "Awfully nice morning this," he said, trying to pose himself in a graceful and indifferent attitude against the door. "It isn't hot and it isn't cold. It's awfully nice."

"Yes," said Em.

"Your cousin, now," said Gregory in an aimless sort of way—"I suppose she's shut up in her room writing letters."

"No," said Em.

"Gone for a drive, I expect? Nice morning for a drive."

"No."

"Gone to see the ostriches, I suppose?"

"No." After a little silence Em added, "I saw her go by the kraals to the 'kopje.'"

Gregory crossed and uncrossed his legs.

"Well, I think I'll just go and have a look about," he said, "and see how things are getting on before I go to the camps. Good-bye; so long."

Em left for a while the bags she was folding and went to the window, the same through which, years before, Bonaparte had watched the slouching figure cross the yard. Gregory walked to the pigsty first, and contemplated the pigs for a few seconds; then turned round, and stood looking fixedly at the wall of the fuel-house as though he thought it wanted repairing; then he started off suddenly with the evident intention of going to the ostrich-camps; then paused, hesitated, and finally walked off in the direction of the 'kopje.'

Then Em went back to the corner, and folded more sacks.

On the other side of the 'kopje' Gregory caught sight of a white tail waving among the stones, and a succession of short, frantic barks told where Doss was engaged in howling imploringly to a lizard who had crept between two stones, and who had not the slightest intention of re-sunning himself at that particular moment.

The dog's mistress sat higher up, under the shelving rock, her face bent over a volume of plays upon her knee. As Gregory mounted the stones she started violently and looked up; then resumed her book.

"I hope I am not troubling you," said Gregory as he reached her side. "If I am I will go away. I just——"

"No; you may stay."

"I fear I startled you."

"Yes; your step was firmer than it generally is. I thought it was that of some one else."

"Who could it be but me?" asked Gregory, seating himself on a stone at her feet.

"Do you suppose you are the only man who would find any-thing to attract him to this 'kopje'?"

"Oh, no," said Gregory.

He was not going to argue that point with her, nor any other; but no old Boer was likely to take the trouble of climbing the 'kopje,' and who else was there?

She continued the study of her book.

"Miss Lyndall," he said at last, "I don't know why it is you never talk to me."

"We had a long conversation yesterday," she said without looking up.

"Yes; but you ask me questions about sheep and oxen. I don't call that talking. You used to talk to Waldo, now," he said, in an aggrieved tone of voice. "I've heard you when I came in, and then you've just left off. You treated me like that from the first day; and you couldn't tell from just looking at me that I couldn't talk about the things you like. I'm sure I know as much about such things as Waldo does," said Gregory, in exceeding bitterness of spirit.

"I do not know which things you refer to. If you will enlighten me I am quite prepared to speak of them," she said, reading as she spoke.

"Oh, you never used to ask Waldo like that," said Gregory, in a more sorely aggrieved tone than ever. "You used just to begin."

"Well, let me see," she said closing her book and folding her hands on it. "There at the foot of the 'kopje' goes a Kaffir; he has nothing on but a blanket; he is a splendid fellow—six feet high, with a magnificent pair of legs. In his leather bag he is going to fetch his rations, and I suppose to kick his wife with his beautiful legs when he gets home. He has a right to; he bought her for two oxen. There is a lean dog going after him, to whom I suppose he never gives more than a bone from which he has sucked the marrow; but his dog loves him, as his wife does. There is something of the master about him in spite of his blackness and wool. See how he brandishes his stick and holds up his head!"

"Oh, but aren't you making fun?" said Gregory, looking doubtfully from her to the Kaffir herd, who rounded the 'kopje.'

"No; I am very serious. He is the most interesting and intelligent thing I can see just now, except, perhaps, Doss. He is profoundly suggestive. Will his race melt away in the heat of a collision with a higher? Are the men of the future to see his bones only in museums—a vestige of one link that spanned between the dog and the white man? He wakes thoughts that run far out into the future and back into the past."[1]

Gregory was not quite sure how to take these remarks. Being about a Kaffir, they appeared to be of the nature of a joke; but, being seriously spoken, they appeared earnest: so he half laughed and half not, to be on the safe side.

"I've often thought so myself. It's funny we should both think the same; I knew we should if once we talked. But there are other things—love, now," he added. "I wonder if we would think alike about that. I wrote an essay on love once; the master said it was the best I ever wrote, and I can remember the first sentence still— 'Love is something that you feel in your heart.'"

"That was a trenchant remark. Can't you remember any more?"

"No," said Gregory, regretfully; "I've forgotten the rest. But tell me what do you think about love?"

A look, half of abstraction, half amusement, played on her lips.

"I don't know much about love," she said, "and I do not like to talk of things I do not understand; but I have heard two opinions. Some say the Devil carried the seed from hell, and planted it on the earth to plague men and make them sin; and some say, that when all the plants in the garden of Eden were pulled up by the roots, one bush that the angels had planted was left growing, and it spread its seed over the whole earth, and its name is love. I do not know which is right—perhaps both. There are different species that go under the same name. There is a love that begins in the head,

---

1   According to Peter Bowler, Spencer believed that "social progress actually improves human nature, so that those races that have not advanced as far as the Europeans already have been left behind as living fossils, doomed to extinction." Spencer's idea of "survival of the fittest" allowed evolutionists to view non-white races as intermediate stages between apes and Europeans (see *Evolution: the History of an Idea*, University of California Press, 1989, 104; 299-306). Gerald Monsman notes that "frequent comparison of natives to animals in nineteenth century accounts is not simply an inconsequential rhetorical formula, but an indication of an ingrained way of looking at the native" (see "Writing the Self on the Imperial Frontier: Olive Schreiner and the Stories of Africa, *The Bucknell Review*, 37 [1993]:150). Lyndall's tone here is ironic, however, and Schreiner most often treats Africans as an oppressed labor force rather than a biologically inferior branch of humanity. See Paula Krebs, "Olive Schreiner's Racialization of South Africa." *Victorian Studies* 40 (Spring 1997): 427-45.

and goes down to the heart, and grows slowly; but it lasts till death, and asks less than it gives. There is another love, that blots out wisdom, that is sweet with the sweetness of life and bitter with the bitterness of death, lasting for an hour; but it is worth having lived a whole life for that hour. I cannot tell, perhaps the old monks were right when they tried to root love out; perhaps the poets are right when they try to water it. It is a blood-red flower, with the colour of sin; but there is always the scent of a god about it."

Gregory would have made a remark; but she said, without noticing,

"There are as many kinds of loves as there are flowers: everlastings that never wither; speedwells that wait for the wind to fan them out of life; blood-red mountain-lillies that pour their voluptuous sweetness out for one day, and lie in the dust at night. There is no flower has the charm of all—the speedwell's purity, the everlasting's strength, the mountain-lily's warmth; but who knows whether there is no love that holds all—friendship, passion, worship?

"Such a love," she said, in her sweetest voice, "will fall on the surface of strong, cold, selfish life as the sunlight falls on a torpid winter world; there, where the trees are bare, and the ground frozen, till it rings to the step like iron, and the water is solid, and the air is sharp as a two-edged knife, that cuts the unwary. But, when its sun shines on it, through its whole dead crust a throbbing yearning wakes: the trees feel him, and every knot and bud swell, aching to open to him. The brown seeds, who have slept deep under the ground, feel him, and he gives them strength, till they break through the frozen earth, and lift two tiny, trembling green hands in love to him. And he touches the water, till down to its depths it feels him and melts, and it flows, and the things, strange sweet things that were locked up in it, it sings as it runs, for love of him. Each plant tries to bear at least one fragrant little flower for him; and the world that was dead lives, and the heart that was dead and self-centred throbs, with an upward, outward yearning, and it has become that which it seemed impossible ever to become. There, does that satisfy you?" she asked, looking down at Gregory. "Is that how you like me to talk?"

"Oh, yes," said Gregory, "that is what I have already thought. We have the same thoughts about everything. How strange!"

"Very," said Lyndall, working with her little toe at a stone in the ground before her.

Gregory felt he must sustain the conversation. The only thing he could think of was to recite a piece of poetry. He knew he had learnt many about love; but the only thing that would come into his mind now was the 'Battle *of Hohenlinden*'[1] and '*Not a drum was heard*,'[2] neither of which seemed to bear directly on the subject on hand.

But unexpected relief came to him from Doss, who, too deeply lost in contemplation of his crevice, was surprised by the sudden descent of the stone Lyndall's foot had loosened, which, rolling against his little front paw, carried away a piece of white skin. Doss stood on three legs, holding up the paw with an expression of extreme self-commiseration; he then proceeded to hop slowly upwards in search of sympathy.

"You have hurt that dog," said Gregory.

"Have I?" she replied indifferently, and re-opened the book, as though to resume her study of the play.

"He's a nasty, snappish little cur!" said Gregory, calculating from her manner that the remark would be endorsed. "He snapped at my horse's tail yesterday, and nearly made it throw me. I wonder his master didn't take him, instead of leaving him here to be a nuisance to all of us!"

Lyndall seemed absorbed in her play; but he ventured another remark.

"Do you think now, Miss Lyndall, that he'll ever have anything in the world,—that German, I mean,—money enough to support a wife on, and all that sort of thing? *I* don't. He's what *I* call a soft."

She was spreading her skirt out softly with her left hand for the dog to lie down on it.

"I think I *should* be rather astonished if he ever became a respectable member of society," she said. "I don't expect to see him the possessor of bank-shares, the chairman of a divisional council, and the father of a large family; wearing a black hat, and going to church twice on a Sunday. He would rather astonish me if he came to such an end."

"Yes; I don't expect *anything* of him either," said Gregory, zealously.

"Well, I don't know," said Lyndall; "there are some small things I rather look to him for. If he were to invent wings, or carve a stat-

---

1 Poem by Thomas Campbell (1777-1844).
2 First words of "The Burial of Sir John Moore at Corunna" by Charles Wolfe (1791-1823).

ue that one might look at for half-an-hour without wanting to look at something else, I should not be surprised. He may do some little thing of that kind perhaps, when he has done fermenting and the sediment has all gone to the bottom."

Gregory felt that what she said was not wholly intended as blame.

"Well, I don't know," he said sulkily; "to me he looks like a fool. To walk about always in that dead-and-alive sort of way, muttering to himself like an old Kaffir witch-doctor! He works hard enough, but it's always as though he didn't know what he was doing. You don't know how he looks to a person who sees him for the first time."

Lyndall was softly touching the little sore foot as she read, and Doss, to show he liked it, licked her hand.

"But, Miss Lyndall," persisted Gregory, "what do you really think of him?"

"I think," said Lyndall, "that he is like a thorn-tree which grows up very quietly, without any one's caring for it, and one day suddenly breaks out into yellow blossoms."

"And what do you think I am like?" asked Gregory hopefully.

Lyndall looked up from her book.

"Like a little tin duck floating on a dish of water, that comes after a piece of bread stuck on a needle, and the more the needle pricks it the more it comes on."

"Oh, you *are* making fun of me now, you really are!" said Gregory, feeling wretched. "You *are* making fun, aren't you, now?"

"Partly. It is always diverting to make comparisons."

"Yes; but you don't compare me to anything nice, and you do other people. What is Em like, now?"

"The accompaniment of a song. She fills up the gaps in other people's lives, and is always number two; but I think she is like many accompaniments—a great deal better than the song she is to accompany."

"She is not half so good as you are?" said Gregory, with a burst of uncontrollable ardour.

"She is so much better than I, that her little finger has more goodness in it than my whole body. I hope you may not live to find out the truth of that fact."

"You are like an angel," he said, the blood rushing to his head and face.

"Yes, probably; angels are of many orders."

"You are the one being that I love?" said Gregory, quivering; "I thought I loved before, but I know now! Do not be angry with me. I know you could never like me; but, if I might but always be near you to serve you, I would be utterly, utterly happy. I would ask nothing in return! If you could only take everything I have and use it; I want nothing but to be of use to you."

She looked at him for a few moments.

"How do you know," she said slowly, "that you could not do something to serve me? You could serve me by giving me your name."

He started, and turned his burning face to her.

"You are very cruel; you are ridiculing me," he said.

"No, I am not, Gregory. What I am saying is plain, matter-of-fact business. If you are willing to give me your name within three weeks' time, I am willing to marry you; if not, well. I want nothing more than your name. That is a clear proposal, is it not?"

He looked up. Was it contempt, loathing, pity, that moved in the eyes above? He could not tell; but he stooped over the little foot and kissed it.

She smiled.

"Do you really mean it?" he whispered.

"Yes. You wish to serve me, and to have nothing in return!—you shall have what you wish." She held out her fingers for Doss to lick.— "Do you see this dog? He licks my hand because I love him; and I allow him to. Where I do not love I do not allow it. I believe you love me; I too could love so, that to lie under the foot of the thing I loved would be more heaven than to lie in the breast of another. Come! Let us go. Carry the dog," she added; "he will not bite you if I put him in your arms. So—do not let his foot hang down."

They descended the 'kopje.' At the bottom he whispered,—

"Would you not take my arm, the path is very rough?"

She rested her fingers lightly on it.

"I may yet change my mind about marrying you before the time comes. It is very likely. Mark you!" she said, turning round on him; "I remember your words:—*You will give everything, and expect nothing. The knowledge that you are serving me is to be your reward; and you will have that. You will serve me, and greatly. The reasons I have for marrying you I need not inform you of now; you will probably discover some of them before long."

"I only want to be of some use to you," he said.

It seemed to Gregory that there were pulses in the soles of his feet, and the ground shimmered as on a summer's day. They walked round the foot of the 'kopje,' and past the Kaffir huts. An old Kaffir maid knelt at the door of one grinding 'mealies.' That she should see him walking so made his heart beat so fast that the hand on his arm felt its pulsation. It seemed that she must envy him.

Just then Em, looked out again at the back window and saw them coming. She cried bitterly all the while she sorted the skins.

But that night when Lyndall had blown her candle out, and half turned round to sleep, the door of Em's bedroom opened.

"I want to say good night to you, Lyndall," she said, coming to the bedside and kneeling down.

"I thought you were asleep," Lyndall replied.

"Yes, I have been asleep; but I had such a vivid dream," she said, holding the other's hands, "and that awoke me. I never had so vivid a dream before.

"It seemed I was a little girl again, and I came somewhere into a large room. On a bed in the corner there was something lying dressed in white, and its little eyes were shut, and its little face was like wax. I thought it was a doll, and I ran forward to take it; but some one held up her finger and said, 'Hush! it is a little dead baby.' And I said, 'Oh, I must go and call Lyndall, that she may look at it also.'

"And they put their faces close down to my ear and whispered, 'It is Lyndall's baby.'

"And I said, 'She cannot be grown up yet; she is only a little girl! Where is she?' And I went to look for you, but I could not find you.

"And when I came to some people who were dressed in black, I asked them where you were, and they looked down at their black clothes, and shook their heads, and said nothing; and I could not find you anywhere. And then I awoke.

"Lyndall," she said, putting her face down upon the hands she held, "it made me think about that time when we were little girls and used to play together, when I loved you better than anything else in the world. It isn't any one's fault that they love you; they can't help it. And it isn't your fault; you don't make them love you. I know it."

"Thank you, dear," Lyndall said. "It is nice to be loved, but it would be better to be good."

Then they wished good night, and Em went back to her room. Long after Lyndall lay in the dark thinking, thinking, thinking; and as she turned round wearily to sleep she muttered,

"There are some wiser in their sleeping than in their waking."

Chapter IX.
Lyndall's Stranger.

A fire is burning in the unused hearth of the cabin. The fuel blazes up, and lights the black rafters, and warms the faded red lions on the quilt, and fills the little room with a glow of warmth and light made brighter by contrast, for outside the night is chill and misty.

Before the open fireplace sits a stranger, his tall slight figure reposing in the broken armchair, his keen blue eyes studying the fire from beneath delicately pencilled, drooping eyelids. One white hand plays thoughtfully with a heavy flaxen moustache; yet once he starts, and for an instant the languid lids raise themselves: there is a keen, intent look upon the face as he listens for something. Then he leans back in his chair, fills his glass from the silver flask in his bag, and resumes his old posture.

Presently the door opens noiselessly. It is Lyndall, followed by Doss. Quietly as she enters, he hears her, and turns.

"I thought you were not coming."

"I waited till all had gone to bed. I could not come before."

She removed the shawl that enveloped her, and the stranger rose to offer her his chair; but she took her seat on a low pile of sacks before the window.

"I hardly see why I should be outlawed after this fashion," he said, re-seating himself and drawing his chair a little nearer to her; "these are hardly the quarters one expects to find after travelling a hundred miles in answer to an invitation."

"I said, 'Come if you wish.'"

"And I did wish. You give me a cold reception."

"I could not take you to the house. Questions would be asked which I could not answer without prevarication."

"Your conscience is growing to have a certain virgin tenderness," he said, in a low melodious voice.

"I have no conscience. I spoke one deliberate lie this evening. I said the man who had come looked rough, we had best not have him in the house; therefore I brought him here. It was a deliberate lie, and I hate lies. I tell them if I must but they hurt me."

"Well, you do not tell lies to yourself, at all events. You are candid, so far."

She interrupted him.

"You got my short letter?"

"Yes; that is why I come. You sent a very foolish reply, you must take it back. Who is this fellow you talk of marrying?"

"A young farmer."

"Lives here?"

"Yes; he has gone to town to get things for our wedding."

"What kind of a fellow is he?"

"A fool."

"And you would rather marry him than me?"

"Yes; because you are not one."

"That is a novel reason for refusing to marry a man," he said, leaning his elbow on the table, and watching her keenly.

"It is a wise one," she said shortly. "If I marry him I shall shake him off my hand when it suits me. If I remained with him for twelve months he would never have dared to kiss my hand. As far as I wish he should come, he comes, and no further. Would you ask me what you might and what you might not do?"

Her companion raised the moustache with a caressing movement from his lip and smiled. It was not a question that stood in need of any answer.

"Why do you wish to enter on this semblance of marriage?"

"Because there is only one point on which I have a conscience. I have told you so."

"Then why not marry me?"

"Because if once you have me you would hold me fast. I shall never be free again." She drew a long low breath.

"What have you done with the ring I gave you?" he said.

"Sometimes I wear it; then I take it off and wish to throw it into the fire; the next day I put it on again, and sometimes I kiss it."

"So you do love me a little?"

"If you were not something more to me than any other man in the world, do you think—" she paused. "I love you when I see you; but when you are away from me I hate you."

"Then I fear I must be singularly invisible at the present moment," he said. "Possibly if you were to look less fixedly into the fire you might perceive me."

He moved his chair slightly so as to come between her and the firelight. She raised her eyes to his face.

"If you do love me," he asked her, "why will you not marry me?"

"Because, if I had been married to you for a year, I should have come to my senses, and seen that your hands and your voice are like the hands and the voice of any other man. I cannot quite see that now. But it is all madness. You call into activity one part of my nature; there is a higher part that you know nothing of, that you never touch. If I married you, afterwards it would rise and assert itself, and I should hate you always, as I do now sometimes."

"I like you when you grow metaphysical and analytical," he said, leaning his face upon his hand. "Go a little further in your analysis; say, 'I love you with the right ventricle of my heart, but not the left, and with the left auricle of my heart, but not the right; and, this being the case, my affection for you is not of a duly elevated, intellectual, and spiritual nature.' I like you when you get philosophical."

She looked quietly at him; he was trying to turn her own weapons against her.

"You are acting foolishly, Lyndall," he said, suddenly changing his manner, and speaking earnestly, "most foolishly. You are acting like a little child; I am surprised at you. It is all very well to have ideals and theories; but you know as well as any one can that they must not be carried into the practical world. I love you. I do not pretend that it is in any high, super-human sense; I do not say that I should like you as well if you were ugly and deformed, or that I should continue to prize you whatever your treatment of me might be, or to love you though you were a spirit without any body at all. That is sentimentality for beardless boys. Every one not a mere child (and you are not a child, except in years) knows what love between a man and a woman means. I love you with that love. I should not have believed it possible that I could have brought myself twice to ask of any woman to be my wife, more especially one without wealth, without position, and who—"

"Yes—go on. Do not grow sorry for me. Say what you were going to— 'who has put herself into my power, and who has lost the right of meeting me on equal terms.' Say what you think. At least we two may speak the truth to one another."

Then she added after a pause,

"I believe you do love me, as much as you possibly could love anything; and I believe that when you ask me to marry you you are performing the most generous act you ever have performed in the course of your life, or ever will; but, at the same time, if I had required your generosity, it would not have been shown me. If, when I got your letter a month ago, hinting at your willingness to marry me, I had at once written, imploring you to come, you would have read the letter. 'Poor little Devil!' you would have said, and tore it up. The next week you would have sailed for Europe, and have sent me a cheque for a hundred and fifty pounds (which I would have thrown in the fire), and I would have heard no more of you." The stranger smiled. "But because I declined your proposal, and wrote that in three weeks I should be married to another, then what you call love woke up. Your man's love is a child's love for butterflies. You follow till you have the thing, and break it. If you have broken one wing, and the thing flies still, then you love it more than ever, and follow till you break both; then you are satisfied when it lies still on the ground."

"You are profoundly wise in the ways of the world; you have seen far into life," he said.

He might as well have sneered at the firelight.

"I have seen enough to tell me that you love me because you cannot bear to be resisted, and want to master me. You liked me at first because I treated you and all men with indifference. You resolved to have me because I seemed unattainable. That is all your love means."

He felt a strong inclination to stoop down and kiss the little lips that defied him; but he restrained himself. He said quietly, "And you loved me——?"

"Because you are strong. You are the first man I ever was afraid of. And"—a dreamy look came into her face—"because I like to experience, I like to try. You don't understand that."

He smiled.

"Well, since you will not marry me, may I inquire what your intentions are, the plan you wrote of. You asked me to come and hear it, and I have come."

"I said, 'Come if you wish'—If you agree to it, well; if not, I marry on Monday."

"Well?"

She was still looking beyond him at the fire.

"I cannot marry you," she said slowly, "because I cannot be tied; but, if you wish, you may take me away with you, and take care of me; then when we do not love any more we can say good-bye. I will not go down country," she added; "I will not go to Europe. You must take me to the Transvaal. That is out of the world. People we meet there we need not see again in our future lives."

"Oh, my darling," he said, bending tenderly, and holding his hand out to her, "why will you not give yourself entirely to me? One day you will desert me and go to another."

She shook her head without looking at him.

"No, life is too long. But I will go with you."

"When?"

"To-morrow. I have told them that before daylight I go to the next farm. I will write from the town and tell them the facts. I do not want them to trouble me; I want to shake myself free of these old surroundings; I want them to lose sight of me. You can understand that is necessary for me."

He seemed lost in consideration; then he said,

"It is better to have you on those conditions than not at all. If you *will* have it, let it be so."

He sat looking at her. On her face was the weary look that rested there so often now when she sat alone. Two months had not passed since they parted; but the time had set its mark on her. He looked at her carefully, from the brown, smooth head to the little crossed feet on the floor. A worn look had grown over the little face, and it made its charm for him stronger. For pain and time, which trace deep lines and write a story on a human face, have a strangely different effect on one face and another. The face that is only fair, even very fair, they mar and flaw; but the face whose beauty is the harmony between that which speaks from within and the form through which it speaks, power is added by all that causes the outer man to bear more deeply the impress of the inner. The pretty woman fades with the roses in her cheeks, and the girl-hood that lasts an hour; the beautiful woman finds her fulness of bloom only when a past has written itself on her, and her power is then most irresistible when it seems going.

From under their half-closed lids the keen eyes looked down at her. Her shoulders were bent; for a moment the little figure had forgotten its queenly bearing, and drooped wearily; the wide dark eyes watched the fire very softly.

It certainly was not in her power to resist him, nor any strength in her that made his own at that moment grow soft as he looked at her.

He touched one little hand that rested on her knee.

"Poor little thing!" he said; "you are only a child."

She did not draw her hand away from his, and looked up at him.

"You are very tired?"

"Yes."

She looked into his eyes as a little child might whom a long day's play had saddened.

He lifted her gently up, and sat her on his knee.

"Poor little thing!" he said.

She turned her face to his shoulder, and buried it against his neck; he wound his strong arm about her, and held her close to him. When she had sat for a long while, he drew with his hand the face down, and held it against his arm. He kissed it, and then put it back in its old resting-place.

"Don't you want to talk to me?"

"No."

"Have you forgotten the night in the avenue?"

He could feel that she shook her head.

"Do you want to be quiet now?"

"Yes."

They sat quite still, excepting that only sometimes he raised her fingers softly to his mouth.

Doss, who had been asleep in the corner, waking suddenly, planted himself before them, his wiry legs moving nervously, his yellow eyes filled with anxiety. He was not at all sure that she was not being retained in her present position against her will, and was not a little relieved when she sat up and held out her hand for the shawl.

"I must go," she said.

The stranger wrapped the shawl very carefully about her.

"Keep it close around your face, Lyndall; it is very damp outside. Shall I walk with you to the house?"

"No. Lie down and rest; I will come and wake you at three o'clock."

She lifted her face that he might kiss it, and, when he had kissed it once, she still held it that he might kiss it again. Then he let her out. He had seated himself at the fire-place, when she re-opened the door.

"Have you forgotten anything?"

"No."

She gave one long, lingering look at the old room. When she was gone, and the door shut, the stranger filled his glass, and sat at the table sipping it thoughtfully.

The night outside was misty and damp; the faint moonlight, trying to force its way through the thick air, made darkly visible the outlines of the buildings. The stones and walls were moist, and now and then a drop, slowly collecting, fell from the eaves to the ground. Doss, not liking the change from the cabin's warmth, ran quickly to the kitchen door-step; but his mistress walked slowly past him, and took her way up the winding footpath that ran beside the stone wall of the camps. When she came to the end of the last camp, she threaded her way among the stones and bushes till she reached the German's grave. Why she had come there she hardly knew; she stood looking down. Suddenly she bent and put one hand on the face of a wet stone.

"I shall never come to you again," she said.

Then she knelt on the ground, and leaned her face upon the stones.

"Dear old man, good old man, I am so tired!" she said (for we will come to the dead to tell secrets we would never have told to the living). "I am so tired. There is light, there is warmth," she wailed; "why am I alone, so hard, so cold? I am so weary of myself! It is eating my soul to its core,—self, self, self! I cannot bear this life! I cannot breathe, I cannot live! Will nothing free me from myself?" She pressed her cheek against the wooden post. "I want to love! I want something great and pure to lift me to itself! Dear old man, I cannot bear it any more! I am so cold, so hard, so hard; will no one help me?"

The water gathered slowly on her shawl, and fell on to the wet stones; but she lay there crying bitterly. For so the living soul will cry to the dead, and the creature to its God; and of all this crying there comes nothing. The lifting up of the hands brings no salvation; redemption is from within, and neither from God nor man: it is wrought out by the soul itself, with suffering and through time.

Doss, on the kitchen door-step, shivered, and wondered where his mistress stayed so long; and once, sitting sadly there in the damp, he had dropped asleep, and dreamed that old Otto gave him a piece of bread, and patted him on the head, and when he woke his teeth chattered, and he moved to another stone to see if it was drier. At last he heard his mistress's step, and they went into the house together. She lit a candle, and walked to the Boer-woman's bedroom. On a nail under the lady in pink hung the key of the wardrobe. She took it down and opened the great press. From a little drawer she took fifty pounds (all she had in the world), relocked the door, and turned to hang up the key. Then she paused, hesitated. The marks of tears were still on her face, but she smiled.

"Fifty pounds for a lover! A noble reward!" she said, and opened the wardrobe and returned the notes to the drawer, where Em might find them.

Once in her own room, she arranged the few articles she intended to take to-morrow, burnt her old letters, and then went back to the front room to look at the time. There were two hours yet before she must call him. She sat down at the dressing-table to wait, and leaned her elbows on it, and buried her face in her hands. The glass reflected the little brown head with its even parting, and the tiny hands on which it rested. "One day I will love something utterly, and then I will be better," she said once. Presently she looked up. The large dark eyes from the glass looked back at her. She looked deep into them.

"We are all alone, you and I," she whispered; "no one helps us, no one understands us; but we will help ourselves." The eyes looked back at her. There was a world of assurance in their still depths. So they had looked at her ever since she could remember, when it was but a small child's face above a blue pinafore. "We shall never be quite alone, you and I," she said; "we shall always be together, as we were when we were little."

The beautiful eyes looked into the depths of her soul.

"We are not afraid; we will help ourselves!" she said. She stretched out her hand and pressed it over them on the glass. "Dear eyes! we will never be quite alone till they part us; —till then!"

Chapter X.
Gregory Rose Has An Idea.

Gregory Rose was in the loft putting it neat. Outside the rain poured; a six months' drought had broken, and the thirsty plain was drenched with water. What it could not swallow ran off in mad rivulets to the great 'sloot,' that now foamed like an angry river across the flat. Even the little furrow between the farmhouse and the kraals was now a stream, knee-deep, which almost bore away the Kaffir-women which crossed it. It had rained for twenty-four hours, and still the rain poured on. The fowls had collected—a melancholy crowd—in and about the waggon-house, and the solitary gander, who alone had survived the six months' want of water, walked hither and thither, printing his webbed foot-marks on the mud, to have them washed out the next instant by the pelting rain, which at eleven o'clock still beat on the walls and roofs with unabated ardour.

Gregory, as he worked in the loft, took no notice of it beyond stuffing a sack into the broken pane to keep it out; and, in spite of the pelt and patter, Em's clear voice might be heard through the open trap-door from the dining-room, where she sat at work, singing the 'Blue Water'—

"And take me away,
And take me away,
And take me away,
To the Blue Water"—

that quaint, childish song of the people, that has a world of sweetness, and sad, vague yearning when sung over and over dreamily by a woman's voice as she sits alone at her work. But Gregory heard neither that nor yet the loud laughter of the Kaffir maids, that every now and again broke through from the kitchen, where they joked and worked. Of late Gregory had grown strangely impervious to the sounds and sights about him. His lease had run out, but Em had said, "Do not renew it; I need one to help me; just stay on." And, she had added, "You must not remain in your own little house; live with me; you can look after my ostriches better so."

And Gregory did not thank her. What difference did it make to him, paying rent or not, living there or not; it was all one. But yet he came. Em wished that he would still sometimes talk of the strength and master-right of man; but Gregory was as one smitten on the cheek-bone. She might do what she pleased, he would find no fault, had no word to say. He had forgotten that it is man's right to rule. On that rainy morning he had lighted his pipe at the kitchen fire, and when breakfast was over stood in the front door watching the water rush down the road till the pipe died out in his mouth. Em saw she must do something for him, and found him a large calico duster. He had sometimes talked of putting the loft neat, and today she could find nothing else for him to do. So she had the ladder put to the trap-door that he need not go out in the wet, and Gregory with the broom and duster mounted to the loft. Once at work he worked hard. He dusted down the very rafters, and cleaned the broken candle-moulds and bent forks that had stuck in the thatch for twenty years. He placed the black bottles neatly in rows on an old box in the corner, and piled the skins on one another, and sorted the rubbish in all the boxes; and at eleven o'clock his work was almost done. He seated himself on the packing-case which had once held Waldo's books, and proceeded to examine the contents of another which he had not yet looked at. It was carelessly nailed down. He loosened one plank, and began to lift out various articles of female attire—old-fashioned caps, aprons, dresses with long pointed bodies such as he remembered to have seen his mother wear when he was a little child. He shook them out carefully to see there were no moths, and then sat down to fold them up again one by one. They had belonged to Em's mother, and the box, as packed at her death, had stood untouched and forgotten these long years. She must have been a tall woman, that mother of Em's, for when he stood up to shake out a dress the neck was on a level with his, and the skirt touched the ground. Gregory laid a night-cap out on his knee, and began rolling up the strings; but presently his fingers moved slower and slower, then his chin rested on his breast, and finally the imploring blue eyes were fixed on the frill abstractedly. When Em's voice called to him from the foot of the ladder he started, and threw the night-cap behind him.

She was only come to tell him that his cup of soup was ready; and, when he could hear that she was gone, he picked up the night-cap again, and a great brown sun-kapje—just such a 'kapje' and such a dress as one of those he remembered to have seen a sister-of-mercy wear. Gregory's mind was very full of thought. He took down a fragment of an old looking-glass from behind a beam, and put the 'kapje' on. His beard looked somewhat grotesque under it; he put up his hand to hide it—that was better. The blue eyes looked out with the mild gentleness that became eyes looking out from under a 'kapje.' Next he took the brown dress, and, looking round furtively, slipped it over his head. He had just got his arms in the sleeves, and was trying to hook up the back, when an increase in the patter of the rain at the window made him drag it off hastily. When he perceived there was no one coming he tumbled the things back into the box, and, covering it carefully, went down the ladder.

Em was still at her work, trying to adjust a new needle in the machine. Gregory drank his soup, and then sat before her, an awful and mysterious look in his eyes.

"I am going to town to-morrow," he said.

"I'm almost afraid you won't be able to go," said Em, who was intent on her needle; "I don't think it is going to leave off to-day."

"I am going," said Gregory.

Em looked up.

"But the 'sloots' are as full as rivers—you cannot go. We can wait for the post," she said.

"I am not going for the post," said Gregory impressively.

Em looked for explanation; none came.

"When will you be back?"

"I am not coming back."

"Are you going to your friends?"

Gregory waited, then caught her by the wrist.

"Look here, Em," he said between his teeth, "I can't stand it any more. I am going to her."

Since that day, when he had come home and found Lyndall

gone, he had never talked of her; but Em knew who it was who needed to be spoken of by no name.

She said, when he had released her hand,

"But you do not know where she is?"

"Yes, I do. She was in Bloemfontein when I heard last. I will go there, and I will find out where she went then, and then, and then! I will have her."

Em turned the wheel quickly, and the ill-adjusted needle sprang into twenty fragments.

"Gregory," she said, "she does not want us; she told us so clearly in the letter she wrote." A flush rose on her face as she spoke. "It will only be pain to you, Gregory. Will she like to have you near her?"

There was an answer he might have made, but it was his secret, and he did not choose to share it. He said only,

"I am going."

"Will you be gone long, Gregory?"

"I do not know; perhaps I shall never come back. Do what you please with my things. I cannot stay here!"

He rose from his seat.

"People say, forget, forget!" he cried, pacing the room. "They are mad! they are fools! Do they say so to men who are dying of thirst—forget, forget? Why is it only to us they say so! It is a lie to say that time makes it easy; it is afterwards, afterwards that it eats in at your heart!

"All these months," he cried bitterly, "I have lived here quietly, day after day, as if I cared for what I ate, and what I drank, and what I did! I care for nothing! I cannot bear it! I will not! Forget! Forget!" ejaculated Gregory. "You can forget all the world, but you cannot forget yourself. When one thing is more to you than yourself, how are you to forget it?

"I read," he said— "yes; and then I come to a word she used, and it is all back with me again! I go to count my sheep, and I see her face before me, and I stand and let the sheep run by. I look at you, and in your smile, a something at the corner of your lips, I see her. How can I forget her when, whenever I turn, she is there, and not there? I cannot, I will not, live where I do not see her.

"I know what you think," he said, turning upon Em. "You think I am mad; you think I am going to see whether she will not like me! I am not so foolish. I should have known at first she never could suffer me. Who am I, what am I, that she should look at me? It was right that she left me; right that she should not look at me.

If any one says it is not, it is a lie! I am not going to speak to her,"
he added— "only to see her; only to stand sometimes in a place
where she has stood before."

Chapter XI.
An Unfinished Letter.

Gregory Rose had been gone seven months. Em sat alone on a
white sheepskin before the fire.

The August night-wind, weird and shrill, howled round the
chimneys and through the crannies, and in walls and doors, and
uttered a long low cry as it forced its way among the clefts of the
stones on the 'kopje.' It was a wild night. The prickly-pear tree, stiff
and upright as it held its arms, felt the wind's might, and knocked
its flat leaves heavily together, till great branches broke off. The
Kaffirs, as they slept in their straw huts, whispered one to another
that before morning there would not be an armful of thatch left
on the roofs; and the beams of the waggon-house creaked and
groaned as if it were heavy work to resist the importunity of the
wind.

Em had not gone to bed. Who could sleep on a night like this?
So in the dining-room she had lighted a fire, and sat on the ground
before it, turning the roaster-cakes that lay on the coals to bake. It
would save work in the morning; and she blew out the light
because the wind through the window-chinks made it flicker and
run; and she sat singing to herself as she watched the cakes. They
lay at one end of the wide hearth on a bed of coals, and at the other
end a fire burnt up steadily, casting its amber glow over Em's light
hair and black dress, with the ruffle of crape about the neck, and
over the white curls of the sheepskin on which she sat.

Louder and more fiercely yet howled the storm; but Em sang
on, and heard nothing but the words of her song, and heard them
only faintly, as something restful. It was an old, childish song she
had often heard her mother sing long ago—

> Where the reeds dance by the river,
> Where the willow's song is said,
> On the face of the morning water,
> Is reflected a white flower's head.

She folded her hands and sang the next verse dreamily—

Where the reeds shake by the river,
Where the moonlight's sheen is shed,
On the face of the sleeping water,
Two leaves of a white flower float dead.
Dead, Dead, Dead!

She echoed the refrain softly till it died away, and then repeated it. It was as if, unknown to herself, it harmonized with the pictures and thoughts that sat with her there alone in the fire-light. She turned the cakes over, while the wind hurled down a row of bricks from the gable, and made the walls tremble.

Presently she paused and listened; there was a sound as of something knocking at the back-doorway. But the wind had raised its level higher, and she went on with her work. At last the sound was repeated. Then she rose, lit the candle at the fire, and went to see. Only to satisfy herself, she said, that nothing could be out on such a night.

She opened the door a little way, and held the light behind her to defend it from the wind. The figure of a tall man stood there, and before she could speak he had pushed his way in, and was forcing the door to close behind him.

"Waldo!" she cried in astonishment.

He had been gone more than a year and a half.

"You did not expect to see me," he answered, as he turned towards her; "I should have slept in the out-house, and not troubled you to-night; but through the shutter I saw glimmerings of a light."

"Come into the fire," she said; "it is a terrific night for any creature to be out. Shall we not go and fetch your things in first?" she added.

"I have nothing but this," he said, motioning to the little bundle in his hand.

"Your horse?"

"Is dead."

He sat down on the bench before the fire.

"The cakes are almost ready," she said; "I will get you something to eat. Where have you been wandering all this while?"

"Up and down, up and down," he answered wearily; "and now the whim has seized me to come back here. Em," he said, putting his hand on her arm as she passed him, "have you heard from Lyndall lately?"

"Yes," said Em, turning quickly from him.

"Where is she? I had one letter from her, but that is almost a year ago now—just when she left. Where is she?"

"In the Transvaal. I will go and get you some supper; we can talk afterwards."

"Can you give me her exact address? I want to write to her."

But Em had gone into the next room.

When food was on the table she knelt down before the fire, turning the cakes, babbling restlessly, eagerly, now of this, now of that. She was glad to see him—Tant' Sannie was coming soon to show her her new baby—he must stay on the farm now, and help her. And Waldo himself was well content to eat his meal in silence, asking no more questions.

"Gregory is coming back next week," she said; "he will have been gone just a hundred and three days to-morrow. I had a letter from him yesterday."

"Where has he been?"

But his companion stooped to lift a cake from the fire.

"How the wind blows! One can hardly hear one's own voice," she said. "Take this warm cake; no one's cakes are like mine. Why, you have eaten nothing!"

"I am a little weary," he said; "the wind was mad to-night."

He folded his arms, and rested his head against the fire-place, whilst she removed the dishes from the table. On the mantelpiece stood an ink-pot and some sheets of paper. Presently he took them down and turned up the corner of the table-cloth.

"I will write a few lines," he said, "till you are ready to sit down and talk."

Em, as she shook out the table-cloth, watched him bending intently over his paper. He had changed much. His face had grown thinner; his cheeks were almost hollow, though they were covered by a dark growth of beard.

She sat down on the skin beside him, and felt the little bundle on the bench; it was painfully small and soft. Perhaps it held a shirt and a book, but nothing more. The old black hat had a piece of unhemmed muslin twisted round it, and on his elbow was a large patch so fixed on with yellow thread that her heart ached. Only his hair was not changed, and hung in silky beautiful waves almost to his shoulders. To-morrow she would take the ragged edge off his collar, and put a new band round his hat. She did not interrupt him, but she wondered how it was that he sat to write so intently after his long weary walk. He was not tired now; his pen hurried quickly and restlessly over the paper, and his eye was bright.

Presently Em raised her hand to her breast, where lay the letter yesterday had brought her. Soon she had forgotten him, as entirely as he had forgotten her; each was in his own world with his own. He was writing to Lyndall. He would tell her all he had seen, all he had done, though it were nothing worth relating. He seemed to have come back to her, and to be talking to her now he sat there in the old house.

"——and then I got to the next town, and my horse was tired, so I could go no further, and looked for work. A shopkeeper agreed to hire me as salesman. He made me sign a promise to remain six months, and he gave me a little empty room at the back of the store to sleep in. I had still three pounds of my own, and when you have just come from the country three pounds seems a great deal.

"When I had been in the shop three days I wanted to go away again. A clerk in a shop has the lowest work to do of all people. It is much better to break stones: you have the blue sky above you, and only the stones to bend to. I asked my master to let me go, and I offered to give him my two pounds, and the bag of mealies I had bought with the other pound; but he would not.

"I found out afterwards he was only giving me half as much as he gave to the others—that was why. I had fear when I looked at the other clerks that I would at last become like them. All day they were bowing and smirking to the women who came in; smiling, when all they wanted was to get their money from them. They used to run and fetch the dresses and ribbons to show them, and they seemed to me like worms with oil on. There was one respectable thing in that store—it was the Kaffir storeman. His work was to load and unload, and he never needed to smile except when he liked, and he never told lies.

"The other clerks gave me the name of Old Salvation; but there was one person I liked very much. He was clerk in another store. He often went past the door. He seemed to me not like others—his face was bright and fresh like a little child's. When he came to the shop I felt I liked him. One day I saw a book in his pocket, and that made me feel near him. I asked him if he was fond of reading, and he said yes, when there was nothing else to do. The next day he came to me, and asked me if I did not feel lonely; he never saw me going out with the other fellows; he would come and see me that evening, he said.

"I was glad, and bought some meat and flour, because the grey mare and I always ate mealies; it is the cheapest thing; when you boil it hard you can't eat much of it. I made some cakes, and I folded my great coat on the box to make it soft for him; and at last he came.

"'You've got a rummy place here,' he said.

"You see there was nothing in it but packing-cases for furniture, and it was rather empty. While I was putting the food on the box he looked at my books; he read their names out aloud. 'Elementary Physiology,' 'First Principles.'

"'Golly!' he said; 'I've got a lot of dry stuff like that at home I got for Sunday school prizes; but I only keep them to light my pipe with now; they come in handy for that.' Then he asked me if I had ever read a book called the 'Blackeyed Creole.' 'That is the style for me,' he said; 'there where the fellow takes the nigger-girl by the arm, and the other fellow cuts it off! That's what I like.'

"But what he said after that I don't remember, only it made me feel as if I were having a bad dream, and I wanted to be far away.

"When he had finished eating he did not stay long: he had to go and see some girls home from a prayer-meeting; and he asked how it was he never saw me walking out with any on Sunday afternoons. He said he had lots of sweethearts, and he was going to see one the next Wednesday on a farm, and he asked me to lend my mare. I told him she was very old. But he said it didn't matter; he would come the next day to fetch her.

"After he was gone my little room got back to its old look. I loved it so; I was so glad to get into it at night, and it seemed to be reproaching me for bringing him there. The next day he took the grey mare. On Thursday he did not bring her back, and on Friday I found the saddle and bridle standing at my door.

In the afternoon he looked into the shop, and called out, 'Hope you got your saddle, Farber? Your bag-of-bones kicked out six miles from this. I'll send you a couple of shillings tomorrow, though the old hide wasn't worth it. Good morning.'

"But I sprang over the counter, and got him by his throat. My father was so gentle with her; he never would ride her up hill, and now this fellow had murdered her! I asked him where he had killed her, and I shook him till he slipped out of my hand. He stood in the door grinning.

"'It didn't take much to kill *that* bag-of-bones, whose master sleeps in a packing-case, and waits till his company's finished to eat on the plate. Shouldn't wonder if you fed her on sugar-bags,' he said; 'and, if you think I've jumped her, you'd better go and look yourself. You'll find her along the road by the 'aas-vogels'[1] that are eating her.'

"I caught him by his collar, and I lifted him from the ground, and I threw him out into the street, half-way across it. I heard the bookkeeper say to the clerk that there was always the devil in those mum fellows; but they never called me Salvation after that.

"I am writing to you of very small things, but there is nothing else to tell; it has been all small and you will like it. Whenever anything has happened I have always thought I would tell it to you. The back thought in my mind is always you. After that only one old man came to visit me. I had seen him in the streets often; he always wore very dirty black clothes, and a hat with crape round it, and he had one eye, so I noticed him. One day he came to my room with a subscription-list for a minister's salary. When I said I had nothing to give he looked at me with his one eye.

"'Young man,' he said, 'how is it I never see you in the house of the Lord?' I thought he was trying to do good, so I felt sorry for him, and I told him I never went to chapel. 'Young man,' he said, 'it grieves me to hear such godless words from the lips of one so young—so far gone in the paths of destruction. Young man, if you forget God, God will forget you. There is a seat on the right-hand side as you go at the bottom door that you may get. If you are given over to the enjoyment and frivolities of this world, what will become of your never-dying soul?'

"He would not go till I gave him half-a-crown for the minister's salary. Afterwards I heard he was the man who collected the pew-rents, and got a per-centage. I didn't get to know any one else.

"When my time in that shop was done I hired myself to drive one of a transport-rider's waggons.

"That first morning, when I sat in the front and called to my oxen, and saw nothing about me but the hills with the blue coming down to them, and the karroo bushes, I was drunk; I laughed; my heart was beating till it hurt me. I shut my eyes tight, that when I opened them I might see there were no shelves about me. There must be a beauty in buying and selling if there is beauty in everything; but it is very ugly to me. My life as transport-rider would have been the best life in the world if I had had only one waggon to drive. My master told me he would drive one, I the other, and he would hire another person to drive the third. But the first day

---

1 Vultures.

I drove two to help him, and after that he let me drive all three. Whenever we came to an hotel he stopped behind to get a drink, and when he rode up to the waggons he could never stand; the Hottentot and I used to lift him up. We always travelled all night, and used to 'out-span' for five or six hours in the heat of the day to rest. I planned that I would lie under the waggon and read for an hour or two every day before I went to sleep, and I did for the first two or three; but after that I only wanted to sleep like the rest, and I packed my books away. When you have three waggons to look after all night, you are sometimes so tired you can hardly stand. At first when I walked along driving my waggons in the night it was glorious; the stars had never looked so beautiful to me; and on the dark nights when we rode through the bush there were will-o'-the-wisps dancing on each side of the road. I found out that even the damp and dark are beautiful. But I soon changed, and saw nothing but the road and my oxen. I only wished for a smooth piece of road, so that I might sit at the front and doze. At the places where we 'out-spanned' there were sometimes rare plants and flowers, the festoons hanging from the bush-trees, and nuts and insects, such as we never see here; but after a little while I never looked at them—I was too tired. I ate as much as I could, and then lay down on my face under the waggon till the boy came to wake me to 'in-span,' and then we drove on again all night; so it went, so it went. I think sometimes when we walked by my oxen I called to them in my sleep, for I know I thought of nothing; I was like an animal. My body was strong and well to work, but my brain was dead. If you have not felt it, Lyndall, you cannot understand it. You may work, and work, and work, till you are only a body, not a soul. Now, when I see one of those evil-looking men that come from Europe—navvies,[1] with the beast-like, sunken face, different from any Kaffir's—I know what brought that look into their eyes; and if I have only one inch of tobacco I give them half. It is work, grinding mechanical work, that they or their ancestors have done, that has made them into beasts. You may work a man's body so that his soul dies. Work is good. I have worked at the old farm from the sun's rising till its setting, but I have had time to think, and time to feel. You may work a man so that all but the animal in him is gone; and that grows stronger with physical labour. You may work a man till he is a devil. I know it, because I have felt it. You will never

---

1 Workers in excavation or construction of large earth-works.

understand the change that came over me. No one but I will ever know how great it was. But I was never miserable; when I could keep my oxen from sticking fast, and when I could find a place to lie down in, I had all I wanted. After I had driven eight months a rainy season came. For eighteen hours out of the twenty-four we worked in the wet. The mud went up to the axles sometimes, and we had to dig the wheels out, and we never went far in a day. My master swore at me more than ever, but when he had done he always offered me his brandy-flask. When I first came he had offered it me, and I had always refused; but now I drank as my oxen did when I gave them water—without thinking. At last I bought brandy for myself whenever we passed an hotel.

"One Sunday we 'out-spanned' on the banks of a swollen river to wait for its going down. It was drizzling still, so I lay under the waggon on the mud. There was no dry place any where; and all the dung was wet, so there was no fire to cook food. My little flask was filled with brandy, and I drank some and went to sleep. When I woke it was drizzling still, so I drank some more. I was stiff and cold; and my master, who lay by me, offered me his flask, because mine was empty. I drank some, and then I thought I would go and see if the river was going down. I remember that I walked to the road, and it seemed to be going away from me. When I woke up I was lying by a little bush on the bank of the river. It was afternoon; all the clouds had gone, and the sky was deep blue. The Bushman boy was grilling ribs at the fire. He looked at me, and grinned from ear to ear. 'Master was a little nice,' he said, 'and lay down in the road. Something might ride over master, so I carried him there.' He grinned at me again. It was as though he said, 'You and I are comrades. I have lain in a road too. I know all about it.' When I turned my head from him I saw the earth, so pure after the rain, so green, so fresh, so blue;—and I was a drunken carrier, whom his leader had picked up in the mud, and laid at the roadside to sleep out his drink. I remembered my old life, and I remembered you. I saw how, one day, you would read in the papers—'A German carrier, named Waldo Farber, was killed through falling from his waggon, being instantly crushed under the wheel. Deceased was supposed to have been drunk at the time of the accident.' There are those notices in the paper every month. I sat up, and I took the brandy-flask out of my pocket, and I flung it as far as I could into the dark water. The Hottentot boy ran down to see if he could catch it; it had sunk to the bottom. I never drank again. But, Lyndall, sin looks much more terrible to those who look at it than to those who do it. A convict, or a man who drinks, seems something so far off and horrible when we see him; but to himself he seems quite near to us, and like us. We wonder what kind of a creature he is; but he is just we, ourselves. We are only the wood, the knife that carves on us is the circumstance.

"I do not know why I kept on working so hard for that master. I think it was as the oxen come every day and stand by the yokes; they do not know why. Perhaps I would have been with him still; but one day we started with loads for the Diamond Fields. The oxen were very thin now, and they had been standing about in the yoke all day without food while the waggons were being loaded. Not far from the town was a hill. When we came to the foot the first waggon stuck fast. I tried for a little while to urge the oxen, but I soon saw the one 'span' could never pull it up. I went to the other waggon to loosen that 'span' to join them on in front, but the transport-rider, who was lying at the back of the waggon, jumped out.

"'They shall bring it up the hill; and if half of them die for it they shall do it alone,' he said.

"He was not drunk, but in a bad temper, for he had been drunk the night before. He swore at me, and told me to take the whip and help him. We tried for a little time, then I told him it was no use, they could never do it. He swore louder, and called to the leaders to come on with their whips, and together they lashed. There was one ox, a black ox, so thin that the ridge of his backbone almost cut through his flesh.

"'It is you, Devil, is it, that will not pull?' the transport-rider said. 'I will show you something.' He looked like a Devil.

"He told the boys to leave off flogging, and he held the ox by the horn, and took up a round stone and knocked its nose with it till the blood came. When he had done they called to the oxen and took up their whips again, and the oxen strained with their backs bent, but the waggon did not move an inch.

"'So you won't, won't you?' he said. 'I'll help you.'

"He took out his clasp-knife, and ran it into the leg of the trembling ox three times, up to the hilt. Then he put the knife in his pocket, and they took their whips. The oxen's flanks quivered, and they foamed at the mouth. Straining, they moved the waggon a few feet forward, then stood with bent backs to keep it from sliding back. From the black ox's nostril foam and blood were streaming on to the ground. It turned its head in its anguish and looked at me with its great starting eyes. It was praying for help in its agony and weakness, and they took their whips again. The creature bellowed out aloud. If there is a God, it was calling to its Maker for help. Then a stream of clear blood burst from both nostrils; it fell on to the ground, and the waggon slipped back. The man walked up to it.

"'You are going to lie down, Devil, are you? We'll see you don't take it too easy.'

"The thing was just dying. He opened his clasp-knife and stooped down over it. I do not know what I did then. But afterwards I know I had him on the stones, and I was kneeling on him. The boys dragged me off. I wish they had not. I left him standing in the sand in the road, shaking himself, and I walked back to the town. I took nothing from that accursed waggon, so I had only two shillings. But it did not matter. The next day I got work at a wholesale store. My work was to pack and unpack goods, and to carry boxes, and I had only to work from six in the morning till six in the evening; so I had plenty of time. I hired a little room, and subscribed to a library, so I had everything I needed; and in the week of Christmas holidays I went to see the sea. I walked all night, Lyndall, to escape the heat, and a little after sunrise I got to the top of a high hill. Before me was a long, low, blue, monotonous mountain. I walked looking at it, but I was thinking of the sea I wanted to see. At last I wondered what that curious blue thing might be; then it struck me it was the sea! I would have turned back again, only I was too tired. I wonder if all the things we long to see—the churches, the pictures, the men in Europe—will disappoint us so! You see I had dreamed of it so long. When I was a little boy, minding sheep behind the 'kopje,' I used to see the waves stretching out as far as the eye could reach in the sunlight. My sea! Is the ideal always more beautiful than the real?

"I got to the beach that afternoon, and I saw the water run up and down on the sand, and I saw the white foam breakers; they were pretty, but I thought I would go back the next day. It was not my sea.

"But I began to like it when I sat by it that night in the moonlight; and the next day I liked it better; and before I left I loved it. It was not like the sky and stars that talk of what has no beginning and no end; but it is so human. Of all the things I have ever seen, only the sea is like a human being; the sky is not, nor the earth. But the sea is always moving, always something deep in itself is stirring it. It never rests; it is always wanting, wanting, wanting. It hurries on; and then it creeps back slowly without having reached, moaning. It is always asking a question, and it never gets the answer. I can hear it in the day and in the night; the white foam breakers are saying that which I think. I walk alone with them when there is no one to see me, and I sing with them. I lie down on the sand and watch them with my eyes half shut. The sky is better, but it is so high above our heads. I love the sea. Sometimes we must look down too. After five days I went back to Grahamstown.

"I had glorious books, and in the night I could sit in my little room and read them; but I was lonely. Books are not the same things when you are living among people. I cannot tell why, but they are dead. On the farm they would have been living beings to me; but here, where there were so many people about me, I wanted some one to belong to me. I was lonely. I wanted something that was flesh and blood. Once on this farm there came a stranger: I did not ask his name, but he sat among the 'karroo' and talked with me. Now, wherever I have travelled I have looked for him— in hotels, in streets, in, passenger waggons as they rushed in, through the open windows of houses I have looked for him, but I have not found him—never heard a voice like his. One day I went to the Botanic Gardens. It was a half-holiday, and the band was to play. I stood in the long raised avenue and looked down. There were many flowers, and ladies and children were walking about beautifully dressed. At last the music began. I had not heard such music before. At first it was slow and even, like the everyday life, when we walk through it without thought or feeling; then it grew faster, then it paused, hesitated, then it was quite still for an instant, and then it burst out. Lyndall, they made heaven right when they made it all music. It takes you up and carries you away, away, till you have the things you longed for; you are up close to them. You have got out into a large, free, open place. I could not see anything while it was playing; I stood with my head against my tree; but, when it was done, I saw that there were ladies sitting close to me on a wooden bench, and the stranger who had talked to me that day in the karroo was sitting between them. The ladies were very pretty, and their dresses beautiful. I do not think they had been listening to the music, for they were talking and laughing very softly. I heard all they said, and could even smell the rose on the breast of one. I was afraid he would see me; so I went to the other side of the tree, and soon they got up and began to pace up and down in the avenue. All the time the music played they chatted, and he carried on his arm the scarf of the prettiest lady. I did not hear the music; I tried to catch the sound of his voice each time he went by. When I was listening to the music I did not know I was badly dressed; now I felt so ashamed of myself. I never knew before what a low, horrible thing I was, dressed in tan-cord. That day on the farm, when we sat on the ground under the thorn-trees, I thought he quite belonged to me; now, I saw he was not mine. But he was still as beautiful. His brown eyes are more beautiful than any one's eyes, except yours.

"At last they turned to go, and I walked after them. When they got out of the gate he helped the ladies into a phaeton, and stood for a moment with his foot on the step talking to them. He had a little cane in his hand, and an Italian greyhound ran after him. Just when they drove away one of the ladies dropped her whip.

"'Pick it up, fellow,' she said; and when I brought it her she threw sixpence on the ground. I might have gone back to the garden then; but I did not want music; I wanted clothes, and to be fashionable and fine. I felt that my hands were coarse, and that I was vulgar. I never tried to see him again.

"I stayed in my situation four months after that, but I was not happy. I had no rest. The people about me pressed on me, and made me dissatisfied. I could not forget them. Even when I did not see them they pressed on me, and made me miserable. I did not love books; I wanted people. When I walked home under the shady trees in the street I could not be happy, for when I passed the houses I heard music, and saw faces between the curtains. I did not want any of them, but I wanted some one for mine, for me. I could not help it. I wanted a finer life.

"Only one day something made me happy. A nurse came to the store with a little girl belonging to one of our clerks. While the maid went into the office to give a message to its father, the little child stood looking at me. Presently she came close to me and peeped up into my face.

"'Nice curls, pretty curls,' she said; 'I like curls.'

"She felt my hair all over with her little hands. When I put out my arm she let me take her and sit her on my knee. She kissed me with her soft mouth. We were happy till the nurse-girl came and shook her, and asked her if she was not ashamed to sit on the knee of that strange man. But I do not think my little one minded. She laughed at me as she went out.

"If the world was all children I could like it; but men and women draw me so strangely, and then press me away, till I am in agony. I was not meant to live among people. Perhaps some day, when I am grown older, I will be able to go and live among them and look at them as I look at the rocks and bushes, without letting them disturb me, and take myself from me; but not now. So I grew miserable; a kind of fever seemed to eat me; I could not rest, or read, or think; so I came back here. I know you were not here, but it seemed as though I should be nearer you; and it is you I want— you that the other people suggest to me, but cannot give."

He had filled all the sheets he had taken, and now lifted down the last from the mantelpiece. Em had dropped asleep, and lay slumbering peacefully on the skin before the fire. Out of doors the storm still raged, but in a fitful manner, as though growing half weary of itself. He bent over his paper again, with eager flushed cheek, and wrote on.

"It has been a delightful journey, this journey home. I have walked on foot. The evening before last, when it was just sunset, I was a little footsore and thirsty, and went out of the road to look for water. I went down into a deep little 'kloof.'[1] Some trees ran along the bottom, and I thought I should find water there. The sun had quite set when I got to the bottom of it. It was very still—not a leaf was stirring anywhere. In the bed of the mountain torrent I thought I might find water. I came to the bank, and leaped down into the dry bed. The floor on which I stood was of fine white sand, and the banks rose on every side like the walls of a room. Above there was a precipice of rocks, and a tiny stream of water oozed from them and fell slowly on to the flat stone below. Each drop you could hear fall like a little silver bell. There was one among the trees on the bank that stood cut out against the white sky. All the other trees were silent; but this one shook and trembled against the sky. Everything else was still; but those leaves were quivering, quivering. I stood on the sand; I could not go away. When it was quite dark, and the stars had come, I crept out. Does it seem strange to you that it should have made me so happy? It is because I cannot tell you how near I felt to things that we cannot see but we always feel. To-night has been a wild, stormy night. I have been walking across the plain for hours in the dark. I have liked the wind, because I have seemed forcing my way through to you. I knew you were not here, but I would hear of you. When I used to sit on the transport waggon half-sleeping, I used to start awake because your hands were on me. In my lodgings, many nights I have blown the light out, and sat in the dark, that I might see your

1 Gorge.

face start out more distinctly. Sometimes it was the little girl's face who used to come to me behind the 'kopje' when I minded sheep, and sit by me in her blue pinafore; sometimes it was older. I love both. I am very helpless, I shall never do anything; but you will work, and I will take your work for mine. Sometimes such a sudden gladness seizes me when I remember that somewhere in the world you are living and working. You are my very own; nothing else is my own so. When I have finished I am going to look at your room door——"

He wrote; and the wind, which had spent its fury, moaned round and round the house, most like a tired child weary with crying.

Em woke up, and sat before the fire, rubbing her eyes, and listening, as it sobbed about the gables, and wandered away over the long stone walls.

"How quiet it has grown now," she said, and sighed herself, partly from weariness and partly from sympathy with the tired wind. He did not answer her; he was lost in his letter.

She rose slowly after a time, and rested her hand on his shoulder.

"You have many letters to write," she said.

"No," he answered; "it is only one to Lyndall."

She turned away, and stood long before the fire looking into it. If you have a deadly fruit to give, it will not grow sweeter by keeping.

"Waldo, dear," she said, putting her hand on his, "leave off writing."

He threw back the dark hair from his forehead and looked at her.

"It is no use writing any more," she said.

"Why not?" he asked.

She put her hand over the papers he had written.

"Waldo," she said, "Lyndall is dead."

Chapter XII.
Gregory's Womanhood.

Slowly over the flat came a cart. On the back seat sat Gregory, his arms folded, his hat drawn over his eyes. A Kaffir boy sat on the front seat driving, and at his feet sat Doss, who, now and again, lifted his nose and eyes above the level of the splashboard, to look at the surrounding country; and then, with an exceedingly knowing wink of his left eye, turned to his companions, thereby intimating that he clearly perceived his whereabouts. No one noticed the cart coming. Waldo, who was at work at his carpenter's table in the waggon-house, saw nothing, till chancing to look down he perceived Doss standing before him, the legs trembling, the little nose wrinkled, and a series of short suffocating barks giving utterance to his joy at reunion.

Em, whose eyes had ached with looking out across the plain, was now at work in a back room, and knew nothing till, looking up, she saw Gregory, with his straw hat and blue eyes, standing in the doorway. He greeted her quietly, hung his hat up in its old place behind the door, and for any change in his manner or appearance he might have been gone only the day before to fetch letters from the town. Only his beard was gone, and his face was grown thinner. He took off his leather gaiters, said the afternoon was hot and the roads dusty, and asked for some tea. They talked of wool, and the cattle, and the sheep, and Em gave him the pile of letters that had come for him during the months of absence, but of the thing that lay at their hearts neither said anything. Then he went out to look at the kraals, and at supper Em gave him hot cakes and coffee. They talked about the servants, and then ate their meal in quiet. She asked no questions. When it was ended Gregory went into the front room, and lay in the dark on the sofa.

"Do you not want a light?" Em asked, venturing to look in.

"No," he answered; then presently called to her, "Come and sit here; I want to talk to you."

She came and sat on a footstool near him.

"Do you wish to hear anything?" he asked.

She whispered, "Yes, if it does not hurt you."

"What difference does it make to me?" he said. "If I talk or am silent, is there any change?"

Yet he lay quiet for a long time. The light through the open door showed him to her, where he lay, with his arm thrown across his eyes. At last he spoke. Perhaps it was a relief to him to speak.

To Bloemfontein in the Free State, to which through an agent he had traced them, Gregory had gone. At the hotel where Lyndall and her stranger had stayed he put up; he was shown the very room in which they had slept. The coloured boy who had driven them to the next town told him in which house they had boarded, and Gregory went on. In that town he found they had left the cart, and bought a spider and four greys, and Gregory's heart rejoiced. Now indeed it would be easy to trace their course. And he turned his steps northwards.

At the farmhouses where he stopped the 'Ooms' and 'Tantes' remembered clearly the spider with its four grey horses. At one place the Boer-wife told how the tall, blue-eyed Englishman had bought milk, and asked the way to the next farm. At the next farm the Englishman had bought a bunch of flowers, and given half-a-crown for them to the little girl. It was quite true; the Boer-mother made her get it out of the box and show it. At the next place they had slept. Here they told him that the great bull-dog who hated all strangers, had walked in the evening and laid its head on the lady's lap. So at every place he heard something, and traced them step by step.

At one desolate farm the Boer had a good deal to tell. The lady had said she liked a waggon that stood before the door. Without asking the price the Englishman had offered a hundred and fifty pounds for the old thing, and bought oxen worth ten pounds for sixteen. The Dutchman chuckled, for he had the 'Salt-reim's'[1] money in the box under his bed. Gregory laughed too, in silence; he could not lose sight of them now, so slowly they would have to move with that cumbrous ox-waggon. Yet, when that evening came, and he reached a little wayside inn, no one could tell him anything of the travellers.

The master, a surly creature, half-stupid with Boer-brandy, sat on the bench before the door smoking. Gregory sat beside him, questioning, but he smoked on. He remembered nothing of such strangers. How should he know who had been there months and months before? He smoked on. Gregory, very weary, tried to awake his memory, said that the lady he was seeking for was very beautiful, had a little mouth, and tiny, very tiny, feet. The man only smoked on as sullenly as at first. What were little, very little, mouths and feet to him. But his daughter leaned out in the window above. She was dirty and lazy, and liked to loll there when travellers came, to hear the men talk, but she had a soft heart. Presently a hand came out of the window, and a pair of velvet slippers touched his shoulder, tiny slippers with black flowers. He pulled them out of her hand. Only one woman's feet had worn them, he knew that.

---

1 Salt-reim is a variation on the derogatory term "soutpiel," meaning an Englishman with one foot in South Africa and another in England so that his cock dangled in the salt waters of the Mediterranean.

"Left here last summer by a lady," said the girl; "might be the one you are looking for. Never saw any feet so small."

Gregory rose and questioned her.

They might have come in a waggon and spider, she could not tell. But the gentleman was very handsome, tall, lovely figure, blue eyes, wore gloves always when he went out. An English officer, perhaps; no Africander, certainly.

Gregory stopped her.

The lady? Well, she was pretty, rather, the girl said; very cold, dull air, silent. They stayed for, it might be, five days; slept in the wing over against the 'stoep'; quarrelled sometimes, she thought—the lady. She had seen everything when she went in to wait. One day the gentleman touched her hair; she drew back from him as though his fingers poisoned her. Went to the other end of the room if he came to sit near her. Walked out alone. Cold wife for such a handsome husband, the girl thought; she evidently pitied him, he was such a beautiful man. They went away early one morning, how or in which way, the girl could not tell.

Gregory inquired of the servants, but nothing more was to be learnt; so the next morning he saddled his horse and went on. At the farms he came to the good old 'Ooms' and 'Tantes' asked him to have coffee, and the little shoeless children peeped out at the stranger from behind ovens and gables; but no one had seen what he asked for. This way and that he rode to pick up the thread he had dropped; but the spider and the waggon, the little lady and the handsome gentleman, no one had seen. In the towns he fared yet worse.

Once indeed hope came to him. On the 'stoep' of an hotel at which he stayed the night in a certain little village, there walked a gentleman, grave and kindly-looking. It was not hard to open conversation with him about the weather, and then—Had he ever seen such and such people, a gentleman and lady, a spider and waggon, arrive at that place? The kindly gentleman shook his head. What was the lady like, he inquired.

Gregory painted. Hair like silken floss, small mouth, underlip very full and pink, upper lip pink but very thin and curled; there were four white spots on the nail of her right hand forefinger, and her eyebrows were very delicately curved.

The gentleman looked thoughtful, as trying to remember.

"Yes; and a rose-bud tinge in the cheeks; hands like lilies, and perfectly seraphic smile."

"That is she! that is she!" cried Gregory.

Who else could it be? He asked where she had gone to. The gentleman most thoughtfully stroked his beard. He would try to remember. Were not her ears———. Here such a violent fit of coughing seized him that he ran away into the house. An ill-fed clerk and a dirty barman standing in the doorway laughed aloud. Gregory wondered if they could be laughing at the gentleman's cough, and then he heard some one laughing in the room into which the gentleman had gone. He must follow him and try to learn more; but he soon found that there was nothing more to be learnt there. Poor Gregory!

Backwards and forwards, backwards and forwards, from the dirty little hotel where he had dropped the thread, to this farm and to that, rode Gregory, till his heart was sick and tired. That from that spot the waggon might have gone its own way and the spider another was an idea that did not occur to him. At last he saw it was no use lingering in that neighbourhood, and pressed on.

One day, coming to a little town, his horses knocked up, and he resolved to rest them there. The little hotel of the town was a bright and sunny place, like the jovial face of the clean little woman who kept it, and who trotted about talking always—talking to the customers in the tap-room, and to the maids in the kitchen, and to the passers-by when she could hail them from the windows; talking, as good-natured women with large mouths and small noses always do, in season and out.

There was a little front parlour in the hotel, kept for strangers who wanted to be alone. Gregory sat there to eat his breakfast, and the landlady dusted the room and talked of the great finds at the Diamond Fields, and the badness of maid-servants, and the shameful conduct of the Dutch parson in that town to the English inhabitants. Gregory ate his breakfast and listened to nothing. He had asked his one question, had had his answer; now she might talk on.

Presently a door in the corner opened and a woman came out—a Mozambiquer, with a red handkerchief twisted round her head. She carried in her hand a tray, with a slice of toast crumbled fine, and a half-filled cup of coffee, and an egg broken open, but not eaten. Her ebony face grinned complacently as she shut the door softly and said "Good morning."

The landlady began to talk to her.

"You are not going to leave her really, Ayah, are you?" she said. "The maids say so; but I'm sure you wouldn't do such a thing."

The Mozambiquer grinned.

"Husband says I must go home."

"But she hasn't got any one else, and won't have any one else. Come now," said the landlady, "I've no time to be sitting always in a sick room, not if I was paid anything for it."

The Mozambiquer only showed her white teeth good-naturedly for answer, and went out, and the landlady followed her.

Gregory, glad to be alone, watched the sunshine as it came over the fuchsias in the window, and ran up and down on the panelled door in the corner. The Mozambiquer had closed it loosely behind her, and presently something touched it inside. It moved a little, then it was still, then moved again; then through the gap a small nose appeared, and a yellow ear overlapping one eye; then the whole head obtruded, placed itself critically on one side, wrinkled its nose disapprovingly at Gregory, and withdrew. Through the half-open door came a faint scent of vinegar, and the room was dark and still.

Presently the landlady came back.

"Left the door open," she said, bustling to shut it; "but a darkey will be a darkey, and never carries a head on its shoulders like other folks. Not ill, I hope, sir?" she said, looking at Gregory when she had shut the bed-room door.

"No," said Gregory, "no."

The landlady began putting the things together.

"Who," asked Gregory, "is in that room?"

Glad to have a little innocent piece of gossip to relate, and some one willing to hear it, the landlady made the most of a little story as she cleared the table. Six months before a lady had come alone to the hotel in a waggon, with only a coloured leader and driver. Eight days after a little baby had been born. If Gregory stood up and looked out at the window he would see a blue gum-tree in the graveyard; close by it was a little grave. The baby was buried there. A tiny thing, only lived two hours, and the mother herself almost went with it. After a while she was better; but one day she got up out of bed, dressed herself without saying a word to any one, and went out. It was a drizzly day; a little time after some one saw her sitting on the wet ground under the blue gum-tree, with the rain dripping from her hat and shawl. They went to fetch her, but she would not come until she chose. When she did she had gone to bed, and had not risen again from it; never would, the doctor said.

She was very patient, poor thing. When you went in to ask her how she was she said always "Better," or "Nearly well!" and lay still in the darkened room, and never troubled any one. The Mozambiquer took care of her, and she would not allow any one else to touch her; would not so much as allow any one else to see her foot uncovered. She was strange in many ways, but she paid well, poor thing; and now the Mozambiquer was going, and she would have to take up with some one else.

The landlady prattled on pleasantly, and now carried away the tray with the breakfast-things. When she was gone Gregory leaned his head on his hands, but he did not think long.

Before dinner he had ridden out of the town to where on a rise a number of transport-waggons were out-spanned. The Dutchman driver of one wondered at the stranger's eagerness to free himself of his horses. Stolen perhaps; but it was worth his while to buy them at so low a price. So the horses changed masters, and Gregory walked off with his saddle-bags slung across his arm. Once out of sight of the waggons he struck out of the road and walked across the 'veld,'[1] the dry, flowering grasses waving everywhere about him; half way across the plain he came to a deep gully which the rain torrents had washed out, but which was now dry. Gregory sprang down into its red bed. It was a safe place, and quiet. When he had looked about him he sat down under the shade of an over-hanging bank and fanned himself with his hat, for the afternoon was hot, and he had walked fast. At his feet the dusty ants ran about, and the high red bank before him was covered by a network of roots and fibres washed bare by the rains. Above his head rose the clear blue African sky; at his side were the saddle-bags full of women's clothing. Gregory looked up half plaintively into the blue sky.

"Am I, am I Gregory Nazianzen Rose?" he said.

It was all so strange, he sitting there in that 'sloot' in that up-country plain—strange as the fantastic, changing shapes in a summer cloud. At last, tired out, he fell asleep, with his head against the bank. When he woke the shadow had stretched across the 'sloot,' and the sun was on the edge of the plain. Now he must be up and doing. He drew from his breast pocket a little sixpenny looking-glass, and hung it on one of the roots that stuck out from the bank. Then he dressed himself in one of the old-fashioned gowns and a great pinked-out collar. Then he took out a razor. Tuft by tuft the soft brown beard fell down into the sand, and the little ants took it to line their nests with. Then the glass showed a face surrounded

---

1 Open countryside.

by a frilled cap, white as a woman's, with a little mouth, a very short upper lip, and a receding chin.

Presently a rather tall woman's figure was making its way across the 'veld.' As it passed a hollowed-out ant-heap it knelt down, and stuffed in the saddle-bags with the man's clothing, closing up the ant-hill with bits of ground to look as natural as possible. Like a sinner hiding his deed of sin, the hider started once and looked round, but yet there was no one near save a 'meerkat,' who had lifted herself out of her hole and sat on her hind legs watching. He did not like that even she should see, and when he rose she dived away into her hole. Then he walked on leisurely, that the dusk might have reached the village streets before he walked there. The first house was the smith's, and before the open door two idle urchins lolled. As he hurried up the street in the gathering gloom he heard them laugh long and loudly behind him. He glanced round fearingly, and would almost have fled, but that the strange skirts clung about his legs. And after all it was only a spark that had alighted on the head of one, and not the strange figure they laughed at.

The door of the hotel stood wide open, and the light fell out into the street. He knocked, and the landlady came. She peered out to look for the cart that had brought the traveller; but Gregory's heart was brave now he was so near the quiet room. He told her he had come with the transport waggons that stood outside the town.

He had walked in, and wanted lodgings for the night.

It was a deliberate lie, glibly told; he would have told fifty, though the recording angel had stood in the next room with his pen dipped in the ink. What was it to him? He remembered that she lay there saying always, 'I am better.'

The landlady put his supper in the little parlour where he had sat in the morning. When it was on the table she sat down in the rocking-chair, as her fashion was, to knit and talk, that she might gather news for her customers in the tap-room. In the white face under the queer, deep-fringed cap she saw nothing of the morning's traveller. The new-comer was communicative. She was a nurse by profession, she said; had come to the Transvaal, hearing that good nurses were needed there. She had not yet found work. The landlady did not perhaps know whether there would be any for her in that town?

The landlady put down her knitting and smote her fat hands together.

If it wasn't the very finger of God's Providence, as though you saw it hanging out of the sky, she said. Here was a lady ill and needing a new nurse that very day, and not able to get one to her mind, and now—well, if it wasn't enough to convert all the atheists and freethinkers in the Transvaal she didn't know!

Then the landlady proceeded to detail facts.

"I'm sure you will suit her," she added; "you're just the kind. She has heaps of money to pay you with; has everything that money can buy. And I got a letter with a cheque in it for fifty pounds the other day from some one, who says I'm to spend it for her, and not to let her know. She is asleep now, but I'll take you in to look at her."

The landlady opened the door of the next room, and Gregory followed her. A table stood near the bed, and a lamp burning low stood on it; the bed was a great four-poster with white curtains, and the quilt was of rich crimson satin. But Gregory stood just inside the door with his head bent low, and saw no further.

"Come nearer! I'll turn the lamp up a bit, that you can have a look at her. A pretty thing, isn't it?" said the landlady.

Near the foot of the bed was a dent in the crimson quilt, and out of it Doss's small head and bright eyes looked knowingly.

"See how the lips move; she is in pain," said the landlady.

Then Gregory looked up at what lay on the cushion. A little white, white face, transparent as an angel's, with a cloth bound round the forehead, and with soft short hair tossed about on the pillow.

"We had to cut it off," said the woman, touching it with her fore-finger. "Soft as silk, like a wax doll's."

But Gregory's heart was bleeding.

"Never get up again, the doctor says," said the landlady.

Gregory uttered one word. In an instant the beautiful eyes opened widely, looked round the room and into the dark corners.

"Who is here? Whom did I hear speak?"

Gregory had sunk back behind the curtain; the landlady drew it aside, and pulled him forward.

"Only this lady, ma'am—a nurse by profession. She is willing to stay and take care of you, if you can come to terms with her."

Lyndall raised herself on her elbow, and cast one keen scrutinizing glance over him.

"Have I never seen you before?" she asked.

"No."

She fell back wearily.

"Perhaps you would like to arrange the terms between yourselves," said the landlady. "Here is a chair. I will be back presently."

Gregory sat down, with bent head and quick breath. She did not speak, and lay with half-closed eyes, seeming to have forgotten him.

"Will you turn the lamp down a little?" she said at last; "I cannot bear the light."

Then his heart grew braver in the shadow, and he spoke. Nursing was to him, he said, his chosen life's work. He wanted no money: if——She stopped him.

"I take no service for which I do not pay," she said. "What I gave to my last nurse I will give to you; if you do not like it you may go."

And Gregory muttered humbly, he would take it.

Afterwards she tried to turn herself. He lifted her. Ah! a shrunken little body, he could feel its weakness as he touched it. His hands were to him glorified for what they had done.

"Thank you! that is so nice. Other people hurt me when they touch me," she said. "Thank you!" Then after a little while she repeated humbly, "Thank you; they hurt me so."

Gregory sat down trembling. His little ewe-lamb, could they hurt her?

The doctor said of Gregory four days after, "She is the most experienced nurse I ever came in contact with."

Gregory, standing in the passage, heard it, and laughed in his heart. What need had he of experience? Experience teaches us in a millennium what passion teaches us in an hour. A Kaffir studies all his life the discerning of distant sounds; but he will never hear my step, when my love hears it, coming to her window over the short grass.

At first Gregory's heart was sore when day by day the body grew lighter, and the mouth he fed took less; but afterwards he grew accustomed to it, and was happy. For passion has *one* cry, one only—"Oh, to touch thee, Beloved!"

In that quiet room Lyndall lay on the bed with the dog at her feet, and Gregory sat in his dark corner watching.

She seldom slept, and through those long, long days she would lie watching the round streak of sunlight that came through the knot in the shutter, or the massive lion's paw on which the wardrobe rested. What thoughts were in those eyes? Gregory wondered; he dared not ask.

Sometimes Doss where he lay on her feet would dream that

they two were in the cart, tearing over the 'veld,' with the black horses snorting, and the wind in their faces; and he would start up in his sleep and bark aloud. Then awaking, he would lick his mistress's hand almost remorsefully, and slink quietly down into his place.

Gregory thought she had no pain, she never groaned; only sometimes, when the light was near her, he thought he could see slight contractions about her lips and eyebrows.

He slept on the sofa outside her door.

One night he thought he heard a sound, and, opening it softly, he looked in. She was crying out aloud, as if she and her pain were alone in the world. The light fell on the red quilt, and the little hands that were clasped over the head. The wide-open eyes were looking up, and the heavy drops fell slowly from them.

"I cannot bear any more, not any more," she said in a deep voice. "Oh God, God! Have I not borne in silence? Have I not endured these long, long months? But now, now, oh God, I cannot!"

Gregory knelt in the doorway listening.

"I do not ask for wisdom, not human love, not work, not knowledge, not for all things I have longed for," she cried; "only a little freedom from pain! only one little hour without pain! Then I will suffer again."

She sat up, and bit the little hand Gregory loved.

He crept away to the front door, and stood looking out at the quiet starlight. When he came back she was lying in her usual posture, the quiet eyes looking at the lion's claw. He came close to the bed.

"You have much pain to-night?" he asked her.

"No, not much."

"Can I do anything for you?"

"No, nothing."

She still drew her lips together, and motioned with her fingers towards the dog who lay sleeping at her feet. Gregory lifted him and laid him at her side. She made Gregory turn open the bosom of her night-dress that the dog might put his black muzzle between her breasts. She crossed her arms over him. Gregory left them lying there together.

The next day, when they asked her how she was, she answered "Better."

"Some one ought to tell her," said the landlady; "we can't let her soul go out into eternity not knowing, especially when I don't think it was all right about the child. You ought to go and tell her, Doctor."

So, the little doctor, edged on and on, went in at last. When he came out of the room he shook his fist in the landlady's face.

"Next time you have any Devil's work to do, do it yourself," he said, and shook his fist in her face again, and went away swearing.

When Gregory went into the bed-room he only found her moved, her body curled up, and drawn close to the wall. He dared not disturb her. At last, after a long time, she turned.

"Bring me food," she said, "I want to eat. Two eggs, and toast, and meat—two large slices of toast, please."

Wondering, Gregory brought a tray with all that she had asked for.

"Sit me up, and put it close to me," she said; "I am going to eat it all." She tried to draw the things near her with her fingers, and re-arranged the plates. She cut the toast into long strips, broke open both eggs, put a tiny morsel of bread into her own mouth, and fed the dog with pieces of meat put into his jaws with her fingers.

"Is it twelve o'clock yet?" she said; "I think I do not generally eat so early. Put it away, please, *carefully*—no, do not take it away—only on the table. When the clock strikes twelve I will eat it."

She lay down trembling. After a little while she said,

"Give me my clothes."

He looked at her.

"Yes; I am going to dress to-morrow. I should get up now but it is rather late. Put them on that chair. My collars are in the little box, my boots behind the door."

Her eyes followed him intently as he collected the articles one by one, and placed them on the chair as she directed.

"Put it nearer," she said; "I cannot see it;" and she lay watching the clothes, with her hand under her cheek.

"Now open the shutter wide," she said; "I am going to read."

The old, old tone was again in the sweet voice. He obeyed her; and opened the shutter, and raised her up among the pillows.

"Now bring my books to me," she said, motioning eagerly with her fingers; "the large book, and the reviews, and the plays; I want them all."

He piled them round her on the bed; she drew them greedily closer, her eyes very bright, but her face as white as a mountain lily.

"Now the big one off the drawers. No, you need not help me to hold my book," she said; "I can hold it for myself."

Gregory went back to his corner, and for a little time the restless turning over of leaves was to be heard.

"Will you open the window," she said, almost querulously, "and throw this book out? It is so utterly foolish. I thought it was a valuable book; but the words are merely strung together, they make no sense. Yes—so!" she said with approval, seeing him fling it out into the street. "I must have been very foolish when I thought that book good."

Then she turned to read, and leaned her little elbows resolutely on the great volume, and knit her brows. This was Shakespeare— it must mean something.

"I wish you would take a handkerchief and tie it tight round my head, it aches so."

He had not been long in his seat when he saw drops fall from beneath the hands that shaded the eyes, on to the page.

"I am not accustomed to so much light, it makes my head swim a little," she said. "Go out and close the shutter."

When he came back, she lay shrivelled up among the pillows.

He heard no sound of weeping; but the shoulders shook. He darkened the room completely.

When Gregory went to his sofa that night, she told him to wake her early; she would be dressed before breakfast. Nevertheless, when morning came, she said it was a little cold, and lay all day watching her clothes upon the chair. Still she sent for her oxen in the country; they would start on Monday and go down to the Colony.

In the afternoon she told him to open the window wide, and draw the bed near it.

It was a leaden afternoon, the dull rain-clouds rested close to the roofs of the houses, and the little street was silent and deserted. Now and then a gust of wind eddying round caught up the dried leaves, whirled them hither and thither under the trees, and dropped them again into the gutter: then all was quiet. She lay looking out. Presently the bell of the church began to toll, and up the village street came a long procession. They were carrying an old man to his last resting-place. She followed them with her eyes till they turned in among the trees at the gate.

"Who was that?" she asked.

"An old man," he answered, "a very old man; they say he was ninety-four; but his name I do not know."

She mused a while, looking out with fixed eyes.

"That is why the bell rang so cheerfully," she said. "When the old die it is well; they have had their time. It is when the young die that the bells weep drops of blood."

"But the old love life?" he said; for it was sweet to hear her speak.

She raised herself on her elbow.

"They love life, they do not want to die," she answered; "but what of that? They have had their time. They knew that a man's life is three-score years and ten; they should have made their plans accordingly! But the young," she said, "the young, cut down, cruelly, when they have not seen, when they have not known—when they have not found—it is for them that the bells weep blood. I heard in the ringing it was an old man. When the old die——Listen to the bell! it is laughing—'It is right, it is right: he has had his time.' They cannot ring so for the young."

She fell back exhausted; the hot light died from her eyes, and she lay looking out into the street. By-and-bye stragglers from the funeral began to come back and disappear here and there among the houses; then all was quiet, and the night began to settle down upon the village street. Afterwards, when the room was almost dark, so that they could not see each other's faces, she said, "It will rain to-night;" and moved restlessly on the pillows. "How terrible when the rain falls down on you."

He wondered what she meant, and they sat on in the still darkening room. She moved again.

"Will you presently take my cloak—the new grey cloak from behind the door—and go out with it. You will find a little grave at the foot of the tall blue gum-tree; the water drips off the long pointed leaves; you must cover it up with that."

She moved restlessly as though in pain.

Gregory assented, and there was silence again. It was the first time she had ever spoken of her child.

"It was so small," she said; "it lived such a little while—only three hours. They laid it close by me, but I never saw it; I could feel it by me." She waited; "Its feet were so cold; I took them in my hand to make them warm, and my hand closed right over them they were so little." There was an uneven trembling in the voice. "It crept close to me; it wanted to drink, it wanted to be warm." She hardened herself—"I did not love it; its father was not my prince; I did not care for it; but it was so little." She moved her hand. "They might have kissed it, one of them, before they put it in. It never did any one any harm in all its little life. They might have kissed it, one of them."

Gregory felt that some one was sobbing in the room.

Late on in the evening, when the shutter was closed and the lamp lighted, and the rain-drops beat on the roof, he took the cloak from behind the door and went away with it. On his way back he called at the village post-office and brought back a letter. In the hall he stood reading the address. How could he fail to know whose hand had written it? Had he not long ago studied those characters on the torn fragments of paper in the old parlour? A burning pain was at Gregory's heart. If now, now at the last, one should come, should step in between! He carried the letter into the bedroom and gave it her. "Bring me the lamp nearer," she said. When she had read it she asked for her desk.

Then Gregory sat down in the lamp-light on the other side of the curtain, and heard the pencil move on the paper. When he looked round the curtain she was lying on the pillow musing. The open letter lay at her side; she glanced at it with soft eyes. The man with the languid eyelids must have been strangely moved before his hand set down those words: "Let me come back to you! My darling, let me put my hand round you, and guard you from all the world. As my wife they shall never touch you. I have learnt to love you more wisely, more tenderly, than of old; you shall have perfect freedom. Lyndall, grand little woman, for your own sake be my wife!

"Why did you send that money back to me? You are cruel to me; it is not rightly done."

She rolled the little red pencil softly between her fingers, and her face grew very soft. Yet—

"It cannot be," she wrote; "I thank you much for the love you have shown me; but I cannot listen. You will call me mad, foolish—the world would do so; but I know what I need and the kind of path I must walk in. I cannot marry you. I will always love you for the sake of what lay by me those three hours; but there it ends. I must know and see. I cannot be bound to one whom I love as I love you. I am not afraid of the world—I will fight the world. One day—perhaps it may be far off—I shall find what I have wanted all my life; something nobler, stronger than I, before which I can kneel down. You lose nothing by not having me now; I am a weak, selfish, erring woman. One day I shall find something to worship and then I shall be—"

"Nurse," she said; "take my desk away; I am suddenly so sleepy; I will write more to-morrow." She turned her face to the pillow; it was the sudden drowsiness of great weakness. She had dropped asleep in a moment, and Gregory moved the desk softly, and then sat in the chair watching. Hour after hour passed, but he had no wish for rest, and sat on, hearing the rain cease, and the still night settle down everywhere. At a quarter-past twelve he rose, and took a last look at the bed where she lay sleeping so peacefully; then he turned to go to his couch. Before he had reached the door she had started up and was calling him back.

"You are sure you have put it up?" she said, with a look of blank terror at the window. "It will not fall open in the night, the shutter—you are sure?"

He comforted her. Yes, it was tightly fastened.

"Even if it is shut," she said in a whisper, "you cannot keep it out! You feel it coming in at four o'clock, creeping, creeping, up, up; deadly cold!" She shuddered.

He thought she was wandering, and laid her little trembling body down among the blankets.

"I dreamed just now that it was not put up," she said, looking into his eyes; "and it crept right in and I was alone with it."

"What do you fear?" he asked tenderly.

"The Grey Dawn," she said, glancing round at the window. "I was never afraid of anything, never when I was a little child, but I have always been afraid of that. You will not let it come in to me?"

"No, no; I will stay with you," he continued.

But she was growing calmer, "No; you must go to bed. I only awoke with a start; you must be tired. I am childish, that is all;" but she shivered again.

He sat down beside her. After some time she said, "Will you not rub my feet?"

He knelt down at the foot of the bed and took the tiny foot in his hand; it was swollen and unsightly now, but as he touched it he bent down and covered it with kisses.

"It makes it better when you kiss it; thank you. What makes you all love me so?" Then dreamily she muttered to herself: "Not utterly bad, not quite bad—what makes them all love me so?"

Kneeling there, rubbing softly, with his cheek pressed against the little foot, Gregory dropped to sleep at last. How long he knelt there he could not tell; but when he started up awake she was not looking at him. The eyes were fixed on the far corner, gazing wide and intent, with an unearthly light.

He looked round fearfully. What did she see there? God's angels come to call her? Something fearful? He saw only the purple curtain with the shadows that fell from it. Softly he whispered, asking what she saw there.

And she said, in a voice strangely unlike her own, "I see the vision of a poor weak soul striving after good. It was not cut short; and, in the end, it learnt, through tears and much pain, that holiness is an infinite compassion for others; that greatness is to take the common things of life and walk truly among them; that"—she moved her white hand and laid it on her forehead—"happiness is a great love and much serving. It was not cut short; and it loved what it had learnt—it loved—and——"

Was that all she saw in the corner?

Gregory told the landlady the next morning that she had been wandering all night. Yet, when he came in to give her her breakfast, she was sitting up against the pillows, looking as he had not seen her look before.

"Put it close to me," she said, "and when I have had breakfast I am going to dress."

She finished all he had brought her eagerly.

"I am sitting up quite by myself," she said, "Give me his meat;" and she fed the dog herself, cutting his food small for him. She moved to the side of the bed.

"Now bring the chair near and dress me. It is being in this room so long, and looking at that miserable little bit of sunshine that comes in through the shutter, that is making me so ill. Always that lion's paw!" she said, with a look of disgust at it. "Come and dress me." Gregory knelt on the floor before her, and tried to draw on one stocking, but the little swollen foot refused to be covered.

"It is very funny that I should have grown so fat since I have been so ill," she said, peering down curiously. "Perhaps it is want of exercise?" She looked troubled and said again, "Perhaps it is want of exercise." She wanted Gregory to say so too. But he only found a larger pair; and then tried to force the shoes, oh so tenderly! on to her little feet.

"There," she said, looking down at them when they were on, with the delight of a small child over its first shoes, "I could walk far now. How nice it looks!"

"No," she said, seeing the soft gown he had prepared for her, "I will not put that on. Get one of my white dresses—the one with the pink bows. I do not even want to think I have been ill. It is thinking and thinking of things that makes them real," she said. "When you draw your mind together, and resolve that a thing shall not be, it gives way before you; it is not. Everything is possible if one is resolved," she said. She drew in her little lips together, and Gregory obeyed her; she was so small and slight now it was like

dressing a small doll. He would have lifted her down from the bed
when he had finished, but she pushed him from her, laughing very
softly. It was the first time she had laughed in those long dreary
months.

"No, no; I can get down myself," she said, slipping cautiously on
to the floor. "You see!" She cast a defiant glance of triumph when
she stood there. "Hold the curtain up high, I want to look at
myself."

He raised it, and stood holding it. She looked into the glass on
the opposite wall. Such a queenly little figure in its pink and white.
Such a transparent little face, refined by suffering into an almost
angel-like beauty. The face looked at her; she looked back, laughing softly. Doss, quivering with excitement, ran round her, barking.
She took one step towards the door, balancing herself with outstretched hands.

"I am nearly there," she said.

Then she groped blindly.

"Oh, I cannot see! I cannot see! Where am I?" she cried.

When Gregory reached her she had fallen with her face against
the sharp foot of the wardrobe and cut her forehead. Very tenderly he raised the little crushed heap of muslin and ribbons, and laid
it on the bed. Doss climbed up, and sat looking down at it. Very
softly Gregory's hands disrobed her.

"You will be stronger to-morrow, and then we shall try again,"
he said, but she neither looked at him nor stirred.

When he had undressed her, and laid her in bed, Doss stretched
himself across her feet and lay whining softly.

So she lay all that morning, and all that afternoon.

Again and again Gregory crept close to the bedside and looked
at her; but she did not speak to him. Was it stupor or was it sleep
that shone under those half-closed eyelids? Gregory could not tell.

At last in the evening he bent over her.

"The oxen have come," he said; "we can start to-morrow if you
like. Shall I get the waggon ready to-night?"

Twice he repeated his question. Then she looked up at him, and
Gregory saw that all hope had died out of the beautiful eyes. It was
not stupor that shone there, it was despair.

"Yes, let us go," she said.

"It makes no difference," said the doctor; "staying or going; it is
close now."

So the next day Gregory carried her out in his arms to the waggon which stood 'in-spanned' before the door. As he laid her down

on the 'kartel' she looked far out across the plain. For the first time she spoke that day

"That blue mountain, far away; let us stop when we get to it, not before." She closed her eyes again. He drew the sails down before and behind, and the waggon rolled away slowly. The landlady and the niggers stood to watch it from the 'stoep.'

Very silently the great waggon rolled along the grass-covered plain. The driver on the front box did not clap his whip or call to his oxen, and Gregory sat beside him with folded arms. Behind them, in the closed waggon, she lay with the dog at her feet, very quiet, with folded hands. He, Gregory, dared not be in there. Like Hagar, when she laid her treasure down in the wilderness, he sat afar off:—"For Hagar said, 'Let me not see the death of the child.'"[1]

Evening came, and yet the blue mountain was not reached, and all the next day they rode on slowly, but still it was far off. Only at evening they reached it; not blue now, but low and brown, covered with long waving grasses and rough stones. They drew the waggon up close to its foot for the night. It was a sheltered, warm spot.

When the dark night had come, when the tired oxen were tied to the wheels, and the driver and leader had rolled themselves in their blankets before the fire, and gone to sleep, then Gregory fastened down the sails of the waggon securely. He fixed a long candle near the head of the bed, and lay down himself on the floor of the waggon near the back. He leaned his head against the 'kartel,' and listened to the chewing of the tired oxen, and to the crackling of the fire, till, overpowered by weariness, he fell into a heavy sleep. Then all was very still in the waggon. The dog slept on his mistress's feet, and only two mosquitoes, creeping in through a gap in the front sail, buzzed drearily round.

The night was grown very old when from a long, peaceful sleep Lyndall awoke. The candle burnt at her head, the dog lay on her feet; but he shivered; it seemed as though a coldness struck up to him from his resting-place. She lay with folded hands, looking upwards; and she heard the oxen chewing, and she saw the two mosquitoes buzzing drearily round and round, and her thoughts,— her thoughts ran far back into the past.

Through these months of anguish a mist had rested on her mind; it was rolled together now, and the old clear intellect awoke

---

1 Genesis 21:16.

from its long torpor. It looked back into the past; it saw the present; there was no future now. The old strong soul gathered itself together for the last time; it knew where it stood.

Slowly raising herself on her elbow, she took from the sail a glass that hung pinned there. Her fingers were stiff and cold. She put the pillow on her breast, and stood the glass against it. Then the white face on the pillow looked into the white face in the glass. They had looked at each other often so before. It had been a child's face once, looking out above its blue pinafore; it had been a woman's face, with a dim shadow in the eyes, and a something which had said, "We are not afraid, you and I; we are together; we will fight, you and I." Now to-night it had come to this. The dying eyes on the pillow looked into the dying eyes in the glass; they knew that their hour had come. She raised one hand and pressed the stiff fingers against the glass. They were growing very stiff. She tried to speak to it, but she would never speak again. Only, the wonderful yearning light was in the eyes still. The body was dead now, but the soul, clear and unclouded, looked forth.

Then slowly, without a sound, the beautiful eyes closed. The dead face that the glass reflected was a thing of marvellous beauty and tranquillity. The Grey Dawn crept in over it and saw it lying there.

Had she found what she sought for—something to worship? Had she ceased from being? Who shall tell us? There is a veil of terrible mist over the face of the Hereafter.

Chapter XIII.
Dreams.

"Tell me what a soul desires, and I will tell you what it is." So runs the phrase.

"Tell me what a man dreams, and I will tell you what he loves." That also has its truth.

For, ever from the earliest childhood to the latest age, day by day, and step by step, the busy waking life is followed and reflected by the life of dreams—waking dreams, sleeping dreams. Weird, misty, and distorted as the inverted image of a mirage, or a figure seen through the mountain mist, they are still the reflections of a reality.

On the night when Gregory told his story, Waldo sat alone before the fire, his untasted supper before him. He was weary after his day's work—too weary to eat. He put the plate down on the floor for Doss, who licked it clean, and then went back to his corner. After a time the master threw himself across the foot of the bed without undressing, and fell asleep there. He slept so long that the candle burnt itself out, and the room was in darkness. But he dreamed a lovely dream as he lay there.

In his dream, to his right rose high mountains, their tops crowned with snow, their sides clothed with bush and bathed in the sunshine. At their feet was the sea, blue and breezy, bluer than any earthly sea, like the sea he had dreamed of in his boyhood. In the narrow forest that ran between the mountains and the sea the air was rich with the scent of the honey-creeper that hung from dark green bushes, and through the velvety grass little streams ran purling down into the sea. He sat on a high square rock among the bushes, and Lyndall sat by him and sang to him. She was only a small child, with a blue pinafore, and a grave, grave, little face. He was looking up at the mountains, then suddenly when he looked round she was gone. He slipped down from his rock, and went to look for her, but he found only her little footmarks: he found them on the bright green grass, and in the moist sand, and there where the little streams ran purling down into the sea. In and out, in and out, and among the bushes where the honey-creeper hung, he went looking for her. At last, far off, in the sunshine, he saw her gathering shells upon the sand. She was not a child now, but a woman, and the sun shone on her soft brown hair, and in her white dress she put the shells she gathered. She was stooping, but when she heard his step she stood up, holding her skirt close about her, and waited for his coming. One hand she put in his, and together they walked on over the glittering sand and pink sea-shells; and they heard the leaves talking, and they heard the waters babbling on their way to the sea, and they heard the sea singing to itself, singing, singing.

At last they came to a place where was a long reach of pure white sand: there she stood still, and dropped on to the sand one by one the shells that she had gathered. Then she looked up into his face with her beautiful eyes. She said nothing; but she lifted one hand and laid it softly on his forehead; the other she laid on his heart.

With a cry of suppressed agony Waldo sprang from the bed, flung open the upper half of the door, and leaned out, breathing heavily.

Great God! it might be only a dream, but the pain was very real, as though a knife ran through his heart, as though some treacherous murderer crept on him in the dark! The strong man drew his breath like a frightened woman.

"Only a dream, but the pain was very real," he muttered, as he pressed his right hand upon his breast. Then he folded his arms on the door, and stood looking out into the starlight.

The dream was with him still; the woman who was his friend was not separated from him by years—only that very night he had seen her. He looked up into the night sky that all his life long had mingled itself with his existence. There were a thousand faces that he loved looking down at him, a thousand stars in their glory, in crowns, and circles, and solitary grandeur. To the man they were not less dear than to the boy they had been not less mysterious; yet he looked up at them and shuddered; at last turned away from them with horror. Such countless multitudes, stretching out far into space, and yet not in one of them all was she! Though he searched through them all, to the farthest, faintest point of light, nowhere should he ever say, "She is here!" To-morrow's sun would rise and gild the world's mountains, and shine into its thousand valleys; it would set and the stars creep out again. Year after year, century after century, the old changes of nature would go on, day and night, summer and winter, seed-time and harvest; but in none of them all would she have part!

He shut the door to keep out their hideous shining, and because the dark was intolerable lit a candle, and paced the little room, faster and faster yet. He saw before him the long ages of eternity that would roll on, on, on, and never bring her. She would exist no more. A dark mist filled the little room.

"Oh, little hand! oh, little voice! oh, little form!" he cried; "oh, little soul that walked with mine! oh, little soul, that looked so fearlessly down into the depths, do you exist no more for ever—for all time?" He cried more bitterly: "It is for this hour—this—that men blind reason, and crush out thought! For this hour—this, this—they barter truth and knowledge, take any lie, any creed, so it does not whisper to them of the dead that they are dead! Oh, God! God! for a Hereafter!"

Pain made his soul weak; it cried for the old faith. They are the tears that fall into the new-made grave that cement the power of the priest. For the cry of the soul that loves and loses is this, only this: "Bridge over Death; blend the Here with the Hereafter; cause the mortal to robe himself in immortality; let me not say of my Dead that it is dead! I will believe all else, bear all else, endure all else!"

Muttering to himself, Waldo walked with bent head, the mist in his eyes.

To the soul's wild cry for its own there are many answers. He began to think of them. Was not there one of them all from which he might suck one drop of comfort?

"You shall see her again," says the Christian, the true Bible Christian. "Yes, you shall see her again. '*And I saw the dead, great and small, stand before God. And the books were opened, and the dead were judged from those things which were written in the books. And whosoever was not found written in the book of life was cast into the lake of fire, which is the second death.*'[1] Yes, you shall see her again. She died so—with her knee unbent, with her hand unraised, with a prayer unuttered, in the pride of her intellect and the strength of her youth. She loved and she was loved; but she said no prayer to God; she cried for no mercy; she repented of no sin! Yes; you *shall* see her again."

In his bitterness Waldo laughed low:

Ah, he had long ceased to hearken to the hellish voice.

But yet another speaks.

"You shall see her again," says the nineteenth-century Christian, deep into whose soul modern unbelief and thought have crept, though he knows it not. He it is who uses his Bible as the pearl-fishers use their shells, sorting out gems from refuse; he sets his pearls after his own fashion, and he sets them well. "Do not fear," he says; "hell and judgment are not. God is love. I know that beyond this blue sky above us is a love as widespreading over all. The All-Father will show her to you again; not spirit only—the little hands, the little feet you loved, you shall lie down and kiss them if you will. Christ arose, and did eat and drink, so shall she arise. The dead, all the dead, raised incorruptible! God is love. You shall see her again."

It is a heavenly song, this of the nineteenth-century Christian. A man might dry his tears to listen to it, but for this one thing,—Waldo muttered to himself confusedly:—

"The thing I loved was a woman proud and young; it had a mother once, who, dying, kissed her little baby, and prayed God that she might see it again. If it had lived the loved thing would itself have had a son, who, when he closed the weary eyes and smoothed the wrinkled forehead of his mother, would have prayed God to see that old face smile again in the Hereafter. To the son

---

1   Revelations 20:12-14.

heaven will be no heaven if the sweet worn face is not in one of the choirs, he will look for it through the phalanx of God's glorified angels; and the youth will look for the maid, and the mother for the baby. 'And whose then shall she be at the resurrection of the dead?'"[1]

"Ah God! ah God! a beautiful dream," he cried; "but can any one dream it not sleeping?"

Waldo paced on, moaning in agony and longing. He heard the Transcendentalist's[2] high answer.

"What have you to do with flesh, the gross and miserable garment in which spirit hides itself? You shall see her again. But the hand, the foot, the forehead you loved, you shall see no more. The loves, the fears, the frailties that are born with the flesh, with the flesh they shall die. Let them die! There is that in man that cannot die,—a seed, a germ, an embryo, a spiritual essence. Higher than she was on earth, as the tree is higher than the seed, the man than the embryo, so shall you behold her; changed, glorified!"

High words, ringing well; they are the offering of jewels to the hungry, of gold to the man who dies for bread. Bread is corruptible, gold is incorruptible; bread is light, gold is heavy; bread is common, gold is rare; but the hungry man will barter all your mines for one morsel of bread. Around God's throne there may be choirs and companies of angels, cherubim and seraphim, rising tier above tier, but not for one of them all does the soul cry aloud. Only perhaps for a little human woman full of sin, that it once loved.

"Change is death, change is death," he cried. "I want no angel, only she; no holier and no better, with all her sins upon her, so give her me or give me nothing!"

And, truly, does not the heart love its own with the strongest passion for their very frailties? Heaven might keep its angels if men were but left to men.

"Change is death," he cried, "change is death! Who dares to say the body never dies, because it turns again to grass and flowers? And yet they dare to say the spirit never dies, because in space

1 Variation on the question posed by the Sadducees to Christ. See Matthew 20:28.
2 Nineteenth-century philosophers and writers who believed in the underlying unity of creation and the essential goodness of humankind. Schreiner appreciated the Transcendentalist essays of Ralph Waldo Emerson, for whom Waldo may have been named.

some strange unearthly being may have sprung up upon its ruins. Leave me! Leave me!" he cried in frantic bitterness. "Give me back what I have lost, or give me nothing."

For the soul's fierce cry for immortality is this,—only this:— Return to me after death the thing as it was before. Leave me in the Hereafter the being that I am today. Rob me of the thoughts, the feelings, the desires that are my life, and you have left nothing to take. Your immortality is annihilation; your Hereafter is a lie.

Waldo flung open the door, and walked out into the starlight, his pain-stricken thoughts ever driving him on as he paced there.

"There must be a Hereafter because man longs for it?" he whispered. "Is not all life from the cradle to the grave one long yearning for that which we never touch? There must be a Hereafter because we cannot think of any end to life. Can we think of a beginning? Is it easier to say 'I was not' than to say 'I shall not be'? And yet, where were we ninety years ago? Dreams, dreams! Ah, all dreams and lies! No ground anywhere."

He went back into the cabin and walked there. Hour after hour passed, and he was dreaming.

For, mark you, men will dream; the most that can be asked of them is but that the dream be not in too glaring discord with the thing they know. He walked with bent head.

All dies, all dies! the roses are red with the matter that once reddened the cheek of the child; the flowers bloom the fairest on the last year's battle-ground; the work of death's finger cunningly wreathed over is at the heart of all things, even of the living. Death's finger is everywhere. The rocks are built up of a life that was. Bodies, thoughts, and loves die: from where springs that whisper to the tiny soul of man, "You shall not die"? Ah, is there no truth of which this dream is shadow?

He fell into perfect silence. And, at last, as he walked there with his bent head, his soul passed down the steps of contemplation into that vast land where there is always peace; that land where the soul, gazing long, loses all consciousness of its little self, and almost feels its hand on the old mystery of Universal Unity that surrounds it.

"No death, no death," he muttered; "there is that which never dies—which abides. It is but the individual that perishes, the whole remains. It is but the organism that vanishes, the atoms are there. It is but the man that dies, the Universal Whole of which he is part reworks him into its inmost self. Ah, what matter that man's day be short!—that the sunrise sees him, and the sunset sees his grave; that of which he is but the breath has breathed him forth and drawn him back again. That abides we abide."

For the little soul that cries aloud for continued personal existence for itself and its beloved, there is no help. For the soul which knows itself no more as a unit, but as a part of the Universal Unity of which the Beloved also is a part; which feels within itself the throb of the Universal Life; for that soul there is no death.

"Let us die, beloved, you and I, that we may pass on for ever through the Universal Life!" In that deep world of contemplation all fierce desires die out, and peace comes down. He, Waldo, as he walked there, saw no more the world that was about him; cried out no more for the thing that he had lost. His soul rested. Was it only John, think you, who saw the heavens open?[1] The dreamers see it every day.

Long years before the father had walked in the little cabin, and seen choirs of angels, and a prince like unto men, but clothed in immortality. The son's knowledge was not as the father's; therefore, the dream was new-tinted, but the sweetness was all there, the infinite peace, that men find not in the little cankered kingdom of the tangible. The bars of the real are set close about us; we cannot open our wings but they are stuck against them, and drop bleeding. But, when we glide between the bars into the great unknown beyond, we may sail for ever in the glorious blue, seeing nothing but our own shadows.

So age succeeds age, and dream succeeds dream, and of the joy of the dreamer no man knoweth but he who dreameth.

Our fathers had their dream; we have ours; the generation that follows will have its own. Without dreams and phantoms man cannot exist.

Chapter XIV.
Waldo Goes Out to Sit in the Sunshine.

It had been a princely day. The long morning had melted slowly into a rich afternoon. Rains had covered the 'karroo' with a heavy coat of green that hid the red earth everywhere. In the very chinks of the stone walls dark green leaves hung out, and beauty and growth had crept even into the beds of the sandy furrows and lined

---

1 Revelations 21:2.

them with weeds. On the broken sod-walls of the old pigsty chick-weeds flourished, and ice-plants lifted their transparent leaves. Waldo was at work in the waggon-house again. He was making a kitchen-table for Em. As the long curls gathered in heaps before his plane, he paused for an instant now and again to throw one down to a small naked nigger, who had crept from its mother, who stood churning in the sunshine, and had crawled into the waggon-house. From time to time the little animal lifted its fat hand as it expected a fresh shower of curls; till Doss, jealous of his master's noticing any other small creature but himself, would catch the curl in his mouth and roll the little Kaffir over in the sawdust, much to that small animal's contentment. It was too lazy an after-noon to be really ill-natured, so Doss satisfied himself with snapping at the little nigger's fingers, and sitting on him till he laughed. Waldo, as he worked, glanced down at them now and then, and smiled; but he never looked out across the plain. He was conscious without looking of that broad green earth; it made his work pleasant to him. Near the shadow at the gable the mother of the little nigger stood churning. Slowly she raised and let fall the stick in her hands, murmuring to herself a sleepy chant such as her people love; it sounded like the humming of far-off bees.

A different life showed itself in the front of the house, where Tant' Sannie's cart stood ready inspanned, and the Boer-woman herself sat in the front room drinking coffee. She had come to visit her step-daughter, probably for the last time, as she now weighed two hundred and sixty pounds, and was not easily able to move. On a chair sat her mild young husband nursing the baby—a pudding-faced, weak-eyed child.

"You take it and get into the cart with it," said Tant' Sannie. "What do you want here, listening to our woman's talk?"

The young man arose, and meekly went out with the baby.

"I'm very glad you are going to be married, my child," said Tant' Sannie, as she drained the last drop from her coffee cup. "I wouldn't say so while that boy was here, it would make him too conceited; but marriage is the finest thing in the world. I've been at it three times, and if it pleased God to take this husband from me I should have another. There's nothing like it, my child; nothing."

"Perhaps it might not suit all people, at all times, as well as it suits you, Tant' Sannie," said Em. There was a little shade of weariness in the voice.

"Not suit every one!" said Tant' Sannie. "If the beloved Redeemer didn't mean men to have wives what did He make women for? That's what I say. If a woman's old enough to marry, and doesn't, she's sinning against the Lord—it's a wanting to know better than Him. What, does she think the Lord took all that trouble in making her for nothing? It's evident He wants babies, otherwise why does He send them? Not that I've done much in that way myself," said Tant' Sannie sorrowfully; "but I've done my best."

She rose with some difficulty from her chair, and began moving slowly towards the door.

"It's a strange thing," she said, "but you can't love a man till you've had a baby by him. Now there's that boy there—when we were first married if he only sneezed in the night I boxed his ears; now if he lets his pipe-ash come on my milkcloths I don't think of laying a finger on him. There's nothing like being married," said Tant' Sannie, as she puffed toward the door. "If a woman's got a baby and a husband she's got the best things the Lord can give her; if only the baby doesn't have convulsions. As for a husband, it's very much the same who one has. Some men are fat, and some men are thin; some men drink brandy, and some men drink gin; but it all comes to the same thing in the end; it's all one. A man's a man, you know."

Here they came upon Gregory, who was sitting in the shade before the house. Tant' Sannie shook hands with him.

"I'm glad you're going to get married," she said. "I hope you'll have as many children in five years as a cow has calves, and more too. I think I'll just go and have a look at your soap-pot before I start," she said, turning to Em. "Not that I believe in this new plan of putting soda in the pot. If the dear Father had meant soda to be put into soap what would He have made milk-bushes for, and stuck them all over the 'veld' as thick as lambs in the lambing season?"

She waddled off after Em in the direction of the built-in soap-pot, leaving Gregory as they found him, with his dead pipe lying on the bench beside him, and his blue eyes gazing out far across the flat, like one who sits on the sea-shore watching that which is fading, fading from him. Against his breast was a letter found in a desk addressed to himself, but never posted. It held only four words: "You must marry Em." He wore it in a black bag round his neck. It was the only letter she had ever written to him.

"You see if the sheep don't have the scab this year!" said Tant' Sannie as she waddled after Em. "It's with all these new inventions that the wrath of God must fall on us. What were the children of Israel punished for, if it wasn't for making a golden calf? I may have my sins, but I do remember the tenth commandment: 'Honour thy father and thy mother that it may be well with thee, and that thou mayst live long in the land which the Lord thy God giveth thee!' It's all very well to say we honour them, and then to be finding out things that they never knew, and doing things in a way that they never did them! *My* mother boiled soap with bushes, and I will boil soap with bushes. If the wrath of God is to fall upon this land," said Tant' Sannie, with the serenity of conscious virtue, "it shall not be through me. Let them make their steam-waggons and their fire-carriages; let them go on as though the dear Lord didn't know what he was about when He gave horses and oxen legs,—the destruction of the Lord will follow them. I don't know how such people read their Bibles. When do we hear of Moses or Noah riding in a rail-way? The Lord sent fire-carriages out of heaven in those days: there's no chance of His sending them for us if we go on in this way," said Tant' Sannie sorrowfully, thinking of the splendid chance which this generation had lost.

Arrived at the soap-pot she looked over into it thoughtfully.

"Depend upon it you'll get the itch, or some other disease; the blessing of the Lord'll never rest upon it," said the Boer-woman. Then suddenly she broke forth. "And she eighty-two, and goats, and rams, and eight thousand morgen, and the rams real angora, and two thousand sheep, and a short-horn bull," said Tant' Sannie, standing upright and planting a hand on each hip.

Em looked at her in silent wonder. Had connubial bliss and the joys of motherhood really turned the old Boer-woman's head?

"Yes," said Tant' Sannie; "I had almost forgotten to tell you. By the Lord if I had him here! We were walking to church last Sacrament Sunday, Piet and I. Close in front of us was old Tant' Trana, with dropsy and cancer, and can't live eight months. Walking by her was something with its hands under its coat-tails, flap, flap, flap; and its chin in the air, and a stick-up collar, and the black hat on the very back of the head. I knew him! 'Who's that?' I asked. 'The rich Englishman that Tant' Trana married last week.' 'Rich Englishman! I'll rich Englishman him' I said; 'I'll tell Tant' Trana a thing or two.' My fingers were just in his little white curls. If it hadn't been the blessed Sacrament, he wouldn't have walked so 'sourka, sourka, courka,' any more. But I thought, Wait till I've had it, and then———. But he, sly fox, son of Satan, seed of the Amalekite,[1] he

---

1 Amalekites were enemies of the Israelites. See 1 Samuel, Chapter 30.

saw me looking at him in the church. The blessed Sacrament wasn't half over when he takes Tant' Trana by the arm, and out they go. I clap my baby down to its father, and I go after them. But," said Tant' Sannie, regretfully, "I couldn't get up to them; I am too fat. When I got to the corner he was pulling Tant' Trana up into the cart. 'Tant' Trana,' I said, 'you've married a Kaffir's dog, a Hottentot's brakje.' I hadn't any more breath. He winked at me; he winked at me," said Tant' Sannie, her sides shaking with indignation, "first with one eye, and then with the other, and then drove away. Child of the Amalekite!" said Tant' Sannie, "if it hadn't been the blessed Sacrament. Lord, Lord, Lord!"

Here the little Bush-girl came running to say that the horses would stand no longer, and still breathing out vengeance against her old adversary she laboured towards the cart. Shaking hands and affectionately kissing Em, she was with some difficulty drawn up. Then slowly the cart rolled away, the good Boer-woman putting her head out between the sails to smile and nod. Em stood watching it for a time, then as the sun dazzled her eyes she turned away. There was no use in going to sit with Gregory: he liked best sitting there alone, staring across the green karroo; and till the maid had done churning there was nothing to do; so Em walked away to the waggon-house, and climbed on to the end of Waldo's table, and sat there, swinging one little foot slowly to and fro, while the wooden curls from the plane heaped themselves up against her black print dress.

"Waldo," she said at last, "Gregory has given me the money he got for the waggon and oxen, and I have fifty pounds besides that once belonged to some one. I know what they would have liked to have done with it. You must take it and go to some place and study for a year or two."

"No, little one, I will not take it," he said, as he planed slowly away; "the time was when I would have been very grateful to any one who would have given me a little money, a little help, a little power of gaining knowledge. But now, I have gone so far alone I may go on to the end. I don't want it, little one."

She did not seem pained at his refusal, but swung her foot to and fro, the little old wrinkled forehead more wrinkled up than ever.

"Why is it always so, Waldo, always so?" she said; "we long for things, and long for them, and pray for them; we would give all we have to come near to them, but we never reach them. Then at last, too late, just when we don't want them any more, when all the sweetness is taken out of them, then, they come. We don't want them then," she said, folding her hands resignedly on her little apron. After a while she added; "I remember once, very long ago, when I was a very little girl, my mother had a work-box full of coloured reels. I always wanted to play with them, but she would never let me. At last one day she said I might take the box. I was so glad I hardly knew what to do. I ran round the house, and sat down with it on the back steps. But when I opened the box all the cottons were taken out."

She sat for a while longer, till the Kaffir maid had finished churning, and was carrying the butter towards the house. Then Em prepared to slip off the table, but first she laid her little hand on Waldo's. He stopped his planing and looked up.

"Gregory is going to the town to-morrow. He is going to give in our banns to the minister; we are going to be married in three weeks."

Waldo lifted her very gently from the table. He did not congratulate her; perhaps he thought of the empty box, but he kissed her forehead gravely.

She walked away towards the house, but stopped when she had got half-way. "I will bring you a glass of buttermilk when it is cool," she called out; and soon her clear voice came ringing out through the back windows as she sang the "Blue Water" to herself, and washed the butter.

Waldo did not wait till she returned. Perhaps he had at last really grown weary of work; perhaps he felt the waggon-house chilly (for he had shuddered two or three times), though that was hardly likely in that warm summer weather; or, perhaps, and most probably, one of his old dreaming fits had come upon him suddenly. He put his tools carefully together, ready for to-morrow, and walked slowly out. At the side of the waggon-house there was a world of bright sunshine, and a hen with her chickens was scratching among the gravel. Waldo seated himself near them with his back against the red-brick wall. The long afternoon was half spent, and the 'kopje' was just beginning to cast its shadow over the round-headed yellow flowers that grew between it and the farmhouse. Among the flowers the white butterflies hovered, and on the old 'kraal' mounds three white kids gambolled, and at the door of one of the huts an old grey-headed Kaffir-woman sat on the ground mending her mats. A balmy, restful, peacefulness seemed to reign everywhere. Even the old hen seemed well satisfied. She scratched among the stones and called to her chickens when she found a treasure; and all the while tucked to herself with intense inward satisfaction. Waldo, as he sat with his knees drawn up to his chin and his arms folded on them, looked at it all and smiled. An evil world, a deceitful, treacherous, mirage-like world, it might be; but a lovely world for all that, and to sit there gloating in the sunlight was perfect. It was worth having been a little child, and having cried and prayed, so one might sit there. He moved his hands as though he were washing them in the sunshine. There will always be something worth living for while there are shimmery afternoons. Waldo chuckled with intense inward satisfaction as the old hen had done; she, over the insects and the warmth; he, over the old brick-walls, and the haze, and the little bushes. Beauty is God's wine, with which he recompenses the souls that love him; he makes them drunk.

The fellow looked, and at last stretched out one hand to a little ice-plant that grew on the sod-wall of the sty; not as though he would have picked it, but as it were in a friendly greeting. He loved it. One little leaf of the ice-plant stood upright, and the sun shone through it. He could see every little crystal cell like a drop of ice in the transparent green, and it thrilled him.

There are only rare times when a man's soul can see Nature. So long as any passion holds its revel there, the eyes are holden that they should not see her.

Go out if you will, and walk alone on the hill-side in the evening, but if your favourite child lies ill at home, or your lover comes to-morrow, or at your heart there lies a scheme for the holding of wealth, then you will return as you went out; you will have seen nothing. For Nature, ever, like the old Hebrew God, cries out, "Thou shalt have no other gods before me." Only then, when there comes a pause, a blank in your life, when the old idol is broken, when the old hope is dead, when the old desire is crushed, then the Divine compensation of Nature is made manifest. She shows herself to you. So near she draws you, that the blood seems to flow from her to you, through a still uncut cord: you feel the throb of her life.

When that day comes, that you sit down broken, without one human creature to whom you cling, with your loves the dead and the living-dead; when the very thirst for knowledge through long-continued thwarting has grown dull; when in the present there is no craving, and in the future no hope, then, oh, with a beneficent tenderness, Nature enfolds you.

Then the large white snowflakes as they flutter down, softly, one by one, whisper soothingly, "rest, poor heart, rest!" It is as though our mother smoothed our hair, and we are comforted.

And yellow-legged bees as they hum make a dreamy lyric; and the light on the brown stone wall is a great work of art; and the glitter through the leaves makes the pulses beat.

Well to die then; for, if you live, so surely as the years come, so surely as the spring succeeds the winter, so surely will passions arise. They will creep back, one by one, into the bosom that has cast them forth, and fasten there again, and peace will go. Desire, ambition, and the fierce agonizing flood of love for the living—they will spring again. Then Nature will draw down her veil: with all your longing you shall not be able to raise one corner; you cannot bring back those peaceful days. Well to die then!

Sitting there with his arms folded on his knees, and his hat slouched down over his face, Waldo looked out into the yellow sunshine that tinted even the very air with the colour of ripe corn, and was happy.

He was an uncouth creature with small learning, and no prospect in the future but that of making endless tables and stone walls, yet it seemed to him as he sat there that life was a rare and very rich thing. He rubbed his hands in the sunshine. Ah, to live on so, year after year, how well! Always in the present; letting each day glide, bringing its own labour, and its own beauty; the gradual lighting up of the hills, night and the stars, firelight and the coals! To live on so, calmly, far from the paths of men; and to look at the lives of clouds and insects; to look deep into the heart of flowers, and see how lovingly the pistil and the stamens nestle there together; and to see in the thorn-pods how the little seeds suck their life through the delicate curled-up string, and how the little embryo sleeps inside! Well, how well, to sit so on one side, taking no part in the world's life; but when great men blossom into books looking into those flowers also, to see how the world of men too opens beautifully, leaf after leaf. Ah! life is delicious; well to live long, and see the darkness breaking, and the day coming! The day when soul shall not thrust back soul that would come to it; when men shall not be driven to seek solitude, because of the crying-out of their hearts for love and sympathy. Well to live long and see the new time breaking. Well to live long; life is sweet, sweet, sweet! In his breast pocket, where of old the broken slate used to be, there was now a little dancing shoe of his friend who was sleeping. He could feel it when he folded his arm tight against his breast; and that was well also. He drew his hat lower over his eyes, and sat so motionless that the chickens thought he was asleep, and gathered closer around him. One even ventured to peck at his boot; but he ran away quickly. Tiny, yellow fellow that he was, he knew that men were dangerous; even sleeping they might awake. But Waldo did not sleep, and coming back from his sunshiny dream, stretched out his hand for the tiny thing to mount. But the chicken eyed the hand askance, and then ran off to hide under its mother's wing, and from beneath it it sometimes put out its round head to peep at the great figure sitting there. Presently its brothers ran off after a little white moth, and it ran out to join them; and when the moth fluttered away over their heads they stood looking up disappointed, and then ran back to their mother.

Waldo through his half-closed eyes looked at them. Thinking, fearing, craving, those tiny sparks of brother life, what were they, so real there in that old yard on that sunshiny afternoon? A few years—where would they be? Strange little brother spirits! He stretched his hand towards them, for his heart went out to them; but not one of the little creatures came nearer him, and he watched them gravely for a time; then he smiled, and began muttering to himself after his old fashion. Afterwards he folded his arms upon his knees, and rested his forehead on them. And so he sat there in the yellow sunshine, muttering, muttering, muttering to himself.

It was not very long after when Em came out at the backdoor with a towel thrown across her head, and in her hand a cup of milk.

"Ah," she said, coming close to him, "he is sleeping now. He will find it when he wakes, and be glad of it."

She put it down upon the ground beside him. The mother hen was at work still among the stones, but the chickens had climbed about him, and were perching on him. One stood upon his shoulder, and rubbed its little head softly against his black curls; another tried to balance itself on the very edge of the old felt hat. One tiny fellow stood upon his hand, and tried to crow; another had nestled itself down comfortably on the old coat-sleeve, and gone to sleep there.

Em did not drive them away; but she covered the glass softly at his side. "He will wake soon," she said, "and be glad of it."

But the chickens were wiser.

THE END.

Appendix A: Historical Contexts

1. James Anthony Froude, from *Two Lectures on South Africa*, 1880

[James Anthony Froude (1818-1894) wrote extensively on history and literature and other topics. He was also the friend and biographer of Thomas Carlyle, a prominent Victorian writer of controversial political views. In the 1870s, Froude traveled twice to South Africa to gather information and represent the views of the Secretary for the Colonies, Lord Carnarvon. The following excerpt is from a lecture given in Edinburgh five years after his return. At the time of his travels to South Africa, the British colonies and the Dutch states were very mistrustful of each other and of the intentions of the British government. On his second trip, Froude's mission had been to get all parties to agree on a conference to discuss native affairs and the possibility of forming a confederation of South African states. Although Froude was able to appeal successfully to many of the colonists, he was not able to convince the Colonial government officials. A conference was held in England in 1876, but since it was not attended by representatives from the Cape or the Transvaal, no resolution on confederation could be reached. Froude remained an advocate for reconciliation between the Dutch states and the British colonies and for justice for the native peoples.]

***

What I shall have to say has nothing to do with party politics. I know your rule here; and if you had no such rule, nothing could be more misleading than to treat the troubles which have arisen at the Cape of Good Hope as the results of a Liberal policy or of a Conservative policy. Neither are Liberals specially to blame nor Conservatives; we are merely reaping the harvest now of seventy years of mismanagement. Tory statesmen and Whig statesmen have alike borne their part in it, and we cannot throw stories at one another. The mistakes of both have risen from the simplest of causes. They have been attempting to govern a country six thousand miles off, of which they did not know anything, and took no pains to learn anything; and yet (we ought not, perhaps, to wonder at it) they never suspected their own ignorance. They have had certain fixed ideas, not always consistent, that the Dutch were a very wicked people; that the natives were innocent and harmless, or would be if the Dutch would let them alone.

Under the impression of these ideas they have attempted alternately to coerce the Dutch or to leave them to govern themselves; to protect the natives or make war upon them, and annex their territories. At one time we have insisted that the South Africans shall act as we please. Then we have told them to do as they please and to trouble us with their affairs no further. The story of our rule at the Cape is a story of vacillation varied with tyranny, which can be paralleled only in the history of our rule in Ireland. We say of our treatment of Ireland that if we had lived in the days of our fathers we would not have been partakers of their evil deeds. I am afraid that, like the Jews, we are showing ourselves our fathers' sons, and are treading in their steps and imitating their example with the most filial devoutness.

Therefore I am not going to quarrel especially with anything which this Government has done or the late Government or any Government. I am going simply to tell you what the state of South Africa was when I was there, why I went out, what persons I saw, what they said to me, and what came of it. You will then, I think, be at least able to understand how all these wonderful wars and annexations have been brought about, and why they have not brought South Africa a step nearer to quiet and content.

I will begin with the briefest possible account of these South African settlements, what they are and how they came into our possession.

We speak of South Africa as an English colony. It is not a colony. It is a conquered country, of which we took possession for our own purposes against the wish of its proper owners. English colonists have since settled there: but South Africa is Dutch. The laws are Dutch, the language, over the greater part of it, is Dutch. The Dutch occupied it more than two hundred years ago. They subdued the Hottentots, they destroyed the wild beasts. They built farmhouses and towns. They planted trees and vineyards. Forests of oak and pine introduced from Holland still speak for their industry. I have myself been a guest in Dutch houses in the interior which were built far back in the last century. English colonists go to South Africa to make money, and come back with it. To the Dutch settlers it is still a home, the only home they have. There they planted themselves, there they took root, and raised their families. There they mean to stay. It is their country. They feel for it as you do for Scotland or the French for France. They look on us as intruders. They hope to have it again one day for themselves, and the Dutch are a tough, stubborn, independent people, as the Spaniards and Austrians found to their cost when they tried to master them in Europe.

How, then, did we come by South Africa? After the French revolution the armies of the Convention overran Holland. It became for a time a French province, and the Dutch colonies, it was feared, would share the misfortunes of the mother-country. The Cape was on the high road to India. The Cape was then as important to England as the Suez Canal is now. At the extreme point of the African continent there is a land-locked bay: it is the one harbour where a naval arsenal can be made for several thousand miles. An enemy possession of Simon's Bay could interrupt the entire ocean traffic between Europe and the East. For this reason we took it. For this reason we are obliged to keep it. The Suez Canal may be blocked any day, and we may be driven back on the old route.

We occupied the Cape in 1795. The party in Holland who were opposed to France approved. The Cape colonists made slight resistance. It was understood that we went there only as a garrison, and that on the peace it would be restored. At the Peace of Amiens it was in fact restored; but war broke out again immediately, and we went back. This time the colonists did not admit us so quietly. They armed; they fought gallantly for their liberties; they were defeated, and they submitted a second time. We said that we should go away again when the war was finally over. It would have been better, I think, both for us and for South Africa if we had gone away. A high-spirited population never willingly submits to be ruled by strangers. The conqueror forgets. The conquered does not forget, and nourishes hopes which spring again when opportunity offers. The English, however, when in possession of places which they find convenient, are apt to stay there. We had got hold of the Cape; we wished to keep our hold, and at the Congress of Vienna it was arranged as we desired. The Dutch colonists were not consulted.

★★★

Naturally enough when [Lord Carnarvon] took up his work the state of things in South Africa drew his attention. I happened to mention to him that I was about to travel, and was undecided where to go. He told me that he was perplexed by the reports which reached him from the Cape of Good Hope. Natal had been in conflagration; trouble was growing about the Diamond Fields; evidently mischief was at work of some kind. He said he should like to hear from some unprejudiced person what it all meant, and what was the cause of it. He suggested that if I wished to turn my travels to some account I might make a tour through South Africa, of course on my own responsibility, and tell him what I thought about it.

It was in this way that I came to be concerned in these matters, and that I am now speaking to you about them here in Edinburgh. The Proposal suited me well enough. Lord Carnarvon gave me letters, and I went out in the summer of 1874 and reached Cape Town in September. I have no leisure time now for the picturesque. Cape Town is a wonderfully beautiful place, and that is all that I can say about it. I found everybody abusing Bishop Colenso.[1] He had just left on his way to England; we had crossed each other on the voyage. My letters gave me access to the politicians. Mr. Molteno, who was then Premier, was gracious and communicative, and talked to me very freely about the state of the country. He spoke moderately of what had happened in Natal. He thought that there had been far too much violence; but still there had been a real danger, which could not be neglected. He had felt it his duty to support the Natal Government, as any difference of opinion might excite the natives elsewhere. He protested strongly against English interference; if the Colony was to bear the burden of its own defence, the Colony must be allowed its own native policy.

This seemed only reasonable.

He next spoke of the Diamond Fields, where I was better

---

1   J.W. Colenso, Anglican Bishop of Natal, is an important figure in religious controversies as well as politics. For writing a critical examination of the Pentateuch, the Church tried to excommunicate him. Later Colenso defended Chief Langalibalele from trumped up charges by the settlers which resulted in his imprisonment and the confiscation of his people's lands. Unable to get a fair hearing in Natal, Bishop Colenso went to England, met with Lord Carnarvon and returned to South Africa in 1875 with some promises of redress for the natives. Trouble between the settlers and the natives, especially after his defense of Langalibalele, weakened Colenso's relationship with his congregation, but he was never forced to retire.

informed, for I had been studying the Blue-books and I could appreciate what Mr. Molteno said. He regretted very strongly the action of the High Commissioner towards the Dutch States. He had himself, he said, opposed the annexation of the Diamond Fields, and if he could he would have prevented it. The quarrel, he thought, was being needlessly and unwisely exasperated. It was not his business to interfere; but he wished with all his heart that the Imperial Government would adopt more moderate measures, the Dutch people all over the country being greatly irritated. He declined to say what he thought we ought to do. He was cautious of committing himself; but his condemnation of the proceedings of the High Commissioner was as emphatic as words could make it.

But I was to see the actual scene of the disturbance with my own eyes. I went on to Natal, and thence through the Transvaal, the Diamond Fields, and the Orange Free State. I cannot here describe my journey. I will tell you only the general impressions which I formed. Langalibalele[1] of course was the one subject in Natal. Three of his sons and several hundreds of his tribe were in Maritzburg gaol, as convicts at hard labor. They had not been tried, and they had been in confinement for a year. I saw them and heard their story. The interpreter, who had no prejudice in their favour, was satisfied that they were speaking truth. The account they gave me was the same as that which Bishop Colenso gave, and which England afterwards found to be true.

The Natal people were proud of their achievement, and were furious that it should be called in question. They said that they would have responsible government, like the Cape. A party among them desired to join the Free State and be independent. Responsible government meant that they were to take their own defence upon themselves. That I see is what the English papers now say that they ought to do. Colonists, it is perfectly true, ought to be prepared to defend themselves. But I could wish that the English papers would remember that Natal is not an English colony any more than the Cape. It is only the last, or rather it was then only the last, of the conquests which we had made from the Dutch.

---

1 Some of Langalibalele's men were paid illegally in guns instead of wages, and their chief was called to account. He refused to answer the charges and was sentenced to death, and later to relocation.

There are but ten thousand English there all told. Many of these are no better than the mean whites in the Southern States of the Union. The utmost that they could do would be to bring into the field seven or eight hundred men badly armed and undrilled. We ourselves had to send twenty thousand regular troops there to deal with the Zulus, and the effect of responsible government could only be that they would provoke a war in some foolish panic, and if Natal was still British territory, we should be obliged to go to their help after all, to save the survivors, if any survivors were left. The Dutch would not help them. The Dutch would say that if we chose to take the country we must protect it.

★★★

My own business was to enquire into the circumstances of the annexation [of the Diamond Fields, formerly part of the Orange Free State]. Half the diggers openly called it robbery, and would have preferred to belong to the Free State. I enquired what had become of Waterboer, the Griqua chief, in whose name we had occupied the place. It appeared that we had cracked the nut, kept the kernel, and given Waterboer the shell. He was away somewhere on a slip of wilderness which had been allowed for himself and his tribe. We had taken away the diamond mine from the Free States on the ground that it belonged to Waterboer; we had then turned out Waterboer and kept it ourselves. Across the lines of the original dispute appeared the figures of persons who had been speculating inland; of some who had made great fortunes; of others who bad missed the fortunes, and were ready to split on their luckier rivals. I was in a spider's web spun out of a thousand cross twinings, and where the truth was I could not pretend to judge. I asked one man who was behind the scenes to tell me whether Waterboer's claims had any basis in them. 'Not a fraction,' he said; 'the whole business has been a trick and a swindle. I will prove it so before any arbitrator in the world.'

My own conclusion, after hearing all that could be said, was that I was among a people whose only language on the subject was an infinite conjugation of the verb to lie. As the witnesses flatly contradicted each other, half of them must have lied. I could only regret that the English good name had been soiled by contact with so dirty a business and we had broken our solemn word too. We have heard much lately about treaties and the faith of treaties. In modern European history no treaty has been ever broken with more deliberate shamelessness than the treaty of Aliwal was broken by us when we annexed the Diamond Fields.

I had still to visit Bloemfontein, the capital of the Orange Free State itself, about seventy miles from the mine. The President, Mr. Brand, I found in no better humour towards England than his brother President in Pretoria. President Burgers was smooth and polished; you could see no further than the surface of him, and then only the outside objects reflected upon it. President Brand was a blunt and straightforward Dutchman, who said what he meant, and was incapable of uttering a single word which he did not mean. To me, when I first saw him, he spoke with dignity and some sternness. The English, a great powerful nation, had been pleased, he said, to break faith with a small weak Republic. They had robbed the Orange Free State, and they had justified themselves by charging the Free State with crimes which it had not committed. He had asked for the arbitration of a foreign Power; and he had been told that England would not submit her actions to the judgment of foreigners; he had tried other means of obtaining redress but they had all failed. He had sent round a protest to the Great Powers, but he could not pretend to resist by force. His people would have resisted, but he had forbidden them; he would not sanction needless bloodshed. I found that he believed that there was a real Providence in this world, and that an unjust action would not be allowed to prevail.

It was not for me to admit that my own Government had been as unrighteous as President Brand maintained. He, on his part, did not seem to care much whether we came to an arrangement with him or not. He thought, like President Burgers, that our day was nearly over in South Africa. History, he said, showed that all colonies became independent sooner or later. Meanwhile, I suppose he relied on his friends in the Cape Parliament. They could not undo the annexation, but they would protect him from further violence.

Mr. Brand had discharged his resentment upon me as the first Englishman that came in his way; I liked him none the worse for it, and after a few days we became more intimate. He wished to go into his injuries in detail. As well as I could I avoided this. I told him that whether the annexation had been justifiable or not, there would now be an insuperable difficulty in undoing it; but I was sure that the English Government had no bad intentions against him, and that if he could suggest any other way in which good feeling could be restored between us, I believed the Government would meet him half way.

With all their stubbornness the Dutch have a vein of sentiment in them. Mr. Brand seemed to think that his people would be satisfied if we would acknowledge that we had done them wrong. He did not ask to have the mine restored to him; he knew that it was impossible. A fair boundary, with some trifling compensation, would meet his wishes; and in return he said, like the Boers in the Transvaal, that if we wished it he would then make some modifications in his native administration. He was already, indeed, trying experiments in this direction, and going as far as he dared. Part with his independence, however, he never would. He was sworn to maintain it, and he would maintain it. The friend and ally of English he was willing to be; its subject never.

That is the true Boer feeling; and no threats, no cajoling, no force, no interest will ever alter it. Such a feeling, I think, deserves to be respected.

★★★

The Colonial Office had long been anxious to confederate the States of South Africa, and to form a self-governed Dominion there like that which had succeeded so well in Canada. If the Republics could be induced to join, all difficulty would be at an end. The mine would still be English, to whatever province it might be attached. The advantages of such an arrangement were obvious at home, and we are apt to assume that, our views being always reasonable, other people will see things as we do. Other people, unfortunately, are not always reasonable. The Dutch States I knew to be most unreasonably fond of independence. The Cape Dutch, everywhere object to our presence at the Cape in any shape. The two Republics were free of us, and I thought it most unlikely that with their own consent they would come back under our flag. They were ready, if they were well treated, for an alliance with us; they were willing to modify their native administration to please us. The Queen's subjects they would not agree to be for any bribe that we might hold out to them.

Nor did I think the colony would like Confederation. At present it had all the advantages of the situation. The trade of the interior States passed through the colonial ports; duties were levied there on every bale of goods that passed up to the Free States and the Diamond Fields. The colony kept those duties; it keeps them still. Under confederation it would have to account for them. The colony was rich; it was out of harm's way; Natal might be in danger from the natives; the Cape Colony was in little danger, if in any. Why should the Cape make itself responsible for keeping the peace in Natal and in the interior States? The colony, I thought, would relieve us of the Diamond Fields if the dispute with the Free States could be first arranged—more than this I did not think it would do.

★★★

Meanwhile the Government at home was anxious to realise the feeling which had arisen in favour of Confederation. An enabling Bill was passed through Parliament, in spite of the efforts of the Irish members, and Sir Bartle Frere went out as Governor to carry it into act. The Cabinet was in too great a hurry. Confederations may grow, but they cannot be manufactured. All the Acts of Parliament in the world will not ripen the harvest a day before its time. The Cabinet believed, unluckily, that the harvest was ripe already, and that they had only to gather it. The state of the Transvaal was partly our own fault, for it was we who had supplied the natives with guns and powder. The situation was tempting; for the Transvaal seemed the key of the political position. With the Transvaal in our hands there could be no more negotiations with other nations. The Orange Free State would be surrounded by British territory, and would soon be tired of its independence. Why not take the Transvaal then? Nothing would better please the old enemies of the Boers. English settlers and traders there wished it, for the security of their property. No one knows less, I think, of the feelings of the Dutch than their English neighbours, and all English people habitually believe what they wish. It seemed a mere act of humanity to step in and prevent a war between the Boers and the natives. Lord Carnarvon, with the entire conviction that the Boers themselves desired it, allowed the Transvaal to be taken over, as it was called, in the Queen's name.

Those who really understood South Africa knew what must follow. If we had wished to gain the affection of the Dutch people for ever, Providence had given us the opportunity. A small loan of money and a public offer of help to the Dutch Republic, if it was in extremities, would have shot the South African States into one as easily as if they had been so many balls of quicksilver. If Lord Carnarvon had wished to do this, English prejudice would perhaps have forbidden him; but I think he might have waited. If the danger to the Transvaal was as real and as near as Lord Carnarvon was led to believe, the Boers in a few months would have appealed to him for assistance, and he could have made his own terms. They could not then have said that they were annexed against their will. They could not then have said, as they say now, that they did not want our help, and that they could have successfully defended themselves.

Annexation, unasked for would certainly revive the bitter feelings of the Dutch in the Cape Colony. It would forfeit all that had been gained by the settlement of the Diamond Fields affair, and it would again entangle the Imperial Government in the concerns of the interior of the continent. The Cape Colony would only undertake the defence of the interior frontier, if it was obliged to undertake it. If we chose to take it upon ourselves, they would be only too happy to see us charged with the burden, and Confederation would only be further off than ever. We had just extricated ourselves out of this position by the engagement of the Cape to take the Diamond Fields. Why should we plunge into it again? If the object was to prevent a struggle with the natives, the chances were that the struggle would come notwithstanding. The difference would only be that the business of killing the natives would fall on us and not on the Dutch.

Notwithstanding these objections, the annexation was persisted in, and the Zulu War immediately followed.

It was not the first war which Sir Bartle Frere had begun in South Africa. Sir Bartle Frere had gone out, as I said, to confederate the South African States. If the Cape Colony was to undertake the defence of the country, the object should have been to diminish as far as possible the responsibilities which would be thrown upon the Colony. The Government at home had just added to these responsibilities on one side by taking the Transvaal. Sir Bartle Frere, in his capacity of High Commissioner, made War on Kreli, the chief of the Kaffirs, and annexed Kaffraria, adding about half a million to the number of natives whom the Colony would be expected to govern. Kaffraria is naturally rich. It is, or it might be, the garden of South Africa. No doubt many of the colonists looked on it with covetous eyes. It is easy to make a war if you wish for it. Kreli had done us no harm. Some difference had risen between Kreli's people and a tribe who were under our protection. It was a mere police case, but perhaps the High Commissioner thought that the way to Confederation would be made more easy if the independent native chiefs in the neighbourhood of the Colony were brought into subjection. Demands were made on Kreli which he could not accept. War followed. It cost the Colony a million. How much it cost us I do not know. It spread along the frontier up to the Kei, and down the Orange River. Vast numbers of men have been destroyed. Women and children have been killed in cold blood. Kreli is still at large, but his country has been taken from him. This war is but just over. The last stage of it was the storming of the stronghold of a Basuto chief named Morosi. Morosi himself was killed.

When the Kaffir war was half finished, Sir Bartle Frere went on to Natal to settle with the Zulus. The Zulus are the noblest and bravest of all the African tribes so far as we yet know them. They and their king Cetewayo had always been good neighbors to the English in Natal, and as long as the Boers had the Transvaal it was our policy to be on good terms with Cetewayo. The Zulus are a warlike people, as we know to our cost. They were proud of their independence, and determined to maintain it, and they kept up a large army. I do not see that they were to be blamed for this. I mentioned that there was a disputed frontier between them and the Boers. The cause of our taking the Transvaal was to prevent the Boers and the Zulus from fighting. When the Transvaal became ours the frontier had still to be settled. A Commission was appointed to arrange it, one member of which was my distinguished and gallant friend Colonel Durnford, who was killed at Isandwana. The Commissioners reported in favour of the line claimed by the Zulus. But some Dutch farmers had located themselves on the Zulu side of it, and Sir Bartle decided that Cetewayo must be content with his sovereignty, and must leave these Boers in possession of the land. As the Boers were in a bad humour with us for having taken away their liberty, it was thought, perhaps, that a sop of this kind would please them. Cetewayo would not agree to this; and as there was no longer any Transvaal Republic against which his army might be useful, we discovered that he had no need of an army. It had been always an anxiety to the people in Natal; they did not like exerting themselves, or taxing themselves, to keep up a force of their own. I think the force of police which was kept up by Natal amounted to about 200 men. Cetewayo had 40,000 or 50,000. It would be more agreeable to the Natalians, and perhaps Sir Bartle thought that the Cape Colony would be more ready to take charge of Natal, if this army of Cetewayo's was broken up. So Cetewayo was treated as Kreli had been. There was no difficulty in

finding an excuse. The Tugela River only divides Natal from Zululand; fugitives from either side were in the habit of crossing to the
other. Some Zulu runaways had come over into Natal, and had
been pursued and taken back. Reparation might have been
demanded fairly; but Cetewayo was told at the same time that, as
British territory now lapped him round, his army was unnecessary.
If used at all, it could only be used against us. This was very likely
true. Cetewayo, seeing us swallowing so much territory, thought it
as well, naturally enough, to be on his guard against us; but a reason like this Sir Bartle could not recognise. The Kaffir war had
brought a larger number of British troops into South Africa than
are usually maintained there. The opportunity was a favourable
one; and Sir Bartle sent an ultimatum to Cetewayo requiring,
among other demands, that his regiments should be disbanded. Of
course he knew that the brave, proud chief could give him but one
answer. He would have redressed any wrong which had been committed by his people; he could not lay down his arms at the com-
mand of a British Governor. A friend of mine lately visited Cetewayo in his prison at Cape Town, and asked him if he did not
regret having disobeyed Sir Bartle's commands. Cetewayo replied
that had he known all that would happen he would have given the
same reply. A brave man might know that he would be beaten, but
he would still fight, rather than submit like a coward. His people all
felt as he did.

I think you in Scotland ought to have some sympathy with
Cetewayo and his Zulus.

★★★

In that case 'we have made our bed,' as they say, 'and we must
lie upon it.' We have chosen for our own amusement to take Kaffraria, to take the Transvaal, to conquer Zululand. It will be bad
for us in every way to be led to suppose that we can send troops
and annex territories wholesale, and then thrust the trouble of
them upon others. If we eat an unwholesome supper we must not
expect our neighbours to suffer the indigestion. We must bear the
indigestion ourselves, and it is very good that we should. We shall
be more careful what we eat thereafter. I have been considering
nothing but our own interests. But the natives, too, have a right
to be considered. If we invade them and overthrow their chiefs,
the least that we can do is to provide them with a tolerable government in return. A tolerable government means one that shall

be just and strong. The Colony cannot provide such a government. We can—and we only. The natives will resist the colonists, because they believe that they are a match for them. British magistrates they will not resist, because they know that the power of Great Britain lies behind. I am sorry that circumstances or our own folly have forced us into an expensive position. But being there we must honourably make the best of it. Kaffraria, Basuto Land, Natal, and the Protectorate over Zululand will then remain in the hands of the Crown, and the Crown will have to keep them till the natives can be sufficiently educated to be trusted with the franchise. The experiment can thus be tried whether any of the native races in South Africa are capable of real civilization. Under a South African Dominion, under the rule of the colonists, they would be doomed to inevitable degradation. Under such a rule as that which we maintain in India they will have a chance of rising, if it be in them to rise. The Kaffirs have long taught us to respect and fear them as a brave and honourable tribe. The Zulus have earned a bigger distinction: they have defeated an English General in the open field. They will multiply—either to be our credit or to be our shame. War among themselves kept their numbers down. When they can no longer fight, they will increase as the Irish increased. If we can succeed in educating them, no more honourable achievement will have to be recorded by the future historian of the British Empire. If we fail, we fail: but we shall have failed in an enterprise which even to have attempted will in some way redeem the stain of our dark and discreditable conquests.

The Transvaal, in spite of prejudices about the British flag, I still hope that we shall restore to its lawful owners.

2. Olive Schreiner, from *Thoughts on South Africa*, 1891

[This essay was first published in London (*Fortnightly Review*) and South Africa (*Cape Times*) in 1891. It was republished along with several other essays in a book of the same title in 1923. Although the essay argues for South African national identity, it also defines race as the most important obstacle to unity. Unfortunately, Schreiner never addressed the history or lives of black South Africans. Her other essays are primarily concerned with analyzing the culture of the Boers.]

South Africa: Its Natural Features, its Diverse Peoples,
its Political Status: The Problem

There are artists who, loving their work, when they have finished
it, put it aside for years, that, after the lapse of time, returning to
it and reviewing it from the standpoint of distance, they may
judge of it in a manner which was not possible while the passion
of creation and the link of unbroken emotion bound them to
it.

What the artist does intentionally, life often does for us fortu-
itously in other relationships.

It may be questioned whether a man has ever been able to form
an adequate conception of his mother's face in its relation to others, till after long years of absence he has returned to it, and,
whether he will or no, there flashes on him the consciousness of its
beauty, nobility, weariness, or age as compared with that of others;
a thing which was not possible to him, when it rose for him every
morning as the sun, and mingled itself with all the experiences of
his day.

What is true of the personal mother is yet more true of the
man's native land. It has shaped all his experiences; it has lain as the
background to all his consciousness; it has modified his sensations
and emotions. He can no more pass a calm, relative judgment on
it, than an artist can upon the work he is creating, or a child, at the
breast can analyze the face above it. The incapacity of peoples to
pass judgments on the surroundings from which they have never
been separated is familiar to every traveller. The mayor of the little
German town does not take you to see the costumes of the peas-
ants, nor the old church, nor the Dürer over the altar; but drags you
away to see the new row of gas-lamps in the village street. The costumes, the church, the picture are unique in Europe and the world;
better gas-lamps flame before every butcher's shop in London and
Paris; but the lamps are new and have cost him much; he cannot
view them objectively. The inhabitant of one of the rarest and
fairest towns in the colonies or on earth does not boast to you of
his oaks and grapes, or ask you what you think of his mountain, or
explain to you the marvellous mixture of races in his streets; but he
is anxious to know what you think of his docks and small public
buildings. He has not the emotional detachment necessary for the
forming of a large critical judgment. A certain distance is necessary
to the seeing of great wholes clearly. It is not by any chance that
the most scientific exposition of American Democracy is the work

of a Frenchman, that the best history of the French Revolution is by an Englishman, or that the finest history of English literature is the work of a Frenchman.[1] Distance is essential for a keen, salient survey, which shall take in large outlines and mark prominent characteristics.

It is customary to ridicule the traveller who passes rapidly through a country, and then writes his impression of it. The truth is he sees much that is hidden for ever from the eyes of the inhabitants. Habit and custom have blinded them. They are indignant when it is said that their land is arid, that it has few running streams, that its population is scanty, and that vegetables are scarce; and they are amused and surprised when he descants for three pages on the glorious rarity of their air, and the scientific interest of their mingled peoples: yet these are the prominent external features which differentiate their land from all others.

Nevertheless, there is a sense in which the people of a country are justified in their contempt of the bird's-eye view of the stranger. There is a certain knowledge of a land which is only to be gained by one born in it, or brought into long-continued, close, personal contact with it, and which in its perfection is perhaps never obtained by any man with regard to a country which he has not inhabited before he was thirty. It is the subjective emotional sympathy with its nature, and the comprehension not merely of the vices and virtues of its people, but of the how and why of their existence, which is possible to a man only with regard to a country that is more or less his own. The stranger sees the barren scene, but of the emotion which that barren mountain is capable of awakening in the man who lives under its shadow he knows nothing. He marks the curious custom, but of the social condition which originated it, and the passions concerned in its maintenance, he understands absolutely nothing.

This subtle, sympathetic, subjective knowledge of a land and people is that which is essential to the artist, and to the great leader of men. Without it no artist has ever greatly portrayed a land or a people, no great statesman or reformer has ever led or guided a nation or race....

---

1 Alexis de Tocqueville (1805-1859) wrote *Democracy in America* (1835-1840); Thomas Carlyle (1795-1881) wrote *The French Revolution* (1837); and Hippolyte Taine (1828-1893) wrote *History of English Literature* (1863-64, translated 1871).

Both forms of knowledge are essential to the true understanding of a country. And if it may be said that no man understands a thing till he has coldly criticized it, it may also be said that no man knows a thing till he has loved it.

★★★

For the right understanding of the South African people and their problem, the first requisite is a clear comprehension of their land.

Taking the term South Africa to include all the country south from the Zambesi and Lake N'gami to Cape Agulhas, it may be said that few territories possess more varied natural features; nevertheless, through it all, from Walfish Bay to Algoa Bay, from the Zambesi to Cape Town, there is in it a certain unity. No South African set down in any part of it could fall to recognize it as his native land and he could hardly mistake any other for it.

The most noticeable feature in first looking at it, is the strip of lowland country running along the entire south and east coast, and bordered everywhere inland by high mountain ranges.

In the Western Province the coast belt consists of chains of huge mountains forming a network over a tract of country some hundreds of miles in extent, the mountains having at their feet level valleys or small plains. They are composed of igneous though stratified rock, covered by little soil, and showing signs of titanic subterranean action; many of them seem to have been hurled up by one convulsive act; bare strata of rock thousands feet in extent are raised on end) their jagged edges forming the summits of vast mountain ranges. In the still, peaceful valleys at the feet of these mountains are running streams; in the spring the African heath covers them with red, pink and white bells, and the small wine-farms dot the sides of the valleys with their white houses and green fields, dwarfed under the high, bare mountains. Here and there are little towns and villages, built as only the old Dutch-Huguenots knew how to build, the long, straight streets lined with trees on either hand, and streams of water running down them; and the old thatch-roofed, gabled, white-washed, green-shuttered houses standing back, with their stone stoeps,[1] under the deep shade of the trees, and with their vineyards and orchards behind

---

1 Stoep = veranda. [Author's note]

them. No one can build such towns now. They are as unique as their mountains.

Perhaps one sees the Western Province to best advantage in the Hex River Valley, with its mountains of solid rock rising up thousands of feet on either hand, the vast strata contorted into fantastic shapes, and below them the smiling valley with its sprinkling of wine-farms. Hardly less characteristic is Cape Town itself, the capital of the Province and of the whole Colony, which lies on its promontory at the extreme end of the continent. In a valley between two mountains, one high, flat and of pure rock, its stupendous front overhanging the town, the other lower and rounded, its cliff worn away everywhere but on one mighty head which it rears into the blue, the town lies, with its flat-roofed houses and long straight streets, on a bay as blue and delicately curved as that of Naples.

Here it was that the wandering Hottentots on the shore saw the first sails creep across the waters of their blue bay. Here it was that in 1652 Jan Anthony van Riebeek, the servant of the Dutch East Indian Company, landed with his dependents and built the first houses and made the first gardens. The fort which they built in those early days may still be seen near the sea shore; the small block-houses which you may still see on the spurs of the mountain, a disputed tradition says, were used in those days as outlook towers against the incursions of possible foes.

Here the Dutch East Indian Company imported its slaves, often from Madagascar, English slave-ships bringing them. Here, Peter Kolben tells us that, about the year 1712, he saw a slave burnt to death. They are, says he, speaking of the slaves, "most detestable and wicked wretches," and "'tis now and then a most difficult thing to keep them in order." This slave had tried to burn down his master's house; they tied him to an upright post by a chain which allowed him to make one turn about it. "Then," said Peter Kolben, "was kindled a fire round about him, just beyond the stretch of the chain; the flames rose high; the heat was vehement; he ran for some time to-and-again about the post, but gave not one cry. Being half roasted he sank down, and said (speaking in Portuguese), *Dios mio Pays (O God, my Father)*, and then expired."

These things have passed away now, as the elephant and hippopotami have passed from the slopes of Table Mountain, and the thumb-screw and the rack and stake from Europe, and as other things will pass away yet.

★★★

The population of the Western Province is partly English and partly Boer or Dutch-Huguenot, the descendants of the Dutch East Indian Company's servants and settlers, and of a large number of French Huguenots who arrived in the Colony about 1687, driven from France by the Revocation of the Edict of Nantes, and who, winnowed by the unerring flail of religious persecution, form, perhaps, the finest element that has ever been added to the population of South Africa. The labouring classes are, as elsewhere in South Africa, coloured, and here largely half-castes, the descendants of the first Dutch residents and their slaves, or much more rarely of blended Dutch and Hottentot blood. In Cape Town itself are found also Malays, Chinamen, Hindus, and the representatives of all European nations.

If leaving Cape Town we go a few hundred miles eastward, along the coast, we shall find the lowland belt assume new characteristics. The hills, though high, are softer and more rounded, covered completely with soil and grass; or their sides, and even summits, are clothed in bush, stretching for ten or twenty or forty miles....

In this bush it is particularly easy to lose yourself. As you pass round clump after clump, there are always others o exactly the same shape before you, and you sometimes find you have gone two or three times round the same mass of vegetation. Oxen once lost in this bush are not easily discovered for days, though hidden behind the next clump, and it is almost hopeless to look for them unless one can gain an eminence and oversee a wide stretch of country. In this bush several Europeans have lost their lives during the last fifteen years.

★★★

Eighty years ago it was alive with elephant, lion, bushbuck and wild animals of all kinds. Now, the elephant is extinct, except where artificially preserved; bush-buck are scarce; a few large leopards may still be found in sequestered kloofs, and wild cats and monkeys and parrots are yet abundant, but a lion has not been seen for forty years. Thousands of small birds feed on the berries that abound here, and fifty small birds may sometimes be heard chirping in the depths of one kunee tree. Eighty years ago, the inhabitants of this tract were warlike Kaffir tribes of the Bantu race. They have not been exterminated as the Hottentots and Bushmen in the west have largely been, but are still found as the servants on farms and in towns. The white inhabitants at the present day are mainly English, the descendants largely of a group of emigrants who landed here in 1820, and who proved themselves one of the most entirely successful and satisfactory bodies of emigrants whom England has ever sent forth.

Here and there throughout the entire tract are scattered small English towns and villages; and thriving farms, where sheep and agriculture go together, are hidden away in the bush.

To see this land typically one should outspan one's wagon on the top of a height on a hot summer's day, when not a creature is stirring, and the sun pours down its rays on the flaccid, dust-covered leaves of the bushes. When the leader has gone to take the oxen to water and the driver has gone to lie down behind the bushes, if you stand up on the front chest of the wagon, and look out, as far as your eye can reach, you will see over hills and dales, the bush stretching, silent, motionless, and hot. Not a sound is to be heard; your hand blisters on the tent of the wagon; suddenly a cicada from a clump of bush at your right sets up its keen, shrill cry; it is glorying in the heat and the solitude of the bush. You listen to it in the unbroken silence, till you and it seem to be alone in the world.

Not less characteristic is the bush, when, as a little child, you travel through it at-night. The ox-wagon creaks slowly along the sandy road in the dark, the driver walks beside it and calls at intervals to his tired oxen; you look out across the wagon-chest, and, as the wagon moves along, the dark outlines of the bushes on either side seem to move too; now a great clump comes nearer and nearer like a vast animal; then, as you peer into the dark, they seem like great ruined castles co in to topple over you; and you creep closer down behind the wagon-chest. Against the dark night sky to the right, on the ridge of the hill, are the gaunt forms of aloes standing like a row of men keeping watch. You remembered all the stories you had heard of Kaffir wars and men shot down and stabbed, as they passed along hill-sides; and then a will-o'-the-wisp comes out from some dried-up torrent bed, and far before you dances in and out among the bushes, now in sight and now gone. You are not afraid; but you are glad when the people in the wagon begin to sing hymns; and more glad yet when at half-past nine it stops, drawn up beside a great clump of bush at the roadside. The tired oxen are taken from the yoke, and you climb out and light a fire and gather from afar and near stumps of dried elephant's food and euphorbia, and throw them on the fire, and the flame leaps up high. Then you all sit down beside the ruddy blaze; and away off the driver and leader have lighted their fire, and are talking to each other in Kaffir as they boll the coffee and roast the meat. The light from your own fire blazes up and lights the great, dusty body of the wagon, and the tired oxen, as they lie tied to their yokes, chewing the cud; and it glints on the bush with its dark-green leaves behind you, and on the faces round the fire; and you laugh, and talk; and forget the stories of Kaffir wars, and the great wild bush stretching about you.

★★★

If we return to the Western districts of the Cape Colony, and leaving the coast belt, climb one of the high mountain ranges that here, as everywhere else, bound the coast belt separating it from the centre of the country, we shall find to our surprise that on reaching its summit, we make hardly any descent on the other side; and that what appeared from the south to be a high mountain range was merely the edge of a vast plateau. We shall find ourselves on an undulating plain, bounded on every side by small fantastic hills. The air is dry and clear; so light that we draw a long breath to make sure we are breathing it aright. The sky above is a more transparent blue than nearer the coast, and seems higher. There is not a blade of grass to be seen growing anywhere; the red sand is covered with bushes a few inches high, clothed with small, hard leaves of dull, olive-green; here and there is an ice-plant, or a stapelia with fleshy, cactus-like leaves, or a rod-like milk bush. As far as the eye can reach, there is often not a tree or a shrub more than two feet high; and far, in the distance, rising abruptly out of the plain, are perhaps two solitary flat-topped mountains; nearer at hand are small conical hillocks, made of round iron-stones piled so regularly on one another that they seem the work of man rather than nature. In the still, clear air you can see the rocks on a hill ten miles off as if they were beside you; the stillness is so intense that you can hear the heaving of your own breast. This is the Karoo. To the stranger, oppressive, weird, fantastic, it is to the man who has lived with it a scene for the loss of which no other on earth compensates.

As you travel through it after fifteen, twenty, or fifty miles, you may come upon a farm. The house, a small brown or white speck in the vast landscape, lies at the foot of a range of hills or a small "kopje," with its sheep kraals on the slope behind it, of large brown squares, enclosed by low stone walls. Sometimes there is a garden before the house also enclosed by stone walls, and containing fruit trees, and there is a dam with willow trees planted beside; sometimes there is no dam and no garden, and the little brown mud house stands there baking in the sun with its kraals behind it; the only water for men or beasts coming from some small unseen spring.

Throughout the Karoo there are few running streams the waters of any fountains which may exist are quickly drunk up by the dry soil, and men and animals are largely dependent on artificial dams filled by rain-water. The farmer makes his livelihood from flocks of sheep which wander over the Karoo, and which in good years flourish on its short dry bushes.

In the spring, in those years when rain has fallen, for two months the Karoo is a flower garden. As far as the eye can reach, stretch blots of white and yellow and purple fig flowers; 1 every foot of Karoo sand is broken open by small flowering lilies and waxflowers; in a space a few feet square you may sometimes gather fifty kinds of flowers. In the crevices of the rocks little flowering plants are growing. At the end of two months it is over; the bulbs have died back into the ground by millions, the fig blossoms are withered, the Karoo assumes the red and brown tints which it wears for all the rest of the year.

Sometimes there is no spring. At intervals of a few years great droughts occur, when for thirteen months the sky is cloudless. The Karoo bushes drop their leaves and are dry withered stalks, the fountains fail, and the dams are floored with dry baked mud, which splits up into little squares, the sheep and goats die by hundreds, and the Karoo is a desert.

★★★

To see the Karoo rightly one should saddle one's horse and ride away from some solitary farm-house. For twenty miles you may ride without seeing a living thing, nor passing even a herd of sheep or goats, or a korhaan or mierkat. At midday you off-saddle in a narrow plain between two low hills, that widen out at the further end into a wider plain, from which rise two conical, solitary, flat-topped hills; and the horizon is bounded by a purple mountain thirty miles off. You put your saddle down beside a milk bush and tie the halter round the horse's knee, that he may go and feed upon the bushes; and you seat yourself beside your saddle on the ground. The milk bush gives little shade, and the midday sun shines hot upon you. In the red sand at your feet the ants are running to and fro, carrying away the crumbs that may have fallen from your saddle-bag; and in the stillness you can hear your horse break the twigs from the bushes as he feeds; he moves further off, and you cannot hear even that. Then you notice on the red sand a little to the right, at the foot of a Karoo bush, a scaly lizard, with his head raised, and his belly palpitating on the red sand, watching you. He is a tiny fellow, three inches long. You move, and he is gone like a flash of light across the sand. By and by the ants have carried away the crumbs, and they too are gone. You sit alone with the sun beating down on you. As the plain lies to-day, so it has lain for long countless ages. Those sharp stones on the edge of the rise to your right, with their points turned to the sky, for how many centuries have they lain there, their edges as sharp and fresh to-day as though they had been broken but yesterday? Those motionless hills; the very knotted Karoo stem at your hand, for how many generations have the leaves sprouted and fallen from its gnarled stalk? The Bushman and the wild buck have crept over the scene; they have gone, and the Englishman with his horse and gun have come; but plain lines with its sharp stones turned to the sky unchanged through the centuries. Those two stones standing loosely one upon another have stood so for thousands of years, because there was no hand to sever them.

It is not fear one feels, with that clear, blue sky above one; that which creeps over one is not dread. It was amid such scenes as these, amid such motionless, immeasurable silences, that the Oriental mind first framed its noblest conception of the unknown, the "I am that I am" of the Hebrew.[1]

Nor less wonderful is the Karoo at night, when the Milky Way forms a white band across the sky; and you stand alone outside, and sec the velvety, blue-black vault rising slowly on one side of the horizon and sinking on the other; and the silence is so intense you seem almost to hear the stars move. Nor is it less wonderful on moonlight nights, when you sit alone on a kopje; and the moon has arisen and the light is pouring over the plain; then even the stones are beautiful; and what you have believed of human love and fellowship—and never grasped—seems all possible to you.

And not less rare is the sunrise, when the hills, which have been purple in the dawn, turn suddenly to gold, and the rays of light

---

1 Exodus 3:14.

shoot fifty miles across the plain and make every drop on the ice-plants sparkle.

Nor less wonderful are the sunsets, when you go out at evening after the day's work. The fierce heat is over; as you walk, a cool breath touches your cheek; you look up and all the hills are turned pink and purple, and a curious light lies on the top of the Karoo bushes; they are all gilded; then it vanishes, and along the horizon there are bars of gold and crimson against a pale emerald sky; and there everything begins to turn grey.

In the Karoo there are also mirages. As you travel along the great plains, such as those between Beaufort and De Aar, you continually see, in hot weather, far off on the horizon, lakes with the sunlight sparkling on the water; there are islands and palm trees and domes and minarets and snow-capped mountains. If you remain for half an hour they do not change. Why the mirage should always take the shape of lakes, islands, and palm trees, is something which science, in giving us its cause, has not accounted for.

★★★

Crossing the Vaal River, we shall find to the north the Transvaal Republic. This is a tract of country of great extent and diversity. In part of it we have bush, in part high grass tablelands; on the east a low lying, moist, fever-haunted district. On the whole it is of great fertility. On the ridges of the high tablelands, lie the great Johannesburg gold-mines, which have drawn men from all parts of the earth. There are probably about eight black men to each white, the white population being probably divided between those of Boer, and English or other European extraction in the proportion of one to one; but no accurate census has yet been taken. The largest city, Johannesburg, is mainly English, the farming population Dutch-Huguenot.

If, leaving the Transvaal Republic, we cross the Limpopo, we shall find ourselves in the country known as Matabele and Mashonaland.

Bounded on the north by the Zambesi, the largest and only truly navigable river in South Africa, whose falls are the largest in the world, and further by Lake N'Gami and its low-lying territory, and on the West by the Kalahari, and on the cast by the strip of low country claimed by Portugal. To the extreme left it is largely flat and arid, like the greater part of South Africa; the central position has mountain and bush, while along the low-lying riverbeds it is fever-haunted, to the cast is a high healthy tableland, well watered and wooded.

It is the land of Livingstone.[1] Some of us remember on hot Sunday afternoons, as little children, when no more worldly book than missionary travels was allowed us, how we sat on our stools and looked out into the sunshine and dreamed of that land. Of the Garden Island, where the smoke of the mighty falls goes up, whose roar is heard twenty-five miles off; of hippopotami playing in the water, and of elephants and lions, and white rhinoceroses. We had heard of a man on the north of the Limpopo, who once saw three lions lying under the trees on the grass like calves, and he walked straight past them, and they looked at him and did nothing. We had heard of great ruins—ruins which lay there overgrown with weeds and trees. From there we believed the Queen of Sheba brought the peacocks and the gold for King Solomon. We meditated over it deeply. Yes, we should go and see it. Up a valley, a great white rhinoceros would wade with its feet in the water; on each side under the trees zebras and antelopes would stand quietly feeding on the green grass. We would creep up quietly and look at them. No one but we would ever have seen them before. We would not disturb them. We would see the giraffes pick the top leaves from the trees, and elephant-cows walk along with their little calves at their sides. At night round the fire we would hear the lions roar, and the wild dogs how], and sleep with our feet to the fire, and the stars above us; we would plant seeds on the Garden island; we would pass lions and they should not eat us; we would climb over the ruins where the Queen of Sheba stood! We almost dropped the book from our knees and rose to go. In that land there were no Sunday afternoons and no boredom; you could do as you liked. The very names Zambesi and Limpopo drew us, with the lure of the unknown.

Even to-day there is still much to be learnt with regard to these lands. To the west it is inhabited by the Bamangwato, under their chief Kame; in the centre by the brave warlike Matabele, under the chief Lobengula; in the east by the mild, industrious Mashonas, on whom the Matabele raid; and there are to-day the men of the, British South Africa Company looking for gold.

---

1 David Livingstone (1813-1873) was Britain's most famous missionary and explorer. He traveled through most of the continent of Africa on various expeditions. He believed that Christianity and commerce would bring civilization to all parts of Africa. His *Missionary Travels and Researches* (1857) was a popular book.

It is more than possible that if we went there now we should not find all we have dreamed of. Elephants are scarce; Selous says he has killed the last white rhinoceros; if we met a lion he might eat us; the hippopotami will soon be driven away from the Victoria Falls; the ruins may not be three thousand years old; boredom and Sunday afternoons may exist there as elsewhere, and the gold may need much washing from the sand; but it is certain that in these auriferous regions will ultimately spring up dense populations. It is from the territories north of the Vaal and south of the Zambesi, in this moister climate, with its more navigable rivers, that civilization in its coarser proportions will first unroll itself. More Southern Africa may produce better men; our greatest poet may yet be born in the Karoo; our great artist in the valley of the Paarl; our great thinker among the keen airs of Basutoland; neither wealth nor dense population have a tendency to produce the finest individuals; but it is in the north-east of Southern Africa that mineral wealth and vast populations with all that they signify for good and evil will probably first arise.

To understand the view taken in South Africa of the opening up of these lands, it is necessary to turn back from the present day to the Europe of the sixteenth century, when the hearts and eyes of men were turned to the new world, and each man who crossed the seas carried with him the hearts and thoughts of the thousands who remained. There is no explanation to be given of these sudden movements of entire peoples in a given direction. Their scientific causes are as subtle as those which govern the migrations of the lemmings. Some lead and the rest follow.

★★★

This, then, is South Africa; the country which the South African regards as his native land. To the superficial observer nothing would be more unlike than its differing parts; between the falls of the Zambesi with their spray-drenched forest and their banks, unchanged by civilization as when the eye of Livingstone first beheld them more than thirty years ago, and a little Eastern Province town, with its narrow, conventional life; between the wilds of Namaqualand, where the little Bushman still sits down behind his bush to cook his supper of animal entrails and lies down with the stars over him, and the white house and tree-lined streets of the Paarl; between the Kalahari, where under a thorn tree groups of antelopes are gathered in the moonlight, and the gambling saloons and music-halls of Johannesburg and Kimberley; between the kraals of Kaffirland, where the Kaffir boys are holding their "abakweta" dances in the moonlight with whitened faces, and the drawing-rooms of Cape Town, where women in low dresses sit aimlessly talking, there seems little in common.

Nevertheless, through the whole of South Africa there runs a certain unity. It is not only that geraniums and plumbago, flat-topped mountains, aloes and cuphorbla are peculiar to our land, and that sand and rocks abound everywhere; nor is it even that the land is everywhere young, and full of promise; but there is a certain colossal plentitude, a certain large freedom in all its natural proportions, which is truly characteristic of South Africa. If Nature here wishes to make a mountain, she runs a range for five hundred miles; if a plain, she levels eighty; if a rock, she tilts five thousand feet of strata on end; our skies are higher and more intensely blue; our waves larger than others; our rivers fiercer. There is nothing measured, small nor petty in South Africa.

Many years ago, we travelled from Port Elizabeth to Graham-stown in a post-cart with a woman who had just come from England. All day we had travelled up through the bush, and at noon came out on a height where, before us, as far as the eye could reach, over hill and dale, without sign of human habitation or break, stretched the bush. She began to sob; and, in reply to our questionings, could only reply, almost inarticulately: "Oh! It's so terrible! There's so much of it! There's so much!"

It is this "so much" for which the South African yearns when he leaves his native land. The lane, the pond, the cottage with roses climbing over the porch, the old woman going down the lane in her red cloak driving her cow, the parks with the boards of warning, the hill with the church and ruin beyond, oppress and suffocate us. Amid the arts of Florence and Venice, the civilizations of London and Paris, in crowded drawing-rooms, surrounded by all that wealth, culture and human fellowship can give, there comes back to us the remembrance of still Karoo nights, when we stood alone under the stars, and of wide breezy plains, where we rode and we return. Europe cannot satisfy us.

The sharp business man who makes money at the "Fields" and goes to end his life in Europe, comes back at the end of two years. You ask him why he returned. He looks at you in a curious way, and, with his head aside, replies meditatively: "There's no room there, you know. It's so free here." Neither can you entrap him into further explanations; South Africa is like a great fascinating woman; those who see her for the first time wonder at the power she exercises, and those who come close to her fall under it and never leave her for anything smaller, because she liberates them.

If we turn from the land itself, to examine more closely the people who inhabit it, we shall be struck in the first place by the marvellous diversity of races found among us.

For not only are the South Africans not of one national variety (a fact not surprising when the extent of our country is taken into consideration); not only do we belong to the most distinct branches of the human family to be found anywhere on the surface of the globe, representing the most widely different stages in human development, from the Bushman with his ape-like body, flat forehead and primitive domestic institutions, to the nineteenth-century Englishman fresh from Oxford, with the latest views on social and political development, and the financial Jew; but we are more or less a mixture of these astonishingly diverse types. We are not a collection of small, and, though closely contiguous, yet distinct peoples; we are a more or less homogeneous blend of heterogeneous social particles in different stages of development and of cohesion with one another, underlying and overlaying each other like the varying strata of confused geological formations.

It is this fact which lies at the core of the social and political problem of South Africa, and which makes it at the same time the most complex and difficult, and the most interesting, with which a people has ever been called upon to deal.

★★★

A nation, like an individual, is a combination of units in the nation the units are persons; in the individual body they are cells. The single cell, alone and uncombined, is capable only of the simplest forms of development; the solitary amœboid germ can undergo no high development, as it floats unconnected in the water or air; it is only when cells are combined in close and vital union with others, and there is interaction, that high development is possible. The highly differentiated complex cells that go to form a human eye or brain are possible only as parts of a larger interacting organism, a long-continued and close interaction between millions of cells, and could come into being in no other way.

Yet more is the analogous fact true with regard to human beings. Alone and divided from his fellows, the individual man is capable of only the very lowest form of development. The accounts of persons who have been lost in infancy and grown up alone, apart from any organization or interaction with their fellows, shows in the extremest form how very low is the natural condition of the human amœboid. Speechless, knowledgeless, its very hands incapable of performing the simplest operation which the veriest child in the lowest organized society learns to perform (as we imagine intuitively), such an individuality impresses on us, in its extremest form, a lesson which all human history teaches us in other shapes.

Great men, great actions, great arts, great developments, are impossible without those closely united, interacting organic combinations of men which we call nations, using that word in its largest sense, and to include all organized, centralized, interacting masses of humans and to exclude such as are inorganic and only united in name or by force. The organically united nation is the only known matrix in which the human being can attain to full development. A Plato, an Aristotle, a Shakespeare, a Michael Angelo, implying as much the existence of a Greece, an England, or an Italy, are as impossible without them as an eye or brain imply and would be impossible without a whole human organism. They are the efflorescence of the nations.

Without the closely united, interacting, organically bound body of humans, no great men, no highly developed masses.

Therefore, in all ages, and rightly, men have set the highest value on the maintenance of their social organization, and have regarded as a greater evil than any which could afflict them personally the destruction of their organism as a whole. The individual particles may be left untouched (as in the case of Poland), but they suffer more deeply from the loss of interaction and organized union than had they separately been individually destroyed.

Nor is it only the particles composing a national organism that gain by its maintenance in health and unity. From a wider standpoint it is of importance to humanity as a whole. The virile organized individuality of Greece, of Rome, of England (while it remained an organized unity and had not begun to dissolve itself into an inchoate trading firm, seeking to dominate by force peoples and lands in all parts of the world for trade purposes), and of France has bequeathed almost as much to humanity at large as to its own members; and an old, diseased or disorganized nationality, or a young, shapeless, unorganized mass of humans, however healthy the individual units composing it may be, is a mass without the capability of full development or of adding to the common fund of humanity.

The first need of an unorganized mass of humans is to attain to some form of vital organization. This must precede the fullest development of the individual units, and must adjust itself before any complex internal growth can begin.

Painfully trite as these observations are, it is necessary to keep them in mind when dealing with the South African question.

Were the political states into which South Africa is to-day divided—not highly organized and developed nations, bound together by bonds of race, language, religion and long-continued interaction into organic wholes, for that is impossible—but, did they possess, however sporadically and embryonically, the germs from which national life and unity might develop itself, if without the union of race, language and ideas which goes to form the ideally united people, there were at least this one condition, from which national life and unity might be expected to develop itself: that, divided from each other as the inhabitants of each of one state might be in race, religion, language and interest, they were yet more nearly united to the majority of their fellows within their state on these matters, than with large masses of the peoples *immediately beyond their borders*—if this were so, then the problem of South Africa would not only not be what it is; it would be reversed. Our problem would then be: *How can each separate state into which South Africa is divided be maintained in its integrity and so strengthened that it may most quickly attain to full national unity and organization?* For so would the benefit of national life be most quickly and simply attained by the peoples of South Africa.

★★★

... there is no *a priori* reason, if our political states possessed the least germ of organic unity or nationality, why the ultimate form of organization in South Africa should not be that of half a dozen distinct nations. The question is:

Does such a germ exist ?

We believe the most temporary survey will prove that it does not.

Short as is the time at our disposal, let us rapidly glance at a few of our states to see if any germ of national life lies at their core.

Let us take first the Cape Colony, as the oldest, best organized, most important, and most powerful of our divisions; one whose boundaries, except at the northeast, are tolerably well defined, and which has a centralized form of political government. There are in the Colony, roughly speaking, a million and a half of men. One million of these are natives, Hottentots, and half-castes, but mainly Bantus, of the Chuana or Kaffir races; the remaining half million are divided between men of English and other European descent speaking English, and the men of Boer descent, often speaking the "Taal." Now not only are these peoples who form our population not united to each other by race, language, creed or custom but, and this is a far more important fact, each division forming our population is far more closely connected by all these ties to masses of humans beyond our borders than to their fellow Cape Colonists within. Thus, our Bantus and Chuanas are absolutely one in race, language and sympathy with countless of thousands of Kaffirs and Chuanas of Kaffirland, Basutoland, the Free State, and even Transvaal. They are far more closely bound to these fellows of theirs in other states than to the white men in their own. The same may be said of the white population. Not only are they not bound to the native population in their state, but the Cape Colonial Englishman is absolutely identical with those in the Transvaal, Zambesia, Free State and Natal; and the Boer of the Cape Colony is absolutely identical with the, Boers of these different states; he is only artificially divided by a political line from his friends and kinsfolk in the Transvaal, Free State or Natal. Race, language, creed, tradition, which in the true national state form centripetal forces, binding its parts to one centre, in such a state become centrifugal, driving them from it and the political boundaries are so crossed and recrossed by these lines of union that they are rendered void.

★★★

Viewed thus, we see that the States of South Africa are not, taken isolatedly, national; their boundaries are of the nature of electoral, cantonal, fiscal, political divisions; *of immense importance, and by all means to be preserved, as such divisions are,* but not to be mistaken for those deeper, subtler and organic divisions from which the life of great nations takes its rise. There is far more resemblance between the population of the Transvaal and that of the Colony, Free State, or Natal, than between the populations of Yorkshire and Surrey; there is far more subtle, deep-lying, organic difference between Normandy and Bordeaux than between Natal and the Cape Colony. In looking at the political divisions of South Africa, one is irresistibly reminded of a well-known English village, in which the boys on the one side of the street threw stones at the boys on the other, because the parish boundary ran down the centre. Great nations are not founded on such differences as these.

But, it might be yet asked: "If our peoples are so mingled that our states cannot become the foundation of healthy national life, would it not be possible in so large and sparsely peopled a country to redivide our races, giving to each its territory?" Apart from the physical impossibilities which render such a proposal ridiculous, if, by some almighty force, all our natives could be gathered into one territory, our Boers in another, and our Englishmen into a third, no sooner would that force be removed than we should remingle in the old manner, the native as labourer craving the products of our civilization, the Boer as farmer, and the Englishman, Jews and other newcomers as speculators and builders of railroads, and introducers of commerce. A natural want binds and blends our races. But there is a subtler reason why such racial divisions are not even thinkable. The blending has now gone too far. There is hardly a civilized roof in South Africa that covers people of only one nation; in our households, in our families, in our very persons we are mingled.

Let us take a typical Cape household before us at the moment. The father of the household is an Englishman; the mother a so-called Boer, of half Dutch and half French blood, with a French name; the children are of the three nationalities; the governess is a German; the cook is a Half-caste, partly Boer and partly the descendant of the old slaves; the housemaid is a Half-caste, partly Hottentot, and whose father was perhaps an English soldier; the little nurse girl is a pure Hottentot; the boy who cleans the boots and waits, a Kaffir; and the groom is a Basuto. This household is a type of thousands of others to be found everywhere in South Africa.

★★★

What then shall be said of the South African problem as a whole? Is it impossible for the South African peoples to attain to any form of unity, organization, and national life? Must we for ever remain a vast, inchoate, invertebrate mass of humans, divided horizontally into layers of race, mutually antagonistic, and vertically severed by lines of political state division, which cut up our races without simplifying our problems, and which add to the bitterness of race conflict the irritation of political division? Is national life and organization unattainable by us?

We believe that no one can impartially study the condition of South Africa and feel that it is so. Impossible as it is that our isolated states should consolidate, and attain to a complete national life, there is a form of organic union which is possible to us. For there is a sense in which all South Africans are one. It is not only that all men born in South Africa, from the Zambesi to the Cape, are bound by the associations of their early years to the same vast, untamed nature; it is not only that South Africa itself, situated at the extremity of the continent, shut off by vast seas and impassable forests from the rest of the world, forces upon its inhabitants a certain union, like that of a crew who, in the same ship, set out on an interminable voyage together; there is a subtle but a very real bond, which unites all South Africans, and differentiates us from all other peoples in the world. *This bond is our mixture of races itself.* It is this which divides South Africans from all other peoples in the world, and makes us one. From Zambesi to the sea the same mixture exists, in slightly varying form, and the same problem is found. Wherever a Dutchman, an Englishman, a Jew, and a native are superimposed, there is that common South African condition through which no dividing line can be drawn. The only form of organization which can be healthily or naturally assumed by us is one which takes cognizance of this universal condition. Great and seemingly insuperable as are for the moment the difficulties which lie in our path on the way to a great, common, national unity, no man can study South Africa without feeling that, in this form, and this alone, is national life and organization attainable by South Africa. Difficult as it may be, it is at once simpler and easier than the consolidation of any separate part. It is the one form of crystallization open to us the one shape we shall assume.

South African unity is not the dream of the visionary; it is not even the forecast of genius, which makes clear and at hand that which only after ages can accomplish it is not even like the splendid vision of that little-understood man, the first Napoleon, of a unified and consolidated Europe, which was fated to failure from the moment of its inception, because dreamed five hundred years before its time. South African unity is a condition the practical necessity for which is daily and hourly forced upon us by the common needs of life: it is the one possible condition which will enable us to solve our internal difficulties: it is the one path open to us. For this unity all great men born in South Africa during the next century will be compelled directly or indirectly to labour; it is this unity which must precede the production of anything great and beautiful by our people as a whole; neither art, nor science, nor literature, nor statecraft will flourish among us as long as we remain in our unorganized form: it is the attainment of this unity which constitutes the problem of South Africa: *How, from our political states and our discordant races, can a great, a healthy, a united, an organized nation be formed?*

★★★

This problem naturally divides itself into two parts. For the moment, the first is the most pressing and absorbing, that of the political union of our states; and it must precede the other. Great as are the difficulties which lie in this path at present, difficulties whose extent can only be understood by one who has deeply studied our internal condition, yet so urgent is the practical need for it, so ripe the time, that there are probably men now living who may see it accomplished. It is impossible to study the South Africa of to-day and doubt that within sixty years there will exist here a great centralized and independent form of government embodying the united political will of the people; that with regard to external defence and the most vital internal problems, South Africa will be politically one; *its state divisions, while developed and intensified in certain directions*, will be relegated to the performance of those invaluable functions of self-government for which they are so admirably fitted. Circumstances and individuals favouring, we may see this accomplished before the next decade is out; it must come at last.

For the moment, the political aspect of our problem is the most pressing; but there is another, deeper and more important, and of which no man now living will see the final solution. A central government, a customs union, a common treasury for purposes of external defence, these are but the shell in which the vital unity of the community must be contained if we are ever to become, not simply a large, but a great, a powerful and a truly progressive people. Day by day, and hour by hour, every man and woman in South Africa, whether they will it or no, labours to produce the final answer which will be given to this question: How, of our divided peoples, can a great, healthy, harmonious and desirable nation be formed?

This is the final problem of South Africa. If we cannot solve it, our fate is sealed. If South Africa is unable so to co-ordinate, and, where she cannot blend, so to harmonize her differing peoples, that if in years to come a foreign foe should land upon her shores, and but six men were left to defend her, two English, two Dutch, two of native extraction: if those six men would not stand shoulder to shoulder, fighting for a land that was their own, in which each felt, widely as he might otherwise be separated from his fellows, that he had a stake—then the fate of South Africa is sealed; the handwriting has already appeared on the wall against us we must take for ever a last place among the nations however large, rich, populous we may become, we shall never be able to look free, united peoples in the face. In past ages empires have existed which were founded on racial hatred and force. Of this type were the great states of antiquity—Egypt, Assyria, Rome, and Greece. They passed away; but for a time they were able to maintain themselves in states of like construction with themselves, only falling when they came into contact with freer and more united peoples.

In the twentieth century it will not be possible for a state constructed after the plan of the ancient world to attain to power and developed greatness, even for a time. In an age in which the nations of the civilized world are with titanic efforts shaping rafts with which to shoot those rapids down which empire after empire, civilization after civilization, have disappeared, and will shoot them and appear below them, free united peoples; if the South Africa of the future is to remain eaten internally by race hatreds, a film of culture and intelligence spread over seething masses of ignorance and brutality, inter-support and union being wholly lacking; then, though it may be our misfortune rather than our fault, our doom is sealed; our place will be wanting among the great, free nations of earth. Neither in art, in science, in material invention, in the discovery of larger and more satisfactory modes of conducting human life, can we stand beside them. A man with an internal disease feeding on his vitals cannot compete with the sound in body and limb.

Taken as a, whole, so vast, so complex, and so beset with difficulty is our South African problem, that it may be truly said that no European nation has had during the last eight hundred years to face anything approaching it in complexity and difficulty. To find any analogy to it we must go back as far as the England of Alfred, when divided Saxons and invading Danes were the elements out of which organic unity had to be constructed. But there are elements in our problem which no European nation has ever had to face, and which no migrating part of a European race has ever had to deal with, in exactly the same form in which they meet us. Our race question is complicated by a question of colour, which presents itself to us in a form more virulent and intense than that in which it has met any modern people. America and India have nothing analogous to it; and it has to be faced in an age which does not allow of the old methods in dealing with alien and so-called inferior peoples. In South Africa the nineteenth century is brought face to face with a prehistoric world.

To understand rightly the difficulty of our problem to grasp the nature of the obstacles which lie in our path to organic union; to understand our crying need of it, and to grasp the grounds we have for hope, it will be necessary to examine closely the different races of which we are composed; and finally, to glance briefly at some of the conditions and individuals that are at the present moment largely influencing the future of South Africa.

Appendix B: Philosophical Contexts

1. Herbert Spencer

[Herbert Spencer (1820-1903) was one of the earliest sociologists and the author of numerous books on a wide variety of topics. In his essay for the *Westminster Review*, Spencer characterizes evolution as a progression from simple to more diverse organisms. His ideas of progress and the perfectibility of humankind were extremely popular in the Victorian era. The second excerpt is from the work that influenced Schreiner's thinking while she wrote the first draft of *African Farm* in South Africa. Although his influence in England had diminished considerably, Spencer publicly condemned the Boer Wars in 1899-1902.]

a. From "Progress: Its Law and Cause," *Westminster Review* April, 1857.

The current conception [of progress] is a teleological one. The phenomena are contemplated solely as bearing on human happiness. Only those changes are held to constitute progress which directly or indirectly tend to heighten human happiness. And they are thought to constitute progress simply *because* they tend to heighten human happiness. But rightly to understand Progress, we must inquire what is the nature of these changes, considered apart from our interests. Ceasing, for example, to regard the successive geological modifications that have taken place in the Earth, as modifications that have gradually fitted it for the habitation of Man, and as *therefore* a geological progress, we must seek to determine the character common to these modifications—the law, to which they all conform. And similarly in every other case. Leaving out of sight concomitants and beneficial consequences, let us ask what Progress is in itself.

★★★

Now, we propose in the first place to show, that this law of organic progress is the law of all progress. Whether it be in the development of the Earth, in the development of Life upon its surface, in the development of Society, of Government, of Manufactures, of

Commerce, of Language, Literature, Science, Art, this same evolution of the simple into the complex, through a process of continuous differentiation holds throughout. From the earliest traceable cosmical changes down to the latest results of civilization, we shall find that the transformation of the homogeneous into the heterogeneous, is that in which Progress essentially consists.

★★★

The deductions which we have drawn from the established truths of geology and the general laws of life, gains immensely in weight on finding it to be in perfect harmony with an induction drawn from direct experience. Just that divergence of many races from one race, which we inferred must have been continually occurring during geologic time, we know to have taken place, during the pre-historic and historic periods, in man and domestic animals. And just that multiplication of effects which we concluded must have produced the first, we see has produced the last. Single causes, as famine, pressure of population, war, have periodically led to further dispersions of mankind and of dependent creatures: each such dispersion initiating new modifications, new varieties of type. Whether all the human races be or be not derived from one stock, philological evidence makes it clear that whole groups of races now easily distinguishable from each other, were originally one race,—that the diffusion of one race in sundry directions into different climates and conditions of existence, has simultaneously produced many modified forms of it. Similarly with domestic animal. Though in some cases—as that of dogs—community of origin will perhaps be disputed, yet in other cases—as that of the Sheep or the cattle of our own country—it will not be questioned that local differences of climate, food, and treatment, have transformed one original breed into numerous breeds now become so far distinct as to produce unstable hybrids. Moreover, through the complication of effects flowing from single causes, we here find, what we before inferred, not an increase of general heterogeneity but also of special heterogeneity. While of the divergent divisions and subdivisions of the human race, many have undergone modifications of detail not constituting an advance; while in some the type may have degraded; in others it has become decidedly more heterogeneous. The civilized European departs more widely from the vertebrate archetype than does the savage. Thus, both the law and the cause of progress, which, from lack of evidence, can be but hypothetically substantiated in respect of the earlier forms of life on our globe, can be actually substantiated in respect of the latest forms.

If the advance of Man towards greater heterogeneity is traceable to the production of many effects by one cause, still more clearly may the advance of Society towards greater heterogeneity be similarly explained.

b. From *First Principles of a New System of Philosophy* (1871)

Chapter 5: The Reconciliation

[In this excerpt, Spencer offers to reconcile Science and Religion by introducing the idea of the "Unknowable," which he understood as the ultimate realm of religion beyond the knowable realms of Science. Schreiner read Spencer's *First Principles* enthusiastically in 1871. In a letter to Havelock Ellis, she later explained that Spencer had helped her to believe in "a unity underlying all nature" (First and Scott, 59).]

We see then that from the first, the faults of both Religion and Science have been the faults of imperfect development. Originally a mere rudiment, each has been growing into a more complete form; the vice of each has in all times been its incompleteness; the disagreements between them have throughout been nothing more than the consequences of their incompleteness; and as they reach their final forms, they come into entire harmony.

The progress of intelligence has throughout been dual. Though it has not seemed so to those who made it, every step in advance has been a step towards both the natural and the supernatural. The better interpretation of each phenomenon has been, on the one hand, the rejection of a cause that was relatively conceivable in its nature but unknown in the order of its actions, and, on the other hand, the adoption of a cause that was known in the order of its actions but relatively inconceivable in its nature. The first advance out of universal fetishism manifestly involved the conception of agencies less assimilable to the familiar agencies of men and animals, and therefore less understood; while, at the same time, such newly-conceived agencies in so far as they were distinguished by their uniform effects, were better understood than those they replaced. All subsequent advances display the same double result. Every deeper and more general power arrived at as a cause of phenomena has been at once less comprehensible than the special ones it superseded, in the sense of being less definitely representable in thought, while it has been more comprehensible in the sense that its actions have been more completely predicable. The progress has thus been as much towards the establishment of a positively unknown as towards the establishment of a positively known. Though as knowledge approaches its culmination, every unaccountable and seemingly supernatural fact is brought into the category of facts that are accountable or natural; yet, at the same time, all accountable or natural facts are proved to be in their ultimate genesis unaccountable and supernatural. And so there arise two antithetical states of mind, answering to the opposite sides of that existence about which we think. While our consciousness of Nature under the one aspect constitutes Science, our consciousness of it under the other aspect constitutes Religion. Otherwise contemplating the facts, we may say that Religion and Science have been undergoing a slow differentiation; and that their ceaseless conflicts have been due to the imperfect separation of their spheres and functions. Religion has, from the first, struggled to unite more or less science with its nescience; Science has, from the first, kept hold of more or less nescience as though it were a part of science. Each has been obliged gradually to relinquish that territory which it wrongly claimed, while it has gained from the other that to which it had a right; and the antagonism between them has been an inevitable accompaniment of this process. A more specific statement will make this clear. Religion, though at the outset it asserted a mystery, also made numerous definite assertions respecting this mystery—professed to know its nature in the minutest detail; and in so far as it claimed positive knowledge, it trespassed upon the province of Science. From the times of early mythologies, when such intimate acquaintance with the mystery was alleged, down to our own days, when but a few abstract and vague propositions are maintained, Religion has been compelled by Science to give up one after another of its dogmas of those assumed conditions which it could not substantiate. In the mean time, Science substituted for the personalities to which Religion ascribed phenomena, certain metaphysical entities; and in doing this it trespassed on the province of Religion; since it classed among the things which it comprehended certain forms of the incomprehensible, partly by the criticism of Religion, which has occasionally called in question its assumptions, and partly as a consequence of spontaneous growth, Science has been obliged to abandon these attempts to include within the boundaries of knowledge that which cannot be known, and has so yielded up to Religion that which of right belonged to it. So long as this process of differentiation is incomplete, more or less of antagonism must continue. Gradually as the limits of possible cognition are established, the causes of conflict will diminish. And a permanent peace will be reached when Science becomes fully convinced that its explanations are proximate and relative, while Religion becomes fully convinced that the mystery it contemplates is ultimate and absolute.

Religion and Science are therefore necessary correlatives. As already hinted, they stand respectively for those two antithetical modes of consciousness which cannot exist asunder. A known cannot be thought of apart from an unknown; nor can an unknown be thought of apart from a known. And by consequence neither can become more distinct without giving greater distinctness to the other. To carry further a metaphor before used, they are the positive and negative poles of thought, of which neither can gain in intensity without increasing the intensity of the other.

***

Thus the consciousness of an Inscrutable Power manifested to us through all phenomena has been growing ever clearer, and must eventually be freed from its imperfections. The certainty that on the one hand such a Power exists, while on the other hand its nature transcends intuition and is beyond imagination, is the certainty towards which intelligence has from the first been progressing. To this conclusion Science inevitably arrives as it reaches its confines; while to this conclusion Religion is irresistibly driven by criticism. And satisfying as it does the demands of the most rigorous logic, at the same time that it gives the religious sentiment the widest possible sphere of action, it is the conclusion we are bound to accept without reserve or qualification.

2. Charles Darwin, from *On the Origin of Species*, 1859

[Although Schreiner's earliest knowledge of evolutionary thought was from Herbert Spencer, she grappled along with other intellectuals of the day to understand the implications of Darwin's theory for human life. The term "struggle for existence," which Darwin reluctantly adapted from Spencer, is explained in this excerpt from chapter three of the first edition of Darwin's work. The last sentence of the chapter suggests the cold comfort of intellectual inquiry that Schreiner's characters confront in the novel.]

We will now discuss in a little more detail the struggle for existence.... Nothing is easier than to admit in words the truth of the universal struggle for life, or more difficult—at least I have found it so—than constantly to bear this conclusion in mind. Yet unless it be thoroughly engrained in the mind, I am convinced that the whole economy of nature, with every fact on distribution, rarity, abundance, extinction, and variation, will be dimly seen or quite misunderstood. We behold the face of nature bright with gladness, we often see superabundance of food; we do not see, or we forget, that the birds which are idly singing round us mostly live on insects or seeds, and are thus constantly destroying life; or we forget how largely these songsters, or their eggs, or their nestlings, are destroyed by birds and beasts of prey; we do not always bear in mind, that though food may be now superabundant, it is not so at all seasons of each recurring year.

I should premise that I use the term Struggle for Existence in a large and metaphorical sense, including dependence of one being on another, and including (which is more important) not only the life of the individual, but success in leaving progeny....

***

A struggle for existence inevitably follows from the high rate at which all organic beings tend to increase. Every being, which during its natural lifetime produces several eggs or seeds, must suffer destruction during some period of its life, and during some season or occasional year, otherwise, on the principle of geometrical increase, its numbers would quickly become so inordinately great that no country could support the product. Hence, as more individuals are produced than can possibly survive, there must in every case be a struggle for existence, either one individual with another of the same species, or with the individuals of distinct species, or with the physical conditions of life. It is the doctrine of Malthus[1]

---

1 In his *An Essay on the Principle of Population* (1788), Thomas Malthus (1766-1834) asserted that populations tend to increase at a greater rate than the food supply.

applied with manifold force to the whole animal and vegetable kingdoms; for in this case there can be no artificial increase of food, and no prudential restraint from marriage.

★★★

When we reflect on this struggle, we may console ourselves with the full belief, that the war of nature is not incessant, that no fear is felt, that death is generally prompt, and that the vigorous, the healthy, and the happy survive and multiply.

Appendix C: Social Contexts

1. John Stuart Mill, from *The Subjection of Women*, 1869 (*Collected Works of John Stuart Mill*, ed. John M. Robson. Toronto: University of Toronto Press, 1984)

[John Stuart Mill (1806-1873) wrote many volumes on politics, economics, and social issues. He was a staunch believer that civilization rests on the rights of individuals. He also believed in the equality of the sexes. In these excerpts, Mill not only argues for the equality of women to men, but he also offers an explanation of the constraints on women's time and energies that keep them from full participation in the labor force. Foreshadowing Schreiner's argument in *Woman and Labor* (1911), Mill predicts the dangers to society if women are not given honorable occupations.]

On the other point which is involved in the just equality of women, their admissibility to all the functions and occupations hitherto retained as the monopoly of the stronger sex, I should anticipate no difficulty in convincing any one who has gone with me on the subject of the equality of women in the family. I believe that their disabilities elsewhere are only clung to in order to maintain their subordination in domestic life; because the generality of the male sex cannot yet tolerate the idea of living with an equal. Were it not for that, I think that almost every one, in the existing state of opinion in politics and political economy, would admit the injustice of excluding half the human race from the greater number of lucrative occupations, and from almost all high social functions; ordaining from their birth either that they are not, and cannot by any possibility become, fit for employments which are legally open to the stupidest and basest of the other sex, or else that however fit they may be, those employments shall be interdicted to them, in order to be preserved for the exclusive benefit of males. In the last two centuries, when (which was seldom the case) any reason beyond the mere existence of the fact was thought to be required to justify the disabilities of women, people seldom assigned as a reason their inferior mental capacity; which, in times when there was a real trial of personal faculties (from which all women were not excluded) in the struggles of public life, no one really believed in. The reason given in those days was not women's unfitness, but the interest of society, by which was meant the interest of men: just as the raison d'état, meaning the convenience of the government, and the support of existing authority, was deemed a sufficient explanation and excuse for the most flagitious crimes. In the present day, power holds a smoother language, and whomsoever it oppresses, always pretends to do so for their own good: accordingly, when anything is forbidden to women, it is thought necessary to say, and desirable to believe, that they are incapable of doing it, and that they depart from their real path of success and happiness when they aspire to it. But to make this reason plausible (I do not say valid), those by whom it is urged must be prepared to carry it to a much greater length than any one ventures to do in the face of present experience. It is not sufficient to maintain that women on the average are less gifted than men on the average, with certain of the higher mental faculties, or that a smaller number of women than of men are fit for occupations and functions of the highest intellectual character. It is necessary to maintain that no women at all are fit for them, and that the most eminent women are inferior in mental faculties to the most mediocre of the men on whom those functions at present devolve. For if the performance of the function is decided either by competition, or by any mode of choice which secures regard to the public interest, there needs to be no apprehension that any important employments will fall into the hands of women inferior to average men, or to the average of their male competitors. The only result would be that there would be fewer women than men in such employments; a result certain to happen in any case, if only from the preference always likely to be felt by the majority of women for the one vocation in which there is nobody to compete with them. Now, the most determined depreciator of women will not venture to deny, that when we add the experience of recent times to that of ages past, women, and not a few merely, but many women, have proved themselves capable of everything, perhaps without a single exception, which is done by men, and of doing it successfully and creditably.

★★★

There are other reasons, besides those which we have now given, that help to explain why women remain behind men, even in the pursuits which are open to both. For one thing, very few women have time for them. This may seem a paradox; it is an undoubted social fact. The time and thoughts of every woman have to satisfy great previous demands on them for things practical. There is, first, the superintendence of the family and the domestic expenditure, which occupies at least one woman in every family, generally the one of mature years and acquired experience; unless the family is so rich as to admit of delegating that task to hired agency, and submitting to all the waste and malversation inseparable from that mode of conducting it. The superintendence of a household, even when not in other respects laborious, is extremely onerous to the thoughts; it requires incessant vigilance, an eye which no detail escapes, and presents questions for consideration and solution, foreseen and unforeseen, at every hour of the day, from which the person responsible for them can hardly ever shake herself free. If a woman is of a rank and circumstances which relieve her in a measure from these cares, she has still devolving on her the management for the whole family of its intercourse with others—of what is called society, and the less the call made on her by the former duty, the greater is always the development of the latter: the dinner parties, concerts, evening parties, morning visits, letter writing, and all that goes with them. All this is over and above the engrossing duty which society imposes exclusively on women, of making themselves charming. A clever woman of the higher ranks finds nearly a sufficient employment of her talents in cultivating the graces of manner and the arts of conversation. To look only at the outward side of the subject: the great and continual exercise of thought which all women who attach any value to dressing well (I do not mean expensively, but with taste, and perception of natural and of artificial convenance) must bestow upon their own dress, perhaps also upon that of their daughters, would alone go a great way towards achieving respectable results in art, or science, or literature, and does actually exhaust much of the time and mental power they might have to spare for either.[1] If it were

---

1 "It appears to be the same right turn of mind which enables a man to acquire the truth, or the just idea of what is right, in the ornaments, as in the more stable principles of art. It has still the same centre of perfection, though it is the centre of a smaller circle.—To illustrate this by the fashion of dress, in which there is allowed to be a good or bad taste. The component parts of dress are continually changing from great to little, from short to long; but the general form still remains: it is still the same general dress which is comparatively fixed, though on a very slender foundation; but it is on this which fashion must rest. He who invents with the most success, or dresses in the best taste, would probably, from the same sagacity employed to greater purposes, have discovered equal skill, or have formed the same correct taste, in the highest labours of art."—Sir Joshua Reynolds' Discourses, Disc. vii. [Author's note]

possible that all this number of little practical interests (which are made great to them) should leave them either much leisure, or much energy and freedom of mind, to be devoted to art or speculation, they must have a much greater original supply of active faculty than the vast majority of men. But this is not all. Independently of the regular offices of life which devolve upon a woman, she is expected to have her time and faculties always at the disposal of everybody. If a man has not a profession to exempt him from such demands, still, if he has a pursuit, he offends nobody by devoting his time to it; occupation is received as a valid excuse for his not answering to every casual demand which may be made on him. Are a woman's occupations, especially her chosen and voluntary ones, ever regarded as excusing her from any of what are termed the calls of society? Scarcely are her most necessary and recognised duties allowed as an exemption. It requires an illness in the family, or something else out of the common way, to entitle her to give her own business the precedence over other people's amusement. She must always be at the beck and call of somebody, generally of everybody. If she has a study or a pursuit, she must snatch any short interval which accidentally occurs to be employed in it. A celebrated woman, in a work which I hope will some day be published, remarks truly that everything a woman does is done at odd times.[1] Is it wonderful, then, if she does not attain the highest eminence in things which require consecutive attention, and the concentration on them of the chief interest of life? Such is philosophy, and such, above all, is art, in which, besides the devotion of the thoughts and feelings, the hand also must be kept in constant exercise to attain high skill.

★★★

What marriage may be in the case of two persons of cultivated faculties, identical in opinions and purposes, between whom there exists that best kind of equality, similarity of powers and capacities with reciprocal superiority in them—so that each can enjoy the luxury of looking up to the other, and can have alternately the pleasure of leading and of being led in the path of development— I will not attempt to describe. To those who can conceive it, there

---

1   Florence Nightingale, *Suggestions for Thought to the Searchers after Truth among the Artizans of England*, 3 vols. (London: printed Eyre and Spottiswoods [not published], 1860), Vol. II, p. 392.) [Editor's note]

is no need; to those who cannot, it would appear the dream of an enthusiast. But I maintain, with the profoundest conviction, that this, and this only, is the ideal of marriage; and that all opinions, customs, and institutions which favour any other notion of it, or turn the conceptions and aspirations connected with it into any other direction, by whatever pretences they may be coloured, are relics of primitive barbarism. The moral regeneration of mankind will only really commence, when the most fundamental of the social relations is placed under the rule of equal justice, and when human beings learn to cultivate their strongest sympathy with an equal in rights and in cultivation

★★★

The injudiciousness of parents, a youth's own inexperience, or the absence of external opportunities for the congenial vocation, and their presence for an uncongenial, condemn numbers of men to pass their lives in doing one thing reluctantly and ill, when there are other things which they could have done well and happily. But on women this sentence is imposed by actual law, and by customs equivalent to law. What, in unenlightened societies, colour, race, religion, or in the case of a conquered country, nationality, are to some men, sex is to all women; a peremptory exclusion from almost all honourable occupations, but either such as cannot be fulfilled by others, or such as those others do not think worthy of their acceptance. Sufferings arising from causes of this nature usually meet with so little sympathy, that few persons are aware of the great amount of unhappiness even now produced by the feeling of a wasted life. The case will be even more frequent, as increased cultivation creates a greater and greater disproportion between the ideas and faculties of women, and the scope which society allows to their activity.

When we consider the positive evil caused to the disqualified half of the human race by their disqualification—first in the loss of the most inspiriting and elevating kind of personal enjoyment, and next in the weariness, disappointment, and profound dissatisfaction with life, which are so often the substitute for it; one feels that among all the lessons which men require for carrying on the struggle against the inevitable imperfections of their lot on earth, there is no lesson which they more need, than not to add to the evils which nature inflicts, by their jealous and prejudiced restrictions on one another. Their vain fears only substitute other and worse evils for those which they are idly apprehensive of: while every restraint on the freedom of conduct of any of their human fellow creatures, (otherwise than by making them responsible for any evil actually caused by it), dries up *pro tanto* the principal fountain of human happiness, and leaves the species less rich, to an inappreciable degree, in all that makes life valuable to the individual human being.

2. Havelock Ellis, from *Studies in the Psychology of Sex: Sex in Relation to Society*, 1910

[Havelock Ellis (1859–1936) was a life-long friend and correspondent with Olive Schreiner. When she met him in London after the publication of *African Farm*, he was still a medical student. He became an early psychologist and wrote on many subjects, including literature and social issues. The following excerpt comes from his seven-volume masterwork. Although Ellis's views initially met with outrage and scandal, his work was later recognized as a milestone in the study of sexuality.]

In civilized societies as they attain maturity, the women tend to acquire a greater and greater degree alike of moral responsibility and economic independence. Any freedom and seeming equality of women, even when it actually assumes the air of superiority, which is not so based, is unreal. It is only on sufferance; it is the freedom accorded to the child, because it asks for it so prettily or may scream if it is refused. This is merely parasitism.[1] The basis of economic independence ensures a more real freedom. Even in societies which by law and custom hold women in strict subordi-

---

1 Olive Schreiner has especially emphasized the evils of parasitism for women. "The increased wealth of the male," she remarks (in "The Woman's Movement of Our Day," *Harper's Bazaar*, Jan 1902), "no more of necessity benefits and raises the female upon whom he expends it, than the increased wealth of his mistress necessarily benefits, mentally or physically, a poodle, because she can then give him a down cushion in place of one of feathers, and chicken in place of beef." Olive Schreiner believes that feminine parasitism is a danger which really threatens society at the present time, and that if it is not averted "the whole body of females in civilized societies must sink into a state of more or less absolute dependence." [Author's note]

nation, the woman who happens to be placed in possession of property enjoys a high degree alike of independence and of responsibility.[1] The growth of a high civilization seems indeed to be so closely identified with the economic freedom and independence of women that it is difficult to say which is cause and which effect. Herodotus, in his fascinating account of Egypt, a land which he regarded as admirable beyond all other lands, noted with surprise that, totally unlike the fashion of Greece, women left the men at home to the management of the loom and went to market to transact the business of commerce.[2] It is the economic factor in social life which secures the moral responsibility of women and which chiefly determines the position of the wife in relation to her husband.[3] In this respect in its late stages civilization returns to the same point it had occupied at the beginning, when, as has already been noted, we find greater equality with men and at the same time greater economic independence.[4]

In all the leading modern civilized countries, for a century past, custom and law have combined to give an ever greater economic independence to women. In some respects England took the lead by inaugurating the great industrial movement which slowly swept

---

1 In Rome and in Japan, Hobhouse notes (*Morals in Evolution*, vol. i, pp. 169, 176), the patriarchal system reached its fullest extension, yet the laws of both these countries placed the husband in a position of practical subjugation to a rich wife. [Author's note]

2 Herodotus, Bk. ii, Ch. XXXV. Herodotus noted that it was the woman and not the man on whom the responsibility for supporting aged parents rested. That alone involved a very high economic position of women. It is not surprising that to some observers, as to Diodorus Siculus, it seemed that the Egyptian woman was mistress over her husband. [Author's note]

3 Hobhouse, Hale, and also Grosse, believe that good economic position of a people involves high position of women. Westermarck (*Moral Ideas*, vol. i, p. 661), here in agreement with Olive Schreiner, thinks this statement cannot be accepted without modification, though agreeing that agricultural life has a good effect on woman's position, because they themselves become actively engaged in it. A good economic position has no real effect in raising woman's position, unless women themselves take a real and not merely parasitic part in it. [Author's note]

4 Westermarck (*Moral Ideas*, vol. i, Ch. XXVI, vol. ii, p. 29) gives numerous references with regard to the considerable proprietary and other privileges of women among savages which tend to be lost at a somewhat higher stage of culture. [Author's note]

women into its ranks,[1] and made inevitable the legal changes which, by 1882, insured to a married woman the possession of her own earnings. The same movement, with its same consequences, is going on elsewhere. In the United States, just as in England, there is a vast army of five million women, rapidly increasing, who earn their own living, and their position in relation to men workers is even better than in England.

★★★

It is undoubtedly true that—partly as a result of ancient traditions and education, partly of genuine feminine characteristics—many women are diffident as to their right to moral responsibility and unwilling to assume it. And an attempt is made to justify their attitude by asserting that woman's part in life is naturally that of self-sacrifice, or, to put the statement in a somewhat more technical form, that women are naturally masochistic; and that there is, as Krafft-Ebing[2] argues, a natural "sexual subjection" of woman. It is by no means clear that this statement is absolutely true, and if it were true it would not serve to abolish the moral responsibility of women.

It thus seems probable that the increase of moral responsibility may tend to make a woman's conduct more intelligible to others;[3] it will in any case certainly tend to make it less the concern of others. This is emphatically the case as regards the relations of sex. In the past men have been invited to excel in many forms of virtue; only one virtue has been open to women. That is no longer possible. To place upon a woman the main responsibility for her own sexual conduct is to deprive that conduct of its conspicuously public character as a virtue or a vice. Sexual union, for a woman as

---

1 The steady rise in the proportion of women among English workers in machine industries began in 1851. There are now, it is estimated, three and a half million women employed in industrial occupations, beside a million and a half domestic servants. (See for details, James Haslam, in a series of papers in the *Englishwoman*, 1909.) [Author's note]

2 Baron Richard Krafft-Ebing (1840-1902) was a professor of psychiatry at Strasbourg and author of *Psychopathia Sexualis* (1886), a treatise on sexual aberrations.

3 "Men will not learn what women are," remarks Rosa Mayreder (*Zur Kritik de Weiblichkeit*, p. 199), "until they have left off prescribing what they ought to be." [Author's note]

much as for a man, is a physiological fact; it may also be a spiritual fact; but it is not a social act. It is, on the contrary, an act which, beyond all other acts, demands retirement and mystery for its accomplishment. That indeed is a general human, almost zoological, fact. Moreover, this demand of mystery is more especially made by woman in virtue of her greater modesty which, we have found reason to believe, has a biological basis. It is not until a child is born or conceived that the community has any right to interest itself in the sexual acts of its members. The sexual act is of no more concern to the community than any other private physiological act. It is an impertinence, if not an outrage, to seek to inquire into it. But the birth of a child is a social act. Not what goes into the womb but what comes out of it concerns society. The community is invited to receive a new citizen. It is entitled to demand that that citizen shall be worthy of a place in its midst and that he shall be properly introduced by a responsible father and a responsible mother. The whole of sexual morality, as Ellen Key[1] has said, revolves round the child.

At this final point in our discussion of sexual morality we may perhaps be able to realize the immensity of the change which has been involved by the development in women of moral responsibility. So long as responsibility was denied to women, so long as a father or a husband, backed up by the community, held himself responsible for a woman's sexual behavior, for her "virtue," it was necessary that the whole of sexual morality should revolve around the entrance to the vagina. It became absolutely essential to the maintenance of morality that all eyes in the community should be constantly directed on to that point, and the whole marriage law had to be adjusted accordingly. That is no longer possible. When a woman assumes her own moral responsibility, in sexual as in other matters, it becomes not only intolerable but meaningless for the community to pry into her most intimate physiological or spiritual acts. She is herself directly responsible to society as soon as she performs a social act, and not before.

In relation to the fact of maternity the realization of all that is involved in the new moral responsibility of women is especially significant. Under a system of morality by which a man is left free

---

1   Ellen Key (1849–1926) was a Swedish feminist whose most famous work was *The Century of the Child* (1900, trans. 1909). She wrote extensively on sex, love and marriage.

to accept the responsibility for his sexual acts while a woman is not equally free to do the like, a premium is placed on sexual acts which have no end in procreation, and a penalty is placed on the acts which lead to procreation. The reason is that it is the former class of acts in which men find chief gratification; it is the latter class in which women find chief gratification. For the tragic part of the old sexual morality in its bearing on women was that while it made men alone morally responsible for sexual acts in which both a man and a woman took part, women were rendered both socially and legally incapable of availing themselves of the fact of masculine responsibility unless they had fulfilled conditions which men had laid down for them, and yet refrained from imposing upon themselves. The act of sexual intercourse, being the sexual act in which men found chief pleasure, was under all circumstances an act of little social gravity; the act of bringing a child into the world, which is for women the most massively gratifying of all sexual acts, was counted a crime unless the mother had before fulfilled the conditions demanded by man. That was perhaps the most unfortunate and certainly the most unnatural of the results of the patriarchal regulation of society. It has never existed in any great State where women have possessed some degree of regulative power.

★★★

With the realization of the moral responsibility of women the natural relations of life spring back to their due biological adjustment. Motherhood is restored to its natural sacredness. It becomes the concern of the woman herself, and not of society nor of any individual, to determine the conditions under which the child shall be conceived. Society is entitled to require that the father shall in every case acknowledge the fact of his paternity, but it must leave the chief responsibility for all the circumstances of child-production to the mother. That is the point of view which is now gaining ground in all civilized lands both in theory and in practice.[1]

---

1 It has been set out, for instance, by Professor Wahrmund in *Ehe und Eherecht*, 1908. I need scarcely refer again to the writings of Ellen Key, which may be said to almost epoch-making in their significance, especially (in German translation) *Ueber Liebe und Ehe* (also French translation), and (in English translation, Putnam, 1908), the valuable, though less important work, *The Century of the Child*. See also Edward Carpenter,

3. Olive Schreiner, from *Woman and Labor*, 1911

[Considered by many feminists at the time as the "Bible of the Woman's Movement," Schreiner's work insists that "We take all labor for our province!" Throughout this treatise, Schreiner treats women's rights in a more radical manner than did the suffragettes. It begins with an historical overview of women's labor. It argues against the idea that in the modern age, women's labor was unnecessary. "Sex parasitism" is Schreiner's term for the social condition in which women's only function is her passive performance as, what we would call, a "sex object." Written during the Boer War (1899-1902) and published just a few years before World War I, Schreiner's work also addresses the role of women in war. If women were involved in government, it would mean the "death of war as a means of arranging human differences," according to Schreiner, not because they are morally superior to men, but because their experiences as child-bearers give them a greater knowledge of the cost of human flesh. In the first excerpt, Schreiner discusses the women's movement. Her description of the life of "an individual young girl" offers another view of Schreiner herself and the character of Lyndall. In the second excerpt, she responds to the idea that women's labor be confined to child-bearing by analyzing the class biases behind such propositions.]

The female labor movement is, in its ultimate essence, an endeavor on the part of a section of the race to save itself from inactivity and degeneration, and this even at the immediate cost of most heavy loss in material comfort and ease to the individuals composing it. The male labor movement is, directly and in the first place, material; and, at least superficially, more or less self-seeking, though its ultimate reaction on society by saving the poorer members from degradation and dependency and want is undoubtedly wholly social and absolutely essential for the health and continued development of the human race. In the woman's labor movement of our day, which has essentially taken its rise among women of the

---

Love's Coming of Age; Forel, *Die Sexuelle Frage* (English translation, abridged, *The Sexual Question*, Rebman, 1908); Bloch, *Sexualleben unsere Zeit* (English translation, *The Sexual Life of Our Time*, Rebman, 1908); Helene Stöcker, *Die Liebe und die Frauen*, 1906; and Paul Lapie, *La Femme dans la Famille*, 1908. [Author's note]

more cultured and wealthy classes, and which consists mainly in a demand to have the doors leading to professional, political, and highly skilled labor thrown open to them, the ultimate end can only be attained at the cost of more or less intense, immediate, personal suffering and renunciation, though eventually, if brought to a satisfactory conclusion, it will undoubtedly tend to the material and physical well-being of woman herself, as well as to that of her male companions and descendants.

The coming half-century will be a time of peculiar strain, as mankind seeks rapidly to adjust moral ideals and social relationships and the general ordering of life to the new and continually unfolding material conditions. If these two great movements of our age, having this as their object, can be brought into close harmony and cooperation, the readjustment will be the sooner and more painlessly accomplished; but, for the moment, the two movements alike in their origin and alike in many of their methods of procedure, remain distinct.

It is this fact, the consciousness on the part of the women taking their share in the woman's movement of our age, that their efforts are not, and cannot be, of immediate advantage to themselves, but that they almost of necessity and immediately lead to loss and renunciation, which gives to this movement its very peculiar tone; setting it apart from the large mass of economic movements, placing it rather in a line with those vast religious developments which at the interval of ages have swept across humanity, irresistibly modifying and reorganizing it.

It is the perception of this fact, that, not for herself, nor even for fellow women alone, but for the benefit of humanity at large, she must seek to readjust herself to life, which lends to the woman's most superficial and seemingly trivial attempt at readjustment a certain dignity and importance.

It is this profound hidden conviction which removes from the sphere of the ridiculous the attitude of even the feeblest woman who waves her poor little "woman's rights" flag on the edge of a platform, and which causes us to forgive even the passionate denunciations, not always wisely thought out, in which she would represent the evils of woman's condition as wrongs intentionally inflicted upon her, where they are merely the inevitable results of ages of social movement.

It is this over-shadowing consciousness of a large impersonal obligation which removes from the sphere of the wholly contemptible and insignificant even the action of the individual young girl, who leaves a home of comfort or luxury for a city garret, where in solitude, and under that stern pressure which is felt by all individuals in arms against the trend of their environment, she seeks to acquire the knowledge necessary for entering on a new form of labor. It is this profound consciousness which makes not less than heroic the figure of the little half-starved student, battling against gigantic odds to take her place beside man in the fields of modern intellectual toil, and which, whether she succeed or fail, makes her a landmark in the course of our human evolution. It is this consciousness of large impersonal ends to be attained, and to the attainment of which each individual is bound to play her part, however small, which removes from the domain of the unnecessary, and raises to importance, the action of each woman who resists the tyranny of fashions in dress or bearing, or custom which impedes her in her strife towards the new adjustment.

It is this consciousness which renders almost of solemn import the efforts of the individual female after physical or mental self-culture and expansion; this which fills with a lofty enthusiasm the heart of the young girl, who, it may be, in some solitary farmhouse, in some distant wild of Africa or America, deep into the night bends over her books, with the passion and fervor with which an early Christian may have bent over the pages of his Scriptures; feeling that, it may be, she fits herself by each increase of knowledge for she knows not what duties towards the world, in the years to come.

It is this consciousness of great impersonal ends, to be brought, even if slowly and imperceptibly, a little nearer by her action, which gives to many a woman strength for renunciation, when she puts from her the lower type of sexual relationship, even if bound up with all the external honor a legal marriage can confer, if it offers her only enervation and parasitism. This consciousness enables her often to accept poverty, toil, and sexual isolation (an isolation more terrible to her than to any male), and renunciation of motherhood, that crowning beatitude of the woman's existence, which, and which alone, fully compensates her for the organic sufferings of womanhood—in the conviction that, by so doing, she makes more possible a fuller and higher attainment of motherhood and wifehood to the women who will follow her.

★★★

It has been stated sometimes, though more often implicitly than in any direct or logical form, (this statement being one it is not easy

to make definitely without its reducing itself to nullity!), that
woman should seek no fields of labor in the new world of social
conditions that is arising about us, as she has her function as child-
bearer: a labor which, by her own showing, is arduous and dangerous, though she may love it as a soldier loves his battle field; that
woman should perform her sex functions only, allowing man or
the state to support her, even when she is only potentially a child-
bearer and bears no children.[1]

There is some difficulty in replying to a theorist so wholly delu-
sive. Not only is he to be met by all the arguments against parasitism of class or race; but, at the present day, when probably much
more than half the world's most laborious and ill-paid labor is still
performed by women, from tea pickers and cocoa tenders in India
and the islands, to the washerwomen, cooks, and drudging labor-
ing men's wives, who, in addition to the sternest and most unend-
ing toil, throw in their child-bearing as a little addition: and when
in some civilized countries women exceed the males in numbers
by one million, so that there would still be one million females for
whom there was no legitimate sexual outlet, though each male in
the nation supported a female, it is somewhat difficult to reply with
gravity to the assertion, "Let Woman be content to be the Divine
Child-bearer, and ask no more."

Were it worth replying gravely to so idle a theorist, we might
answer:—Through all the ages of the past, when, with heavy
womb and hard labor-worn hands, we physically toiled beside
man, bearing up by the labor of our bodies the world about us, it
was never suggested to us, "You, the child-bearers of the race, have
in that one function a labor that equals all others combined; therefore, toil no more in other directions, we pray of you. Neither
plant, nor build, nor bend over the grindstone, nor far into the
night, while we sleep, sit weaving the clothing we and our children
are to wear! Leave it to us, to plant, to reap, to weave, to work, to

---

1   Such a scheme, as has before been stated, was actually put forward by a
    literary man (Karl Pearson, 'Woman and Labor,' *Fortnightly Review*, 329
    [May 1894]) in England some years ago: but he had the sense to state
    that it should apply only to women of the upper classes; the mass of
    laboring women, who form the vast bulk of the English women of the
    present day, being left to their ill-paid drudgery and their child-bearing as
    well! [Author's note]. See Burdett pp. 62–66 on Schreiner's revision of
    Pearson's ideas.

toil for you, O sacred child-bearer! Work no more; every man of the race will work for you!" This cry in all the grim ages of our past toil we never heard.

And to-day the lofty theorist, who to-night stands before the drawing-room fire in spotless shirt-front and perfectly fitting clothes, and exclaims upon the amplitude of woman's work in life as child-bearer, and the mighty value of that labor which exceeds all other, making it unnecessary for her to share man's grosser and lower toils: does he always remember his theory? When walking to-morrow morning, he finds that the elderly house drudge, who rises at dawn while he yet sleeps, to make his tea and clean his boots, has brought his tea late, and polished his boots ill; may he not even sharply condemn her, and assure her she will have to leave unless she works harder and rises earlier? He does not exclaim to her, "Divine child-bearer! Potential mother of the race! Why should you clean my boots or bring up my tea, while I lie warm in bed? Is it not enough you should have the holy and mysterious power of bringing the race to life? Let that content you. Henceforth I shall get up at dawn and make my own tea and clean my own boots, and pay you just the same!" Nor, should his landlady, now about to give birth to her ninth child, send him up a poorly-cooked dinner or forget to bring up his scuttle of coal, does he send for her and thus apostrophize the astonished matron: "Child-bearer of the race! Producer of men! Cannot you be contented with so noble and lofty a function in life without toiling and moiling? Why carry up heavy coal-scuttles from the cellar and bend over hot fires, wearing out nerve and muscle that should be reserved for higher duties? We, we men of the race, will perform its mean, its sordid, its grinding toil! For woman is beauty, peace, repose! Your function is to give life, not to support it by labor. The Mother, the Mother! How wonderful it sounds! Toil no more! Rest is for you; labor and drudgery for us!" Would we not rather assure her that, unless she labored more assiduously and sternly, she would lose his custom and so be unable to pay her month's rent, and perhaps so, with children and an invalid or drunken husband whom she supports, be turned out into the streets? For it is remarkable, that, with theorists of this class, it is not toil, or the amount of toil, crushing alike to brain and body, which the female undertakes that he objects to; it is the form and the amount of the reward. It is not the hand-laboring woman, even in his own society, worn out and prematurely aged at forty with grinding domestic toil that has no beginning and knows no end—

"Man's work is from sun to sun,
But woman's work is never done"—

it is not the haggard, work-worn woman and mother who irons his shirts, or the potential mother who destroys health and youth in the sweater's den[1] where she sews the garments in which he appears so radiantly in the drawing-room who disturbs him.

It is the thought of the woman-doctor with an income of some hundreds a year, who drives round in her carriage to see her patients, or receives them in her consulting-rooms, and who spends the evening smoking and reading before her study fire or receiving her guests; it is the thought of the woman who, as legislator, may loll for perhaps six hours on the padded seat of legislative bench, relieving the tedium now and then by a turn in the billiard- or refreshment-room, when she is not needed to vote or speak; it is the woman as Greek professor, with three or four hundred a year, who gives half a dozen lectures a week, and has leisure to enjoy the society of her husband and children, and to devote to her own study and life of thought; it is she who wrings his heart. It is not the woman, who, on hands and knees, at ten-pence a day, scrubs the floors of the public buildings, or private dwellings, that fills him with anguish for womanhood: that somewhat quadrupedal posture is for him truly feminine, and does not interfere with the ideal of the mother and child-bearer.

---

1 In the nineteenth century, sweater referred to an employer who over-works and underpays his workers.

Appendix D: Literary Contexts

1. Olive Schreiner, from *Dreams*, 1890

[Schreiner's collection of stories was very popular before World War I. Schreiner herself valued this kind of allegorical tale over her other writing. She explained to Arthur Symons, in a conversation he recorded in June 1889, that allegory was true art because it expressed "the passion of abstract ideas" rather than of "merely this man or that" (quoted in Samuel Cronwright Schreiner's *The Life of Olive Schreiner*, p.185). The story that follows reflects views about men and women that Schreiner had held for a long time. In response to Havelock Ellis's criticism of Henrick Ibsen's play *A Doll House* (1879; translated 1889), Schreiner wrote that in the future men and women will walk hand in hand, but "now the fight has oftenest to be fought out alone by both. I think men suffer as much as women from the falseness of the relations" (see *My Other Self*, p. 43).]

"Three Dreams in a Desert"
Under a Mimosa Tree

As I travelled across an African plain the sun shone down hotly. Then I drew my horse up under a mimosa tree, and I took the saddle from him and left him to feed among the parched bushes. And all to right and to left stretched the brown earth. And I sat down under the tree, because the heat beat fiercely, and all along the horizon the air throbbed. And after a while a heavy drowsiness came over me, and I laid my head down against my saddle, and I fell asleep there. And, in my sleep, I had a curious dream.

I thought I stood on the border of a great desert, and the sand blew about everywhere. And I thought I saw two great figures like beasts of burden of the desert, and one lay upon the sand with its neck stretched out, and one stood by it. And I looked curiously at the one that lay upon the ground, for it had a great burden on its back, and the sand was thick about it, so that it seemed to have piled over it for centuries.

And I looked very curiously at it. And there stood one beside me watching. And I said to him, "What is this huge creature who lies here on the sand?"

And he said, "This is woman; she that bears men in her body."

And I said, "Why does she lie here motionless with the sand piled round her?"

And he answered, "Listen, I will tell you! Ages and ages long she has lain here, and the wind has blown over her. The oldest, oldest, oldest man living has never seen her move: the oldest, oldest book records that she lay here then, as she lies here now, with the sand about her. But listen! Older than the oldest book, older than the oldest recorded memory of man, on the Rocks of Language, on the hard-baked clay of Ancient Customs, now crumbling to decay, are found the marks of her footsteps! Side by side with his who stands beside her you may trace them; and you know that she who now lies there once wandered free over the rocks with him."

And I said, "Why does she lie there now?"

And he said, "I take it, ages ago the Age-of-dominion-of-muscular-force found her, and when she stooped low to give suck to her young, and her back was broad, he put his burden of subjection on to it, and tied it on with the broad band of Inevitable Necessity. Then she looked at the earth and the sky, and knew there was no hope for her; and she lay down on the sand with the burden she could not loosen. Ever since she has lain here. And the ages have come, and the ages have gone, but the band of Inevitable Necessity has not been cut."

And I looked and saw in her eyes the terrible patience of the centuries; the ground was wet with her tears, and her nostrils blew up the sand.

And I said, "Has she ever tried to move?"

And he said, "Sometimes a limb has quivered. But she is wise; she knows she cannot rise with the burden on her."

And I said, "Why does not he who stands by her leave her and go on?"

And he said, "He cannot. Look—"

And I saw a broad band passing along the ground from one to the other, and it bound them together.

He said, "While she lies there he must stand and look across the desert. "

And I said, "Does he know why he cannot move?"

And he said, "No."

And I heard a sound of something cracking, and I looked, and I saw the band that bound the burden on to her back broken asunder; and the burden rolled on to the ground.

And I said, "What is this?"

And he said, "The Age-of-muscular-force is dead. The Age-of-nervous-force has killed him with the knife he holds in his hand; and silently and invisibly he has crept up to the woman, and with that knife of Mechanical Invention he has cut the band that bound the burden to her back. The Inevitable Necessity is broken. She might rise now."

And I saw that she still lay motionless on the sand, with her eyes open and her neck stretched out. And she seemed to look for something on the far-off border of the desert that never came. And I wondered if she were awake or asleep. And as I looked her body quivered, and a light came into her eyes, like when a sunbeam breaks into a dark room.

I said, "What is it?"

He whispered, "Hush! the thought has come to her, 'Might I not rise?'"

And I looked. And she raised her head from the sand, and I saw the dent where her neck had lain so long. And she looked at the earth, and she looked at the sky, and she looked at him who stood by her: but he looked out across the desert.

And I saw her body quiver; and she pressed her front knees to the earth, and veins stood out; and I cried, "She 's going to rise!"

But only her sides heaved, and she lay still where she was.

But her head she held up; she did not lay it down again. And he beside me said, "She is very weak. See, her legs have been crushed under her so long."

And I saw the creature struggle: and the drops stood out on her. And I said, "Surely he who stands beside her will help her?"

And he beside me answered, "He cannot help her: she must help herself. Let her struggle till she is strong."

And I cried, "At least he will not hinder her! See, he moves farther bent forward and sleeping there, with the bees flying about her head, down. "

And he answered, "He does not understand. When she moves she draws the band that binds them, and hurts him, and he moves farther from her. The day will come when he will understand and will know what she is doing. Let her once stagger on to her knees. In that day he will stand close to her, and look into her eyes with sympathy."

And she stretched her neck, and the drops fell from her. And the creature rose an inch from the earth and sank back.

And I cried, "Oh, she is too weak! she cannot walk! The long years have taken all her strength from her. Can she never move?"

And he answered me, "See the light in her eyes!"
And slowly the creature staggered on to its knees.

And I awoke: and all to the east and to the west stretched the barren earth, with the dry bushes on it. The ants ran up and down in the red sand, and the heat beat fiercely. I looked up through the thin branches of the tree at the blue sky overhead. I stretched myself, and I mused over the dream I had had. And I fell asleep again, with my head on my saddle. And in the fierce heat I had another dream.

I saw a desert and I saw a woman coming out of it. And she came to the bank of a dark river; and the bank was steep and high.[1] And on it an old man met her, who had a long white beard; and a stick that curled was in his hand, and on it was written Reason. And he asked her what she wanted; and she said, "I am woman; and I am seeking for the land of Freedom."

And he said, "It is before you."

And she said, "I see nothing before me but a dark flowing river, and a bank steep and high, and cuttings here and there with heavy sand in them."

And he said, "And beyond that?"

She said, "I see nothing, but sometimes, when I shade my eyes with my hand, I think I see on the further bank trees and hills, and the sun shining on them!"

He said, "That is the Land of Freedom."

She said, "How am I to get there?"

He said, "There is one way, and one only. Down the banks of Labour through the water of Suffering. There is no other."

She said, "Is there no bridge?"

He answered, "None."

She said, "Is the water deep?"

He said, "Deep."

She said, "Is the floor worn?"

He said, "It is. Your foot may slip at any time, and you may be lost." She said, "Have any crossed already?"

He said, "Some have *tried!*"

She said, "Is there a track to show where the best fording is?"

---

1 The banks of an African river are sometimes a hundred feet high, and consist of deep shifting sands, through which in the course of ages the river has worn its gigantic bed. [Author's note]

He said, "It has to be made."

She shaded her eyes with her hand; and she said, "I will go."

And he said, "You must take off the clothes you wore in the desert: they are dragged down by them who go into the water so clothed."

And she threw from her gladly the mantle of Ancient-received-opinions she wore, for it was worn full of holes. And she took the girdle from her waist that she had treasured so long, and the moths flew out of it in a cloud. And he said, "Take the shoes of dependence off your feet."

And she stood there naked, but for one white garment that clung close to her.

And he said, "That you may keep. So they wear clothes in the Land of Freedom. In the water it buoys; it always swims."

And I saw on its breast was written Truth; and it was white; the sun had not often shone on it; the other clothes had covered it up. And he said, "Take this stick; hold it fast. In that day when it slips from your hand you are lost. Put it down before you; feel your way: where it cannot find a bottom do not set your foot."

And she said, "I am ready; let me go."

And he said, "No—but stay; what is that—in your breast?"

She was silent.

He said, "Open it and let me see."

And she opened it. And against her breast was a tiny thing, who drank from it, and the yellow curls above his forehead pressed against it; and his knees were drawn up to her, and he held her breast fast with his hands.

And Reason said, "Who is he, and what is he doing here?"

And she said, "See his little wings—"

And Reason said, "Put him down."

And she said, "He is asleep, and he is drinking! I will carry him to the Land of Freedom. He has been a child so long, so long, I have carried him. In the Land of Freedom he will be a man. We will walk together there, and his great white wings will overshadow me. He has lisped one word only to me in the desert —'Passion!' I have dreamed he might learn to say 'Friendship' in that land."

And Reason said, "Put him down!"

And she said, "I will carry him so—with one arm, and with the other I will fight the water."

He said, "Lay him down on the ground. When you are in the water you will forget to fight, you will think only of him. Lay him down." He said, "He will not die. When he finds you have left him alone he will open his wings and fly. He will be in the Land of Freedom before you. Those who reach the Land of Freedom, the first hand they see stretching down the bank to help them shall be Love's. He will be a man then, not a child. In your breast he cannot thrive; put him down that he may grow."

And she took her bosom from his mouth, and he bit her, so that the blood ran down on to the earth; and she covered her wound. And she bent and stroked his wings. And I saw the hair on her forehead turned white as snow, and she had changed from youth to age.

And she stood far off on the bank of the river. And she said, "For what do I go to this far land which no one has ever reached? *Oh, I am alone! I am utterly alone!*"

And Reason, that old man, said to her, "Silence! what do your hear?"

And she listened intently, and she said, "I hear a sound of feet, a thousand times ten thousand and thousands of thousands, and they beat this way!"

He said, "They are the feet of those that shall follow you. Lead on! make a track to the water's edge! Where you stand now, the ground will be beaten flat by ten thousand times ten thousand feet." And he said, "Have you seen the locusts how they cross a stream? First one comes down to the water-edge, and it is swept away, and then another comes and then another, and then another, and at last with their bodies piled up a bridge is built and the rest pass over."

She said, "And, of those that come first, some are swept away, and are heard of no more; their bodies do not even build the bridge?"

"And are swept away, and are heard of no more—and what of that?" he said.

"And what of that—" she said.

"They make a track to the water's edge."

"They make a track to the water's edge—." And she said, "Over that bridge which shall be built with our bodies, who will pass?"

He said, "*The entire human race.*"

And the woman grasped her staff.

And I saw her turn down that dark path to the river.

And I awoke; and all about me was the yellow afternoon light: the sinking sun lit up the fingers of the milk bushes; and my horse stood by me quietly feeding. And I turned on my side, and I watched the ants run by thousands in the red sand. I thought I would go on my way now—the afternoon was cooler. Then a drowsiness crept over me again, and I laid back my head and fell asleep.

And I dreamed a dream.

I dreamed I saw a land. And on the hills walked brave women and brave men, hand in hand. And they looked into each other's eyes, and they were not afraid.

And I saw the women also hold each other's hands.

And I said to him beside me, "What place is this?"

And he said, "This is heaven."

And I said, "Where is it?"

And he answered, "On earth."

And I said, "When shall these things be?"

And he answered, "IN THE FUTURE."

And I awoke, and all about me was the sunset light; and on the low hills the sun lay, and a delicious coolness had crept over everything; and the ants were going slowly home. And I walked towards my horse, who stood quietly feeding. Then the sun passed down behind the hills; but I knew that the next day he would rise again.

2. Charles Dilke, from *Problems of Greater Britain*, Vol. 2, 1890

[As a young man, Charles Dilke (1843-1911) traveled widely and became a popular writer. Active in politics, he served as Undersecretary for Foreign Affairs and in 1879 he joined other cabinet members to censure Disraeli's South African policy. As a liberal MP, Dilke supported labor reform, but he was forced to leave politics because of allegations of adultery, which he firmly denied. In 1890 he published his survey of the entire English-speaking world, from which this excerpt is taken. Throughout his life, Dilke was esteemed as an expert in colonial matters.]

In a literary sense the colonies may, indeed, be said to stand now in pretty much the same position in which the United States stood in the time of Tocqueville,[1] and America made a little later a great

---

1 Alexis de Tocqueville (1805-1859) wrote *Democracy in America* (1835-1840).

literary advance. Though it may still be said of the American people that their reading is not over choice, and that they are largely fed upon telegrams and sensational stories, nevertheless the country has produced a powerful literary class and some literary work of the highest merit. In the colonies there is almost as much literary dependence upon England now as there was formerly in the United States; but there is every reason to hope that the universal diffusion of reading, power among the people, and the influence of free libraries, public discussion societies, and other means of rousing intellectual interests, will lead to the same results throughout all Greater Britain which have been witnessed in the United States. While in the richer among the old countries of Europe there is a larger literary class in proportion than can exist in new country, I am disposed to doubt whether the population generally are more literary in their studies than in new countries. It is often said that the people of the colonies are superficial in their tastes, that they like a smattering of literature of an easy type and a smattering of science, but do not read deeply; but I doubt myself whether a careful examination of the statistics of English Free Libraries would show the existence of a better state of things among ourselves. There are, naturally and necessarily, more people with leisure, and more people of the highest cultivation, in proportion to the numbers of the population here than can be the case in the younger countries, and that is all. Olive Schreiner among novelists and for the Cape, Henry Kendall among poets and for Australia, not to speak of statisticians, and of the political essayists of Canada, form the first of a future race of colonial writers; while Markus Clarke and Brunton Stephens of the British-born colonists may be counted as colonial go the colonists themselves, and equally precursors of the colonial literature of the future. Although Adam Lindsay Gordon killed himself, and Markus Clarke died in poverty, and Kendall had little better fate, it may, I think, be safely predicted that the day will come when colonial literature will hold its own with the literature of the mother-country, and letters form an acknowledged and sufficient colonial career. The colonists are no more likely to be content with inferior work in literature and art than they are in other matters. In their newspaper press they expect and obtain, as I have shown, the best. Their universities are remarkable; the organization of secondary instruction admirable; their railway material upon the State lines the most excellent perhaps in the whole World; and although literature and art cannot be called into existence by administrative ability, because they are things of the soul and not merely things of skill, it is impossible to believe that, with their sunlight, their intelligence, their education, their cheerfulness, and their manliness and robustness of mind, the colonies will fulfill the promise that is given by such a work of genius as *The Story of an African Farm*.

Appendix E: Contemporary Reviews

1. Henry Norman, from "Theories and Practice of Modern Fiction," *The Fortnightly Review*, December 1883, xxxiv, 870-86.

[Henry Norman (1858-1939) was a liberal MP, a journalist, and an expert in radio technology. He served as an editor for the *Daily Chronicle* and was a founder of *World's Work*.]

I said just now that from the confused memory of many novels one person and one place stood out most prominently.... the place is a weary flat plain of red sand, broken only by a solitary hillock and a clump, or two of prickly pear-trees; in the distance a ragged boy with a big straw hat is herding a few ewes and lambs, and still farther off a few ungainly ostriches are feeding. A simple scene, truly, but a memorable one to most of the readers of the story of that *African Farm*. In spite of the very masculine name on the title-page[1] it is clearly the work of a woman, and almost equally clearly of a very young one, which makes it all the more remarkable. The hand of the beginner, too, is betrayed by a number of faults of proportion and perspective. The modest title gives no clue to the contents. It is the story of the growth of a human mind cut off from all but the most commonplace influences, facing its own doubts, crushing its own and others' deceits, and at last beating out a music which is not very melodious, but which is thoroughly honest. On the solitary 'Kopje' in the growth of the mind of the little Dutch Waldo, there come up for solution one after another the simple questions of human nature and human action that the world has labelled with many big names; and this young lady historian of Boer life—if the above surmise is correct—faces them as they rise with refreshing temerity, and what is still more surprising and refreshing, she has the right word to say about almost all. Orthodox Christianity, Unitarian Christianity, woman suffrage, marriage, Malthusianism, immortality—they all arise, though not with these names, over the horizon of this African farm. The book

---

1 Schreiner used the pseudonym Ralph Iron for the first editions of *African Farm*.

might well be called the *Romance of the New Ethics*, and to those to whom the New Ethics embodies the hopes and the promises of the future, this novel offers a rare treat, for its author has a just appreciation of the terms and the solution of most of the problems to which this ethics applies. It is, too, an unspeakable relief to escape from the domains of the ordinary novelist—from Homburg and the Highlands, from yachts, clubs, hansoms, and Piccadilly. This book teaches the lesson that wherever there are human hearts beating with natural impulses there is scene enough for all the tragedy and all the comedy of life—that for the delineation of the highest interests of men and women *una domus sufficit*.[1] The characters are all original—we have met none of them before; the style is fresh and full of humour; and, in spite of its occasional youthful lapses, the whole story is of fascinating interest, and, what is more, of great moral power.

2. Canon Malcolm MacColl, from "An Agnostic Novel," *The Spectator* 13 August 1887, 1091-93.

[Malcolm MacColl (1831-1907) was an Anglican cleric who contributed to numerous newspapers and periodicals. His review of *African Farm* was greatly valued by Schreiner herself.]

We owe our readers an apology for our late notice of this very remarkable book. Our excuse is that the title of the book misled us. It seems to promise information about the rearing and management of bullocks and ostriches; but the last thing it suggests is the pathetic story of a troubled soul "crying for the light," and groping its way through pain and sorrow to the inevitable goal of Agnosticism in the case of all who love deeply. The hero of the story dreams one night of the woman he had loved, whom death had snatched away, and rushed out into the night to relieve his pain:—

> "He looked up into the night sky that all his life had mingled with his existence. There were a thousand faces that he loved looking down at him, a thousand stars in their glory, in

---

1   Literally, "one home is enough." For Norman, Schreiner has captured the essence of human life through these otherwise obscure characters.

crowns, and circles, and solitary grandeur. To the man they were not less dear than to the boy they had been mysterious; yet he looked up at them and shuddered; at last he turned away from them with horror. Such countless multitudes, stretching out far into space; and yet not in one of them all was she! Though he searched through them all, to the farthest, faintest point of light, nowhere should he ever say, 'She is here!' To-morrow's sun would rise and gild the world's mountains, and shine into its thousand valleys; it would set and the stars creep out again. Year after year, century after century, the old changes of Nature would go on—day and night, summer and winter, seed-time and harvest; but in none of them all would she have part! He shut the door to keep out the hideous shining, and because the dark was intolerable, lit a candle, and paced the little room faster and faster yet. He saw before him the long ages of eternity that would roll on, on, on, and never bring her. She would exist no more. A dark mist filled the little room. 'Oh, little hand! oh, little voice! oh, little form!' he cried; 'oh, little soul that walked with mine! oh, little soul that looked so fearlessly down into the depths, do you exist no more for ever—for all time?' He cried more bitterly: 'It is for this hour—this—that men blind reason, and crush out thought! For this hour—this, this—they barter truth and knowledge, take any lie, any creed, so it does not whisper to them of the dead that they are dead! Oh, God! God! for a Hereafter!'"

That is the true outcome of Agnosticism in any breast that looks at facts as they are, and not as it would fain have them be. The soul that truly loves, when it has lost the desire of its eyes, cannot face without horror the thought of annihilation,—the thought that never, in all the universe of being, shall it ever more hold sweet converse with the soul that it has lost. Agnosticism is all very well in fair weather, when Nature is smiling and the sea is calm. But when the storm arises, he who rests his hopes upon it finds, like Sinbad the Sailor, that he has cast his anchor not on solid ground, but on the back of a whale, which suddenly sinks beneath him, and leaves him floundering amidst the waves. The value of this book, besides its great literary power, is that it looks Agnosticism fairly in the face. Its heroine acts upon Agnostic principles, and the result is a moral chaos, ending in a wild wail of despair. Two influences are apparent in the shaping of the writer's mind. She was born and bred in the strictest school of Calvinism.[1] Waldo, the hero of the book, is introduced to us as a boy oppressed with the thought of the vast majority of the human race living on forever in misery....We have here probably a chapter of autobiography on the part of the authoress. Her moral sense was revolted by the horrible travesty of Christianity which Calvinism offers, and knowing no other kind of Christianity, she embraced Agnosticism, and in this striking story she carries out its premises to their legitimate conclusions.

The second influence, which appears to have given so somber a hue to her thoughts, and infected her mind with such seemingly hopeless pessimism, is probably due to her surroundings. The local colouring of the story is extremely vivid, and clearly bears the impress of painful personal experience. The scene is laid on a lonely farm in South Africa, and man and nature are alike painted in unattractive and depressing guise. The tendency of ordinary mountain scenery is to raise the spirits, to quicken the imagination, to inspire hope, to point to heaven. The mountains of South Africa, on the other hand, have a depressing influence. They have none of the mystery, the sublimity, the poetry, the aspiration of ordinary mountains. They have no peaks. Their gross bulk, and flat tops, and brown sides are altogether of the earth, and seem to repel and to forbid man's yearning for something beyond the visible and temporal. And the vast plains consist of coarse grass and low scrub, lacking alike the grandeur of the desert and the forest loneliness of the Equatorial regions of the Dark Continent. The farm which gives its name to the story is a Boer homestead, and the Boer of South Africa is a singularly unattractive being. Labour, too, is there presented in its hardest, lowest and most unimaginative form.

[The reviewer introduces Waldo and Lyndall and gives a plot summary that ends with Lyndall's death.]

"Had she found what she sought for?" is the reflection of the authoress on the death of Lyndall; "something to worship? Had she ceased from being? Who shall tell us? There is a veil of terrible mist over the face of the Hereafter." The authoress, indeed, has tried to

---

1 Calvinists believed in predestination and the absolute will of God. In the strictest interpretations of Calvinism, human intelligence, will, faith, or good works were irrelevant to the salvation or damnation of the soul.

raise this veil and peep behind it. But the effort is not successful. The gospel which she preaches from behind the veil carries no conviction; it wears a make-believe smile of peace and satisfaction. But a character like Waldo's could never have found consolation where she makes him find it. His love for Lyndall was passionate, deep, unchangeable, and it was Lyndall that he longed to see again; not an angel, not a spirit glorified out of identity with his lost love, but "a little human woman full of sin, that he once loved." "Give me back what I have lost, or give me nothing!" And it is this man, whose affections are so human and so intensely concentrated, who is presently represented as losing "all consciousness of its little self" in the contemplation of "Universal Unity that surrounds it:"—

"'No death, no death,' he muttered; 'there is that which never dies—which abides. It is but the individual that perishes, the whole remains. It is the organism that vanishes, the atoms are there. It is but the man that dies, the Universal Whole of which he is part reworks him into its inmost self. Ah! What matters that man's day be short?—that the sunrise sees him, and the sunset sees his grave; that of which he is but the breath has breathed him forth and drawn him back again. That abides—we abide ... Let us die, beloved, you and I, that we may pass on for ever through the Universal Life!' In that deep world of contemplation all fierce desires die out, and peace comes down. He, Waldo, as he walked there, saw no more the world that was about him; cried out no more for the thing that he had lost."

No man who loved as Waldo loved could find a moment's comfort in such phantom bliss as this. One might as well bid a thirsty traveller slake his thirst in a painted river. Love cannot be given to a mere abstraction, such as Universal Unity or Universal Life; it must be fixed on a person. Nothing short of a being endowed with will, and intellect, and moral qualities, can attract the love of man. What is Universal Life apart from individual life? There is no such thing. It is a mere chimæra, and it does not become a reality by being printed in capital letters. The only kind of life of which we have any knowledge is life under individual forms, and when death robs us of that, it is the veriest mockery to send us for consolation to a formless, voiceless, impalpable figment of the imagination. "O for the touch of a vanished hand, and the sound of a voice that is still!" That is the irrepressible craving of the soul that has lost what it loved best. The extinction of individual life, disguise it as one may, is for all practical purposes annihilation. And, indeed, the authoress virtually admits it; for having paid her homage to Agnosticism by speaking in the conventional language of its creed, she frankly admits that the consolation in which she makes the soul of Waldo find rest is, after all, nothing better than "a dream." "Without dreams and phantoms man cannot exist." But can he exist on these? The universal experience of mankind answers emphatically, "No."

The truth is, this gifted woman has been driven from her religious and moral moorings,—first by the ghastly theology of Calvinism, and then by the difficulty which she finds in reconciling the facts of the world around her, and especially the injustice done to her own sex, with the doctrine of a God who is omnipotent, compassionate, and just. With regard to Calvinism, all that need be said here is that it is not Christianity at all, but a hideous excrescence essentially foreign to the religion of Christ. The existence of evil, with its attendant misery, is, indeed, the necessary correlative of virtue in a created will. For virtue implies free choice; free choice implies the possibility of making a wrong choice; perseverance in a wrong choice creates habits; habits form character; and a bad character entails misery as a necessary consequence, and may, as far as we can see, become incorrigible. The question is therefore reduced to this dilemma: either virtue or moral goodness, however we choose to phrase it, is impossible; or evil, with its concomitant pain and sorrow, is possible. Omnipotence could not create a being capable of moral goodness without being at the same time capable of sin, and consequently of misery. So far we can see; and we may hope to reach in a higher state of being a point of view where we can see a solution of what now seems a moral enigma. A man inside a large, complex building can have no idea of its architecture. He must be able to "go round about" it, and view it from outside, as the Psalmist did the Temple on Mount Zion, before he can trace its fair lines and harmonious proportions. Now we are inside the method of divine government, in a tiny corner of the great Architect's plan. And are therefore bad judges of its symmetry and the coherence of its parts.

★★★

The world is full of pain, of cruelty, of injustice, of disappointments. Virtue is clad in rags and full of sores, while selfishness is arrayed in purple and fine linen, and faring sumptuously every day.

Wretches who have proved themselves a curse to mankind flourish and prosper, and die peacefully on their pillows; while men eminently qualified in mind and disposition to benefit their race are hurried out of life in the midst of their usefulness by a whiff of cold wind, or the stumbling of a horse, or the folly of a tipsy engine-driver. Or the anomaly may exhibit itself in the possession of splendid talents by persons who use them for the corruption and misery of their fellows. And over all is the terrible, the inevitable doom of death. These are the problems which Christianity does not make; it finds them and offers an explanation and a remedy. Physical science finds them too; but it has no explanations to offer, nor remedy to suggest. It does, however, point to a solution which it cannot itself supply. For it is a doctrine of physical science that instincts which are aboriginal and universal are intended in the economy of Nature to be satisfied. Hunger implies food. The eye implies light. The pinions of the bird imply an atmosphere in which it can fly. Now it is a fact of human consciousness that men live and act as if they were not the mere creatures of a day, emerging for a moment into activity and light, and then passing back into the darkness out of which they came. In the universal heart of humanity is planted an instinct which shrinks from death as from an unnatural catastrophe, and yearns for a life beyond it where the inequalities of this shall be redressed, where wrong shall be righted, where love shall have its fill and the mourners shall be comforted. Another universal instinct is that of prayer. In moment of distress man naturally prays, lifts up imploring eyes to a Being whom he believes able and willing to hear the cries of His creatures. Instincts like these are facts as truly as the instincts of ants and bees and spiders. Are we, then, to resign ourselves to the melancholy conclusion that while the instincts of the lower animals and of ephemeral insects point to corresponding objects, the far-reaching instincts of such a being as man have been bestowed for no other purpose than to torment and mock him? Is Nature to be recognized as a true prophetess up to man, and then to be regarded as a cruel siren who lures him with false hopes, and then turns round and laughs at him? As well believe that there is nothing in space to attract the mariner's compass, as that there is no God who attracts the prayers of human beings.

Another great mistake of the writer of *The African Farm* is her belief that the happiness of woman lies in her being independent. Lyndall does not marry because she will not be "bound." But the truth is that we are all, men and women, not made for independence. We cannot stand alone. Like climbing plants, we need some support outside of ourselves to which we can cling, and thereby raise ourselves. And, indeed, Lyndall recognizes this fact in the touching passage in which, while rejecting the marriage-bond, she cries piteously for "something nobler, stronger than I, before which I can kneel down." And the authoress, with profound insight, brings out, through the instinct of maternity, the love and tenderness and spirit of self-sacrifice which were all the while latent in the nature of the proud, self-centered girl. The idea of the authoress, when she wrote this book, seemed to be that women can only be emancipated and placed in their rightful place by the self-immolation of some pioneers of the sex who will brave the world's scorn, and die, if need be, in sorrow, and under the world's ban, if they can thereby hasten the time when woman shall take her place by man's side as his equal helpmate. We have heard this book described as "immoral" and "blasphemous." This is the exaggeration of prejudice. No bad woman could have written the book. It contains no suggestion of evil. It is evidently the product of a pure and pitying soul, burdened with the consciousness of the evils and sorrows of life and its dark enigmas, and penetrated with a consuming desire to solve the riddle and help forward the advent of a reign of righteousness and love.

3. H. Rider Haggard, from "About Fiction" *Contemporary Review* February 1887, LI, 172-180.

[Sir Henry Rider Haggard (1856-1925) spent six years in South Africa as a young man, and later wrote books on South African history and farming. He is best known, however, for his adventure novels, especially *King Solomon's Mines* (1886) and *She* (1887), both of which are set in Africa.]

Let genius, if genius there be, come forward and speak on its own behalf! But if the reader is inclined to doubt the Propositions that novel writing is becoming every day more difficult and less interesting, let him consult his own mind, and see how many novels proper among the hundreds that have been published within the last five years, and which deal in any way with every day contemporary life, have excited his profound interest. The present writer can at the moment recall but two—one was called "My Trivial Life and Misfortunes," by an unknown author, and the other, "The

Story of a South African Farm," by Ralph Iron. But then neither of these books if examined into would be found to be a novel such as the ordinary writer produces once or twice a year. Both of them are written from within, and not from without; both convey the impression of being the outward and visible result of inward personal suffering on the part of the writer, for in each the key-note is a note of pain. Differing widely from the ordinary run of manufactured books, they owe their chief interest to a certain atmosphere of spiritual intensity, which could not in all probability be even approximately reproduced.

4. Andrew Lang, from "Theological Romances," *Contemporary Review* June 1888, 53, 814–824.

[Andrew Lang (1844–1912) wrote in many genres, including poetry, biography and a history of English literature. He also produced anthropological studies of folklore and mythology and adapted and published several volumes of fairy-tales.]

All this time we have been keeping off the theology of "Robert Elsmere," and I confess that I approach it without enthusiasm. For, after all, any novel written to make a theological point, to advocate theological ideas, is a tract. One may except Miss Schreiner's "Story of a South African Farm." This novel, which begins so well, and tackles Belief, as it were, on first principles, has no theological point to make, no new system to advocate. It is, literally, *Vox clamantis in Deserto*, a voice clamouring in the desert of the African Veldt, complaining, under that iron sky, on those long wastes, that GOD is unsearchable. But it ends in trivialities that would astonish a reader of penny fiction, as when a young man dresses like a young woman that he may nurse the unbelieving lady of his heart in her last illness. This incredulous heroine has a love affair, has even a baby, and refuses to marry its father—why? One scarcely understands.

Select Bibliography

Biographies and Letters

Draznin, Yatta Claire. "My Other Self". The Letters of Olive Schreiner and Havelock Ellis, 1884-1920. New York: Peter Lang, 1992.
First, Ruth and Ann Scott. Olive Schreiner: A Biography. 1980. New Brunswick, NJ: Rutgers UP, 1990.
Schreiner, Samuel Cron Cronwright. The Life of Olive Schreiner. London, T.F. Unwin, 1924.

Criticism

Ardis, Ann L. New Women, New Novels: Feminism and Early Modernism. New Brunswick: Rutgers UP, 1990.
Burdett, Carolyn. Olive Schreiner and the Progress of Feminism: Evolution, Gender, Empire. New York: Palgrave, 2001.
Chrisman, Laura. "Empire, 'race' and feminism at the fin de siecle: the work of George Egerton And Olive Schreiner." Cultural Politics at the Fin de Siecle. Ed. Sally Ledger and Scott McCracken. Cambridge: Cambridge UP, 1995.
Clayton, Cherry. "Olive Schreiner's Paradoxical Pioneer." Women and Writing in South Africa: A Critical Anthology. Ed. Cherry Clayton. Marshalltown: Heinemann SA, 1989. Olive Schreiner. New York: Twayne, 1997.
—. "Forms of Dependence and Control in Olive Schreiner's Fiction." Olive Schreiner and After: Essays on Southern African Literature in honor of Guy Butler. Ed. Guy Butler, Malvern Van Wyk Smith, and Don Maclennan. Capetown: D. Philip, 1983.
Gilmour, Robin. The Novel in the Victorian Age: A Modern Introduction. London: E. Arnold, 1986.
Gorak, Irene. "Olive Schreiner's Colonial Allegory: The Story of an African Farm." Ariel 23 (1992): 53-72.
Haynes, R.D. "Elements of Romanticism in The Story of an African Farm." English Literature in Transition 24 (1981): 59-79.
Krebs, Paula M. "Olive Schreiner's Racialization of South Africa." Victorian Studies 40 (1997): 427-45.

Lenta, Margaret. "Racism, Sexism, and Olive Schreiner's Fiction." *Theoria* 70 (1987): 15-30.

Monsman, Gerald. "Writing the Self on the Imperial Frontier: Olive Schreiner and the Stories of Africa." *The Bucknell Review* 37 (1993): 134-55.

—. "Patterns of Narration and Characterization in Schreiner's *The Story of an African Farm.*" *English Literature in Transition* 28 (1985): 253-70.

—. "Olive Schreiner's Allegorical Vision." *Victorian Review* 18 (1992): 49-62.

—. "The Idea of 'Story' in Olive Schreiner's *Story of an African Farm.*" *Texas Studies in Literature and Language* 29 (1985): 249-69.

Paxton, Nancy L. "*The Story of an African Farm* and the Dynamics of Woman-to-Woman Influence." *Texas Studies in Literature and Language* 30 (1988): 562-81.

Pechey, Graham. "*The Story of an African Farm*: Colonial History and the Discontinuous Text." *Critical Arts* 3 (1983): 65-78.

Pierpont, Claudia Roth. "A critic at large: a woman's place." *The New Yorker* 67 (Jan 27, 1992): 69-83.

Cultural and Historical Backgrounds

On-line Sources

Blue Letter Bible: http://www.blueletterbible.org/
The Cyber Hymnal: http://www.cyberhymnal.org/index.htm#lk
Encyclopedia Britannica: http://search.eb.com/

Books

Bowler, Peter J. *Evolution: The History of an Idea.* Berkeley: U of California Press, 1989.

Dictionary of South African English on Historical Principles. Oxford UP, 1996.

Morrison, Toni. *Playing in the Dark: Whiteness and the Literary Imagination.* Cambridge, MA: Harvard UP, 1992.

Rowbotham, Sheila and Jeffrey Weeks. *Socialism and the New Life: The Personal and Sexual Politics of Edward Carpenter and Havelock Ellis.* London: Pluto Press, 1977.

Thompson, Leonard. *History of South Africa.* New Haven: Yale UP, 1995.